[SCAT JYZE]

Annals of The Jyze Age
____

Jyzeburst

Jyzemelt

Jyze and Jyze Alone

Jyze in Love

Deep Jyze

The Jyze Millennium

Jyze of the Heavenly Year

Scat Jyze

Also by G.P. Sandefjord
____

Have Mercy (a Novel)

Scat Jyze

G.P. Sandefjord

Annal Eight of The Jyze Age

Cover art by GPS
Published by House of Jyze
ISBN 978-0-578-75187-0
Library of Congress CIP Pending
www.HouseOfJyze.com

For Ticiang and Lizzie,

Elgie and Ayize

    Through jyze alone are we able to emerge
from ourselves, to know what another person
sees of a universe which, without jyze, the
landscapes would remain as unknown to us as
those that may exist on the moon.

                    -- Marcel Proust
                    [but he said "art"
                    for "jyze"]

BOOK A

[Scat Jyze : Gray Sheep]

1

New idea -- as I sit here at Z-geist trying to
gather some thoughts. Make this scat jyze the work of a
one-man Full Moon Society. Go at it every month on
full-moon day or close to it. Add entries for the first
day of the year and the last day, also for Christmas,
birthday, and one or two more, maybe Fourth of July,
maybe conception day, maybe a wild-card day or two; and
at an average of roughly ten pages per entry, plus some
room for notes at the back, the blank book of 188 pages
would be full -- like the moon.

So, good. That's the new plan. The concept. For
now anyway. Therefore jump right in before it slips
away.

Late sun, long shadows. A slice of the football
stadium visible a block away because I'm facing south.
Bizarro music, neo post punk, I'd say, but with some
bassoons mixed in (something like that). Only a few
tables occupied. And across the street at my back the
marquee-height Horse of the Heavenly Year has vanished.
It finally got chased off its perch, apparently, above
the entrance to a cowboy bar of a much earlier era. The
building's been sold. Good timing for a new jyze era.

And: suddenly lots of unsettledness in my personal
life. The FBI shows up at the scope office (we're in a
new one now) to check whether we're complying with
security rules. Of course we're not -- never have in
any of our offices except briefly after the last such
inspection maybe five years ago. The firm refuses --
too expensive. So now we may be losing the grand-jury
contract.

[Scat Jyze : Gray Sheep]

    And it gets worse. The feds may confiscate our
computers because they contain "shadows" of secret info
-- mostly grand-jury testimony -- and therefore they
too are not "secure." Also, the feds have no record at
all of me, even though they've cleared me twice over the
years and fingerprinted me three times. So do I want to
run the risk of submitting myself to another
investigation in this crazed right-wing era?
    Well, I might have to. No choice. Money. Time.
It's the same old story: I could never find another job
that would pay as well and leave me as much free time
and offer so many useful perks. Nothing even close!
But will the job still be there for me to hang on to it?
Stay tuned. (Toward the end of next year I'll be
eligible for early-exit Social Security. It's one
possible way to go. But I'd need something to
supplement it.)
    Also I'm in the midst of frantically copying files
in case the feds burst in to haul away the computers.
Third or fourth time for this too. Of biggest concern:
the program I use is very old now. Will I be able to
load it onto another machine? If not, will I be able to
find a new program that can read my current storage
disks? If not, disaster. We're talking somewhere
around twelve thousand pages from the past four decades
-- chrons, urjyze, protojyze, jyze, jyze fiction,
standard fiction, notes and miscellaneous scribblings.
Would a scanner save me? I just don't know.
    (Baseball fans straggling by, many of them
Japanese. Night game ahead. Last series of the year
and it's meaningless now. For the second straight year
our boys swooned in late summer. Just last night they
were eliminated from wild-card contention.)
    And more crunch at the personal level. Today we
learned it's official: our apartment building on the
hilltop (still south hill, yes) is applying to go condo.
Z-wiff spoke with Raphael (landlord) in the garage. The
price range he cited to her for our unit is up about
fifteen percent from his guesstimate of two months ago.
Interest rates are up too, meaning the monthly mortgage

payment would be close to half again what we're
currently paying as renters. Can we swing it? Do we
want to try? We'll have to be moving out either way,
and soon. Our current unit (203) will be remodeled, so
if we want to stay on in the building we'll have to
relocate to the empty unit next door (202). Rather than
move twice we'd probably just buy that unit or maybe the
other one on our floor (201) -- if we could afford to.
The price for either of those other units would be about
the same as that for 203, maybe even a little less.

Stress! It's almost like my all-time stress-out
year of '95. Except -- not really. Nothing could be.
(Well, now just a minute....) But I was unemployed for
much of that year and Mother was dying and so was my
eighteen-year relationship with Lady U. In contrast, as
of this moment I still have a job and relations with Z-
wiff remain splendid and even Mama E's (Z's mother's)
condition seems to have stabilized at a surprisingly
high level: she's regularly watching the soaps now and
keeping us posted on all the latest plot twists.

How splendid with Z-wiff? Unimaginably. Yesterday
was our "fruit & flowers" wedding anniversary of the
solar type: the fourth. (Back on the 11th was the lunar
version, when we became "moongolden": we'd been married
for exactly fifty moons.) We hiked up to the garden
club, site of our wedding reception, for the traditional
annual revisit, nuzzled in the gazebo in the north-side
yard (roses crowding in, squirrels cavorting) and then
moseyed on to our favorite hilltop Chinese place (still
"soon" to be demolished) for dinner. As an anniversary
gift Z-wiff presented me with a photo box displaying
half a dozen very fine color shots of her jazz-warbler
gig -- including three solo numbers! -- performed back
in June at the edgeville club. Miracle we found each
other, yup; as time passes we're only more and more
astounded. -- But blah-blah, I'm a stuck record on
this. Need a stipulation here. Let's have a continuing
rave for the Z-woman!

-- But all the stress. Funny thing, a week ago I
was marveling how everything was fitting into place in

my life as never before. And basically it's still true.
I'm even reaching out to relatives! (And science now
says stress is good for you, at least in some ways, but
as it happens these ways can be lifesaving. Starved
mice, for instance, live much longer because their cells
are continually stressed. That's the theory anyway.
But before deciding to ramp up still further the stress
in our own lives, Z and I would probably want to know
how those starved mice rate their quality of life.)

But even relatives. Three new ones have popped up
in the past eight months, one from each of the paternal
lines and the third from one of the maternals, a
Chandler. Also, second cousin Sverre W. passed through
town on a U.S. tour and interviewed Rob and me for
"Grenjad and Vaehild," the Sandefjord genealogy he's
planning to publish next year (G&V are our paternal
great-great-grandparents). And cousin Erin, who's six
years my junior and grew up in the next Centropolis
suburb to the southwest of ours -- many a holiday dinner
Erin and I shared at the crowded children's table --
she'll be visiting in November after rescheduling at the
last moment; otherwise we'd've met for dinner a week ago
tonight. (I was grateful for the postponement; my
hideaway office was not ready to receive visitors.)

And I'm trying to work my way back into being a
good correspondent. A couple letters a week, that's the
goal. More if time permits. On the docket now are Ann
W., Ken D., Sverre, Lloyd Sandefjord, Patty S., cousin
Kar, brother Jeff, sister Barb. -- She, Barb, sent me a
relatively friendly note in reply to my birthday letter.
I'll go on doing all I can to keep relations open with
her. My hopes are up again, even if only slightly.

*

-- Moved on a few blocks to Z-geist's other
operation, the basement cafe at the ORB (still the only
real bookstore). Officially this cafe here stays open
an hour later than Z-geist does, until eight, but in
fact it's often open much later than that, although
without counter service. The bookstore's closing hour
is ten and in practice the cafe's is usually the same.

[Scat Jyze : Gray Sheep]

   In what other ways is life these days what I always
hoped it would crack up to be? (Am I writing too
strangely or sloppily? Can't be helped! Must not worry
about it!) Well, the existence of friends and a "circle
of support." A couple of kids to "nurture": Kat and new
godson Lwazi, age four months. Always things to do,
places to go, people to meet. (Last weekend Z and I saw
"Homebody: Kabul," live drama on the same stage where
Lady U used to cavort. While admiring the playwright's
intentions and verbal gifts and sharing most of his
political views, I didn't think much of the play itself.
These days I have a better sense of knowing what I'm
doing, where I stand, what the real work is -- and I'm
actually doing that work! (Aiming now to self-publish,
more or less, one of the jyze annals as a Christmas
present for Z-wiff. It's Annal 4, from our meet year,
"Jyze in Love." Hoping the feds' possible computer
seizure won't derail this project. As with all my
writing projects, the word-processing parts of it are
going down on the scope-office machines.))
   And so on. Eating good. Working out. In decent
health as far as I know.
   Favorite corner here. Brick walls behind me and to
my left -- I'm snugged in, out of sight of most of the
cafe, rooted in place back among the displayed canvases.
Like a seated trompe l'oeil sculpture, could say, of an
HQ (historic quarter) drifter. Gooseneck lamp bending
inquisitively, as it appears, over this page. About
twenty feet to my left another table of some serious
personal import: where the Z-woman and I did lunch for
our near-disastrous second date.
   I did answer son Elgie's latest plea for bucks --
the one that came in last month's letter revealing he's
now -- at age thirty -- living in a dorm on campus (he's
wound up at Popeye and Nana's old U in the capital of
country music). Z-wiff helped me see the light on this.
Good grief, I can't be sending money! I'm clinging to
the edge of the precipice myself! Besides, that's not
how I lead my life. That's not the deal. I simply
can't relate to a guy who's forking over monthly $828

payments on a fancy German-made convertible, not to
mention what he lays out for upkeep, fuel, insurance
costs, and probably weekly or maybe even daily wax jobs
as well. He says he'll understand if I can't send money
and I hope he will. But I expect to see a further drop-
off in his already meager communications with us. (Z's
idea is to mail him a health-food package each month.
Sounds good to me, but I doubt we'll stick with it for
long if he's not reciprocating in some way -- and I
don't think he will be. Just a few words would be fine,
an occasional call or e-mail or letter or postcard.)

World conditions? Deteriorating U.S. occupation of
Iraq (the invasion did go down, yes) has forced our two-
fisted cowboy head honcho to crawl to the same UN he
stiffed last year -- now crying for help. Let's hope he
gets none or at least not much. Continuing domestic
economic troubles make the current hard-right cabal look
possibly beatable in next year's elections. Does this
mean the neocons will cook up a new crisis or maybe even
cancel the election? (Martial law, all that: as things
stand now it's probably not too likely but never say it
can't happen here.) The local economy -- ours, J.
City's, still doing its "dot-commie" thing in the U.S.
upper-left corner -- remains bad. Cutbacks galore. But
Z's job looks secure. She's planning to stay with it
five more years, at which point she'll reach the maximum
retirement level with thirty years of service. Then
she'll go for broke on environmental justice, painting,
tutoring, singing, poetry writing -- a long, long list.

Me, I'm "carding" again: meaning I'm altering art
postcards for Z-wiff's amusement. Sixteen so far this
month and I hope I can keep up the pace. About a
hundred to go on the wedding pledge. Maybe for our
anniversary next year we'll throw a "Thousand Cards"
party and declare the pledge fulfilled.

Friends Wei and Alison are off traveling in France.
Earlier this month we hit a lower-north-hill French
restaurant with them and Holly R., the inspiring
political activist and war-tax refuser who'd recently
returned from Palestine. Oh -- and big news from friend

[Scat Jyze : Gray Sheep]

Vic H.: his wife Jean and son Ro got into a nasty
"lovers' quarrel" (in Jean's words) -- Ro tossed an
African drum at her -- which led to his, Ro's, moving
out (at age twenty-two). "The loft within the loft" is
now sadly empty, even its curtains gone. No doubt this
will be reverbing for a while. I still drop by to chat
with Vic (and drink up lots of cheap scotch) every
Tuesday evening. For a ten-day period this month we saw
each other almost daily as I helped him prepare an
application for a foundation grant. He wants to get
back to painting. (His "Cicatrix" book is currently
being considered by several university presses.)
    And now? I'm short a few on filled pages here but
this doesn't mean I can't move on. And I should. It's
Friday night, I've got scoping work to do. For maybe
the last time, who knows. Assuming my computer's still
there. (The new office is two blocks east of the old,
by the way, but otherwise much the same except it's on
the third floor instead of the seventeenth.)

2

    Finally ready to shift this thing into high gear.
It was the sighting of last night's Hunter's Moon,
ringed with high mists, that did it -- straight up and
slightly to the south as I hopped off the last bus from
downtown at half past one in the morning (my usual
return time ever since we started living on the hill).
    So now putting myself on the couch, literally and
figuratively, late in the afternoon, a Friday. Z-wiff's
doing dinner with Aida after work, so I have the place
to myself for a while. But not a real, real long while
I don't think. This might even be the last time I can

do the jyze thing in No. 203. Or then again, maybe not.
All things are hanging in abeyance right now -- so it
seems. Puzzling state. Limbo. The limbo stick
lowering ever more and we're stuck under it bent over
backwards in a permanent shimmy, unable to move in any
direction.

     We're ten days into the month during which we're
supposed to be moving temporarily into No. 202 across
the hall so that this unit we've occupied for almost six
years can be remodeled. But as of now we still don't
have the keys for 202. Only once have we been able to
get through to Raphael (who's currently living back on
the far coast and commuting here once a month and
staying for a week or so), and that was ten days ago.
He ducked most of our questions (this was all by
voicemail) but he did say he'd have Wayne, his right-
hand dude out here, drop by with the keys for 202 "right
away." When they didn't turn up, we started leaving
messages for Wayne. That was four or five days ago.
Now his message box is full. Has he perhaps absconded
with the rent money for Raphael's dozens of tenants?

     All this meaning we may be forced to put off the
move until November. Or maybe there won't be a move.
Or we'll have to -- or want to -- move out of the
building. But move where? Set up house on the sidewalk
or in "the jungle"? All's up in the air at the moment.

     And oddly, same's true with my job. The feds did
finally locate my clearance papers after alleged weeks
of searching. On that score I'm "okay for now," they've
told me, though overdue for another every-five-years
investigation ("we all have to go through them"). But
it's still unknown whether the scope firm will retain
(A) the grand-jury contract and (B) our computers. The
feds are "rereading the contract." Meanwhile we did do
grand jury this week, Naomi and I, same as always.
After all the bluster, shock, phone-tag suspense,
messages urging me to call Mr. X of the U.S. Attorney's
Office, Ms. Y of the FBI. A week of lost afternoons for
the jyze guy. And we did this week's GJ under the same
"inadequate" security measures we've always used.

[Scat Jyze : Gray Sheep]

     (Well, not quite. I did come up with a gambit.
I'm now removing the "security device" from the desktop
computer and locking it in the safe with our laptop.
But to them this isn't a new security measure, because I
implied I've been doing it all along. And I could've
been -- there's no way for them to check and never has
been. I doubt a real computer expert would have much
trouble breaking into our desktop computer even with the
security device locked in the safe. But it sounds good.
They hadn't even known such a device existed. Gives
them something new, another "layer" of security. They
can pretend it's effective. "Oh well, they lock the
security device in the safe, no problem then.")
     But I'm still ready to try loading the software
onto Z's old computer. I should do it anyway,
regardless of what the feds decide. Now that we're in
double abeyance -- that is, suspended in our move to 202
as well as on my job -- I'm thinking I'll be able to
pull it off. Next week. If the abeyances hold.
     So I raved too much last time about relations with
Z-wiff. Or was too glib about them. Because: suddenly
a crisis. She started carrying on about going out
dancing with Aida and Iva K., both of whom are single.
Just the three of them. A pickup fest, in essence,
scheduled for a recently opened downtown jazz & blues
club. So, I bristled. Shades of Lady V. And the Z-
woman backtracked. Hadn't realized I might be upset!
Apologies! And I do choose to go on trusting her. Call
it not an abeyance on this but an aberration. However:
also a little bit of a wake-up call for me. (Shades of
Lady U as well and the first "Indigenes" rehearsals.)
-- Don't want to overdo it, though, because then it
might appear I agree there's something I need to be
awakened from, as if I haven't been treating her right
or something. Huh-uh, not true. No way.
     But could this perhaps be an early sign of, say,
seven-year itch? When we're barely three-quarters of
the way through year six of combined Deephood/marriage?
We'll see. (And so it is too a matter of abeyance.)
-- But stay alert, yeah.

[Scat Jyze : Gray Sheep]

    Quiet building. Quarter to six -- I'm rarely here
at this time on weekdays. Late sun angling in. Several
apartments are empty already, I know, 202 included.
Colorful three-foot-long tinfoil salmon slowly spinning
high above our dining table: it's casting quivery glints
that float along the walls like shards from a disco
ball. Should I get out of here now, take this jyze up
again elsewhere or maybe later right back here when the
moon's shining in? Not a bad idea, either of those.
    (Staring at a big poster Z made for me last night
as a sort of mea-culpa move regarding the attempted jazz
& blues club pickup ploy which my fast work nipped in
the bud. "Save the Last Dance for Me," it says, with a
parenthesis next to "Last" saying "and first and all in
between." And then this in much smaller print, one word
in each letter of the phrase above: "Even murricles have
dangerous moments and I'd rather be on a precipice with
you than any sentient being in the cosmos." So yeah,
even though the last part there might be taken to imply
her G-hub falls short on sentience, forgive her for now
and let's go back to hoping for a strong revival.)
                    *   *
    Fighting with myself tonight for some reason. For
some reason or other. Many possibilities offer
themselves. No matter. At loose ends and 'nuff said.
    Just one rock band grinding it out down below.
Friday night but it's some kind of holiday -- could it
be the abominable Columbus Day? On a Friday? Couldn't
be. Could it? But no school today and the triangle's
showing signs of life. Females strutting around in
courting attire. Males hanging about too, of course,
but most of them around here are such slobs (and I high
on the list to be sure). I'm true to my Z-wiff but
certainly I do look once in a while, by which I mean
check out the babes, though subtly I hope. It's not
just a reflex; it's almost a kind of jyze requirement.
But I can hide or disguise it. Be discreet. At age one
post-Heavenly I should hope so.
    Office door closed. It's still a mess up here.
This too is a matter of abeyances, because it makes no

sense to take things home until I know where home is.
Or a little sense maybe but not enough to warrant the
extra effort it would almost certainly entail later on.
     (Full moon shining down out there in the narrow gap
between very tall buildings. When Z-wiff saw this same
moon last night she thought it looked unusually small.
It appeared that way to me too. Hunter's Moon always
comes as an anticlimax after Harvest Moon, which of
course for Z and me is always swollen extra-large with
its wedding-anniversary significance.)
     Since that anniversary jyzeday three social events
of double-star note:
     ** A dinner at our apartment for our outstanding
new godson Lwazi, age eighteen weeks. His parents,
David and Stacy, and grandmother, Chloris (Stacy's
delightful and dynamic mother, visiting from the
megastate), and Z's friend Rose also attended. Dinner
courtesy of the Malaysian joint. As the only person
present full-bloodedly of the Eurusan tribe I had a lot
of explaining to do about the recent nefarious exploits
of "my people" (and the not-so-recent exploits too,
right, but nothing new there). I presented Lwazi with
my altered version of the "3 Godfathers" lobby poster,
art card size. With its all-Cawk cast (except for one
Latino) would it be a hit or, as Z opined, a very bad
miss? This time for once on racial matters it was Z who
got it wrong. Either that or Lwazi and family put on a
good show. Z went right out the next day and bought a
nice frame for the card and gave it to David at work.
     ** Next, brother Rob at the railcar diner for our
annual joint birthday celebration. The predictable:
books from me for him, CDs from him for me. Same table,
same seats as always -- tradition rules. The neon sign
outside was spinning again despite the burned-out
letters (but only two out of seven this time). Rob
could smoke his pipe indoors in peace. And even not
counting the genealogy-related stuff we had plenty to
talk about. His employer flirting with bankruptcy
again. Our record-breaking warm weather, with the
temperature reaching seventy or above for sixty-one

straight days this past summer. (Rob still keeps
elaborate daily weather records using his own
instruments and so he could confirm, and did, the
weather bureau's accuracy.) This led into our favorite
topic, eco/climate breakdown. Our country's abhorrent
failure to work in meaningful ways to ward off a
catastrophe we're the major cause of worldwide. A
hundred years from now this is what our era will
primarily be remembered for. Of course! Who'll be
around to do the remembering I won't try to speculate.

(Going back, I should mention yet another abeyance:
the revival of my card-altering for the Z-woman has
itself had to be suspended. This makes it almost
certain it won't hit the thousand-card mark by next
September. No fifth-wedding-anniversary celebration of
fulfillment of the pledge. Sixth wedding anniversary
then: that's what I'll aim for.)

(Scat jyze is going well, though, I'll assert.
Yeah! And so I'm planning to buy enough of these cheapo
blank books to cover the rest of my life. How many
fuzzies is that? (They have nifty fuzzy covers.) Hope
for the best, prepare for the worst. Or in this case
why not also prepare for the best? Sixty! Not that I'm
about to race out and buy them all in a day. -- But
mainly I just like the idea of having a big stack of
them around. Something consoling about it.)

** Third, dinner at Jess and Gwen's. Woodsy
secluded southwest-island paradise. But we didn't sleep
over -- thought we'd better hurry back home so we could
start the moving, assuming the keys had arrived as
promised (ha!). Twelve new coats of "cherry cobbler"-
colored paint adorned the high fireplace wall at J&G's.
(Not only did Jess do all the painting but she built the
whole house herself, and from scratch.) First fireplace
fire of the season. Gwen rustled up a feast, and
nothing too spicy (in deference to the sensitive jyzer
gut): chicken, squash, blueberry pie. Jyze City's most
comical cat (the touchingly nerve-damaged Chootchie) was
in fine form, prowling about like a demented prancer.
Gwen's still not pregnant (they're paying five hundred

bucks a pop for artificial insemination) and so they may
settle instead for raising a houseful of Pomeranians.
Best moments for me: after dinner, the couch cluster
before the fire, old blues playing, Chootchie nestled
against my leg, Gwen stroking Jess's hair on the couch
and Z-wiff sprawled out next to them and all three
looking unspeakably gorgeous by firelight. I kept
stealing glances at my own wife!

   -- And for the rest of this entry it'll have to be
down-home jyze (or technically, up-home, on the
hilltop). The promised Moon at the Window. Because the
clock on the digital radio says one a.m. A few last-
second chores before I rush off to the bus stop.

*   *

   -- No moonshine on display. Not now. Maybe a few
hours ago, say about three, or better to say between
three and seven. Now it's just the usual four a.m.
sweet peace, with the occasional low-rider hot rod
ripping it to shreds at high speed twenty-five feet away
down below, though only for a few seconds.

   I in my short-sleeve green henley. Once about a
Great Year back (as a guess) my very best henley of them
all. Only in the past few months has it been limited to
in-house wear. -- And cream-colored hemp shorts. They
look like boxers but they're not; for one thing, they
lack a fly. But I bought them as underwear for the
wedding, along with a matching olive pair, and I'm
trying to get some use out of them. My only below-the-
waist "unners," as Z would say.

   The word from Hal, a construction worker currently
bivouacking up in Raphael's former No. 301 apartment, is
that he told Wayne about our need for the keys but Wayne
"has a lot on his mind these days" and forgot to bring
them. Hal will remind him again tomorrow.

   And tomorrow for us is "Kat day." Second Saturday
every month she spends the night here so Betty can get a
little R&R. Word is she, Kat, likes to hang out with
the fogeys. Last time, though, she crashed very early.
Word is also she's switching boyfriends, from Avery to
Garth. (And from the bedroom right now Z-wiff cries out

17

-- sobs almost -- in a dream. This happens fairly
often, maybe once or twice a month, and especially if
she's been gorging on spices. Usually the words can't
be made out but it sometimes seems she's saying a "no"
or "don't" she doesn't really mean to someone in the
dream. Or maybe that "doesn't really mean" is reading
too much into it. My lewd imagination at work. And
even if it isn't that, she'd undoubtedly say it is.
"The provocateur." She hasn't lost a step on that.

This round only one piece of news about relatives.
Sverre W. resurfaced after a silence of many months, and
his exotically stamped letter from Sweden (otherwise not
very revealing or even personal; he sent an almost
identical one to Rob; but when you think of all the
other relatives he's corresponding with, who can blame
him? -- Although it's true, I'd thought he and I hit it
off well and I was expecting more) -- his letter, I say,
enclosed a five-page excerpt from "Grenjad and Vaehild"
which includes new biographical pages on Rob and me,
among others. The ones about Rob are a bit overly
serious, perhaps, but superbly written: because he did
them himself. In a note he, Rob, mentions he's kept a
voluminous journal all his life and hopes a future
reader or two will want to take a look at it. Maybe I
should ask him to add a footnote saying his older
brother, a/k/a Jyzer G, has done the same. "If you
don't believe mine about something," Rob could write,
"you might want to check out how it squares with his."

Sverre's pages about me are a scream. He wrote
them in his shaky English, basing them on notes he took
when we talked up in the hideaway one afternoon and also
on some other things he heard during his stay, or
thought he heard, or maybe he just made them up out of
thin air. Somehow he has Lady S working as a computer
programmer in a southeastern U.S. state and Elgie called
by that name as an acronymic spelling from the initials
for "Little Guy" (rather than "Little Glen"). And lots
of other howlers like that, only worse. Which is fine
-- at least there's something. Now I'll work up a batch
of elementary revisions and send the pages back and say

[Scat Jyze : Gray Sheep]

I'm ready to have at the whole manuscript whenever he'd
like.

Other news, dish variety. The shocker here is that
our former upstairs neighbors in 303, Doug and Thuy,
have split up, despite having two young kids and a new
house, and Thuy is the splitter. And the man she's
splitting to is Aida's former main dude Kavi, the one
who could never make up his mind about Aida -- Kavi of
the prominent East Indian clothes-importing family and
megabucks. I met him once -- a smooth operator, yes,
but it turned out he can also lay down some real good
lit talk, surprising me and Z as well. And Thuy's the
one who originally introduced him to Aida, and Kavi and
Thuy have remained friends all along. An affair started
up a couple of years ago -- clandestine trips to Mexico
and the like. Doug knew nothing about any of this until
he "stumbled upon" a series of compromising e-mails on
their home computer. Went to his old friend Aida for
advice, which is how I happen to know about it -- she of
course told the whole story to her longtime bestie Z.

Dish! Can't resist this one. Everybody's been
noticing how bedraggled poor Doug looks these days but
thought it was because of financial problems for the new
and improved pan-Asian museum, of which he remains the
director. I've seen him myself -- several times --
moping along the sidewalks of the AQ (Asian quarter) and
decided not to say anything because he appeared so sadly
self-immersed.

-- Saw Ro too, Vic and Jean's kid, at the new
Italian restaurant just outside the entrance to the
hideaway building (former site of the waffle shop). He
was a little shifty-eyed -- not feeling real good about
throwing that drum at his mother, I'd wager, and knowing
I must know about it but not knowing exactly how much I
might know. But he's carrying on with school and living
alone somewhere out in the Yuke, looking for a second
job (and embarrassing his mother by seeking financial
help from her friends -- even begging them for food!).

-- Which just about covers it. For now anyway I
won't try to sort through the pros and cons of passing

along such barefaced gossip. I'll mention this, though:
the man who parlayed his good looks and mondo iron-
pumping talent into movie superstardom has just parlayed
them further into the governorship of the megastate to
the south. Wotta farce! The cowboy cabal in D.C. is
meanwhile hitting the hustings with more lying speeches
in support of its "increasingly troubled foreign policy"
-- as I saw it boldly described in the far-coast paper.
(The other day the ferry we rode to Jess and Gwen's
place was escorted by not just one but two patrol boats,
one on each side, and both bearing mounted deck guns.)
The sorrow. The absurdity. "Dude, Where's My
Country?" (Title of a new book I'm enjoying.)
     Rush to the finish line. Bed dead ahead. (Oops,
sounds bad, like "hetero bed death." -- So scratch
that. Instead: I'm hittin' the hay with my spirit way
up high!) (Right there a line stolen from "Empty Bed
Blues" which jyze tries to use no more than once per J-
book but usually referring to ithyphallic state.)

3

     A few hours ago out this window right here a full
eclipse of the moon. And within moments, just as the
moon rose a bit above the mountains, the eclipse started
to come undone, with a spot on the edge of the disk
lighting up and slowly spreading. Before that, even
after the rising began, no moon could be seen. City
lights, ironically enough, operating in cahoots with
Earth's shadow, kept it dark.
     What's truly different here? The window. Yet it's
almost identical, a mirror image of the one I've been
peering through on Saturday nights (and most other

nights) for almost six years. This is just a year short
of my longest stay in one place as an adult, and that
was at the U Acres house about twenty miles thataway
(southwest) across the drink. (The two longest stays of
my growing-up years were also about seven years, for the
Gatewood Road house starting shortly before I turned
five, and then six years for the upgrade on Cedar Lane.
So for almost half my life I've been literally, and not
just figuratively, could say, at sixes and sevens.)

    -- Truly it's like moving from right brain to left
brain, 203 to 202. Everything's reversed. If the light
switch was to my right there, it's to my left here. No
carpets though. It's colder and noisier than we're used
to, and also darker during all but the early daylight
hours. Otherwise, except for a few quibbles, it's fine.
(Mostly similar quibbles too. Drains are slow, toilets
clog too easily, windows "shed" when it rains -- all
more than a bit annoying actually.)

    For now anyway we're just camping here. "Camping
in." If everything goes well, we'll be moving into 201
somewhere down the line, maybe three or four months from
now, possibly sooner. Depends on whether the city okays
the condoizing plan and the bank approves our loan and
the landlord, Raphael, holds good on his offer. All big
ifs. But I'd still say the odds favor our winding up in
201. In any case that's the one we've decided we want.

    As of today we've been here in 202 one week. All
the major pieces of furniture are in place (same places
as in 203, mirrored) but otherwise it's chaos. Big
stacks of boxes everywhere. A narrow path through the
middle of the "great room" (kitchen/dining/living) leads
to the seating cluster (made up of the couch and two
armchairs) in the front where I hold forth now in the
usual black armchair, with the glass door to the balcony
at my right (yes, in 203 it was to my left).

    -- And later I'll probably be crashing alone on the
foldout bed in Z's room. It's all set up for Kat, but
she, possibly spooked by the new setting here with its
many looming sharp-edged shadows, has wound up sleeping
with Z in our bed tonight. She's "seeing what it's like

to be you, Glen," she informed me in front of Z,
sparking hilarity. For a while I sat in the bedroom
armchair reading, sometimes gazing at the sleeping
"girls." Kat was closest to me. Enough fondness
welling up she could've been a daughter of my own.

Earlier the three of us saw "Lost in Translation"
at a glitzy high-tech downtown multiplex. Two lonely
opposite-sex USAn Cawks in Japan. It was all very
familiar to me even though the selection of "Japanesey"
characteristics added up to a caricature, the typical
wealthy foreigner's take on touristic downtown Tokyo
(with a brief glimpse of a Kyoto temple for variety, and
also a quick view of the iconic volcano from a speeding
bullet train). Still, not as bad as the reviews had me
expecting. An old guy like me, a twenty-something
woman, they succor one another amid all the xeno-ness,
I'll call it, and strike a few sparks but still show
some self-restraint, waddaya know, in deference to their
loyal spouses back home. Z-wiff declared the actor in
the old-guy role to be the spitting image of the jyzer
himself (no comment except -- yeek!).

Earlier this week we saw another film with Kat and
also with Betty, "Discovering Dominga," at a private art
museum on east hill (first movie I've ever seen there).
A Guatemalan orphan raised by a Cawk family in the upper
USAn plains states (maybe a hundred miles down the road
from Betty's home turf) returns to the village where she
was born (probably not far from Kat's birthplace) and
where her parents were among hundreds massacred by
government-sponsored, and therefore U.S.-supported and
-equipped, forces. Kat sat next to me and showed little
reaction even at the most wrenching moments. Afterwards,
outside the theater, she said the movie had "some very
interesting things in it." Then we had to split up.
(Dominga Dominga in the movie didn't much resemble Kat
physically but did strongly remind me of the Ecuadoran
Marta R. -- in appearance, mannerisms, even the way she,
Marta, talked about cultural differences and the
obstacles she faced in trying to adapt to USAn ways --
all this shortly before Lady U came along and displaced

Marta and radically changed my life.)

   -- But what a month it's been. The abeyances. The
move. Last month's jyze session went down, it turned
out, on the last night the 203 apartment was intact.
The next morning the keys for 202 appeared, slipped
anonymously under our door, and we started dismantling.
For three weeks straight I worked on the move at least a
couple of hours a day, with a big flurry toward the end
when we accommodated Raphael's request to be completely
out by the first of the month to let his crew get right
to work on the remodel of 203. (And they did do that --
the past several days I've been listening to them
tearing out our old kitchen cabinets and tossing them to
the ground from the second-floor balcony during what
ordinarily, without all the racket, would be my sleeping
hours.)

   Z-wiff was caught up in a budget crisis at work so
most of the physical part of the move devolved to me.
She laid out lots of bucks, though, including the tab
for five hours of cleaning by Amanda (the same woman who
regularly housecleans for us every four months) and four
hours of moving assistance by two Cawk drifter dudes
recommended by Amanda, Isaiah and Robert, both close to
my age or maybe even a little beyond it (and both with
horrific tales to tell about living in the nearby
greenbelt homeless zone, "the jungle/rez") -- but both
good workers and easy to get along with. (And I'll just
note that Z, as a matter of conscience, pays Amanda the
same hourly amount she makes herself at her city job.
And always has. Pretty damn fine of her if you ask me.)

   -- And it turns out I'm the sentimentalist when it
comes to changes like the one we're going through now.
203 -- "our first and only home so far." Where we began
our period of living together as "Deeps." And even,
shame of shames considering how long it took to happen
-- and Z herself was surprised to remember this -- where
sexually we first consummated. (Or would it be enough
to say we consummated and cut the "sexually" and "first"
as being redundant?) At any rate, yes, no question, she
showed a lot of patience and tolerance back then on the

vexed consummation matter, and thank the gods for that.
(Though I do remember a spate of meltdowns too --
remember them quite well these days, in fact, as I'm
refreshing my memory on that period while revising "Jyze
in Love," the annal for the year we met which I'm still
planning to present in printed form to the Z-woman at
Christmas -- though the move may have slowed me down too
much now to be able to pull it off in a single swoop.
Well-spaced installments might be a better way to go.)

 Meanwhile: I've gone in to be fingerprinted yet
again by the feds as part of my "reclearance." Red
fingerprint ink, young redhead Randi C. rolling my
fingers one by one across the pad as I gazed out at the
stunning fifty-first-floor view from, as it happened,
the largest of the buildings in what I'm thinking of now
as the scope complex, with the dot-com castle prominent
in that view -- "Hey, Randi, that's where I live, on the
hill over there, a block behind that big orange-brick
thing" (a bit over two miles almost due south). In my
bag right now is a fifteen-page form which Randi gave me
to fill out by Monday. Basically the feds want to know
about every single step I've taken in my life, including
any kicks in the womb. No problem -- except I've done
this for them twice before. What if they compare the
answers? Because on many of the dates I'll just be
winging it, as I'm sure I also did for the earlier
versions. (Nor am I pleased about all the time this new
effort will take. Others in the process of being
recleared -- Randi herself for one, she told me -- can
fill in the questionnaire during their work hours and be
paid for doing so. As a self-employed so-called gig
worker I'm stuck with the tab for my own hours.)

 What, me gripe? No I won't. Big picture, right
from the start I've felt terrifically lucky to have this
nightscoping "day job." Twenty-one years now I've hung
on to it. Just hope I can do that for a few more.
-- Not to be repetitious or anything.

 -- Nor have the feds taken away our computers. My
"security device" gambit may have worked. But I think
we're still in abeyance, yes, on that.

[Scat Jyze : Gray Sheep]

     -- What I'd like to do I can't do because of this
fifteen-page FBI form. Tomorrow night must go to
wrestling with that; I can't come back for a second jyze
session. (There's a scoping job too, and Mama E to
visit.) So this is it. What doesn't get done here
doesn't get done. A whole month.
     Let's see. I guess run all the news items together
and hope for the best.
     Cousin Erin was due in last night but had to cancel
out again, and all things considered it was just as
well. She says she'll try again in February.
     I'm up to a full Great Year's worth of blank
fuzzies to be held in reserve for the scat-jyze series,
of which this is Volume 1 I'm working on now. Just had
to do it. I'm going for yin and yang, blue and green,
with red for the Horse Years because fuzzies don't come
in black. Currently I'm waiting for a new shipment of
blues to arrive at chain bookstore #1. (One of my more
bizarre quests, this fuzzy business, gotta say.)
     Did see "Flower Drum Song" with Z at a downtown
theater, a touring company. "Enjoyable." Touching
moment at the end when the all-Asian-ancestry cast
called out one by one the cities of their birth: Seoul,
Kyoto, Hong Kong, Manila, MSM #1, MSM #2, Jyze City (big
cheer).... Otherwise not much of gritty MSM #2
Chinatown or gritty China itself was left in the show.
Glitz instead, boy-girl, immigrant cliches, first
generation versus second generation. But still, nothing
else like it. (And I'm eager to talk about it with Vic,
whom I haven't seen the past couple of weeks owing to
the unending chores associated with moving. But he grew
up in MSM #2 -- to recapitulate from the Jyze Age
annals, that's shorthand for the second-largest
megalopolis in the megastate to the south -- and near
the Chinatown where the play's set; and I myself worked
on the fringes of that same Chinatown for almost two
years in the late sixties. And we both get a big old-
timer-type kick out of revisiting our MSM #2 years.)
     And: one day Z and I arrived for a Mama E visit to
learn she'd "lost" her hearing aid. Mad searches

25

ensued, including going piece by piece through a week's garbage for the whole house. This is a $2500 device, uninsured. Then miraculously it turned up -- hiding under a cup on Mama E's couchside table. None of us had considered that the cup could have a concave bottom. (Dumb, yeah. But in the burst of relief who cared.)

Or the big rain. Really big. Half again as big as any one-day rainfall in recorded J. City history -- over five inches. Floods, mud slides, collapsed houses. In a number of nearby mountain parks damage is so severe it will take up to a decade to bring the parks back to where they were, both figuratively and, in a few cases, literally -- instances where park fixtures, including whole buildings, washed downhill and/or downstream.

Out in the larger world, resistance to the U.S. occupation is still intensifying in Iraq and on balance that's good news, I'd say, despite the immediate horrors. The Iraqi people could wind up being world heroes if their resistance eventually causes the U.S. to back down from its current preventive-war doctrine openly aimed at achieving long-term world domination. (But of course the eco/climate crisis keeps growing "behind the scenes" and the powers that be aren't even acknowledging this fact to say nothing of trying to do something about it. Hey, we USAns wouldn't want to have to give up a single fricking bonbon of the good life -- even as we virtually assure that, thanks primarily to our own extravagance, it'll be a very, very, very bad life, if any life at all, for most of the world, eventually including ourselves, for generations or quite possibly eons to come.)

-- I'm reading a good book about all this, more or less, "The Middle Mind." First one I've come across in a while to point out just why a revival of the sixties counterculture is desperately needed. (What, are you kidding, Jyzer G? But no, I'm serious. And so's the author of "The Middle Mind.")

*   *

Some fifty-four hours later a kwikjyze. I'm still a little loggy from the day of bad sleep that followed

immediately after the two stars above went down. With
our main bed claimed by Kat and Z-wiff, I wound up
crashing on the couch. Then when Z got up around seven
or eight a.m. and Kat stayed on in our bed, I moved to
the opened-up convertible sofa in Z's room where Kat was
originally supposed to sleep.

Bad sleep for me there because of street noise,
uncongenial pillows, unfamiliar underpinnings, and a
stiff and sore neck (itself resulting from another bad
sleep for me a few days earlier in our usual bed, which
is harder now because we've jettisoned my old futon that
made up one of its two layers of "mattress," and
therefore my usual pillow is no longer the correct
thickness so I can "lay my head just right").

And then last night I needed even more time than
expected to finish filling out my "reclearance" form
(regarding "Trusted Position") for the feds. And today
Z took off from work as the first day of a two-day
holiday for herself (tomorrow is the official one:
Veterans Day) to celebrate the end of this year's six-
month-long city-budget ordeal, and that's why I couldn't
come back to these pages this afternoon at home as I'd
hoped to. The return had to wait until past midnight
here at the hideaway, with my night's scoping work
already a wrap (along with an extended dinner hour
during which I finished reading "The Middle Mind," which
at the end makes a surprise pitch for radic-prog
neopragmatism -- and I'm delighted it does, but at the
same time baffled as to how this proposal connects with
all that preceded it).

So why back? Just wanted to mention a few things.

Filling out that form, for one. It occurred to me
that every single reference I cited was someone I'd met
through the Z-spouse. Eight of them in all (you can't
include relatives). -- Or no, there were two, the ninth
and tenth, who, even though technically I met them
through Z, fit better in a different category, since
they're not really her friends: Vic and Jean. (And Vic
and I had one of our best "scotch mist" sessions ever a
few weeks ago, for almost six hours straight. Yet I

wonder: since he's doing no writing now, are we already
past our peak? Also: he took a nasty spill off a ladder
and spent a day in a hospital emergency room; he's lucky
to have escaped with only cuts and bruises. And the
fall happened, talk about symbolism, while he was
clearing out Ro's loft room -- in fact bringing down
Ro's childhood erector set. Yes!)

     Just mention too: Doug and Thuy are both now
"dating" and the people they're doing this with are
each other. But she still wants to go out with other
others (mainly Kavi, who however is out of town for long
spells) and Doug still wants a divorce. All this from
Aida. I've spoken with neither Doug nor Thuy (nor Kavi)
since the split-up.

     Five years and ten months becomes history in the
wink of a jaundiced eye. Here and there in isolated
corners of 203 I came upon items which had been
collecting dust in that same spot since our move-in.
"The Old Bull," for instance: the one I gave Dad as a
Christmas present back in the Mezzu era. Literally blew
it off, I did, just like that, with one breath -- "the
dust of the world." So that the Old Bull could shine
again.

     And that's all. No more time. Got to keep moving.
This is the hideaway and there's a bus to catch.

4

     A few extra pages. Why so? Not only just for the
fun of it. I'd like to fill up a little more of the
fuzzy too. By the end of the year (the lunar year, that
is) I'm hoping it'll reach at least the halfway mark.
Then in all years after this until I can no longer wield

a J-stick, a full fuzzy -- or at least that's the goal.
One each year. Sixty in all if everything were to go
right to an unimaginable degree.

Late Thanksgiving night. Rainy. Couch in the
temporary apartment, 202. Still "camping in." Z groans
in her sleep, not even all that loudly, and I hear it:
sound carries extremely well in here.

Holiday dinner with Wei and Alison. It's a seven-
year tradition now. Alison's swimming pal Mari and
Mari's lawyer son Kirby were also present as usual, and
this time we were unexpectedly joined by Z's former
leadership-institute friend Jessica D., with whom Z had
a falling-out some years ago -- but Jessica has now
become a friend of Alison's. Wei's the master chef.
Harvest abundance but not too much of it, if that even
parses. Mari broke a glass -- Alison's mother's best
stuff -- and for a moment we thought she, Mari, might
come unglued herself as a result. But no.

-- Why do I like these new J-books so much? I mean
the physical books themselves, the fuzzies. Just like
to pick them up, the heft, the feel. The slashy black
handwriting soaking into the cheap paper, page after
page, both sides. Somehow it seems so solid. "Must be
a real story here." More than that: "This right here is
how it is." What it actually amounts to probably falls
so far short of how I perceive it, it's laughable. But
I don't know that for sure. If I don't try to mess with
it too much maybe it won't fall short at all. And
regardless: I like the look of the handwriting. For me
it's like gazing at marvelous Chinese calligraphy except
I composed it myself and I can actually read it (though
a few passages scattered here and there require
considerable effort). In fact this has been one of the
main attractions of jyze for me right from the start.

Bizarre, all this, no doubt. Even more bizarre, my
whole life's wrapped up in it and, again, always has
been, beginning with the chrons around age twenty.
Whoever would've guessed my life would go this way? Or
that I could now be thinking the results are so fine
even if maybe no one else would ever see them that way.

Nor am I saying it doesn't matter to me what others
might think. By and large I suppose I'll never know
anyway. (Does that matter? Sure. But I doubt thinking
so will change anything.)
        -- Left brain, right brain. We may go nuts as we
await the word on the next move. The Z-spouse says
living here is sort of like taking up residence in a
small warehouse without benefit of forklift. Or then
again we might be hunkering down in a fully loaded
moving van parked on a dark side street. (At least
three clocks ticking loudly in this room at present.
Distant train whistle sounding. Meanwhile I'm stuffed
with turkey-day leftovers, including a second slice of
pumpkin pie, a big one, and topped with real whipped
cream. At three a.m. I could no longer resist.)
        A few days back, funny, I locked myself out on the
balcony here while watering the plants. Had to climb
down on our shaky emergency rope ladder (luckily I'd
stashed it out there; in 203 we kept it inside but here
the balcony's a little roomier and we need every spare
inch inside for storage). A forty-degree day and I was
wearing just sweatpants, long-sleeve henley, moccasins.
Rang the buzzers for all the apartments: no one else
home in the whole building, or at least no one willing
to make his or her presence known to me. No money, no
keys, no nuttin', including no "unners." Nearest pay
phone maybe eight blocks distant. Four days' growth of
beard, hair long, unwashed, loose -- I was a monster out
there. Three in the afternoon. Lucked out finally -- a
neighbor I know slightly from the annual block party,
Brian, who lives half a block to the north, came out to
load his car and let me use his cellphone to call Z at
her office. Only the second time I've ever made a call
on a cellphone, and it turned out I couldn't manage it
with my cold hands and had to give a chortling Brian the
number to punch in for me. Z happened to be at her desk
-- also lucky. She caught a ride home with her
coworker Bradley E., who when they pulled up outside
hooted loudly at the sight of me. Knees knocking -- I
was out there pacing around on the sidewalk and doing

calisthenics to keep warm for almost an hour and a half.
     -- Earlier tonight I read a few pages of an
Englishman's diary from the mid seventies. Supposedly
he's that country's best protojyzer of the second half
of the twentieth century. I can see it maybe. But he's
so preposterously civilized. So absurdly high culture.
So unbearably snooty about the uppity lower classes,
women, anybody or anything or any cause, say, that I,
for instance, might think worthy (if I can properly
judge after reading only twenty pages, and of course I
probably can't -- though who knows, maybe his multivolume work is all of a piece, just as I hope mine is).
     Still: my stuff's so different. I never see
anything quite like it. And why is that? Again I'll
never know for sure. It's not that I don't find the
things other jyzer types write about interesting, but
rather I find other things they generally don't write
about more interesting and that's what I want to write
about and generally do write about. Even at this
moment. To me it's not narrow, provincial, self-
absorbed, prosaic, dull, this kind of writing right
here. But I can see how it might seem so to others.
But -- which others? Surely not those who see truly.
Not the readers who want something more than just the
same standard literary stuff -- sustained dialogue,
description, structure, "craftsmanship" -- all that.
     This isn't even parodic, what I'm saying here. Not
intentionally anyway. Because I mean all this. At
least for now. True, I don't necessarily always see
things this way.
     "Annals of The Jyze Age." I'm crazy about all
seven of them. Yes, it's all there, everything I want
in a work of art and I mean at the very highest level.
I'm just nervous about whether I'll be able to bring it
all out, or even a significant part of it, to the point
where it can be seen by someone else. And without, in
the process, ruining what's already there. As I've
noted innumerable times before over the years, yes, but
this is important and bears lots of repeating.
     Scat jyze. Right here. Year of the Rising Sign.

[Scat Jyze : Gray Sheep]

If I make it to another Year of the Rising Sign I'll
then be the same age (two ages really, since East and
West count differently) my friend Vic is this year.
Today by nightscoper upside-down time (NUT) being his
birthday (and that of another local legend as well, the
great Afrusan rock guitarist), and it's again falling on
turkey day as it did the year Vic was born (after his
mother, and he himself in embryonic form, had spent more
than six months locked up in an immigration cell on the
second-most-infamous island in the bay of MSM #2). Vic,
I may not have mentioned before, is one Great Year, as
the Chinese call a cycle of all twelve zodiacal animals,
and ten lunar months (moons) older than me.
       I have a long list of things I'd like to touch on.
But I don't have to do it now. They can all wait for
the next scat-jyze moon. Reminding me: I came across
the term "full-mooner" used as a synonym for "raving
lunatic." Maybe I've seen it before -- it doesn't seem
surprising to me -- but now I'm noticing it. That's
what this scat jyze is: full-mooning. And will continue
to be. With the occasional exception such as tonight,
and even this is only technically an exception.

5

    It's up there all right. Full. Bright. Cold.
This, however, isn't the night I wanted to be looking at
it. Last night would've been much better. Sixty-two
years to the day, it was, maybe even to the hour (close
to it anyway), since the jyzer's conception.
    Pearl Harbor Day. In recent years it's been more
in the public mind (after a long slide) because the
nasty neocons running the show in this country love to

exaggerate the similarities between Pearl Harbor and 9/11. The "fear itself" which that much wiser U.S. supreme leader of Pearl Harbor days famously advised us was the only thing to fear is just what the current regime wants to stir up to the max.

Horrific times, yes. But far worse lie ahead -- our current policies guarantee it.

Meanwhile, this life here. On the human scale. A little jyzin' music, Maestro, if you will.

First note this: the last time around was also an anniverary almost down to the minute and I completely spaced it out. Early morning of the Friday after Thanksgiving -- when Mother died. Eight years ago now. I'd been thinking about it too -- but then the scatting meditation on jyze took over. Still: that this momentary forgetting could happen means it's faded for me, and probably about as much as it ever will. As with Dad, daily dialogue between myself and the departed continues and yet the departing itself is pretty much complete. Can even say this with some equanimity.

At the hideaway. Furnace roaring. Just walked back from the fast-fish place on the waterfront, late dinner. Finally finished the book about the greatest of USAn poets as an early philosophical pragmatist. The writing in this book is stodgily academic but the ideas I like: democracy from the poetic point of view. A spiritual dimension of democracy that can't be separated from either social justice or ecology, among a few other urgent qualities and causes.

-- But the life here and now. Biggest news first: Raphael has given us the okay to move into 201 (yes, another move) starting January 1st, and the condoizing of 1511, our building, almost certainly will be happening. This means if we can pass the credit check for the mortgage, we're in. "Homeowners." We'll be updating the papers for the bank this weekend.

How we learned: I heard echoey voices inside our old apartment, 203, and recognized Raphael's far-coast-accented tones and stepped in (the door was open). It was the first time since Z and I moved out that I'd been

back inside the only home we've ever known together; and
it had indeed been gutted. Sinks, toilets, appliances
torn out, floor sloppily plastered in preparation for
laying the pergo. If I hadn't seized the moment, the
bumbly Raphael probably would've neglected to pass along
the news for weeks. (As far as I could see, only one
item from our time remained in there: the screen door I
hung on the doorway to the balcony. It was dismounted,
the hinges unscrewed for painting, but they'll be
putting it back up, one of the workers said. According
to him it's the only screen door in the building.)

So three more weeks of "camping without forklift in
loaded van parked on dark street," to mash up our
analogies, and then we'll be subjected to another crazy
(and expensive) month of bit-by-bit moving. Yes, we'll
have the whole month again. This time the move should
be much easier because most of our stuff remains in
boxes. On the other hand this time we'll have to unpack
the boxes -- sooner or later.

If. Without mortgage approval we'd have to move
yet again, and it'd be a real one in that case, serious,
involving negotiation of tight staircases and packing
and a short time later unpacking a real van. Not just a
few hundred scoots across the hall. Still: on the whole
I'm feeling pretty good about the way it's all shaking
out. Last summer Z doubted me at first when I assured
her we could pull this off. I asked her to trust me, I
did. "Let me handle that flaky Raphael." Several times
since then she's been about ready to put out a contract
on the man's life. -- But we're not all the way there
yet. Things could still go wrong. It's risky, as I've
said from the start, but I think our chances are good.

-- But then again, how reliable am I for real?
Maybe not too, and especially not these days. The
stressful times have me extra-discombobled. The left-
brain/right-brain/reptile-brain confusions. The changes
in the old milk horse's ritual routine. First I locked
myself out on the balcony. Then, last week, I lost my
bank card. Or maybe it was stolen. Either way, the bad
guys and/or gals got ahold of it and before I even knew

it was missing they'd emptied out my checking account.
Over a thousand bucks. Three large charges at burban-
mall department stores and a miscellaneous series of
smaller ones in J. City itself ($12.07 for gas at a
filling station I occasionally walk by on east hill: for
some reason that figure sticks in my mind).

It hurt. Sickening feeling. But apparently I
won't be losing any money. I called the bank the moment
I noticed the card was missing. The guy at customer
service assured me these losses are almost always
covered. "Or at least they are in your state," he
added, referring to the political entity, not my mental
condition (which at that point was close to apoplectic).
As of today the bank's made me a "temporary loan" of the
amount I'm missing. Next I fill out a bunch of
paperwork while their "very, very good" security team
investigates. How they'll be able to determine I wasn't
the one who charged those big-ticket items I don't know.
Do department stores write down license numbers on the
charge slips maybe? "The only time I've seen these
claims fail to go through is when the claimant" --
that's me -- "failed to fill out the paperwork."

But then: Where am I? What's my address? I had
to give the guy three apartment numbers, and all on the
same floor at the same street address. It must've
sounded suspicious. And he sounded confused. What if
the papers go to 201 before the couple living there
moves out? Maybe that couple doesn't like us too much
right now if they know we'll soon be taking over their
apartment; they might feel we're the ones who're kicking
them out. Maybe, who knows, they'll rip up anything for
us that arrives in the mail. My hunch is they would.

What, me worry? Nah. Just this afternoon I was
making color photocopies of a "We moved" card -- a round
hundred of them, at Z's urging -- which will also serve,
with hand alterations, as our ad-hoc Christmas card this
year. (If ever I had a good excuse for not living up to
my Christmas-card tradition, this is the year.)

Also while at it I photocopied some clips for
Elgie. And earlier, at home, put together a Christmas

present for him, a photo of Z and me taken at her jazz-club gig -- less dismaying of me than's usually the case these days and terrific of her as almost always -- and inserted this in a hilarious blueberry frame she found at a garage sale (metal filaments like vines bearing dozens of bright blue berries). -- Because he did say he "really, really" liked the box of snacks we sent him in September, and especially the blueberry bars.

How do I know that? He called! Full of apologies for blowing us off for three months plus. Talked to Z first while I slept and then later I called him on his cell. And the next day he sent Z an e-mail (a warm and friendly one too, meaning he's finally taking my advice about showing her a little more affection) and the e-mail included a digital photo of his new girlfriend.

What's this? Jenny is dead meat? No, "we're still friends." But he's in love with someone else. Perhaps a coed at his university who snatched his heart just as Nana snatched Popeye's in that same setting? No, an eighteen-year-old Romanian, Brigette -- "Gitti [hard G] to her closest friends" -- whom he met on the internet. In one week they exchanged six hundred e-mails, he informed me, and the next week he paid her a visit. Not in Romania, but in almost as boggling a place: Lahontan. City of my birth! City where his paternal grandparents met and married! -- And of course he'd spaced all that out and could scarcely say a word about what he thought of the place. (How'd he afford this jaunt when his last communication in August said he was living on pennies a month? I dunno. But on this occasion -- for the first time really since his reappearance in my life a couple of years ago now -- I didn't feel he was angling for money (nor did he openly ask for any). So, yes, definitely, things are looking up at least a bit. And the phone talk was more relaxed than most of our previous ones -- on a Sunday evening just as I was about to leave for the scope office, and I stretched out on the chair in our living-room campsite still wearing my heavy outdoor jacket and by the time I hung up found myself soaked in sweat -- but at least not from nerves this time. Or not entirely anyway.)

     So, Gitti. He didn't want us to think him shallow
for mentioning this, he said, but she's six feet tall
and has forty-two-inch legs (which by my computation
leaves just thirty inches for the rest of her) and in
the picture she does look like an elongated, rather
small-headed version of a certain famous Romanian
gymnast. She's living with relatives near Lahontan and
hopes to become a U.S. citizen, perhaps with the help of
some marriageable young man who already is one (not that
she came right out and said this, as far as I know).
She's kind and loving and so are the relatives. She's
fine with Elgie going to med school after law school.

     Is the kid mad? An eighteen-year-old? And he's
almost thirty-one? But then I think of the thirteen-
year-gap between me and Lady U. Or how about the
Eurasian gymnast Lady V -- a big fan of that same
Romanian gymnast -- and barely nineteen years old
herself when I met her. And how old was I then? Almost
twenty-eight. And she was going through a divorce and
had a two-year-old son. -- So Elgie may be mad but he's
also a chip off the old block, or to revive Z's acronym
from last winter: a COOB. A COOB with the same highly
disruptive kind of hormones at the very least.

     (This week he's taking his exams. He seems to be
doing all right in law school. For him it's a hurdle to
clear, that's all, a hoop to jump through. He really
hasn't had time to check out any of the old Hutcheson/
Garrett connections around there. -- Oh, and his car
got smashed up the week he arrived at school. Other
guy's fault though so it's no big deal; insurance is
paying for everything. "It drives better than ever!")

     -- And it's time for my bus break. Home, a few
tasks to attend to, then back for a second act.

     But I'll say this. What's most important of all.
"Jyze in Love" is looking pretty good -- and so's the
actual love in its current phase (except maybe the old
up-and-down sexual cycle is not at this moment as far up
as we'd both prefer). But the writing, I like it a lot.
All the moving's exacting a toll, though, and the

current plan calls for presenting the book to Z in four
installments, with only Part One ("JAMR Jyze") for
Christmas. Other big days for the other parts --
Valentine's Day, her birthday, our meet anniversary,
with her conception day and our wedding anniversary as
fallbacks just in case. And: this also helps solve the
chronic what-to-give-her problem for those occasions.

"Jyze in Love" being Annal 4 of "Annals of The
Jyze Age." I checked at the bookstore to see how the
formatting is done by publishers for other multivolume
series which I view as competitors (well, not really):
"A Dance to the Music of Time," "In Search of Lost Time"
and like that. Got a few new ideas for the layout of
the Christmas-gift chunk.

*   *

Couch. Home. But the pressure's on. Four a.m.
already and tonight I want to try to move my crash time
back half an hour, from five-thirty to five a.m. Also
want to present the Z-wiff with some good good lovin'.
We talked about this last night -- our mutual need and
desire for more of same. (And she indelicately let it
drop that Ray -- Aida's brother -- and Vivienne have
been seeing a marital counselor for months. And she
mentioned the new male potency pill the French call "the
weekender.")

See, pressure. Not that I'll be doing any sex pill
no matter what the French may call it. I don't even
think I need such a pill. I'm good, sez I. But
circumstances are not always good; I prefer to put the
blame on them. And at times I tend to wear myself out.
And when I'm fresh, the wiff's often not around or
she's worn out herself. And so it goes with daily
schedules 120 degrees, give or take, out of sync.

But no excuses. I'd like it to work and I think it
can -- our new timetable, I mean.

But do I really want to be writing about this sort
of stuff? Not too much, no. Haven't I already done
more than enough of that, especially in "Jyze in Love"?
("So then just march on in there," right, "and do what
clearly needs doing." And I'm planning to.)

[Scat Jyze : Gray Sheep]

       My left shoulder's pushing up against Z's cloth
Christmas tree which is perched on the arm of the couch.
On the coffee table next to that stands a poinsettia and
an Advent calendar (gift from Jean just like last year).
And for us that's about it this year as far as seasonal
decor goes. Everything else is boxed somewhere, in one
of the huge stacks looming in every direction. Even if
we knew where something in particular was we'd probably
want to leave it there for the nonce. Keep things as
simple as possible in all this chaos.
       What's new in here since last time? A Japanese
door curtain, split up the middle -- can't remember the
Japanese term for these curtains anymore, and I swear I
did know it at one point -- but it hangs from an
expandable spring rod in the hallway between the
entrance area and the "great room." Its main mission is
to counteract the bad feng shui of this place. Or at
least that's Z's view. Personally I think the feng
shui's all right around here; I just don't like the
place itself. But I do like the curtain. It shows a
woman of the Floating World era, not a Yoshitoshi but --
can't think of the artist's name either. (But knew it
back in the day.) (Nor do I think my memory's going
bad. But why do I bring that up? Did I forget that I
vowed not to? -- And I almost neglected to notice,
until this instant, that I need to assert a jyze-rules
exception, or JRX, for mentioning the ukiyo-e artist's
name considering I don't actually know him personally.)
       Our shaky pal June is down in the megastate right
now, a posh burb of the northernmost megalopolis thereof
(MSM #2, yes), for her son Adam's wedding. Z helped her
write the speech she's pretty much required to deliver
as the groom's mother and even so it's not all that
scintillating (I read a draft). June has yet to pull
out of the depressive tailspin triggered by her failure
to pass the bar exam more than a year ago. And as of
last Friday she's hit the Heavenly Year age (the
Gregorian date for it, that is: her solar birthday).
"The girls" at work threw a party for her. Z and I gave
her an autobiography kit, and way back when her Heavenly

[Scat Jyze : Gray Sheep]

Year was "officially" beginning we presented her with a
personalized Gray Sheep icon to keep on her desk
(because, of course, she was born in the Year of the
Gray Sheep the last time it rolled around sixty years
ago; and that's why this is called her Heavenly Year).
But...will she ever emerge from this depressed state?
It's a miracle she's been able to hang on to her job.
She can barely dress herself, still, and that's no
exaggeration. To say she's "low affect" right now, on
the other hand, is, well, also an exaggeration, yes, but
in the opposite direction -- she's below that, close to
zero affect. I'd like to help her out but -- can't.
Have tried many times and in many ways. Will keep on
trying to the extent she'll let me, but that likely
won't be much. Might be, again, zero.
     Mama E, meanwhile, has been constantly warning us
in recent weeks that her longtime Greek boyfriend Tito
will shoot us if we don't fork over $20,000 to him.
Delusion, sure, but we wonder what's the seed for it.
Her dementia's not usually the raving kind and in fact
her new medication, now finally ramped up to its maximum
dosage (where it'll stay), seems to be helping her a lot
with pain. One moment she'll be working on Christmas
cards, the next she'll be calling us with another grave
warning about Tito. Z-wiff finds all this hard to take
so I'm usually hustled into the breach to talk with Mama
E about it -- taking what she tells us "seriously" but
making it crystal clear we won't pay one red cent to
Tito and we can take care of ourselves, thank you very
much. Or joshing her sometimes -- trying to talk like a
celluloid tough guy, which I know she appreciates -- and
she'll go back to her Christmas cards.
     Speaking of which -- what about my own cards? A
bare-bones list of about twenty (down from thirty-five)
I'd like to send them out to. Short and quick messages.
     Sverre W. wrote again from Stockholm, this time
saying he won't be getting the "Grenjad and Vaehild"
draft to me until late spring. This is good, because
now I can devote most of those newly free January hours
to Part Two of "Jyze in Love" (I'd been planning to do

some heavy G&V editing for Sverre during that period).

Kat here next weekend. Her friend Celine (and
Betty's friend Faye, Celine's mother) has moved to the
megastate, MSM #1, Elgie's town -- Faye's about to take
up domestic-partner-style living with a former high-
school boyfriend down there -- and we all enjoyed the
farewell party Betty threw. Now, though, Z thinks,
Betty "will be emotionally needier." Z's already
dealing with a number of emotionally needy friends these
days. Her compassion and loyalty -- her big heart --
are a wonder to behold, even if they do cause her a
great deal of stress at times -- set those infamous mygs
of hers to swarming something fierce.

*   *

A little more. Next night. It occurred to me I'd
never again have this view on a jyzeday. The night
version, the day version. Then I realized that actually
I would, because I'm sure I'll want to be doing some
holiday jyze this year. We'll still be here in unit 202
then. In fact we've agreed, Z-wiff and I, not even to
think about the move to 201 until after the first of the
year (meaning the Gregorian solar rollover). Or at
least: not to talk about it any more than necessary.

But regardless, the kwikjyze urge was upon me.
-- Tell it slant, you say? No: Tell it jyze! Or maybe
stick a comma in that phrase, to wit: Tell it, jyze!
Testify!

-- At a little past three a.m. Radio down low,
"Making Whoopee." (Didn't do that last night, by the
way, Z and I. Maybe tonight though. Certainly hope so.
A wing and a prayer instead of a "weekender.") -- I try
to be very, very quiet in this place at night. Creep
around in moccasins on tiptoes. Back in 203 the carpets
made tiptoeing unnecessary. In 201, carpetless just
like here, it'll probably be necessary again.

Six years this view or a slightly more southern
version of it. Facing east. Mountains, a narrow slice
of lake, a long ridge about a mile away crowded with
houses. Not a truly impressive view for this city but
still: it means something. But yes, I'm willing to give

it up for the greater quiet and the afternoon sun of
201. But still: I'm attached to the eastern view. The
night version especially. But I've written about the
view and the street down below scores of times during
the Jyze Age, or the second half of it anyway, and so I
think I can dispense with doing that again now.

A few weeks ago a gun battle erupted near the small
hilltop supermarket about eight blocks south and two
blocks southeast of here. Dozens of shots fired. Since
then something new for us: we've spotted a pair of armed
bicycle cops patrolling our end of the hill, and on
several occasions. In hard economic times like these we
see more hooking, more drug dealing, more people living
on the street or in cars or RVs. But only rarely is any
of this all that noticeable unless you're looking for
it. But neither is it a middle-class haven of safety
and security out there. If you're on foot you'd better
stay alert at all times, and especially at night.

Right now the big scare issue is the flu. For that
it's shaping up as one of the worst years in decades.
You feel you're taking your life in your hands riding
the bus up here (now the city's most heavily ridden
route) with its tightly packed crowds of hacking,
coughing, sniffling, sneezing, wheezing late-night
riders, most of them low-income folks, swing-shift
workers set free from the hellhole kitchens of downtown
restaurants at one a.m. (and many of these workers
living in halfway houses up here).

-- But maybe I should wait until next time to go
into the flu situation. By then the chances are good
I'll be able to write about the current version with
some firsthand experience. In fact just today Z was
wondering if a dull pain in the back of her head meant
she was coming down with it. (And speaking of hands: I
always wash mine now with soap and hot water, counting
off twenty seconds before the rinse, after riding the
bus home.)

Camping in. Three more weeks of it. Z tries to
imagine we're staying in one of the ancient streamlined
metal trailers at our coastal honeymoon resort. Makes

it seem more romantic, sez she. (Take that back! sez I.
Can't top this realness right here for romance! Gritty
noir to the max, especially the way the streetlight
illuminates the 202 interior from outside. Such fine
sharp alluring warehouse shadows!)

At the scope office, by the way, the abeyance
abideth. What's going on with the feds? It's puzzling.
Naomi and I are starting to think they just might keep
right on abeying until late spring when two crucial
matters are due to happen almost simultaneously. First,
the scope firm's contract with the feds (for grand jury
and related government work) runs out. Second, the new
federal office building opens for business (so to speak
-- ha! -- but then who else would they open for, as
opposed to against?). Maybe they'll decree that all
scoping must be done there, since free space will be
abundant. It's quite possible we'll never be told
anything directly -- just one day the contract will run
out and the conditions for the next one (to be bid on)
will be different.

By then I'll almost be eligible for Social
Security. So what do I care? (But I do. I want to
hang on to this job for a few more years. Retire at the
standard age of sixty-five and a half or whatever it is
now for my birth-year cohort. By a congressional act
passed a few years ago the age of eligibility is
gradually creeping up, paralleling the increase in life
expectancy. -- Not that I'll really be retiring anyway.
Rather I'll finally be free to do the work I love to do
the way I love to do it -- full time and then some.
-- If, that is, the actuarial odds hold up for me. And
the chances of their doing so, as I can never stop
reminding myself -- just for kicks -- are poorer than
those for many or even most of my cohort owing to the
compromises I've made over the years on medical care (so
as to increase the contemporary hours available for
writing, but of course).)

As of early next week, six years at 1511.
Reminding me of this: not long ago Z happened to be
standing nearby when I set the dryer to run a load. She

pointed out I was using the "permanent press" part of
the dial. I haven't owned a single piece of permanent-
press clothing in at least thirty years. And yet for
six years I've been drying my clothes as if that's what
they were. (Maybe that's why they're so good at
standing up straight all by themselves.)

   I should also note it's been a month of impressive
storms. In-city gusts of sixty-five m.p.h. the other
night. Power was out for days in more remote regions.
With trees thrashing against the walls on two sides of
202 here, and in places against windows, we're well
situated to appreciate the extent of the storminess.
And the windows are shedding even more than before -- on
several days Z and I had to go around mopping the sills
almost nonstop. And the storms blew in quite suddenly:
one day the trees were glorious with fall foliage and
the next day they were stripped bare. We were reminded
again -- as happens most years -- that walking on leaf-
strewn hilly sidewalks in wet weather is hazardous,
sometimes about the same as walking on ice.

   Thinking now. One other first this month. Not
only did I attend a reading at the ORB but I lasted all
the way through it, including the Q&A at the end. The
reader was the author of the very same "The Middle Mind"
which I'd just finished reading myself and liked quite a
bit. Not that I could provide a concise summary of its
argument -- or would even want to be able to, given its
strange way of hanging together. Just I sensed in the
author a spirit somewhat similar to mine. But -- he's
too academic. Also too enamored of the old metafiction
school. Too "experimental." (And I'm the guy who
started a lit mag in college called "The Experimental
Magazine" -- no doubt excessively under the influence of
my pragmatist philosopher hero at that point. (Wish I
could say I gave him proper credit in the magazine.)
-- And for that matter I sometimes like to speak of jyze
itself as being experimental.) -- But I'm still
thinking of reading "The Middle Mind" again to see if
maybe I overlooked something which could push my own
thinking ahead a notch or two. (What still puzzles me:

how did the man get from the Young Marxism of the first
three quarters of the book to the sudden celebration of
neopragmatism at the end? And why is he not more
critical of the serious neoprag shortcomings in the
ecological realm?) (And JRX the "Young Marxism.")
     And this: in talking with Elgie I received some sad
news. Lady S's mother died -- at age ninety-seven. I
should almost call her a "Lady" herself because I lived
with her (in the same small house anyway) for about six
months. I won't even try to go back into all that now
(the thirtieth anniversary of the start of my stay in
Korea is just two months away). But equally sad, in a
sense, Elgie said the death occurred in August but no
one told his mother about it until late November (and so
Elgie didn't know either). The reason: "Big Uncle" was
afraid the news would cause his sister, meaning Lady S,
to suffer another stroke.
     I hear nothing from the lady herself, by the way.
Not even any messages relayed through Elgie. It appears
she's now totally written me off -- as in "never again
will his name pass my lips." Presumably this is because
I'm now married to another woman. Before (for eighteen
years) I was merely living with another woman, so from
time to time Lady S felt she could still call upon me
for advice or financial help beyond what we'd long ago
agreed to (usually these calls and letters came at
intervals of years -- and regardless of the size of the
interval I was only occasionally able to provide the
financial help she wanted, although I think I did all
right on the advice part -- not that she ever followed
any of it so far as I know). -- And so I shouldn't be
surprised by this turn, no. And yet somehow I am.
     What if Elgie decides to get married and invites Z
and me to the wedding? I think it would probably be
best to say no. Let that be his mother's time. We
could invite him and his bride to come up here
afterwards. I suppose. Best to check this out with Z,
though, no question. (She definitely helps me see more
clearly on matters like these.)

[Scat Jyze : Gray Sheep]

6

   Three in the morning on Christmas Eve -- early
Christmas Day by Gregorian measure -- or closer to four
I see now. Just finished wrapping my two presents for
the Z-spouse. There they sit on the couch before me in
white boxes resplendently beribboned in shiny red. I'm
moved, even if she might not be. But will she cry? Oh
god I hope not.
   Very significant gifts, sez I. One, the first half
of Book One ("JAMR Jyze") from "Jyze in Love," all
printed up more or less as I hope the full "Annals of
The Jyze Age" will someday look -- complete with title
pages, cover art, the works. Two, a "Jyze Pledge,"
hand-painted on an eight-by-ten-inch hunk of plywood in
the same color scheme, to deliver the remainder of "Jyze
in Love" in installments on specific dates over the
coming year, with a complete final draft of the book
appearing next Christmas, a fully bound version.
   Will she go for it? I'm sure hopin'. A lot of
work went into this first installment. Even just the
cost of printing it at the copy shop on east hill vastly
exceeded our agreed $25 Christmas-gift limit. (And the
big-haired Cawk dude who helped me put it all together
nearly wept, I swear, when I slipped him an extra fin
before we hit the register. Never before in his three
years on the job, he blubbered, had he been tipped.)
   O Christmas. Standing atop the coffee table next
to me an eleven-story "stupa" or pagoda, I guess I'd
call it, of nesting "Twelve Days of Christmas" boxes
stacked atop each other in order of size, with the
smallest at the pinnacle. This is Z-wiff's spectacular

46

gift -- the boxes dark green, the lettering gold and red -- which she's been setting out one box per night ever since the 14th, each box "personalized" on the outside with humorous loving messages in cartoon bubbles and the inside of each box containing a further message and a small gift. Over and over her magnificent ways of loving and giving take my breath away. (True factual statement, not just sappy stuff.)

This afternoon up to Benita's place with Chinese takeout for Mama E. Sadly it didn't go well. The "I'm sick" litany. And her face still badly bruised on the right side from a fall she took two weeks ago. But on the way back Z and I stopped at Dak and Serafina's to drop off gifts for everyone, and then at the magazine shop and nearby used-book emporium on east hill to feed our PMS (printed material syndrome -- the addiction), and finally at godson Lwazi's on the south end of south hill just to say hello, only to discover no one was home and the gift bags we'd left hanging on their outside doorknob yesterday were still there, so we brought them back with us until we can figure out whassup.

Then at home we opened a couple of gifts just for fun, from Vic and Jean. Nicely wrapped, very thoughtful of them -- some fancy scotch for me and some fancy soap for Z-wiff. Methinks, and Z agrees, we now need to supplement our gifts to them. -- But more on Vic and Jean later. Big story there, Christmas tearjerker type.

*

(I'm almost embarrassed to say I'm drinking a goosed-up "special" version of my usual ceremonial bourbon this year. Just refreshed it. First time ever I've tried the truly upscale stuff, a small bottle spotted on sale at the state liquor store while I was picking up booze gifts yesterday for Vic and Jean -- including a bottle of the sprightly-labeled Mountain Gnome bubbly.) (JRX on that brand name but of course.)

Christmas. Annual jazz great's reading of "The Night Before" just went down on the jazz station. Earlier another jazz great's "Nutcracker," very fine. But I coulda stood more old-time bluesy stuff. For me no Christmas music can top that.

To my right, halfway up the former loft stairs at the near end of the big bookcase, one plant stands out among the diagonal row of half a dozen: a choice pink "moth orchid" Elgie sent us. We were both touched, stepmom Z and I. Maybe he likes us a little after all? Tomorrow we'll try to call him.

Sibs Jeff, Barb, Rob all came through with cards, even notes, even letters (except Jeff, but with him a two-sentence note is the equivalent of a five-page letter from either of the others). Beyond that not much. Jim Q., strangely, returned without explanation the wooden "perennial" card from last year. But then this year I've so far sent out not a single card myself. I've also broken my long-running string of being the only fellow around who still hand-makes his cards. But not really, because I'm planning to alter the "We Moved" cards this weekend and mail them Monday. Moving twice in two months, one of those moves "in progress" right now: a damn good excuse, I'd say, for being a few days late with the cards.

Not really in progress though. In readiness is more like it, or near readiness, or fairly near. We start shifting over to 201 in early January. We're still "camping in." Outside it's still the street and the eastward view. May be like this all the way to the end of the volume if not further.

-- Meanwhile the "War on Terror" intrudes on our holiday, and this time it's collared the Z-woman. The national director of so-called Homeland Security (the Nazi-like name chosen by our Nazi-like neocons) -- the national director calls the police chief here, the police chief calls Z's boss at the utility with a warning that Al Qaeda might be targeting reservoirs over the holidays, so Z is now keeping a utility cellphone with her at all times (including in our bedroom at this very moment) because if the reservoirs are attacked, she's the emergency go-to person for the utility's response. (And the radio issues hourly reports of cancellation of long-distance flights from European to

U.S. cities owing to purported intelligence-monitored "chatter" about another plot resembling the Millennium Bomber's alleged attempt to blow up the MSM #1 airport three years ago -- although for several days back then everyone in J. City thought his target was our own golf-tee icon with the spinning restaurant on top.)

Manipulations galore. Al Qaeda, sure. The Third World a/k/a the Global South and East tries to fight back against centuries of domination and exploitation by the West a/k/a the Global North. But more it's our own government. The way to deal with a world in chaos owing to accelerating (A) eco/climate breakdown and (B) rich/poor gap is simply to be the one on top when the endgame calamities we ourselves have largely caused start to hit. That's how these bozos in charge in our national capital think. (They're clowns am I saying? Better cancel that. These matters are much, much too serious to be invoking mere clowns.)

-- But back to the life here, everyday, how we live like it or not, being shut out (through the ever-deepening corruption of our political system) from any realistic hope of influencing national policy. Quotidiana. My job, for instance. Still hanging fire. Who knows what's going on. Not a word from the feds. Naomi and I just keep on doing what we were doing before, even though we're not supposed, according to those same feds, to be doing it. Yet they're still accepting and paying for what we're producing for them. (From Naomi a nice Christmas bonus. But it's not stopping me from thinking it's time to put in for a raise. First in four or five years -- probably five. I've fallen well behind inflation for that period.) (Mortgage application is in. And Z-wiff's getting cold feet. Understandably, I'd say. Doesn't trust "banana turd," as she's taken to calling Raphael. Wants to bring in a real-estate agent even though it would increase our costs by about twelve grand. Wants a risk-free life! "Precautionary Principle," she calls it. -- But then I can't argue too strenuously: it's mostly her money and her credit we're talking about here.

Personally I'd accept the risk if I could save 12K.)

And here I sit jyzing away. Mr. Vintage Sixty-one Solar Orbits. Like I could care how many anni I've piled up. The whole age business, the briefest mention of it and you're judged to be feeling sorry for yourself. I prefer my "Jyze Age" approach: avoid all mention. So you're going to die -- so like you didn't know? So you are but no one else is? So you're entitled to special pleading just because you're so wonderful?

Vision, I'll admit, getting a bit blurry here. Close to five a.m. on Christmas Eve/Day. Oh so quiet and dark. Somewhere kids are lying awake all aquiver with excitement or even sneaking down to peek at the gift glut. (Not our Kat though. She's blase' now -- and also corralled for ten days back at Betty's family's farm on the high plains. Sunday night we did dinner with her and Betty at their J-town place just before they left. Origami, charades, money for the beautiful one (and she is -- everyone's agreed -- a smile so dazzling we all gasp, sometimes even in sync). Dinah R. the weary cynic was also present. I faux-pas'd in the carving of the chicken. What, you mean someone besides me wants some? So maybe I should cut them in on a few slices before sitting down to eat my own? (What happened was I didn't realize I was the designated carver. I thought we were each to slice off our own chunk and I'd been accorded the honor of going first.)

"Christmas Village" all lit up atop Betty's console. A mix of red and pink globes from the south-end discount mart dangling from tree limbs (not evergreen) outside; a glowing red partridge perched in the pearlike crabapple tree. Betty's voice sexy-hoarse from laryngitis. I gave her the usual preapproved (by Z) "lewd hug" and she reciprocated with amusing gusto.

Poinsettia still here, the same one jyze mentioned last time around. Z's fabulous "Twelve Days" stupa/ pagoda and beautifully made "Noel" Christmas stocking, knee-high, that goes all the way back to her Lahontan grad-school days. My three red-and-green kiri ribbons.

[Scat Jyze : Gray Sheep]

Her two-foot-tall cloth Christmas tree. A gift plate of
cookies home-baked for us by Paz and Tobey. Christmas
rag dolls of Z's from back even further: early
childhood. Otherwise, the same "temporary" 202 mess now
well into its second month, with boxes still stacked to
the ceiling warehouse style and gathering plenty of dust
and cobwebs. "Provisional." "Not worth getting
organized here." Personally I'm digging it.
     -- But the special Christmas entry is not about to
wrap. By no means. Jyze will return with a full report
at the end of the day itself by NUT measure. (Rob and
Gail we won't see until Gregorian Sunday. And later
today it's back to Benita's for another try with Mama E.
I'm wondering if it would be wise to point out to her
that Tito hasn't tried to off us "before Christmas"
despite her incessant warnings that he would.
-- Probably unwise, right.) (As far as we know, if
Tito's still alive at all, he remains holed up somewhere
in the mountain wilds of western Canada.)
     I'm happy to be jyzing away, though, on Christmas
-- the eve, the day, NUT time, Gregorian, whatever.
This tradition goes deep. Yule. Can we drop the Christ
out entirely, please, Son of God, Host of Hosts, Hark
the Herald and all that? Don't I wish. But then again
I don't. Not really. Stick with whatever myth gets you
to the wingding. You can wander off a few feet but best
to stay firmly tethered. -- A coupla days a year only,
though, I'm talking. A simple matter of respect for the
elders, innit, but carried up to the cultural level?
                    *   *
     -- Christmas night NUT style now. Same setting
except I'm facing the chair I was holding down last
night. Couch this time. Booze, jazz, the full twelve-
story stupa (Z prefers that term to pagoda so I say
let's go with it). A few discarded gift wrappings still
lying about.
     (whadja git, whadja git?)
     And no disputing it now, I'm locked into a full
year of churning out chunks of "Jyze in Love." At least
the Z-woman didn't cry. Nor did she seem too impressed

51

or excited, but then that's just how she is when
receiving gifts. She read all the way through the "JAMR
Jyze" chunk (quite rapidly) while sitting in that same
chair as I looked on from right here. Every now and
again she produced a snort or chortle. But what she's
not too polite to admit she's most interested in is the
chunk that comes next, which starts with our "first
meeting" date at the magazine shop in her old hood.

     -- Does this next installment talk about sex? she
wants to know. If it does, then how come she can't talk
about sex (ours) with her friends? (Well, she can, of
course. But back near the beginning I did ask her not
to -- because I was making such a fool of myself at it
in the face of her prodigious talents -- and she's held
to that ever since, or so she says, and I pretty much
believe her. Maybe she's slipped up a few times. If
so, though, nothing's made its way back to me.)

     But right now this jyze, I told her, it isn't
talking with anyone except her. Its wider exposure, if
there's to be any, likely won't come until after we're
gone. And if she's got problems with the story itself,
I want to redo it until they're taken care of. True!
-- But still a potential conflict exists here, no
denying. -- But where there's jyze there's a way.

     Up at Benita's Mama E again was not doing well.
She lasted only about ten minutes at the dining-room
table for the big holiday spread, of which she ate not a
single bite. Z-wiff gave her a stern talking-to but its
effect was brief. And yet guess what: Mama E turns out
to be the only one, other than Z herself, who's given me
a handmade Christmas card this year.

     Tony serving, Clark accompanied by his grandmother
(not too talkative this time), Pauline by her late-
arriving daughter Caroline and two grandsons. Muriel
was away. The chow was good, mostly provided by Z-wiff
via the co-op, ham and chicken, three kinds of dessert,
Christmas pudding included. I skipped breakfast so I
could dig in without inhibition. And did do that. But
not to the extent I'm suffering now. Then we came home
and opened our presents.

[Scat Jyze : Gray Sheep]

     Z's gift for me is a handsome canvas bag with the
Chinese zodiac depicted on it in the form of the U.S.
Postal stamp paper-cutout series, and inside the bag a
coupon worth two hours of time with one of the city's
computer experts, this purchased by her at a workplace
auction. And then in a side bag "for us" a button-
making kit (the pin-on campaign type) and the "narrow"
Japanese calendar for the Monkey Year coming up. In
this way she shows her consideration for her chronically
short-of-funds spouse. -- She's just one heckuva fine
wife, yes she is. Lucky stars, I'm counting 'em and
have been since day one and I think the chances are good
they'll never run out as long as my senses remain intact
enough to recognize them and celebrate them. -- Oh, and
irrespective of all that, a memo to self: never fail to
let her know how appreciated she is.
     Sipping. Leaning my head back to stretch and
eyeing the blooms on Elgie's pink orchid hovering
lepidopterously up there. (Didn't even try to call him
yet. No time during a decent hour.)
     -- News coming on, I shut it off. But will mention
two hits of the bad kind. First, the U.S. occupying
force finally captures the evil Iraqi dictator (our
former ally -- the one we essentially put in power and
later encouraged to attack Iran with arms mostly
supplied by us); second, the U.S. economy seems to be
improving. Both of these hits will help reelect the
sorry current incumbent and so in the long run they're
bad for the country and the world. (Is this a crass
thing to say? No way. We're in Condition Desperate.
And by "we" I mean everyone on the planet, although a
few in the upper echelons of power and wealth still view
themselves as exceptions -- they think they can buy and/
or bully their way out of any conceivable trouble.)
     (Also we've got a mad-cow-disease scare originating
in a farm town just a hundred miles southeast of here.
Front-page stuff worldwide. For a while I'll have to be
laying off the burgers. Of course everything I eat --
me and everyone else, including the most scrupulous of
health freaks -- is riddled if not marbled with risks.)

[Scat Jyze : Gray Sheep]

     And my bank did indeed make me whole again for my
stolen/lost debit card. Or at least the "temporary
loan" is holding so far. It's almost as if I hit the
lotto. I feel I deserve (again almost) to have lost the
thousand bucks for being so careless as to allow the
card to be stolen/lost in the first place (I still don't
know what happened to it and almost certainly never
will), so now in a sense I'm a grand to the good. But
this feeling, I'm sure, will pass quickly. The next
quarterly tax payment is due in January and if my
scoping work doesn't start picking up soon I'll need to
tap the deep reserves again. But assuming we get the
okay on the mortgage, it won't be long before I'll be
needing to tap those same reserves in a much larger way.
Most likely it'll be bye-bye deep reserves. And then
what? A gap of three and a half years until Social
Security kicks in, and that in itself will cover at best
only about two-thirds of my monthly expenses as they
stand now (and assuming no additional medical costs).
     Well, one thing I can say for sure: I owe it to
myself -- but also to others, with Z-wiff and Kat
topping the list -- to stay as healthy as I can.
     -- Christmas tearjerker, promised earlier, is as
simple as they come. Parable-like almost. I was at Vic
and Jean's Tuesday night (the 23rd) and Vic had been
telling me how depressed Jean had been because Ro still
hadn't even contacted them since the blowup back in
October, and now Jean had arrived home after dining out
with friends and was saying pretty much the same thing
(but focusing also on the failure of her fifty-cents-an-
hour raise at A-mart to go through) when a knock sounded
at the door and it was -- Ro! With a sheepish look!
And they wouldn't hear of my leaving. My presence gave
them all someone to deflect the awkwardness onto: that's
my theory. So I became a witness to the reunion. Very
touching indeed. The prodigal son returns at Christmas
-- almost like Elgie back in January of this year after
a much longer separation. (Jean dotes on her only child
so much it's truly shocking to see at times, except
she's such a live wire she soon distracts you from it.)

[Scat Jyze : Gray Sheep]

     All else pales beside that scene. The Z-woman and
I did attend a couple of events in the AQ, one a pan-
Asian museum opening for a show of Filusan historical
photos which triggered many childhood memories for her.
Most evocative of all -- this induced a cascade of Z-
woman tears -- was a photo of a 1930s party much like
the one where her father met her mother (in their case a
group of female hotel workers, mostly of Polish ancestry
(Polusans), invited to a shindig where the men were all
Filusans). Doug T. spoke -- everyone agreed he's
suddenly looking better than he has in years. (But the
divorce is proceeding. And Thuy, his soon-to-be-ex
wife, is joining the staff of the new Filusan city
councilman, Carter C., as is Z's friend, and Aida's
sister, Serafina. This means scuttlebutt about city
politics is certain to become even more plentiful during
Z's and my early-morning "pillow talk.") -- And before
that, an AQ Christmas blowout upstairs at A-mart's
former building (now an emporium for schlocky antiques).
At both of these gatherings I put in "cameos," meeting Z
there on my way in to work.
     (Back to the sex stuff again. Z-wiff seemed to
develop a new depth of empathic concern for her G-hub
after reading an interview with a certain Hollywood
"rogue" actor (of "Easy Rider" fame) now sixty-five or
so, who talked about the "diminution" of his "powers" in
that realm and how "humbling" it's been for him. I,
however, don't feel any such powers I may possess have
necessarily diminished, though I do nonetheless feel
humbled by the fact that to others, meaning Z-wiff, they
sometimes seem to have. In my view it's more a matter
of bad timing or our styles occasionally being out of
whack. Just how it is. I can live with it and I just
hope she can. Nothing new here. Doesn't mean we love
each other one whit less. Can be frustrating at times,
though, I'll acknowledge that. And as soon as we get it
going again, that very fact frequently causes a Z-woman
herpes outbreak. Some kinda irony here. But no
regrets. We've both lived and loved plenty and are
doing so now too but more than ever in the ways that

count most -- and in saying this I'm not just speaking
for myself.)

Busy times ahead. The next month -- oy vey.
Another move! Even harder this time because Z's
patience is already worn micro-thin. Not that she
hasn't been exemplary. But again, except even more so
than last time, I'll be doing the moving, the bulk of
it, and regardless of whether my powers of the heavy-
lifting variety have diminished. Also, I have cards to
make, scoping work to do, the remainder of "JAMR Jyze"
and then all of "20K Jyze" to whip into shape for
Valentine's Day. And I need to be prepared: Z may freak
majorly over any new run-in with Raphael or any new snag
in the mortgage process. At all times I'll be wanting
to have ready at hand my myg protective gear.

But I'm still plenty happy enough, yes I am.
Blessed. (I'm not gloating!) Just think, sixty-two
Christmases. How the hell did I make it this far? And
I even still have a good shot at being the jyzer I've
always wanted to be (although until relatively recently
I lacked the proper term for it). Isn't this a
miracle? But of course it is.

I'm wondering now: a splash more of the special
upscale good stuff? Most likely I'll never taste it
again. So sure, have at it.

7

Here we go again. Jyze is so active lately --
scatting so much. But it's early in the morning of New
Year's Day, Gregorian version, or late New Year's Eve
for me by NUT time, and so a jyzefest pretty much must
break out. Tradition says so. Also pressure of the new

(new scat-jyze rules, that is). Also popular demand.
     This on a night we were snowed in. Or more
accurately, feared in. Fear of snow in our case. In
lots of other cases, here and elsewhere in the Homeland
of the Empire That Now Suddenly Dares To Proclaim It Is
One, fear of the "outs" -- the vast majority of the
world population living outside the techno nations.
Fears on the part of the rulers and their hench
countries. (Not just "theirs" either; even more ours.)
     Orange alert continues. Nonetheless a million
celebrators come out in the main far-coast megalopolis
(FCM #1) under tight security -- metal detectors,
sharpshooters on rooftops, helicopters flappety-flapping
overhead. Here in our provincial capital Jyze City
things are almost as tight. Z and I watched the local
festivities on TV, the golf-tee icon ejacking fireworks
more picturesquely than ever before (and at one point a
roving camera passed by the very spot where Z and I
stood -- we both recognized the bush/tree-trunk setting
-- almost directly under last year's only slightly less
sensational golf-tee-icon eruption).
     The plan had been to dance the year away at a
north-end jazz joint where Leola J. was performing
tonight in a solo show (yes, that Leola J.: Z's longtime
friend and former officemate). But a snowstorm hit last
night and another was predicted for tonight. Z decided
she didn't want to risk the roads. Fine with me -- and
thus our quiet evening at home, catching up on some
reading, listening to "Toast of the Nation" as it rolled
across the time zones, live jazz and blues, a tradition
in itself for me.
     Last night I got caught downtown in the storm.
More than a dozen of us waited a full hour past the
scheduled arrival time for the usual last bus but it
never did show up. At quarter past two we set off as a
group on extremely slippery sidewalks and trudged all
the way to our usual destinations on the hilltop.
Mostly Latino and Chinese immigrants, many inadequately
dressed for the cold. Spirits were high though.
Comical scenes all along the way, slapstick stuff, a

pratfall a minute. Bypassers fighting over the rare
taxicab. Snowballs flying. Several in our group had
never seen snow before. The ascent of the steepest part
of south hill was like a scene from "The Marx Brothers
Do Mt. Everest." (I'm still stiff and sore today. Used
muscles that probably hadn't seen action since the most
recent prior snow emergency roughly a year ago.)

   -- But some big news here on the home front. We've
been "preapproved" for a mortgage. Or I should say Z's
been. When the bank discovered I have no credit record
at all -- zip; blank; nil -- they took my name off the
application, because if it had stayed there, the
turndown would've been automatic. I learned about this
and lots of other details -- many more than I wanted to
hear -- in a forty-minute talk with Audrey, the bank
rep. Her "preapproval" call came in yesterday just as I
was going out the door.

   Strangely, the Z-woman does not seem pleased.
She's in a very odd psychological place right now. I'm
hanging on for dear life. Cutting her all kinds of
slack. And she deserves every slice! (She's asleep
now. The usual: it's four a.m., I'm hunkered down on
the couch and the couch itself is still hunkered down in
unit 202 by the front picture window. However: today's
the day we "officially" start moving into 201, the unit
we're intending to buy. In practice, though, the move
won't begin until later, hopefully sometime next week.)

   At this point I won't even try to go into any of
the financial details. We've got issues about some of
them, Z and I do, but I'm figuring I'll just let her
have her way on pretty much everything. This purchase
will cost me more financially than it needs to (her
also), but rather than grapple with her on how to
proceed I'd prefer to focus my grappling energy
elsewhere. (But once a month for the rest of my life,
most likely, I'll wince: when I'm making out the
needlessly large mortgage check.)

   -- So Gregorian New Year's. As a lifetime follower
of the standard Western solar calendar I'm emotionally
obliged to mark the occasion. But for scat jyze the

year will now and forever more end on Chinese New Year,
meaning the lunar kind. The seleno annus. (Only
yesterday did I suddenly recall that "seleno" is a
prefix meaning "lunar." After deploying it numerous
times in "Heavenly Year," I'd somehow suppressed it for
full-mooner usage. Call it an extended senior moment.)
     No resolutions this year. Nothing specific, that
is. But I still feel the annual end-of-December
upwelling of resolve to do better next year at all the
things I've been wanting to do well at this past year
but haven't, or not well enough. And some more than
others, sure. But why jinx them with namings? They'll
probably be changing anyway. Some, again, if not all.
     Looking back, what kind of year has it been? The
horror of what our country's becoming, that tops all
else. Iraq invasion, political and corporate
corruption, religious craziness, diminishing freedoms,
burgeoning racism and nativism and xenophobia,
polarization of rich and poor, blindness to global eco/
climate disruption and our massive USAn culpability for
it, on and on and on. But -- year Elgie and I reunited.
Year I finished up "Heavenly Year," last of the big jyze
annals (from all of which I'm expecting a lot in the
afterlife if I can live long enough in this life right
here to whip them into publishable shape). Year of the
ongoing quasi-rapprochement with sister Barb. Year of
meeting Sverre W. and commencing work on "Grenjad and
Vaehild." Year of weekly get-togethers with Vic up in
his loft and helping him ready his collection of stories
for publication (at this point the same university
presses are still considering it). Year of at least
maintaining with Mama E. Year of good health for me as
far as I know, knock knock knock on woo-woo-wood. Last
year of living in unit 203 and then the temporary stay
here in 202 as we move toward achieving homeowner status
in our endgame domicile 201. Year of focus on "Jyze in
Love" (though 2004/Green Monkey is the year I'm
expecting it to come fully together). Year of surviving
an FBI scare at the scope office (knock knock knock
again). And best of all, easing past any minor glitches

to get to the real nitty-gritty, another splendid year
-- seventh straight -- with the fabulous Zoelie B. And
featuring her triumphant three-tune solo jazz concert!
     Good stopping point right there. But I'm not done
yet. More to say. So I'll revive the strategy I used
for Christmas and return again at the end of the NUT
day. Split the entry as in olden times. (Yawning
anyway and vision blurring yet again.)
                    *   *
     -- Yeah, back as planned. Time and station the
same as last night. And again it's snowing out there; I
can see it in the glowing cone beneath the streetlight.
Not much new accumulation though. Tiny flakes.
     End of the first full planetary revolution of the
new Euro-American year. And I'm feeling bad because I
still haven't even tried to call Elgie. What's my
excuse anyway? Well, the time never seems right. If
it's good here, it's bad there (which I'm assuming is
Lahontan right now, current abode of the lengthy-limbs-
blessed six-footer Gitti). And I said I'd call "around
Christmas." So I remind myself it's officially only the
eighth day of Christmas. (I'm employing the same scam
for my shamefully delayed Christmas cards.)
     Despite the snow we did motor over to Adele U.'s
this evening for her annual party. I drove -- hey,
what's a little snow to me, a Mentoka/Centropolis boy?
We even, though only at Z's insistence, had chains ready
in the cargo area just in case. And wedged into the
backseat, ready to provide mondo musclepower to
extricate us from a snowdrift if necessary, and probably
scared half to death, were Vic, Jean, and Aida.
     A few others showed up for the party, but not the
usual mob. The spread was still fabulous, though, and
we had it almost all to ourselves. Kit N. put in an
appearance (tough politician -- now president of the J-
town city council) and Z-wiff disliked the way Kit at
one point unceremoniously shoved her leg aside -- Z's
leg -- so she could sit down and talk with Aida. Aida
was meeting Vic and Jean for the first time and
whispered to Z (I learned later) she finds Jean "some

kind of chichi!" It's true the whole affair was a bit
short on the cosmo flash Jean goes for -- Ethiopian
drummers and the like. But I still go for Jean. (Yeah,
even if she sometimes makes me feel I'm a bit short on
cosmo flash myself.) Adele said to Vic and me as we
were leaving, "I hear the two of you are good friends."
Jean: "Not just good friends; they're practically joined
at the hip." "But only one day a week," Vic pointed
out.

     -- All night here big thumpings overhead. When I
went down to fetch the "night paper" I found out why:
the folks up in 302 are moving out under cover of
extreme darkness. (And those folks are, by the way --
just to show we're no rubes down here in 202 -- of bona-
fide Ethiopian descent and they do like drums, or at
least their kids do.) This means the building's now
roughly two-thirds empty. Ciro and his mother (living
directly below us now in 102) may be the only other
tenants left. They're also the only ones in the final
full set of occupants who've been here longer than we
have. Most likely they won't be staying on when the
condo conversion goes through, though, so at that point
we'll become the building seniors in a second way (we've
been the elders all along, except maybe for Ciro's
mother).

     -- This year it was our turn to host brother Rob
and Gail for Christmas dinner. No way could we
entertain here, so instead we met up at the log-cabin
restaurant on the west side -- same spot where we did
dinner with Elgie along with Betty and Kat last January.
The original party of USAn Cawk settler-invaders of what
later became Jyze City landed thereabouts 152 years ago.
We had to take a drafty table right by the entrance on a
very cold night (enh, we're all Norskis or part Norskis,
including even Z -- a tiny part -- so no problem);
otherwise it was a warm and festive setting. During
dessert we opened presents -- to slice away at some
tricky packaging I brought forth the Swiss Army knife
(JRX!) from its rarely visited cranny in my bag. Music
from Rob for me as always, along with an old-timey blues

calendar. Nice wrappings too -- Rob and Gail, as the
longstanding Christmas kudo goes, "really outdid
themselves this year." Z-wiff presented Gail with a
Makah shell necklace and also picked up half the tab for
dinner -- wotta wife! (I picked up the other half,
since it was our turn. Seventy bucks just for half!)
     Z-spouse, I have to say, did, in the end, cry.
Over "Jyze in Love" I'm talking. Who was this guy she
was reading about? Suddenly a naked penis-bearing
stranger's sleeping in her bed! But after another
reading or two the guy began to seem familiar again.
She did offer an unsolicited compliment, or at least I
think it was a compliment: said she noticed the second
time around a "droll sense of humor" which she'd somehow
completely missed the first time. And another time she
said, "You know, this really does read like a novel"
(which is what it boldly calls itself on the cover).
     But then she's been in a state, as I've noted
before. Hanging fire on the mortgage, camping in a
loaded moving van, feeling helpless to help her mother,
suffering a nasty herpes outbreak -- all (and more --
for example, an insufficiently erotically attentive G-
hub) -- all, I say, leading to what we'll forever refer
to as, unless we can somehow manage to suppress all
memory of it, the Boxing Day meltdown of Aught Three.
By Boxing Day plus one, though, she'd gotten herself
together again. Me too. I'm vowing to be an ever
better M'bao (her acronym for "My Beloved and Adored
One," still going strong). It's not even a resolution;
it's already an accomplished fact and therefore all I
have to do is maintain the new status quo. Surely my
basically conservative burban unconscious as instilled
by Mom and Dad and Gatewood itself couldn't object to
that.
     Earlier tonight we worked up our schedule for the
next month. It's brutal. But then we're savvy vets now
-- when it comes to moving or just about anything else.
We shall prevail! (Knocka knocka knocka.)

8

"A BEAUTIFUL MESS" says the headline of this
morning's OMP (original morning paper) lying atop a Z-
geist table. Photo shows a wintry urban scene. Same
kind of scene's showing outside the windows here but a
much-degraded version. You can scarcely see building
walls for the mounds of mud-smeared snow and slush.
Sleet slanting down. "Beauty Becomes Ug-ug-ugly."
     The apartment's too cold for jyzing. A transformer
blew at three a.m. (as I was reading the slush-dampened
far-coast paper) and the northern half of the hilltop
went dark. Power didn't come back on until just before
noon ("Morning Becomes Electric!"). Poor Z-wiff had to
get up in the icy dark and dress for work by
candlelight. For her it was the first extended power
outage ever. Proves she's a city girl for sure.
     I'd been planning to come here anyway, but that was
yesterday. Then in the afternoon the big storm finally
hit after a week of flurries and bad-weather alerts and
very low temperatures. It was also the last day of the
Christmas dozen -- Epiphany! -- as well as the night of
the twelfth full moon of the Gray Sheep Year (which
didn't puff out to its final microdegrees of fullness
until 7:40 in this morning's dark). Perfect time for
jyze to scat, last night was. But the storm prevailed.
     Did finally put in a call to Elgie. Last possible
moment to hold to my "at Christmas" vow. Got his
answering service. No reply as yet.
     Meanwhile a sharp new bend in the steep condo road.
No, two bends. First a fumbly-mumbly call from Raphael
asking us to delay our move until mid month so that

Wayne, who's still his chief handyman, can do some
repair work on the unit (201). Infuriating, this,
because Raphael could've told us weeks earlier instead
of waiting until the last moment (for example, much like
my Christmas call to Elgie, right, shameful). But he
did at least confirm he's ready to go ahead on the sale
to us once the lawyers give the okay.

Zoelie's livid over all this. To be sure! So she
calls Wayne to demand an explanation, and he's mystified
because he's told Raphael he'll need the whole month,
not just fifteen days, for making the 201 repairs --
replacing a couple of windows, oiling the counters,
recalibrating the toilet flushes, and much, much more.
"I want it to be flawless for you." -- How's that
again? Not the kind of thing we're used to hearing!
But the upshot, obviously, is that our 202 camp-in
continues. The rest of this month at least. And who'd
want to bet the steep road to condo heaven won't get
steeper or that we've seen its last switchback?

And otherwise?

No New Year's resolutions. But I've decided I can
acknowledge the existence of four areas where I want to
keep trying to do better: exercise, diet, writing,
sexual loving. Devote at least three hours every day to
writing of one kind or another, jyze of course
included, even newspapers shoved aside if necessary.
The fierce focus must tighten still more (but in all
other ways I'll try to stay laid-back as possible).

Why even say any of this? Why put it in writing?
Just so I can wince later, I guess. "See how scat jyze
runs you through the gauntlet?" (Leaves no hot button
unpushed.)

Holding down a corner of the table: my increasingly
beat-up copy of "The Middle Mind." The red and black
(its two-tone cover). Want to study it until I see
exactly how its author busts his moves -- or fails to.

Eaves dripping out there. Awning fringes too.
Umbrellas bumping along atop galoshes with big pillowy
bundles in between. Arctic gear. You rarely see it
here and very rarely so much of it. Yesterday: folks

crunching and creaking along on snow-packed sidewalks.
The Z-woman mocks me as Mr. Macho Man for tackling
conditions this bad with nothing more substantial for
footwear than my usual chucks. But I'm double-hooding
it, extra-layering it, walking street ruts rather than
sidewalks whenever possible (and during the low-traffic
hours I'm out there it's usually possible).

Vic and I canceled our regular Tuesday get-
together. He and Jean are out of firewood and the loft
temperature's hovering in the low to mid forties. They
lie under mounds of quilts, V&J do, and think back to
the frigidly cold Rome winter when they did the same in
the palazzo and Jean was eight months gone with Ro.

Clinkety-clink of dishes being readied for washing.
Bigger crowd than usual for Z-geist. It's cozy in here.
Music's nicely baroque too. Thanks to the dot-com crash
the techies no longer dominate the place as they once
did. I'm probably the senior patron at the moment and
the grungiest too but both titles are contested and
that's enough for me.

For some odd reason the high brick walls in here
have been artless for the past week or so. Bare brick
and all brick. Between shows? Or has the zeitgeist
itself perhaps ruled that art's dead? Austerity's in
across the board (or brick)?

For jyzeable events we've had Aida's annual New
Year's open house last Saturday night and Kat and
Betty's visit to our place -- bearing delayed Christmas
gifts -- on Sunday.

Aida highly animated and looking good in black
sweater and slacks. But she's embarrassed because her
current inamorata, Mather, has again failed to show.
We've been trying to meet him for more than a year now
and never have. "I'm just unlucky in love," moans Aida.
But she's told Zoelie he's a good fuck (and that's a
quote: Z quoting Aida) (so then does Z-wiff shoot back,
"Hey, old G-hub, he's a good fuck too"? But of course
she's not required to do things like that under our "no
sex talk with others" pact). -- Buffet dinner set up on
a long table in the middle of Aida's living room, folks

seated on chairs around the edges, Charles self-exiled
with the other teens up in his room, a masseur hired for
the evening at work behind the closed study door, all
the women signing up for his deep-body ministrations
(and after receiving them emerging in a visibly melted,
possibly postorgasmic state -- but Z-wiff took a pass,
not liking to be intimately manipulated by strangers).

    David and Stacy appeared with godson Lwazi in tow
and the spunky little lad stole the show. Gnawed on my
thumb for a while. Z-wiff loves to dandle him.
-- Turns out D&S&family did MSM #2 for Christmas,
driving down and back, straight through both ways,
lucking out with the storms (a long stretch of freeway
being all but shut down by a blizzard less than an hour
after they whizzed through on the way back).

    Owing to the icy streets on the hilltop I drove the
venerable Addie O. home from Aida's in her own car, with
the Z-woman following in ours. Good thing I did because
it turned out Addie's defroster was frozen and useless
and I had to drive with my head hanging muttlike out the
window. Addie's the one who used to live in the
"Japanese row" across the street from 1511 -- before it
was emptied by the internment order in 1942. In her
early eighties now, she's still plenty sharp: peppered
me with questions about the status of relations between
Doug and Thuy, her new next-door neighbors (in fact they
learned about the availability of that house from her,
via Aida). Luckily I was loaded with dish on them. Had
to watch myself, though, because some parts of what I
know are confidential and sometimes it's hard to keep
straight what is and what isn't. And this sort of thing
matters plenty to Z, especially if Aida's involved as a
source (as is often the case and was again here).

    -- The next day Kat arrived at 1511 in her plaid-
skirted soccer outfit, fresh from a league game played
indoors because of the weather. Betty showed up moments
later with a bad headache -- sprawled back on Z's chair
for most of the two hours or so of their visit with a
microwave-heated beanbag-like gizmo from her school
nurse's kit pressed against her eyes. Meanwhile Kat was

leaning against me on the couch for much of that time
with my arm locked around her neck. (Z-wiff likes to
see this, I hasten to add. Thinks Kat needs more adult-
male attention and physical contact. And I'm more than
happy to oblige and Kat usually seems pleased also and
so does Betty. Fully authorized and maybe not entirely
innocent but utterly loving and fiercely protective
mutual near-hanky-panky is what this actually is.)

     -- Getting on toward five now. Darkening suddenly
out there and the crowd in here's thinning out. Hello,
here's a country singer on the P.A. for a change of
pace, voice from the deep, still rousing the cons at
that notorious prison down in the megastate. I'll have
to slog on soon -- Z'll be meeting me at the WOC (same
old workout club as always) at half past. I'm still
stiff all over from Monday's round there and also this
most recent bout of long-distance trekking on slushy
sidewalks and streets (several new sets of rarely used
muscles put under severe strain).

     Later, scoping work. Probably won't find an answer
yet to my request for a ten percent raise. I checked
the records and it would be my first increase in exactly
four years. During that time the cost of living in J.
City has gone up well over ten percent. But -- these
are still bad economic times. Technically since I'm
self-employed I don't beg for raises, by the way; what I
do is announce page-rate increases. But I don't want to
price myself out of a job. As it stands I'm already a
little more expensive than the average for scopers who
conduct their operations solely over the internet. But
my turnaround time's much faster, I'm available whenever
needed and on a moment's notice, I'm more experienced
(am I ever!) and probably a better scoper than most or
maybe even all. Naomi wants to keep me happy. But --
perhaps she won't be happy herself and I don't want
that. My guess is she'll go along with the request. Or
she might want to negotiate: do five percent this year
and five more next year, something like that.

     -- And I've cut it about as close as I can. (Hey
-- no more laptops in here right now! I always feel so

much better in a laptop-free cafe environment.) But
onward, yes. (But back later. I'm feeling it now.)
*   *

     "-- But will I be feeling it then?" That should've
been the last line inside those parens at the end.
     Not that I'm not. But it's still cold here in unit
202. And those two cherry popsicles ("ice floes") I
just gobbled down didn't help at all on warming me up.
     At four a.m. Still raining, cold cold rain. No
hope for a viewing of the scat-jyze moon tonight. Last
night we were misted in too and even with the power off
on the hill that mist -- closer to fog really -- was
luminescent, perhaps because of the moon's near-
fullness. (No one but me thinking about the moon right
now. It's the Mars Rover, newly landed, that everyone's
into.) (And JRX that damn Rover.)
     Old wicker chair from the Philippines, on loan to Z
for the past twenty years from Serafina. Cup of tart
pinot noir, made more palatable by stirring in half a
cup of aroniaberry juice. Christmas stuff all still up
-- "Twelve Days" stupa looming atop the table -- but
soon, down. All of it. And here's Alison's copy of
"Life, Paint and Passion," also loaned by her to Z a
while ago, but Z finds she can't get into it. "I don't
like anything," she explains, "that tells me how I
should do creative things, like paint or write poetry or
sing or fuck." Oddly, I like the book. Yet its recipes
are still not for me. For certain others, maybe pretty
good. Among whom Z is not included, though, to repeat.
     "Yes, dear, that's cool." This is Z's stock reply
to pretty much anything I propose these days. Her New
Year's resolution. But I don't think she'll be saying
it to my suggestions on reinvigorating our sex life. As
just suggested, for some reason she's not's so flexible
there. Yet she's the one pushing for reinvigoration.
"Your horny wife." And I by dang intend to come up with
a program she'll go for. It's just that I also want it
to be one I'll go for.
     -- As of seven p.m. power was still out on most of
the west side of J. City, including at Rob and Gail's

68

place. She called with the news. Power failures hit in
big swatches all over town. Our six-hour downtime on
the hilltop was relatively short. (Tonight the delivery
guy handed me the far-coast paper from his car in the
middle of the street as I walked home from the bus stop
in the frozen slush ruts. The sidewalks are still
impassable up here.)

   -- I want to put it on record that I keep a dirty-
clothes hamper under the dining table. This is because
I undress nearby when I arrive home (and shift into more
comfortable sweat clothes). Very revealing, yeah.
Getting nekkid and goose-fleshy. (Can't undress in the
bedroom because Z's asleep in there and she needs to be
fresh for work in the morning.)

   Also note this: I'm using my venerable black
backpack again. It's about fifteen years old and its
like can't be found for sale anymore; all the new bags
are fancier and more ergonomically correct, meaning they
don't work for me. I repaired a worn spot on the bottom
of this one by stitching in some black bookbinding tape
backed with silver duct tape, all on the inside,
virtually undetectable from the outside. But I couldn't
do anything about the partially torn right shoulder
strap. This is why I usually carry the bag on my left
shoulder these days or backwards on the right shoulder
(when I'm not using both straps, that is).

   Modulations. Not until this year -- Gray Sheep
lunar year I'm referring to, since we're still in it --
did I discover the white plastic hamper would fit --
just barely -- under the dining table. Not until a few
months ago did the wear-and-tear on my rust-colored bag
start to make the black one look good again (they're
both the same age and the same discontinued model).

   -- A slipup at the office tonight. The steno
diskette for the job I was supposed to work on wasn't in
the drawer. Nor was the last paycheck for work done in
2003. Nor could I find a reply to my note requesting
(not announcing, not begging for) a page-rate increase.
Once again foul weather's probably the culprit here,
keeping Naomi away from the office, though usually she

leaves me a voicemail if she won't be able to make it
in.

     -- Call it a night now? Maybe so. Guess it's
true, I'm not really feeling it, or at least not as much
as I'd like. (I notice in the rain falling in the
streetlight's illuminated cone the occasional flash of a
snowflake that looks almost like a welder's spark. Or
maybe those are real sparks? Is another transformer
about to explode, as happened one block to the north
last spring?)

     For a final tidbit I'll mention the quote on the
snarly-mouthed U.S. veep's Christmas card. This is the
seriously reactionary and nasty ex-oilman and major
neocon power behind the cabal: the man whom the FBI
ought to be pursuing as Public Enemy No. 1 (though
Gatewood's own Donald R., the secretary of defense, is a
close No. 2). The veep's card quotes something a U.S.
Founding Father said about an empire not being able to
exist if the supreme Christian deity doesn't support it.
(To wit: "And if a sparrow cannot fall to the ground
without His notice, is it probable that an empire can
rise without His aid?" It's ripped from context too,
reversing the meaning, which in essence is that the
Founders need all the help they can get.)

     Dismaying. The kind of thing I can't chase out of
my head, that the seemingly heroic USA of my youth (of
course I'll admit I was massively naive and
underinformed then and am still trying to make up for
the deficit) -- that the USA has come to this.

     -- Two lamps on. Poinsettia still doing fine atop
the coffee table. All the chocolates have long since
disappeared from behind the window shutters of the
special A-mart Advent calendar Jean gave us. Fridge
humming powerfully -- I really notice it now after the
quiet of the blackout hours last night. For an hour or
so I sat right here in the glowy dark with the unzipped
sleeping bag pulled over me, from toes to just below
nose (and Jeep hat on too). "Meditated." As quiet as a
night ever gets around here. No traffic roaring by, no
TVs blasting in nearby apartments, no nuthin'.

[Scat Jyze : Gray Sheep]

9

Closing out the Year of the Gray Sheep. First year
of scat jyze and very successful too, I'll hereby
declare, though it's turning out to be something
different than initially envisioned. In some ways. And
not exactly in the full-mooner sense, no. A bit of
structure here! Regularity! "With room." (As when one
orders coffee, so as to be able later to add cream.)
First the weather. We're back to the normal
winter: chilly, wet, and, as is only right, gray. Out
are cold, slippery, and white. Complaining are -- few.
Even the snowboarders and sledders and skiers prefer to
find their white stuff on out-of-town slopes.
-- But is today really the last day of the Gray
Sheep? Authorities differ. The new moon will appear in
just two and a half hours, most say, but the official
Chinese New Year celebration is tomorrow, that is, the
22nd, not today, the 21st, or today by Nightscoper
Upside-Down Time (NUT), the 20th. It's one more way the
lunar calendar is likable: it's dependent on
interpretation and can befuddle the experts, as indeed
happened at the start of my Heavenly Year exactly
twenty-four moons back. (Gregorian solar time can do
that also but to nowhere near the same extent.)
A notable little calendrical concatenation here.
Yesterday, the 19th, was M.L. King Day (and so Z-wiff as
a public employee was vacationing, but I as a peon in
the private sector could not). Last night -- still
referring to the 19th -- the political primary season
launched with the usual heartland caucuses (producing
lots of drama this year as the out-party struggles to

come up with a viable candidate -- and a surprise winner
emerged, a onetime antiwar protestor who's lately
throttled way back into a moderate liberal). Tonight,
the 20th, the State of the Union address (and I actually
watched part of it -- in living color, no less -- at Vic
and Jean's, just like last year; and also just like
then, what an abomination it was). And then tomorrow,
the 21st, or the 22nd -- "whatever" -- in swings the
Green Monkey Year.

Have news too. Got that raise. The whole ten
percent. "You truly deserve it," Naomi wrote. What's
more: at the urging of the FBI, the scope firm has
finally installed a new office security system, meaning
we now have a chance (probably a good one) of retaining
the grand-jury contract for another five years. And
thus I have a shot (middling if not good) at being able
to support myself with my scoping wages all the way from
here to "retirement." -- A relief, yes. But I'll still
be scraping by from month to month. No bed of gravy or
roses train here. (Cliche dyslexia setting in lots
lately. At times a good malady to have, I say.)

And in comes a card from Ken D. and a holiday
newsletter from his wife, Jo, photos included. They've
aged! -- And since I haven't seen Jo in thirty years,
Ken in thirty-five, in photos or any other way, I
shouldn't be too surprised. And besides, even in their
new more vintage versions they're still looking pretty
damn good and also quite happy. Ken still spouting the
dynamite sports metaphors. Looks like they named a kid
Coltrane -- or it might be a pet; can't tell for sure --
but Ken and I once saw the great man himself perform
live. Resonates doubly, this, because the Z-woman saw
him too, and at the same Centropolis venue during the
same summer of '65 and quite possibly on the same night.
Jazz lover Ken. Without his twin poet's and jazz
lover's encouragements back then maybe no jyze today.

And in comes a call from Elgie. Also a piece of e-
mail on which I'm startled to see the official name he
goes by now is "Glennar P. Sandefjord," just like my
father. (I never put the "P." in there for myself if I

can help it, unless it's preceded by a "G." so the two
together can be read as "Jeep," my old childhood
nickname bestowed by Gramp Perry himself.) To anyone
who's searching on the internet this probably means
Elgie is me, at least for a while. "Hey check this out,
ol' Glen was a DJ in Seoul a few years ago and now in
his dotage he's gone back to school -- to law school!
Just like his old man! He must be crazier'n a coot!"

Gitti, the forty-two-year-old Romanian with the
eighteen-inch legs, is history already. (Or wait, did I
dyslex that too? I did!) -- Elgie's explanation: his
friend Wilson advised him she's too young and
insufficiently educated. So I'd say this kid moves
fast. Heartbreaker! And he's not a kid either! But
then I'm not really in a good position to criticize.
(Z-wiff, though, thinks otherwise: thinks I'm "more the
commitment type." Also thinks it's "a generational
thing." And I'd say in a sense she's right on both
counts: by the time I got to be of the generational
stage I'm in now I'd transitioned more into commitment.
In earlier eras I might've preferred to be the
commitment type, true, but in practice rarely could
manage it for long. -- Of course this could be the case
with Elgie too.)

Other news of the young man: he's taking next year
off from law school, starting in September, so he can
rack up some premed courses. Appears he's leaning more
toward the medical side of his patent-law/medicine
program. He's even talking about becoming a surgeon.
(Wouldn't that mean, I asked, ten more years of school?
His reply: "I can qualify for Social Security at the
same time as surgery!" -- At least he has a sense of
humor.) -- Where's his funding for all this coming
from? I don't know. But he thinks he'll soon be making
thirty K just from a three-month summer job. So
obviously he's either entirely out of my realm or he's
fantasizing like crazy, which would put him right back
into my realm.

Next day he sent the e-mail, mentioned earlier, to
Z-wiff. Had an idea how we could buy a house rather

than a condo. Very cheap, bolt-it-together-yourself
prefab unit, the talk of the web or this or that app or
wherever it is he found it. Z and I are thinking maybe
we haven't done a good job of making our priorities
clear to him. -- But we do like it that he's
communicating. As time goes by it feels more and more
natural. Z even blurted out an invitation on the phone:
"Why don't you come on up here and stay with us for the
fall semester and take the premed courses at the U."
Fine with me. But of course I can't afford to pay his
way and I doubt he can either, thirty-K summer job or
not. That leaves Z. And I suspect she may be
underestimating our early homeowning expenses.

    -- Me, meanwhile, here. Still 202. The couch.
Hanging on in temp fashion just as before. And where's
all this dust coming from anyway? (Lots of hammering
and power-sawing in our old 203 unit -- even with Z's
white-noise machine blasting away it keeps me awake
during the day much more than I'd like. In our supposed
ultimate destination, 201, however, no sign of progress.
But for the time being at least, Z's okay with the
status quo, and so I am too.)

    Big picture? Gray Sheep Year? Guess I've already
pretty much had my say on that. Won't attempt to
evaluate the year by Gray Sheep astrological aspects;
that's not the kind of thing I'm trying to do with this
lunar-year format. I'm just looking for something a
little off-kilter from the standard Western and USAn
ways of carving up time. Looking for something I like.
The animals, the Chinese, the historical resonance for
my own life and the previous jyze volumes, the moon-
revering Tang Dynasty poets, the centrality of the moon
for a nightscoper -- all these I like.

    Also could mention some doings. Dinner at Holly
R.'s with Wei and Alison. Seeing "School of Rock" with
Kat and Betty (and how that movie did bring back my own
youthful foray into rockbanddom, the Nomads, the Worried
Men, "Stranded in the Jungle" and "Alley Oop," "Too Much
Monkey Business," the glory and the agony and the
hormonic if not necessarily harmonic surges, the spurned

jaw-droppingly huge contract with a major record label.
-- Okay, that last part's a crock. But only that part.)
     -- And caught Gavin M., author of "1421," at the
ORB: my second complete sit-through of a reading there.
Already! Even shook his hand and exchanged a few words
with him and therefore the jyze rules allow me to
mention his name (but only the given name and an initial
with a period for the surname). I'm even more convinced
now: the Chinese "discovered" plenty in the early 1400s,
and probably a large part of the world, maybe even
including certain coastal lands in what Europeans later
dubbed the Americas. But historians are still putting
up fierce resistance to this thesis. Few cows could be
more sacred than "Europe discovered the world."
     -- And will Aida, Z's friend, buy a condo in this
building? Our building right here? She's seriously
considering it. A fifty/fifty chance she'll do it, Z
thinks. Dak and Serafina (Aida's sister) are interested
in a unit too, though only for investment purposes.
June may be another candidate for living here. One more
purchaser and "Zoelie and the Friends of Zoelie" could
control the condo council! And the husband of Zoelie
(assuming he'd be ineligible to join the council since
he won't be an official condo owner) (and unofficially
he'll be just a one-third owner) -- the husband, I say,
could be appointed the heavy to guard the door.
     This same Zoelie asked me to assess Mama E's state:
is she deteriorating? I say she is, but not as rapidly
as it might sometimes appear. She's on some powerful
meds that have subduing, not to say zombieizing (at
times), effects. She can still converse, can crack a
joke, can make sharp observations, can take an interest
in life around her, including -- especially -- the
version on her TV screen, and sometimes in unexpected
ways (why hadn't Betty and Kat sent her a Christmas
card, she suddenly demanded to know during our most
recent visit, Sunday). All in all I'd say she's holding
up better than we have any right to expect.
     More? Odds and ends? Well, one day while washing
dishes I was startled to see a chopstick I casually

tossed into the sink disappear straight down a tiny
opening in the grate on the drain. If I tried to throw
it down there like a spear a thousand times from six
inches away I doubt I'd succeed even once. And then a
few nights later I tripped over the telephone extension
cord and quite noisily yanked part of the phone jack out
of the wall, causing Z to lose a couple of hours' sleep.
(These close and cluttered quarters are getting to me.
I have to watch every step I take, as when carrying my
fully loaded backpack into a shop with extremely narrow
aisles and lots of glassware on display -- "china shop,
bull in a," yeah: compare and contrast.)

The famous actress who was Mother's rival for
school beauty queen during their mutual high-school days
in Lahontan died at age eighty-four (which Mother
would've turned next month). On the other hand, the pet
parrot that once belonged to England's cigar-chomping
World War II prime minister was recently found alive and
yakking, not to mention squawking, at age 110 -- exactly
the age Gram S. would've turned two months from now.

And this: I've hit on a way to repair the right-
side strap of my black backpack with heavy-duty black
thread and shiny new black duct tape. It looks a bit
tacky, no question, but now I have hopes I can be
hauling that bag around for another year or two. At
least for all of the Green Monkey Year -- starting, I'll
note, just an hour and ten minutes from now.

Gray Sheep, you're done. You're sheared. Outta
here! See ya in sixty! (Years, that is. -- Or one
Heavenly Year, correct. -- And we do know this renewal
of our acquaintance is within the realm of possibility,
if only by a hair, because at least one human being has
made it to age 122. Which would be my age sixty years
from this moment. And I'll be able to say that for all
the rest of the current Gregorian year. Good
conversation piece fitting right in with the true
zodiac-mad full-mooner cred I'm hereby vowing to
establish once and for all before that Green Monkey can
swing outta here.)

BOOK B

[Scat Jyze : Green Monkey]

10

Squeezing it in. On the run. "Places to do, things to go." Some kind of busy guy. Not that it's truly necessary, the busyness, other than one chooses to make it so. Or better to think one doesn't necessarily choose to do that, but rather one's unconscious does. Not that one can really know how to apportion the blame. (But one can have a pretty good idea, sure.)

Here I am at Z-geist again. Gray day, near to dusk. Just kickin' back. Mellow guy at certain times even if otherwise busy. Just let that ripe fruit fall not too far from the fuzzy. Meanwhile swing by your tail from any available limb of requisite girth.

Or...lots of other possibilities. String theory anyone? Swing theory? Tail theory?

An early opening day this year. Spring eases in on January 22! Stopping by at A-mart on the way down I hoped to see a lion dance or two, there or elsewhere in the AQ. Didn't. But the calligraphers were out in force, including Mr. X, the brushstroke wizard, creator two years ago of a piece of potential cover artwork for "Heavenly Year." Wall hangings, I usually buy one, but not this year. Not even the smallest black-ink-on-red-paper "prosperity" square for ninety-nine cents. Seems I can't get in the mood until we have a more reliably available long-term set of walls at home to hang things on.

Tomorrow, I want to note, the city inspector comes around. Raphael let us know about this in a late phone message -- didn't even meet the legal requirement of forty-eight hours' notice. Z-wiff is fuming over the

diss, of course, as she's done over a number of others
he's dropped on us. Hey, I say, let's just keep hangin'
loose here -- aren't we having a ball? -- all that.
Seems to be working okay so far. But tonight I'll be
the one doing what little pre-inspection cleanup it's
possible to do in our current 202 chaos.

The Z-woman wore her red silk (or silklike anyway,
but I think authentic silk) Chinese jacket to work to
celebrate the new lunar year. Features the animals of
the zodiac, all twelve, and each very stylishly
presented. Hanging there for days in front of the
shower curtain in the bathroom where I could admire it
in the mirror while tooth-brushing. Z counters her
demons by being highly organized and tightly scheduled
(but not by being overly neat, thank the gods). This is
why a born subverter of schedules such as Raphael raises
her every last hackle. Well, one of the reasons anyway.
He's also a blase', overprivileged Eurusan guy from FCM
#1's southern burbs. This makes him something like me,
I suppose -- certainly can't deny I'm largely a product
of the burbs myself, although mine are the northern-
Centropolis kind (probably not all that different from
his) -- but makes him a lot more like brother Jeff.
Jeff morphs in so often when I talk with Raphael,
sometimes I have to look away to reconnect with reality.

Saw Jean at the A-mart floral department. Looked
her up because I needed to talk with Vic about his art
review which was on deadline for the AQ paper and I
couldn't get ahold of him by phone. But then was able
to do so through Jean and the floral-department phone,
some secret signal she uses for him (just as Z does to
reach me). Jean in her bright green A-mart apron,
seeming less harried than usual despite this being one
of the busiest days of the year for her department. She
and Vic, she told me, are throwing a Chinese New Year's
dinner party at ten p.m. for friends of theirs visiting
from MSM #2 and she'll be doing the cooking, so I can't
hang around too long at the loft tonight. But I
couldn't anyway because a heavy scope night lies ahead.
Six o'clock I'm due at the loft. It's five now.

[Scat Jyze : Green Monkey]

    Window table. The guy in the long-sleeved heavy
black cotton shirt and jeans, with the brown ponytail to
mid back (the exact length specified by advanced tail
theory): that's me, the reflected version. The new
Green Monkey Year incarnation, or iteration as some
might say nowadays. Facing east, peering at the main
east-west drag. Railroads up that way, streetcars,
century-old redbrick walls, the equally old black-iron
rooftop fire tower a block away at seventh-floor level.
Empty aluminum tables stand outside on the sidewalk
here, matching chairs. Steady stream of foot traffic,
the usual wintry garb, laptop cases, drifters, artsy
types, many Asian faces. Always feels good to be here.
Not just another franchise coffee joint. Z-geist. The
ghosts. The pulse of the age. Its true name slightly
modified (by me) to honor the Z-woman, whose spirit so
often joins me here (as does the woman herself on
occasion, though probably no more than once a fortnight
on average in the current era).
    One day after our supreme leader tells the Union
how well everything's going in Iraq the CIA leaks an
analysis saying Iraq's on a "path leading to civil war."
    This'll be the year of trying to cast out that same
USAn supreme leader and the neocons and the
fundamentalist loonies, the outrageous swaggery world-
domination schemes, "preventive" wars, Big
Brotherization of the U.S. and the world, outright
denial of global roasting and the various wildly
proliferating eco/climate calamities. Extreme reckless
danger. The out-party has at least a slim chance of
taking power and reversing the demented course we're on
now. The election in November will tell the tale.
(What tale? Yeah, humanity's, I say so. Four more
years like these past four, but this time adding right-
wing control of both houses of the U.S. Congress, and I
don't think a full reversal could happen.)
    The damage is great already. Hundreds of millions
of people severely affected. But it's even bigger than
that. Future of the human race on the line. Can't be
laid-back about this. -- But I'm one of the

beneficiaries. Like the vast majority of USAns, and especially Cawk USAns (Eurusans), I personally profit from these horrific policies, at least in the short run. I may be destitute by Eurusan standards but I still live quite well. who am I to complain? And what good would it do? (Often I think of the author of "Huckleberry Finn" with his magnificent diatribes against USAn imperialism. The country laughed and applauded but usually went in the opposite direction. At least those brilliant rants of his live on, inspiring the ranters of succeeding eras including, to be sure, the Jyze Age.)

For me a year of, especially, moving my work along. "Jyze in Love" for the Z-spouse, other parts of "Annals" just because this is now what I must do, the big work, the masterwork, lifework of the climactic period. Finding enough time to do it will not be easy. Nothing new there. To be able to jyze at all I must be healthy and bringing in enough bucks to support myself and functioning in society to a certain extent and maintaining well with Z -- keeping her happy, yeah, because I love this woman and so must do that to keep myself happy as well. Always I'm searching for new ways to make all these things happen or keep happening. Fine tunings. Minor upheavals. Fresh starts. Jujitsu flips. Fierce inspirations. This year too. No doubt.

The particulars on all this, no need to try to lay them out in advance. That kind of detail of course will almost certainly make up a big part of the year's scat-jyze story. But just a few generalities now won't hurt. To wit: I expect to be writing more letters, working out more, watching my nutrition more, reading newspapers less, rewriting and revising at home more, and (last but not least) loving more and better. -- And so there they are. Now just get on with -- them. Yeah. Exactly.

Any other news? Could mention I sent Evan W., he of the celebrated hand-painted Chinese New Year cards -- Vic tells me he mails out hundreds each year -- sent him, I say, an early Green Monkey New Year's card as an act of tribute which I hope will amuse him. (Have I mentioned this? Evan works in the produce section right

next to Jean's floral zone. Two of the finest painters
anywhere on earth, both of Chinese ancestry, are bumping
into each other daily by the A-mart cucumber bin right
here in J. City: Vic and Evan.) -- From Evan so far, no
card. But Z-wiff added a note to the card I sent him in
which she calls me shameless for "demanding" that my
name be on the envelope as an addressee for his card to
us this year (and not just Z's name, as in all previous
years) (admittedly they did know each other for a couple
of decades before I appeared on the scene).

Kat stayed with us this past weekend. She wrote me
an unsolicited note crowing about whipping me at gin
rummy -- I'm heartened by this. (She also talked
briefly with Elgie on the phone.) -- And when she
arrived home she informed her mother, shocked, "Glen and
Zoelie's TV is black and white! Can you believe it?
They don't even have cable!" (Beats me how she failed
to notice such a glaring deficiency before now.)

And my time is up. I emerge from scat-jyzing, as
is often the case, more than a bit jolted, hyper,
buzzed. Drink lots of coffee at Z-geist. A sip here
and there while mulling, suddenly you're on your second
refill. This is the life!

-- Green Monkey Year, it'll be a live one, I can
sense it. Better yet, I can help make it so. Or anyway
can try. Will.

11

Already I'm feeling a little better. (Aww....)
The lengthy walk in by "the back route," picking my way
a full mile and a half along the torn-up north-south
main drag, then two blocks west. No moon in sight yet,

but if you turn around to search the skies for it while trekking in you see the orange-brick DC castle massively perched atop its steep-sided hill above the high bridge. Its hill and our hill. Our hill of travails right now.

And right here one of the country's "twenty best dives." So a national lads' magazine proclaimed just a few weeks ago, and the story made all the major J. City papers, weeklies as well as dailies. Now I've grabbed a table for myself on the band risers in the back corner, directly beneath a handsome neon sign whose logo features an old-timey fat-tire bicycle much like the one, my first bike, I pedaled so zestily around Gatewood and even points slightly beyond as a boy. Excellent four-seat wooden table, oak I'd say, three planks, the carvings in it so deep you'd almost need four-wheel-drive to travel safely across the tabletop (haw).

Grungy, growly, punky rock playing. The bar, at the far (west) side of the big room, is fairly lively -- two TVs going silently, sports -- but back here it's almost empty. Suitable for a man on a jyze mission. Got my diet soft drink in a can here. The bartender acted almost as if no one had ever asked him for such a lame beverage before. Truth is, though, a joint like this, I still fit right in no matter what I'm drinking.

The bar the tender's patrolling (he in his knit navy blue cap above a classic stubbly mug) is the same one Z-wiff once danced atop. Her fortieth birthday. And a major regret it is I couldn't be present for that. I've heard many a report it was not to be missed. (The "twenty best" award cited the "raunchy amateur bar-top dancers" which are apparently still going at it here -- but probably not too often at this early hour.)

And speaking of celebrations, tonight the long Chinese New Year holiday comes to an end with the Lantern Festival. The moon goes full shortly before one a.m. Yesterday was the first day of spring on another of China's calendars, the ancient agricultural version (and a Chinese year that includes a February 4th at one end or the other -- but especially the front end -- is considered lucky). Two days before that, Punx Phil the

celebrity USAn groundhog espied both sun and moon
shadow, meaning, as we might've guessed anyway, winter's
about to roar back in.

Bringing to mind our state caucuses being held day
after tomorrow. Since last J-day the out-party's poll-
leading presidential candidate has imploded, done in by
his own over-the-top arrogance (I'm sorry to say, though
I never really liked him or most of his surprisingly
conservative platform); and now the lantern-jawed and
thoroughly gelded former antiwar dude -- who's dull,
dull, dull and pompous to boot -- looks to become the
standard-bearer. Assuming he does, I'd give him one
chance in ten of winning in November. Back in the early
seventies I briefly admired the man for daring to speak
out against the carnage after serving in Vietnam (and
causing some of that same carnage himself). After that
the corporate elite began applying the usual power judo
and in no time at all he went pusillanimous. But still:
would that he should win. Hopes and maybe even genuine
chances would rise that the country could steer away
from its current disastrous course.

Which brings me to my latest communication from the
FBI. They want me to sign a statement agreeing to
inform them if my "foreign national" son should try to
influence me in a way that works against national
security. Fortunately they don't bother to define
"national security" -- they leave it to me to do that,
I guess -- so I suppose I can sign it in good
conscience, knowing I'm certainly not about to give up
this job just because of government scare tactics.

More troubling to me, how'd they come up with the
idea Elgie's a "foreign national"? I went to extreme
lengths -- changed my life and brought a lot of grief on
my parents and sister (not that any of it was intended
or that I didn't try to warn them about what might
happen if they let themselves get too involved, as they
soon did) -- went to extreme lengths, I say, precisely
so that Elgie wouldn't be a nonperson in South Korea and
a "foreign national" here. Traveled to Seoul and signed
papers there -- the process took a full year -- making

him a United States citizen at birth (retrospectively,
it's true, but only by some eighteen months, and
purportedly, as a service officer at the U.S. Embassy
explained it to me at the time, to no legal detriment;
and after researching the matter later, Dad the attorney
did confirm this). So what's going on here?

Most likely a glitch has crept in somewhere,
paperwork type. But I don't know this for a fact. If
there is a glitch, could it be of serious import to
Elgie? Z-wiff thinks I should talk with her old friend
Max Y., current head of the local branch of the ACLU.
My choosh is ACLU involvement could easily make matters
worse. -- But I'm thinking on it. Must act, or decide
not to act, soon. Have been trying to reach Elgie, but
without success so far.

I do know Elgie did poorly on his first-semester
grades. He's justifiably worried his 2.4 GPA might
endanger his financial aid. For a while he and Z-wiff
were exchanging e-mails regarding study tips and such.
He's mentioned having problems with classroom
participation -- "feeling shy" -- and so I've bought him
a self-help book about assertiveness and speaking out.
Am sending it for his birthday, coming up on February
19, along with a bobblehead of the extremely tall and
long-legged star of the Jyze City women's pro hoops
team. He'll be thirty-one by Western count. (And he's
still planning to take a leave of absence from law
school next year so he can amass premed credits more
cheaply in MSM #1. I can't imagine the law school would
be too happy about this.)

-- But what is it that's got me downhearted right
now? It's none of the above really. Add-ons, these are
(though clearly they all could rise above that, singly
or together). No, it's the condo situation -- the time
it's taking, the effects it's having on Z-wiff and me.
We're being battered.

But later for the scoop on that. For now it's
enough to say we're still hanging on in 202, waiting to
learn the final purchase price on 201. After much to-
and-fro it still appears we'll be buying the place.

[Scat Jyze : Green Monkey]

        Meanwhile I continue to be a working man. I'm on
the way in now. The scope office is about a mile due
west of here. And the route is all downhill, most of it
within the newly resurgent "east-hill corridor": bars
and pubs, boutiques and head shops (of a sort), hip
restaurants, alt cult such as it is, gays and lezzies
and trannies, movies and books, skateboarders and
piercing palaces and pet groomers. And so: got to get
cracking. Got to blow this dive. Premier dive!
                    *   *
        -- Home now. Dinner done. A last few baked potato
chips rattling in the bowl here. Greasy fingers making
the black matte J-stick barrel shine. Jazz show winding
down, just minutes before the news starts at four a.m.
One big story I already know about from the night paper:
dozens die in stampede at Lantern Festival blowout in
China.
        Tonight was also First Thursday and Z-wiff was out
with Aida doing the HQ artwalk, which they try to hit
together every month. On the sofa opposite a present
for me she must've picked up there: a life-size, more or
less, wooden heart, two-dimensional, with maybe a couple
of dozen metal keys hooked on it, as in "the keys to my
heart." Lotsa keys to this Z-wiff's heart! And it's
true, I could use them right now, every last one. And
even so might not find the ones I need most.
        Just yesterday Aida met with our landlord, the
haplessly disorganized Raphael, to check out a condo.
It's quite possible she'll be living here in the same
building with us (and June still could be also). Aida's
got her eye on Doug and Thuy's old place, 303, directly
above our former unit. But she might be suffering
sticker shock, just as we were at first (and over a much
smaller number). The price for 303 is now up to 200K or
possibly even more. Raphael pulled another fast one on
us, raising prices across the board. (But gosh, who can
blame the guy? If he can command higher prices he
should go for them, of course! This is the USA -- land
of the gouge! And if that also means "withdrawing" his
earlier quote to us, what can we do about it? We

certainly shouldn't be surprised: he did it to us once before. And he is willing to cut us a little deal since we're longtime tenants and we committed to buying long ago. The deal: 201's price is going up only 15K, not 20K as with all the other units.)

Doug and Thuy, by the way, have enlisted for marital counseling. Everyone's stunned. And Thuy and Serafina are battling for control of our local councilperson Carter C.'s two-person office staff (they're the two). (Dish, dish! More dish!)

For one day I was crowing like an idiot. It seemed I had succeeded in holding the price on 201 to 160K. Raphael seemed to be saying that. Z-wiff had no choice but to repeat over and over, "Yes, dear, you were right." Later the same night Raphael slipped a manila envelope under the door -- containing the written confirmation I'd asked for -- and the price he listed there for 201 was 175K. Or really 166K after deducting the real-estate agent's five percent, since we have no agent. (But that same deduction was also supposed to apply at 160K.)

I asked for a reconsideration and supposedly tonight he's been studying the "brief" I submitted. I found some inaccuracies in his numbers. But I doubt it'll go anywhere. We have to decide, Z and I: should we settle for the 165K? It's right at the upper limit of what we can finance while still coming up with a 20 percent down payment. (Without that we'd have to be paying an extra $70 a month for mortgage insurance -- for 30 years. That adds up to $25,200!)

Only yesterday did Wayne, Raphael's handyman, finally start his work on making 201 "flawless for you," as he's told us is his goal. He inadvertently left the door unlocked when he quit for the day and so this morning at five a.m. Z-wiff and I got our first good look at the place. I'm sorry to say Z was not all that impressed. We quarreled a bit. Well, no, she blew up; that's what really happened. Second time in three days. Tensions are high, slack must be cut -- all that. Mygs galore. Tears. Summing up, she's still willing to go ahead with the purchase. "Better the devil you know" is her bottom-line reasoning.

Here's a quick rundown on the drawbacks of our likely new home. From Z's viewpoint: a burglar/rapist could easily climb up to the balcony. The butcherblock kitchen counters would stain too readily. The bathrooms lack storage space. The wall heater in the living-room appears to be that same defective model recalled last year for causing fires. The unit as a whole is smaller than the one we're giving up (which we knew before -- 40 square feet fewer than 203, which has 845). "We'll have to purge," she announced. "Especially books."

For me, I regret the absence of an alcove like the ones in 203 and 202 where I could set up my art worktable. Otherwise it looks okay. And I've got some ideas about where the books could go. (But the lifestyle of the people living above us -- the presence or absence of drums, say, or a basketball-bouncing kid -- will matter a lot.)

We have an appointment with a real-estate lawyer a week from today. In the meantime we're signing nothing. If I'm reading the offering book correctly we have up to three months to make this decision. But we'd like to get it done as soon as possible, for fear of prices rising even higher. And this prolonged campers' life in 202 is wearing on us -- it's fraying nerves we didn't even know we had.

(After an extensive search we managed to locate Z's official name-change papers from the early eighties when she stopped being Louise and took on her current name that combines parts of her father's and mother's names (this was shortly after her father's death -- and since jyze has gone into this in depth in previous annals it won't do so again now). Anyway: with the paper confirming her identity she was able to cash in an old life-insurance policy for $4,000, and that will make the difference in our being able to come up with the 20 percent down payment (for which I'm supplying all of my remaining nest egg from Mother's estate: 25K).

-- During an extremely glum moment in the middle of

one of the quarrels I reflected on how ill-prepared I'd
be if Z-wiff ever decided to dump me. She's the basket
into which I've put all my eggs (or metaphorically
better to say fired my pollywogs, innit?), and not just
the financial ones. -- Could it happen? Z dump me? Of
course it could! This is the USA! And in this respect
I'd even say the USA's doing all right. -- But will it
happen? I don't think so. Certainly not if I can help
it. Nor is she threatening it. But she's not well
pleased with me these days. Except once in a while.
Nothing like as often as before. At best I seem to be a
waning attraction, something like a former hit TV show
in its fifth or sixth season.

     But on our "before the personal deities"
anniversary she came up with a terrific present: a map
of the stars for the night of our "before the community"
wedding. Once we establish ourselves in 201 (or
wherever!) we'll be decorating the margins of the map
("personalizing it") and framing it and hanging it on
the wall next to our bed. Or at least that was the plan
before the quarrels started up again.
                              *
     A week ago last night the godparents of Lwazi
gathered with his parents and grandmother at the largest
and best of the downtown jazz venues to celebrate his
mother's thirty-ninth birthday (the exact moment of
which -- the hour and minute of her birth -- occurred
while we were there, and we all sent up a hullabaloo).
An African "World Music" sensation and his band were
performing. They were just okay, I thought. (And
yesterday Z-wiff and Lwazi's father got into it at work.
These days she's going off on everyone! But today they
staged -- maybe literally -- a tearful reconciliation.)
     And in the midst of all this battling I'm doing
what I can to ready the next installment of "Jyze in
Love" for its promised presentation a week from
Saturday, Valentine's Day.
     -- Why am I so tired right now? Losing sleep over
the quarrels and then today, ironically enough I
suppose, losing more sleep over the pounding coming from

201, the smaller bedroom there, Wayne hard at "making it
flawless" on the other side of the wall just a foot or
two from where I was trying to sleep.

For a few days last week, until the rains washed it
away, a candle was burning in a cardboard box in the
center span of the high bridge which I walk across on
most days, a makeshift memorial for "A.J.," a twelve-
year-old girl (Afrusan, it appeared from the photo,
though maybe also part Asian or Cawk or Native or a more
complicated mixture). Apparently she jumped to her
death there during the holidays, with no media report of
the incident at all so far as I'm aware. When Z-wiff
learned about the memorial she helped keep it going by
supplying new candles. -- One more instance showing why
it's all worth it anyway, the fights, everything.

12

Coupla geezers falling apart. Z-wiff with her
headaches and back and knee pain, me with my hip pointer
or maybe it's something worse than that (too early to
say). And so here I sit at the dining table because the
hip can't take armchairs right now. Still in the
"temporary" apartment, 202, where, just as before except
even more so, "it's like camping in a loaded...
without..." -- yeah. But there is news. Good and bad.

Baddest first. Reporter Naomi's husband, Larry,
the assistant U.S. attorney, was just this week
diagnosed with a brain tumor. Prognosis: "grim" (Naomi
breaking down on the phone as she told me about it).
Consequence for me is that I'm out of a job for "an
extended period" -- maybe two months. I may've found a
little proofreading work to pick up some of the slack

but otherwise Z-wiff will be carrying me for the nonce.
(After the condo deal closes I'll repay her by canceling
the requisite number of her repayments to me of the
deep-reserve funds I've loaned her to cover most of her
share of the down payment. -- And if that's not
perfectly clear, it's still as clear as I can make it in
-- counting now -- thirty-six words or less.)

    Has me thinking about mortality. I actually know
Larry a little bit. Just talked with him on the phone a
week ago while trying to reach Naomi: he was down with a
flu-related headache, as he thought at the time. Over
the past twenty-four years I've scoped thousands of
pages of his grand-jury questionings. Once gave him a
copy of "Chandler-Hutcheson Memorials" to read because
he was developing an interest in genealogy. But he's
way too straight for us to be friends. A prosecutor,
are you kidding me? Far-coast guy, I'm pretty sure.
Centrist out-party type -- his career sidetracked by
this current administration with its legions of neocon
and fundamentalist reactionaries. Made his rep in the
god-awful racist and anti-counterculture War on Drugs.
Softball ump. Three kids by Naomi and a couple more by
his first wife. Often in the past year he's been the
one to drop off Naomi's corrections for me to "final";
his office is fifty stories up in the other highrise at
the scope center (as I'm calling it), the much larger
Building No. 2 as opposed to No. 1 where I work.

    The attorney general himself -- the one for the
whole country -- was just hospitalized with severe
pancreatitis. I mention this because his symptoms sound
a lot like mine, although his are apparently more
intense. Could I be in the early stages of what he's
got? Quite helpfully, though, the newspapers have been
printing body diagrams showing just where the pancreas
is, what it's connected to, etc. Swelling, back pain on
the left side, fever, sweats -- that's me! But fairly
mild so far. I'm hoping it's just a pinched nerve and
I'm imagining the rest or have some sort of flu in
addition. But the suddenness of Larry's illness has me
shaking about what might happen with my own.

(Privately. Nothing about any of this so far to Z-wiff,
except "hip pain, sort of like an old football hip
pointer." She's already got worries enough.)
     Full-moon tales! Rounds of luna tunes!
     Other bad news too, but later for that. Let's go
to the good. Or is it really all that good? Don't know
yet because it's not in writing, though it soon will be,
or should be. But Raphael has offered us a $2700
"credit" if we'll accept his 165K price on unit 201.
That amount would cover the difference between the down
payment for 165K and the one for 152K, the previous
price he'd given us. And overall we'd be saving 17K
from the official market price, and the other units will
all be selling at market, or more likely above current
market, since the market's shooting up so fast. (Front-
page OMP headline: "AREA HOUSING SHORTAGE" -- prices,
having already gone through the roof, are now rocketing
into the clouds.)
     If the papers do get signed I'm gonna take full
credit for the 17K savings. Z-wiff opted out of dealing
with Raphael long ago. We do have a lawyer now, though,
Marc A., and while it's true he hasn't done much for us
legally he's had a calming influence on Z and I'm very
grateful for that. (His wife is Filusan and he's Cawk
-- Ireusan -- and Serafina's husband Dak recommended
him to us; he's known Marc's wife for years.)
     A month of hammering, sawing, other construction
sounds ripping through the building, loud music blasting
-- much like the previous month. Some ten weeks after
201 was supposed to be ready, Wayne's still putting
those flaw-zapping final touches on the place. Of
course he's also tending to many other projects around
the building. But he's told Raphael he wants to get
back to work on our present "temporary" unit, 202,
"soon," so it's quite possible (here I go again) we'll
be outta here, and in over there, by the end of this
month. Supposedly the official marketing date for the
building as a whole is just a couple of weeks away.
Raphael's back from the far coast again, clipping the
hedges and performing various other cosmetic tasks to

make the place as presentable as possible. (Of course
he's not doing that right at this moment, 2:20 a.m.
Presumably he's asleep upstairs in his old unit, 301.)
     June won't be living here. She's saying she can't
afford to buy a unit without first selling her house out
in the northern burbs, and apparently she can't pull
herself together enough to do that. Or is she thinking
she'd lose too much face by living with us (we witnesses
of her bar-exam failure and consequent tailspin)? Hard
to say.   -- And Aida too may be getting cold feet.
She's offered 190K for unit 303, which is currently
priced at a boggling 209K. Her son Charles (sixteen
now) is pressuring her to stay on in their present
house, five miles south at the other end of our hill.
It would be nice for Z and Aida to be close to each
other -- just one floor apart! -- but then again, as Z
herself says, that may be just a bit too close. If I
had a vote on the matter and I could somehow keep it
quiet I'd come down firmly on the "too close" side.
     Once we've settled in at 201 Elgie could be paying
us a visit. He's still planning to take a year off from
law school to rack up premed credits. If he can find
the right courses at the U up here or some other school
in the area he'll live with us for a semester, probably
starting in September. Z-wiff likes the idea and is
willing to sacrifice her bedroom/study for that period.
(Some kind of wife she is, yes. I'm blessed. If I ever
sound like I'm complaining, that's just my own
grumpiness speaking. Or maybe it's my fear that I'm
letting her down. Or of course it could be because
we're in the middle of a squabble -- but usually those
occur a lot less frequently than they have been during
this maddening "camping in" period.)
     It was mass birthday month for the young'uns.
Elgie turned thirty-one, Kat fourteen, and Lwazi eight
months. Elgie didn't have much to say in response to
the gifts we sent, but then neither did Kat regarding
the ones we gave her in person. Lwazi did the best of
the three, though the handwriting in his thank-you note
did look like his mother's. But then -- so it goes. Z-

wiff didn't have much to say herself in response to the Valentine's installment of "Jyze in Love," and Elgie blew off Kat's birthday entirely. Kat was staying with us on Valentine's Day (by coincidence; for the past year she's been coming over on the second weekend of each month and that's where V-Day fell this month) so I bought roses and balloons for her and Betty as well as Z-wiff. A late night of gin rummy with Kat followed, after a serious "conference" about what high school she'll attend. She had a list of eight possibles and we talked at length about the pros and cons of each. A week later she decided in favor of one that hadn't even made the list of eight. (Another week after that we did dinner at Betty and Kat's for Kat's birthday. Barbecued ribs, very good. I gave Kat "The Pen Commandments," a book about writing, after reading it myself. (Can anyone tell?) Lately she's been playing lots of eye games -- seductive "locks" -- with both Z and me. She's learning fast, Z sez. -- But we already knew that.)

Last Saturday was another birthday: my mother's. She'd've been eighty-four. (If she'd been born a few hours later, after Leap Day began, she'd've been twenty-one.) Z-wiff often says she wishes she could talk with my mother and pump her for tips on what makes me tick and how to deal with some of my more difficult personas (or just call them major flaws). Fully appreciates ol' Mom's deep ongoing influence in my life. Also identifies with her in certain ways because I've pointed out their many similarities, hers and Z's -- uppermost among them feistiness and high drama and political/ consumerist activism and hyperactive amygdalas and a keen glamour-puss sense of "where the boys are" (not to mention their similar oddball left-handed -- "sinister" -- perspectives on just about everything).

Lwazi's been facing some worrisome health problems -- three hospital stays in the past two months, the most serious for a respiratory ailment. Is it because of chemicals in the house? Something in Stacy's breast milk? David's frantic over it. (And we're not the most attentive of godparents. Z-wiff sees David at work

every day, though, so that helps. -- Otherwise the
scheduling's too tough. My being a night worker makes
it more so. So do D&S's child-care requirements.)
     Meanwhile: brother Rob's employer declares
bankruptcy. Finally, after months, even years of
rumors. But the store where he's working is still open.
An article in the OMP referred to the classical-music
department there as being "best on the West Coast"
-- indirectly citing brother Rob's efforts as being the
main reason.
     Z-wiff points out: all three Sandefjord boys are
"vocationally challenged." In each case the wife is
the financial rock. (And the Sandefjord girl's no
different. As far as we know Barb's still unemployed --
has been for something like eighteen months now.)
     But -- it's dinnertime. Break time. Be back right
afterwards. Had to work too hard to clear space here at
the 202 dining table not to take full advantage of it.
(Sez Z-wiff: "I just love so much to make a mess!"
-- And lately she's been outdoing herself. Dirty dishes
piled everywhere in the kitchen, a seven-year high, I'd
say, and not a single one of them mine. -- How can I be
sure of this? Because I use only one plate, one bowl,
one glass, one mug, and they're all right here on the
table. But it's comforting to know things can't get any
worse since we're completely out of clean dishes.)
                              *
     So. Incoherent. Pedestrian. Dull. Can see I'm
in top form. But does jyze even care tonight? Must
not. In any event better not if it wants to keep going
here. And it does.
     Three slices of peanut-butter toast for dinner,
along with several spoonfuls of cranberry sauce and the
usual dozen or so vites & supps. (Do they make me any
healthier? I still say yes. For that matter as long as
I'm around to say this it'll be true or at least can't
be proven to be otherwise -- they accomplish what they
set out to do -- so I'm okay with these various pills
and capsules (there's also a morning batch just slightly
smaller) and probably will remain so all the way to the

end, or close to it, however long or short a span that
may be.)

Brought up "the night paper." Double-bagged in
royal blue plastic, still wet. Didn't water the hallway
plants this time. Only four units in the building are
occupied now and two of the other three had loud music
playing at this very late, for them, hour. Construction
materials and appliances fill all the unused parking
stalls in the garage. Among leftover items in one of
those stalls is a motorized red Jeep, child size but
fairly large, maybe even ridable for me. And I'd love
to liberate it. Or at least have my picture taken
behind the wheel as if I were on a mad joyride, knees
sticking way up and the Jeep logo visible. Ideal for a
Christmas card from someone whose childhood nickname was
"Jeep." That's me! But better not try to squeeze
myself into something that size right now -- have
trouble enough just folding myself into the Z-mobile.

Evan W.'s Monkey Year card did finally arrive, by
the way. My appeal worked. He even referred to it,
minimally. Addressed the card to "Z & G" as my card
"demanded," to use Z's term, rather than just to her as
in all previous years. The Monkey in the card, however,
is not Green. Is it possible I'm more deeply into the
Chinese zodiac than Evan, a Chiusan, is?

But with Vic, sorry to say, a rejection slip for
his manuscript from his preferred university press
(which is our local one). I had to nurse him out of his
disappointment and bitterness -- to him it's pretty much
as it was fifty years ago when his pioneering Chinatown
mural in MSM #2 was attacked. (And Jean thanked me for
the nursing. She was lying in bed listening to our
conversation, it turned out. However briefly, she likes
me better again, it appears.) (Today Z-wiff picked up a
pair of bottles of Worcestershire sauce for Jean at our
main south-end discount mart. And earlier Vic and Jean
-- Jean, really -- gave us a teak foldout table as a
housewarming present -- same kind Vic and I always use
at their place for our Tuesday-night eats and drinks.)
-- And last Sunday Vic's friend Bruce O., the bookseller

at the grand arcade in the HQ, was profiled at length in
the combined local Sunday paper's magazine, with a fine
cover photo showing him looking spunky in his infamous
floppy yellow snap-brim rain hat.

-- Z-wiff's Valentine rose is quivering right in
front of my nose here. I hadn't noticed before. It's
amazing how things can become invisible when the clutter
level is this high.

Today was blessedly low stress. An hour of loving
when I woke up -- very careful kind. (And no, I'm still
not out of the woods on loving. The nadir was about two
weeks ago. At that point Z-wiff resuscitated the
"quintessent" lover Bradley mainly for purposes of
invidious comparison, it would seem -- resuscitated
verbally, that is, in a few tall tales resembling the
kind fishermen tell. In real life she hasn't seen him
or heard anything about him in eight or nine years --
about the same as my last contact with Lady U.)

Then out to the Yuke, some low-cost browsing at the
usual magazine shop and the U bookstore. Until I start
making a regular salary again -- or rather, bringing in
something close to the amount I need to live on -- no
more buying of PM, or printed material. -- And since we
were in the area anyway, we hit a north-end branch of
Z's co-op for grub. (As it looks now I'll run out of
cash by the end of the month.)

A historic or at least highly notable moment for Z:
she ran into another former main squeeze, Brian S., on a
downtown sidewalk. Several times she's told me he was
her favorite of them all (but just slightly below
"quintessent" as a shagmaster). She's always blamed
herself for losing him: she insisted he agree on their
having an open relationship in which she could see other
men. And she did take up with other men, at least "a
few." And before long he wanted out. Their time
together was just short of two and a half years (in the
late seventies) -- her personal best before our current
ongoing run. Now he operates some sort of "wealth-
management business." Wears a suit and tie. Is
seriously balding and married with two kids. Cracked

her up by saying marriage is "an interesting
institution." ("Thank god I'm married to someone who
would never say something so banal," she told me -- but
in fact I've said that very thing any number of times.
In jest, true, usually; but does that make it any less
banal? And might not that also be how Brian was saying
it? Or then again maybe this was exactly Z's point.)
     I have an ex-lover story of my own to tell, though
it's just a shadow of hers about Brian. The new issue
of the only Japanese magazine I've ever subscribed to
has photos by Yosh M. and also a review of a new book by
him, "The Streets of Kyoto." The review says he's no
longer the owner of the cafe where I used to hang out in
that city and where I met Maruko, one of my own
"quintessents" for sure, who later (as I understand
from Evan W.) became Yosh's wife and probably still is.
(Evan's wife, Moeko, grew up in Kyoto herself and Evan
met her there and used to hang out at that same cafe.)
     Other good stuff? It's been the month of the gay-
marriage breakout. The new mayor of my former projected
lifetime home city (in these pages a/k/a MSM #2 as well
as my city No. 2/7) shocks everyone and wows many, Z and
me of course included, by permitting such marriages to
take place there. Other municipalities quickly follow
suit. Right-wingers are outraged, the cowboy president
announces his support for a constitutional amendment
restricting marriage to "a man and a woman." (The
lantern-jawed former antiwar veteran will now almost
certainly be the out-party's candidate. And the alleged
spoiler of the 2000 election has jumped in again,
undaunted, as a third-party candidate, and I say good
for him. And the cabal's across-the-board outrages
continue. And Iraq is a tragic mess. And Pakistan is
caught red-handed peddling nukes around the world and
our hypocritical supreme leader does nothing -- because
he's supposedly about to launch a big military push to
nail the Saudi terrorist chieftain of Al Qaeda in the
"outlaw" region of Pakistan and needs the support of
the Pakistani government to do this. Oh, some
fascinating stuff; it just might be a horse race after

all, the cowboy incumbent and the former antiwar
challenger. And then? If by a miracle the latter
should win? Would he just make USAn world domination
look more palatable to the rest of the West? Would he
try to do anything at all about the truly serious
matters? -- At least with him there would be a slim
hope. As always, "lesser evil" talk will be abundant.)
     -- But I didn't intend to go into politics when I
brought up "other stuff." I was thinking more of the
big boot-sock caper. One day while checking out a new
drugstore downtown I stumbled across a "bargain bin" of
my old primo brand of boot socks, identical to the ones
I gave up wearing twenty years ago because they had
become so expensive. And indeed the normal price for
the ones I found on sale was seven bucks a pair -- but
now marked down to an absurdly low buck fifty! I bought
three dozen pairs (one dozen for Rob). (This was before
my job went poof.)
     And attended another concert given by Leola J. (and
two other students of the superb Tetra Y.) at the
edgeville jazz club. This brought back fine memories of
last summer when Z-wiff was one of the warblers there.
(But this time was better in at least one way because
she was sitting right next to me, singing in my ear.)
     -- So much for the second moon of the Green Monkey.
(What moon? Haven't seen it in weeks, it seems.)
Almost time for two more ibuprofen. Am I maybe over the
hump on this "hip pointer" thing? I can hope. Also can
worry. I'm at that age. The slightest thing goes
wrong, it could be the start of something serious, it
could even be lights out. I can think of any number of
scary candidates as possible sources of this pain.
-- Oh well. Have I lived right and thus do I stand
ready to pass proudly from the scene? I suppose.
Certainly I've lived pretty much the way I wanted to,
insofar as financial constraints have permitted me to.
Or that's how I see it. Anyone else who wants to
testify on the matter can form a line out in the hall.
     (Z-spouse muttering in the bedroom. In her sleep?
Calling me? Wanting to testify? -- Now just silence.)

[Scat Jyze : Green Monkey]

       -- Say Naomi's out two months. It'd be a good
period for me to have extra free time -- at least
there's that to be said for it. Time for moving. Time
for setting up Z's old computer in the hideaway (it's
raring to go right now if I can just figure out how to
load my antique scoping program onto it). And it's
always true I could use more time for my own work.
       One other possibility. This summer on my sixty-
second birthday (solar) I become eligible for Social
Security. If no job turns up I could opt for the dole.
But would rather not. It wouldn't even pay my three
rents (apartment, office, storage unit). I'd still need
to be looking for work.
       But I don't want to be thinking about this kind of
stuff now. What's getting into me? So stop right here.
(But first mention Z's lunar birthday is day after
tomorrow and I'm nowhere near ready for it.)

13

       Some scat for the vernal equinox. Special edition.
With colossal clutter all around -- dining table. Three
a.m. Yes, it's still life in the same loaded moving
van, and yes, it's now packed fuller than ever. But
I'll say it one more time and be pretty doggone sure I
mean it: the move is near.
       Didn't say "end is near." On that (my status as a
living organism) the jury's still out. The "injury"'s
not worse but neither is it noticeably better. Still a
sporadically swelling gut/hip, left flank. I'm still
gobbling ibuprofen. Yet actually hurting mostly just
when I sit -- as now. Lying down is good in at least
some positions, standing's okay, walking's best of all.

[Scat Jyze : Green Monkey]

So again suspend judgment. (I'm not in denial
here. I'm aware of the risks and the trade-offs
involved in dealing or not dealing with them.) "Wait
and see." Could be a growth in there somewhere and
could be I'm letting it get out of hand by waiting on
it. If so, that's how it will be. (But not forever.
First, though, I have to see something that means it's
serious business for sure. Blood, lump, blocked bowel,
inability to walk or copulate -- something like that.)
So drop the matter for now.
-- On the house, movement. On the job, no news
except for the makeshift. Details in a moment.
First, a happy-birthday wish for Z. We're five
days past the actual day (solar). That was lovely: a
Monday Z took off, and she decided she wanted to reprise
our celebrated (in "The Z&G Story") "sailor/hooker"
stroll up the avenue which jyze calls "the low road."
We did that, after a brief stop to deliver a transcript
during which I bought a corsage at an in-building flower
shop and then surprised her with it in the car. Then
the stroll, with extensive canoodling in most every
doorway. Cherry trees gorgeously abloom on the hillside
steps and terraces outside the shop where we stopped for
coffee for me and tea for her. Then my old lucky spot,
the overlook at the park by the public market, the vast
waterfront/bay/sound/mountains panorama. Then the art
store just north of the market, then the alley outside
my old B-2 digs, then up to the place she chose for
dinner, the one-eyed Greek eatery (which moved a couple
of years ago from low road to edge road). Still a good
artsy joint -- Z found herself coveting a "Black Flag"
objet-trouve sculpture/painting hanging for sale on the
wall near our booth and just might go back to buy it if
closing on the condo doesn't leave us wearing barrels.
Very early on her birthday -- like two a.m. -- I
hit the usual east-hill copy shop to put together
installment three, "20K Jyze," of "Jyze in Love." Left
the finished booklet out on the couch for her to read
while I was still asleep in the morning. Can't be sure
but I think she liked it quite a bit. At least no big

complaints. And she did say the narrator (that's Jyzer
G, of course) came off as "very likable." But I'll be
sad if she thinks the character "Zoelie B." comes off as
anything less than fabulous.

Her nephew Jacob called a couple of times; that
pleased her. Elgie left her a message and then sent a
gift certificate for the dot-com book peddler
headquartered in the DC castle a block and a half from
our apartment; that pleased her too and pleased me maybe
even more, and this despite the fact that we both detest
the dot-com itself. But the birthday dinner with Mama E
in her room at Benita's did not go well. For Mama E it
was an "I'm in pain" day -- the phrase repeated over and
over, and little else said (she called to apologize the
next day -- the real birthday -- and yesterday we took
her in to see Doc F and x-rays are scheduled -- it's her
stomach -- and a newly retweaked medication regime is
now in place). (And the vegan chocolate-coconut
birthday cake Z picked out was not so tasty, though I
wound up eating way too much of it anyway.)

And the condo? The offering papers finally
arrived. The price is $164,605 (the number's seared
into my synapses) and we get $2700 in closing costs
deducted from that. Our mouthpiece (legal beagle) Marc
A. has been vetting the papers all week and tomorrow at
three we'll be talking with him by conference call (if
we can rig our phone right). Audrey G., the bank rep,
was out of town at a crucial juncture but we did manage
to cajole her into sending, to Eli T., Raphael's lawyer,
a copy of the "preapproval qualification letter" on the
mortgage. Meanwhile interest rates are back down near
their thirty-year low at five and a quarter percent,
half a point lower than when we first talked with the
bank and they estimated our monthly charge at $820 or
so. Since we're now planning to make a bigger down
payment (twenty percent) our monthly charge will likely
be about $780. That's just $35 more per month than
we've paid in rent on 203 for the past six years.

And the crews keep working away here at 1511. Unit
entrance doors and common-area halls and stairwells are

painted (no longer are the doors varnished natural wood; now they're dark gray). Some fancy wrought-iron patio furniture (rental no doubt) has materialized outside the entrance-lobby door. Just last night a big sign went up above the newly landscaped front "garden" saying "The Ettore -- Units Now Selling -- from $174,900." Sounds kind of classy, "The Ettore," and that's because it is. Ettore is Raphael's father's first name. Raphael himself picked it. This is the first we've heard of it. Who knew he had such a mushy patriarchal streak?

And when I arrived home I found a sign taped on the door of 202: "This unit occupied -- DO NOT ENTER." For prospective buyers, I guess. In any event, I entered. (This same sign rides the doors of the other occupied units too -- four in all, including 202.)

But it appears we won't be controlling the condo council. June's out. Aida's out (saying the price is too high and Raphael too flaky). Sylva S., the state rep (Aida's good friend) who was interested for a few days and even dropped by to inspect our unit, is out also. Dak's out. A couple of Dak's friends who briefly expressed interest are probably out. Most likely it's just us. Unlike the others we can't just say no.

-- Is a baby bird living in the vent pipe for our stove fan here in 202? Z thinks so. Wants me to figure out how to reach in there and grab it "because you have long arms." So far I haven't even heard it. Is she maybe hearing the wind flip a squeaky outdoor vent flap? But as a former insulation inspector she should know the difference. (Her two current chief concerns about our new place have to do with access to the water heater, which is blocked by the refrigerator -- so she wants that on wheels -- and the possibility, still unallayed, that the wall heater for the living room is the same hazardous recalled model we used to have in 203.)

Of roaches, though, I know she's not imagining things. I saw one scurry under the mat here when I sat down to start up the jyze. (They're probably our doing too. It's virtually impossible to keep the place clean

under such wretched circumstances as have befallen us.
-- Not that it would necessarily be all that clean even
if it were possible. But for sure it would be cleaner
than it is, and we've never had roaches before.)

Okay. That's it for house chat. Now for a quick
segue to my employment situation.

First, I've heard nothing more from Naomi. I don't
know if Larry's alive or dead. My hunch is he's alive
-- but I think this only because I've seen nothing in
the obits or on the bulletin board at the scope office
(where I sneak in occasionally at night to use their
machines for working on my own stuff -- and this becomes
a bit riskier every time I do it).

Second, I'm proofreading part-time for a young
court reporter Naomi turned me on to. Tanya L. By
happenstance her picture's in one of today's local
papers (to be specific, in the FAP: former afternoon
paper) in a big feature about J-towners whose spouses
have been deployed to Iraq. She prays a lot, it says --
relies on her Christian faith to help her survive the
ordeal. Her husband's an architect; they've been
married just one year less than Z and me. This
proofreading pays very poorly -- not much more than ten
bucks an hour -- and is so sporadic I'll be lucky to
average $150 a week. (The reporting firm Tanya works
for, by the way, is a subsidiary of the big law firm
where Olwen's son Trent was a clerk until he was laid
off last year -- top two floors of a huge black
monstrosity of a highrise occupying a full block between
the high road and the very high road but conveniently
located for me about eight blocks from the hideaway.)

So far I'm holding off on hunting for more scoping
work. My old "client," reporter Verna, may be looking
for a scoper (Naomi hipped me to this too) but I
don't want to commit myself to anything major before I
have a better idea what Naomi's long-term status will
be. My fear is I'll suddenly find myself with too much
work. (But more realistically it'll be too little. And
I doubt Verna would provide consistent work for very
long. At best it would be occasional bursts.)

[Scat Jyze : Green Monkey]

     At any rate: try not to worry about any of this --
if I can help it -- until after the move's complete,
and I'm guessing that won't be until the end of April,
just short of six weeks from now. So again: put the
"suspend" spin on it. Not denial.
     (Good book I'm reading, "Song for Uncle Tom," et
al., by a Japusan writer I've admired for years. He
grew up first in the same northern burbs of Centropolis
where I did and then within a mile or so of the Z-
woman's childhood stomping grounds in the city itself.)
     Tomorrow right after the conference call with Marc
we head over to David and Stacy's to babysit for Lwazi
-- first time. (Kid's doing better now; respiratory
troubles mostly cleared up.)
     Night's not that old yet. Much more I could say.
As always! But Z's stirring and I need to tend to some
other things. Scattered scat this has been. Spring
officially underway as of five hours ago. Just a wee
sliver of moon out there and tomorrow night none at all
-- must be why these ravings fall so short of the full-
moon kind.
     So I'll save those other tales or more likely just
release them back into the wild. -- Jyzed out so kwik!

                        14

     Lucky spot. Do I need it? Its beneficence? Maybe
so. But I don't know that yet. And am asking for it
anyway.
     Corridor of sunlight laid across the bay. First
alfresco jyze in quite a while. Got me a second-tier
table, one row back from the fence, so I can't see much
of the waterfront down below. None of it, actually,

except for the upper reaches of the metal sculpture
tower rising maybe two hundred feet offshore. Lots of
folks out in the park here to soak up some early-season
rays. Rush-hour traffic sizzling by on the viaduct down
below, two tugboats slowly spinning a fully loaded
container ship near the dry docks to the southwest.
Couple of gulls wheeling by overhead, and now a madly
cawing crow.
     Lots going on. (Isn't it always so? And don't I
always observe thusly? It seems it's become part of the
drill.) (Rumble and screech of a train rolling by at
the tunnel entrance under the viaduct. Someone not too
far away behind me is coughing up a storm. -- Ship's
now spun around 180 degrees and it's heading out.)
     Also much is still in abeyance.
     And a notable cluster of days and dates. Yesterday
clocks sprang ahead an hour or otherwise it would be too
dark to jyze out here at this time of day (in short
sleeves no less -- and even with a breeze off the
water). The Gregorian numbers on yesterday were
maximally unlucky in certain Asian countries (including
the only countries besides the U.S. I've ever lived in)
and maybe elsewhere too: 04/04/04.
     Today, "March Madness" finale, playing live on TV
right now (as freighter and tugboat in tandem edge past
the sight line of the sculpture tower, freighter winning
by a nose -- and the glittery corridor of reflected sun
is creeping all but imperceptibly -- or sidling I could
say -- in the same direction). Tomorrow, home opener
for the baseballers, huge crowd expected; my day will be
altered some because of it.
     And so: whassup?
     Herezit.
     (But first say the five two-by-six planks making up
the surface of this squarish anchored table are not just
newly varnished but newly emplaced, and very recently
I'd say, because they bear not a single engraving, no
initials carved in, no graffiti, nothing -- only two or
three traces of birdshit plopped thereon. This must be
the maiden jyze voyage on their expanse, meaning that of

the planks. -- As another pair of shreeing gulls swoops
by. Freighter now long gone. A ferry in, a ferry out.
Land forms of a past chapter of my life occupy the far
western horizon. If they still have anything to say to
me I guess I've become incapable of hearing it.)

First, a quick summary. The move-in at 201 is
underway as of yesterday. Mama E's been through a
series of crises. My left side's still swollen and
sometimes painfully so. The neocon cabal's push for
goosed-up empire amassment (or just call it extended
armed hegemony with universal wealth-extraction rights)
looks to be in ever-deepening trouble. Jean got mugged
and Vic got dissed. -- On all of which more later.
Twice later. One setting to come a surprise.

(And here's a guy scavenging aluminum cans. Rolls
up a red wire cart, bends down into the trash barrel and
tosses cans back over his shoulder into the cart in a
practiced, unerring way, very quickly, a cross between a
juggler and a dog digging a hole. Black quilted jacket
-- the guy looks Latino with some African mixed in and
is dressed well enough I'd wager he's a resident in the
public market's low-income housing. And now he's taking
a break at another of the tables. Picking his nose, in
fact, decorously shielding the operation with his free
hand. Wouldn't want to upset any of the high-class
types at other tables, of whom he may even think I'm
one. And if he does, he's right, or soon will be.
Condo man!)

Best day: arrival of the bank's "good-faith
estimate." It was a thick sheaf of papers and at first
I just glanced through it -- quickly locked it back in
the mailbox because I was late to meet Z at the WOC.
But then returned for a second look to check what the
monthly payment would be. Let out a whoop: $737!
That's more than forty bucks less than we'd been
expecting to pay! It's even eight bucks less than the
monthly rent we coughed up for all those years on 203!

Z didn't whoop at the news. She fears offending
the gods. But the fact is we're getting a steal here.
On the day they hit the market four of the six available

units sold, and ours is the fifth. Further: the others
are all going for 190K or more. We're paying 164K!
Raphael, the owner, suddenly can't figure out how he let
this happen. "You're going to have 25 grand of instant
equity!"

     So, yeah, I'm crowing. Why the heck not? I may be
on my last legs anyway so why bother with humility?
-- But can still handle most of the moving from 202 to
201, I think, so long as I don't overdo it.

     -- Sun and corridor almost joined now, and both
close to the edge of the building to the north --
restaurant folks peering out from behind dark glass.
(Another Latino guy's been hanging about -- is singing
now and in Spanish. Baseball cap worn backwards, orange
V-neck sweater. Right next to him, lined up at the
railing, Russian tourists posing for a photo: two burly
black-haired men, a blond woman, a blond little girl.
"Wait until the ferry can be in the picture," I'd bet
the woman just said in Russian -- while pointing out at
it. The two men must be brothers. Same high degree of
probability, I'd say, as when people see Rob and me
together (but Jeff and me or Jeff and Rob, much lower).)

     Complicated world. Snug and smug little corner of
it here. J-town's leading expat Brit scribbler wrote a
piece for the combined Sunday paper (OMP/FAP) decrying
the town's fascination with its own natural beauty. It
leads to provincial attitudes, sez he. People around
here, for instance, don't even necessarily dress up to
go to the symphony. Horrors! And "everyone," he adds,
goes to bed at ten p.m.! He wants us to be more like
FCM #1 or London -- somehow failing to mention he moved
here precisely to get away from the latter. (Z-wiff
didn't like the piece either. Too often "provincialism"
is just another word for difference. We're both opposed
to J-town's losing its grip on its difference. -- But a
move's afoot to jack the town up to the next level of
urbanity. And it's coming mostly from the alternative
weekly papers! More density! Build big! Wear
expensive noir outfits to piano lounges to bask in the
mawko swill of the neo-crooners!)

[Scat Jyze : Green Monkey]

    -- And now just half the golden corridor is
visible. The building's shadow is creeping from right
to left across the table. Aluminum scavenger, guy in
backward baseball cap, me -- we're the only ones left at
the tables (of which this corner of the park offers only
four at present).
    The shadow's also swallowed my backpack, down by my
right foot. What's in the pack itself? A transcript I
picked up at Tanya L.'s forty-fourth-floor office on the
way here and will proofread tonight and return to her
tomorrow afternoon. Last month I earned $160
proofreading. Peanuts, yeah. But it's helping me
stagger to the end of this month unaided on nonrental
expenses. And for next month I have my $1100 state tax
refund, which is now in. So by the end of May I'll need
to know what kind of future Naomi's seeing for herself
in court reporting, if any, in order that I can make
some decisions. As of now I've still heard nothing
about Larry's status after his brain surgery.
    -- Just a shred of gold remains. Shadow line has
crept to within an inch of the buttons on my shirt, to
their left. I lean right to try to keep warm in the
sun. Coupla minutes more, lights out.
    I'll outsmart 'em, leave now.
                    *   *
    -- And here's the surprise. Or one of them,
rather, and not the one I was thinking about before.
    But first the setting. Dining table, 202, "The
Ettore." Last go-round for jyze in this unit, I'd say,
and this time it's far less likely I'll be wrong. Our
move-in date for 201 is the 16th of this month, and the
closing date on the sale is the 27th. And it's still
the tightly and yet haphazardly loaded moving van in
here, little changed (and even less cleaned) over the
six months we've been occupying it, so to speak, except
of course most of the piles and mounds and stacks have
grown higher. The vaseful of fresh-cut tulips standing
a foot from my left elbow, however, tends to confirm
it's no longer October.
    Jazz station quietly playing, "night paper" already

perused. Everything my eye falls upon around here these days triggers the question "How and when in the overall process am I going to move that to 201?" (We're getting rid of the big green lazyboy-type chair Gerry and Leola gave us, by the way, and also Mother and Dad's old Crest Electronics console, battleship size almost, one of the last major material links -- in my possession anyway -- to the full-family era at 636 Cedar in Gatewood before Dad's death. Not enough room for either of these behemoths in 201 since it's forty square feet smaller.)

And I was wrong about the full moon. It hit its max about twenty-three hours ago. In other words, last night. So that should've been scat-jyze night. And if it had been it would've been not only 04/04/04 -- if I'd started early enough -- but also (and here comes the surprise) the exact tenth anniversary of jyze.

Another bungle on my part. I'd been thinking the jyze anniversary was April 21st. Why, who knows. But then I saw a newspaper headline -- "10 YEARS GONE," about a grunge great's suicide -- and I thought I remembered jyze started up a week or two before that. So I researched the matter.

It's turned out to be a whole lot bigger than I expected, jyze has. Changed my life. Will change other lives too, I'm hoping. Probably not a great many but maybe a few.

-- This table here, most of it's currently given over to stacks of paper bearing on the purchase of the condo. Near chaos. Dealings virtually daily not just with Raphael and Wayne but with Audrey the banker, Eli the lawyer (Raphael's), Marc the lawyer (ours), and a bunch of lesser players such as Dee the inspector, Ethan the other banker, Cuarto the carpenter and his son Mario, on and on. "One crisis after another." Z-wiff frequently reaching out in panic for her three how-to books on buying a house or condo. Mygs swarming as we've rarely seen them swarm before. I in "frantic calming mode" (Z's phrase) but in any event plenty distracted myself. Z leaves a near-full quart of ice cream on the stove overnight, I leave the burner turned on all day. Way too many gaffes like these.

Neither of us has ever bought a condo (or a house) before. So I'd say we're doing all right. What remains of the process looks fairly cut and dried.

Meanwhile Mama E's been a load. Severe stomach pain has led to a series of tests. Z picks her up and drives her down to the medical center on east hill, I join them there upon arising and then on my own drive Mama E back home afterwards, giving poor Z a little respite. After her latest trip Mama E was so zonked on tranquilizers she swallowed part of her dentures -- half swallowed actually -- and had to be rushed to the emergency room by ambulance. Luckily, because the timing was such that we couldn't be reached immediately, Tony and Benita at the AFH were able to handle it. Turned out okay; no esophageal operation was necessary. But no more wearing an upper denture for Mama E. She eats only soft food so she should be all right, at least at the forward end of her digestive system. What's up with her stomach and intestines we still don't know. (Same could be said for the farther end of my own digestive tract and the nearby "hip pointer" area.)

Three o'clock news headlines come on. Massive Shiite uprisings in Iraq, will more U.S. troops be sent over? 9/11 hearings are starting to look more serious. It's quickening, all right, the political situation. But the best that can result from the upcoming U.S. election, even if the challenger should beat the steep odds and oust the incumbent, is a small step in the right direction. The truly serious questions are at least as unlikely to be addressed by the challenger as by the incumbent -- the long-term ones, I mean. But no matter, this is still a crucial election.

Unit 202. Will I miss anything about it? The view, a little bit. The sunrises before I go to bed. The ability to glance down and check whether the newspaper-delivery vehicle -- bicycle, motorcycle, van, car, pickup, whatever's current -- has arrived. (In the future I'll be forced to go by hearing alone and may not be able to make out the distinctive thonks and thuds of the tossed newspapers and so probably will be forced to embark on much more frequent trips downstairs, many fruitless, in hopes of preempting newspaper rip-offs.)

Anything else? The balcony here is a bit roomier, yes, but we haven't been able to use it much, especially not after the hexed day I locked myself out there.

Possibly I'll remember this as the last place I lived where I was still, or anyway could live as if I were still, fully healthy. But -- please, no.

(Do I have any new theories about what's wrong with me? Not really. Could be bladder, colon, stomach, pancreas, prostate, hernia, displaced or pinched nerve, no doubt many other maladies. Sore areas along the back muscles on my left side give me a little hope. Failure of the bulge to go away is worrisome. Pain's not as bad as it was early on, but perhaps only because I've learned to move in ways that don't aggravate the injury or the malfunction, the growth, whatever it is. Lucky thing I'm not doing any scoping now because long spells seated before a screen with my arms raised are highly aggravating, just about the worst thing I can do short of attempting to squeeze into a child's Jeep. -- That I never did do, by the way, but I probably would've tried if the Jeep hadn't disappeared from the parking space before I could get around to it.)

-- Never mind. Dullsville again. I hate to write about this failing-health stuff and I'd hate even more to be asked to read it.

And so I'll take a double break here. Dinner. But not in the dining area. In the kitchen, standing.

*   *

-- And now the other surprise. It's our new condo! In an unoccupied, "blank-slate" state, bare, with touch-up work still to be done here and there but most of it minor. Sheetrocking of the underside of the balcony above ours is the most major. Labels need to be removed from the outside panes of the new windows (and they're all new), caulk needs to be applied in both bathrooms (one of which is half size, just as in 202 and 203).

Blond pergo floors -- look sort of like white pine.

113

[Scat Jyze : Green Monkey]

Walls all painted a very light gray, I'll call it. A
big "great room" with a bedroom to the south and another
to the east branching off the short entrance hallway,
and the kitchen separated from the rest of the "great
room" by a high L-shaped counter just like the ones in
202 and 203. I'm sitting now in the southwest corner of
the south bedroom -- and of the house itself -- and this
will be our future "master" bedroom (the other one,
which is about the same size, will become Z's room to do
with as she pleases). A stack of banker boxes stands in
the corner here, another in the closet; those and the
wooden folding chair I'm sitting on are all I've brought
over so far. Except for peeking in from the doorways,
the other rooms and the balcony are still out of bounds.

A window to my left, another at my back. Four a.m.
Aside from a row of outdoor nightlights on the four-
story apartment building behind ours -- visible to the
west through the leafy high hedge at the back of "The
Ettore"'s shallow backyard -- nothing but darkness.

And I don't want to describe too much anyway. Just
to be here. At the start. Or before the start really.

-- Hesitation. Should I go check on the Z-woman?
Thought I heard a noise out there. Left the door of 202
unlocked. She might even lock it, thinking I had to go
back downtown. And I left my keys over there.

*

-- Back. Brought the keys. But she was awake and
I heard her unwrapping something in the bedroom, maybe
earplugs or medicine of some sort. Nor would I be
surprised if she showed up in here at any moment.

Jyze lives dangerously.

So anyway, this unit 201 is where I'll probably be
hanging out for the rest of my days (nights) and if I'm
lucky this is where I'll die. Right here -- this very
room. In my sleep, please, if possible.

Very quiet in here. Hum of the fridge from the far
side of the "great room" and that's it. (I'm trying to
picture myself stretched out on a bed here, my last day
on this earth, Z-wiff closing my mindlessly staring
eyes. Ooh, ghoulish! Morbid! -- Not that I'm a denier

114

of death. No. Rather I'd prefer to think it's "always already here" in every jyze word. "Immortality project." So then get on with it already! -- But I do want to mention this left-flank swelling I've been talking about in recent months has become something like a small one-sided love handle. It can't be too conspicuous because Z-wiff hasn't even noticed it yet. If she had she would've remarked on it for sure.)

Should mention -- what? Our "meet anniversary," the annual return to the ur-primal scene which had to be aborted because the cafe's been converted into a sitdown restaurant, quite fancy, and it's not open Mondays and the 29th was a Monday. But we had a lovely time regardless. Dinner at a restaurant we've always liked but now it's moved to a new location, far superior to the previous one even though the rest of Z's old hood is now too modernized and yuppified for our taste, too infested with tech spirit and Cawk condescension. Our seventh anniversary. So does the infamous itch start or end on that day? (As the eighth year begins.)

Then Vic and Jean. First Vic was traumatized while serving as a -- but here she is, Z-wiff in the flesh (but robed and slippered) ---

*

Do I know this Z or do I know this Z?

She had a funny story to tell about Raphael buzzing our apartment because he was locked out of the building. But the 202 intercom doesn't work -- nor does the one here -- so how could she have known it was Raphael down there and not an even worse monster? Eventually he came around to the front of the house, yelled up at 202. In good time she buzzed him in. He never did drop by to explain or to thank her. I tell her we've got to expect even weirder behavior from the guy because now he's thinking we somehow tricked him into giving us twenty-five grand. (Why else would he grant us such a good deal? We must've bamboozled him.)

And went right back to bed, she did. Just now I mean. Didn't even ask me to lock the door. She realized this was one of those "Hydes of Jyze" times.

And yet kindly refrained from pointing out I'm not
wearing my official "Hydes of Jyze" hat (Jeep hat).
     -- So Vic and Jean, real quick now. In his day job
Vic's collecting tickets from entering Rotarians on St.
Patrick's Day at the convention center and one of them
says, "So solly, no tickee," to the uproarious amusement
of several other Rotarian buddies. All Cawks, of
course. Brought back a lifetime's worth of such
intentional insults -- and worse -- for Vic. He called
me in a highly agitated state and we talked for an hour.
Z-wiff feared the incident would bring on a heart attack
for Vic, who's seventy-four now and already has plenty
of health problems, including with his ticker. Over the
next couple of weeks he worked on a story about the
incident, draft after draft -- to add to one of his
manuscripts, I guess, though it doesn't really seem
suitable for either of them. So maybe it'll become the
start of a third. An exciting thought!
     Then Jean. One day as she was walking home from
work at six p.m., a purse-snatcher hit her from behind.
Even though knocked down to the sidewalk, she fiercely
clung to the purse while being dragged on the cement
some eight or ten feet before he wrenched it away from
her and fled. This was right outside the HQ's premier
comedy club (of all places) and several customers there
saw it happen through the front window but no one came
out to help until the snatcher was long gone. Classic
USAn situation: TV movies on the theme appear regularly,
roughly one per decade (not that I've ever watched one).
Jean was bruised and pretty badly scraped up, and a
recent back injury was aggravated. -- And all this just
four blocks from the loft.
     The next day I was due to drop by but Vic said we'd
better go out somewhere instead. After toughing out the
first night Jean was badly shook up for several days.
But by the following Tuesday she was the usual vivacious
host again -- showing off her grotesquely black-and-blue
"conversation piece" right hand and forearm. (Wish I
could ease my way in a little closer to her so I could
know the intimate Jean. But she puts up barriers to

that. Still -- this was a shocker.)
     Saturday night the Z-woman and I went over to Betty
and Kat's for dinner and to watch the video of the movie
"13." Another shocker. Next-door neighbor Trudy was
also present, she in her late seventies, very straight
-- jaw dropping at all the wild and sordid teen behavior
in the movie. "I've seen a lot worse," Kat sniffed at
the end (but never did elaborate). Right now Kat at
least appears to be in a calm and steady phase. The
thought of her getting caught in a downward spiral like
that of the girl in the movie -- sex, drugs, violence --
makes us all shudder. For sure that sort of stuff can
be hard for kids to avoid these days. A graphic
demonstration of how all you can do as a parent is your
best and then trust. "Pray." Did it get through or
didn't it? -- Admittedly neither Z-wiff nor I know much
about this sort of thing except from the other side,
when we were the ones being worried about.
     -- Bird cries now. I'm startled by the echoey
sound of my own foot as I shift positions. All this
emptiness here in 201 -- about to be filled. And for a
good long time, I'm hoping.

15

     A jyze perfunk. Real kwik. Already it's 5:05 a.m.
and I've just finished the last little bits of moving
(perishables from the fridge). Now here I sit in the
empty echoey 202, the unit soon to be, for us, history
(but history preserved right next door to the new
present, 201, true -- so always poised, even if
basically inaccessible, to stir memories of the
turbulent transitional months, as could also be said of

203 but for a much longer transitional period).

One chair remaining in the place and nothing else other than some cleaning supplies for Amanda, who's due to arrive at noon to help us whip the place into righteous shape (our request for Raphael to return the full cleaning deposit will soon follow). I sit on the one chair, directly beneath the dangling dining-area light fixture. Birds cheep -- early ones. Looking east to the mountains (last time for this view from within "The Ettore" except maybe while visiting neighbors). No sign of dawn. But dawn is coming, yes it is.

And oh my aching side. Not just the ongoing swelling but a new ding as of two days ago, same general posterior left flank area. Related, I suspect. Will I live or die, be crippled or what? Still don't know. But as far as I can tell, all internal organs are functioning passably well. Still, I couldn't offer much help today to the two guys from the day-labor pickup site, Amanda's buddies, Sheldon and Luke. But the move went smoothly anyway. Or maybe even because.

So here's an end of something that really feels like the end of something, just because of the emptiness of the rooms, the cabinet doors all hanging open, a smaller yet still haunted emptiness obtaining inside each cabinet as well. Where the furnishings of our lives were, the Z-spouse's and mine, to the point we didn't even notice them, now they're all gone and yet I'm seeing them as I didn't before but in negative, so to say. Standard stuff to be sure, except for the overtly transitory nature of the stay. "Camping without forklift" -- or however that went. Could be I've cited the various versions of it a bit more than they deserve.

End of at least one trail here: apartments I've lived in. Forty-year trail as of four months from now (at which point I'll also mark the twenty-fifth anniversary of my arrival in Jyze City with Lady U). Now I'm a homeowner -- one-third homeowner to be exact. Except for technically, and in two senses. First, because the sale doesn't officially close until the 27th, eleven days from now. Second, my name won't be on

the mortgage or any of the other ownership papers. For
these eleven days we'll (technically) be renting our own
new home -- unit 201 -- and my name will still be on the
rental papers (for real!). And in both cases I'll still
be paying, and within a few bucks of the same amount.

Z-wiff's asleep over there. Her first words to me
when I arrived at our new digs at three a.m.: "You can
see straight from the bed to the entrance area! It
ruins the feng shui!" "But surely it's fixable!" sez I.
And tomorrow the fixing will start in earnest, that item
and a long clipboard list of others. She'll head off,
for instance, to a north-end discount emporium in search
of a bathroom cabinet. Or actually we initiated that
particular search last night at the big south-end home
center. Nothing quite right there, though. (I suspect
by the time the list goes onto a third page -- it's near
the bottom of page two now -- we'll be lowering our
standards across the board.) -- Then, after the home
center, burgers at an alehouse in the same area. Bad
service and Z-wiff was cranky about it. I was in too
much low-level hip pain even to notice, or almost.

So now in 201 stuff's piled everywhere just as it
once was here, and in many cases, again, up to the
ceiling or close to it. The next big objective is to
find someone who can anchor our two large bookcases
(sections of my old loft) which will stick out at right
angles from the walls in the southern third of the
"great room" and in effect serve as partitions breaking
up the space. They're funky and I'm sure good old
Raphael will think we're low-rent in putting them up,
but regardless they'll do the job just fine. Raphael
wants this Ettore to be a classy place. Wants "all" of
our plants to go too -- thinks they'll make for water
damage. But what the hell: we're owners now, or will be
in eleven days. It's a done deal! So no more taking
this claptrap from Raphael. (He's still disgruntled
over failing to reap even more bucks from our unit.)

Silhouettes of houses and trees and hills emerging
outside the windows now, traffic sounds increasing, the
usual heralds of dawn -- except this is the last I'll be

seeing and hearing them from this angle. A train
whistle blows and I'm reminded Z-wiff said she heard
quite a few of those from the bed in 201 as she tried to
get to sleep earlier tonight. Now we're on the side of
the house facing the railroad yards a mile or so to the
west -- and the prevailing winds come from that
direction, west or more like southwest. Soon should
also be able to hear the roar of the crowds from the two
stadiums, football and baseball, both just past the rail
yards. Foghorns from the harbor as well. Maybe even
truck horns from the north-south freeway on the west
side of the hill, just as I can hear them now from the
east-west freeway on the east side of the hill.

     So I'll move on. "Move on." Move out too. For
good! And forever! To the unit next door!

16

     Upstairs at the primo javahaus. Sun slanting in on
the table, northwest corner of the triangular upper-
level deck. Coupla Eurusan cartoonists hunched over a
laptop at one neighboring table; an Asiusan cool guy in
shades slouched back from his laptop at another table;
an Afrusan studenty woman likewise hunched over her
laptop at a third. Laptop diversity! Yay! What more
can we ask for in this life? -- And some good punky
rock playing too, I like -- on Cinco de Mayo, a/k/a FF
Day, First Fuck, for Z and me. It took us only a whole
goddamn year and a month and six days to get there.

     Again this round I'm a little late regarding the
scat-jyze moon. If twelve hours either side of the
moment of max fullness is optimal, I'm now maybe thirty-
two hours past the outer limit. But last night at one

a.m. what gorgeous near-fullness hung ten or fifteen
degrees above the DC castle standing floodlit athwart
its far hilltop (our hilltop) as I drove due south down
the high-bridge road heading straight toward it. This
after printing up and binding installment four of "Jyze
in Love" (titled "Jyzin' with Z") at the usual copy shop
and with admirable quickness, making it home just as the
last bus rolled by -- which is to say, normal time.

     Presented the booklet this a.m. Z read it this
afternoon, four p.m., after coming home from work early,
exhausted by directing preparations for Friday's Race
Dialogue Day (or Race Polylogue as it almost was called)
at our hilltop high school, which is eighty-some percent
"students of color" with the languages spoken in their
homes numbering more than forty. Per usual Z showed
little reaction to the new jyze pages except for a few
chortles and exactly two guffaws. Tells me she likes
the sex parts best. Lets me know she views herself as
having been a "saint" back then for putting up with my
shameful 401 days of penile foozles. Wants to see the
jyze account for the day of the first foozle surmounted,
so to speak -- but that of course came the next year,
outside the "Jyze in Love" domain. It was the 5th of
May to be exact, year of Jyze Age Annal 5, "Deep Jyze,"
FF Day -- six years ago today.

     First jyze presentation in the new condo. Yup,
we're officially recognized owners now. Or rather she
is. I had to sign a quitclaim relinquishing any right
to it should she die -- instead it goes to her estate.
We'll be asking Marc the lawyer for reassurance that the
bank can never screw me over on this. I'm supposed to
be calling him. But I keep finding excuses to put it
off. I don't like to be insisting on the protection of
property rights, even (or especially) if they're my own.
(But the fact is I anted up the last 25K of my deep
reserves so we could make the down payment. My cupboard
is now bare. But old Mom would be pleased to know what
the money went for -- the money she left me. A big
chunk of it originally coming from Dad's life-insurance
policy, and I'm sure he'd be pleased too, even if

wondering what in hell took me so long. -- Just like on
FF, correct, and for that matter maybe on jyze itself.)
     The big day was the 26th as it turned out. I
picked up Z at three and we drove down to the real-
estate company's office in a swanky part of town out
past east hill. Glorious sunny afternoon. "Closing."
A tall skinny blond fellow named Preston, bogglingly
congenial, presented the papers. My name appeared on
some of them after all, but the given part was
misspelled -- "Gelnnar" -- sort of like my original
toddler pronunciation of it, "Gunnah," and not that far
from great-great-gramp's "Grenjad." Had to correct
"Gelnnar" on every document and initial the changes.
     For Z-wiff our condo is the first "house" anyone in
her family has ever owned, at least as far as she knows.
First for her for sure. Thus her extreme nervousness
about it -- superstitiousness too -- as we scratched and
clawed our way through the long run-up.
     The worst moment came right after our move-out from
202. Raphael noticed our roach traps there and hit the
roof. He and Z engaged in a bit of a shout-down. Z
came to me in a fury -- "You said you'd deal with him."
So, did. Hey Raphael, we didn't want roaches either!
An intense discussion, and most of it took place in our
old apartment, No. 203, now empty but totally remodeled
(with dark pergo floors -- ugh). He was calling in an
exterminator, he declared, nostrils flaring. Fine,
Raphael, of course; do what you gotta do. I'd have to
get up in the morning, he warned, to let him into our
place. Hey, no problem, Raphael; I get up all the time
to pee anyway. (Actually not true.) -- And just today,
I'll note, the exterminator made his last visit.
     Turned out the roaches were coming from Ciro's
apartment, 102, directly below 202. The place was
infested. Wayne, Raphael's handyman, told me all about
it. From Raphael not even a word of apology.
     (Darkening up here. Every table occupied at dusk.
All students now, I'd say, except for me, the ancient
holding forth in the corner. Sage chin-scratching looks
I deliver to keep them puzzling. And I don't doubt some

wonder what this black stick is I keep pushing across
the inner surface of this blank fuzzy. Maybe a
revolutionary new product from one of the digital
colossi? Designed to look awesomely old school?)

   (In his report the appraiser struggles to explain
why our unit sold for 35K less than the nearly identical
ones above and below us. "Cooperative tenants who
bargained" was what he came up with. But then it's
true, that was the essence of it -- if he'd added the
word "shrewdly." That's me, cooperative, shrewd
bargainer. If only I'd known forty years ago I could do
this! -- But I never would've even tried back then.
And won't again now or ever. Needed to do it this once
so I'd be sure to have a place to curl up and expire in.
Me and Z. As well as to do all those things that will
come before the serious curling-up phase begins,
preferably lots and lots and lots of such things.)

   How'm I meanwhile doing on health? Just hanging in
there. No change I'm aware of since last jyze report.
But I've been able to function pretty much normally for
another full lunar orbit, which is encouraging.

   And -- I now have an idea what my work future
holds. A letter from Naomi arrived the other day, the
first I've heard from her in over two Gregorian months.
Larry's prognosis is better than expected, she says: not
eighteen months to live but five years. First, though,
a second craniotomy. This means she won't be able to
return to work until September. But she is coming back.
And at that point I'll have my old job again. (Unless,
of course, something else goes wrong, with Larry, with
the U.S. Attorney's Office or the FBI, with Naomi, with
me or Z or -- clearly most at risk of all -- Mama E.)

   Between now and September I'll essentially be on
vacation. The proofreading for Tanya L. will continue
but probably won't amount to much (in the past month
it's been a grand total of fourteen hours). Instead Z-
wiff will carry me, thus repaying some of the bucks I
put up for her share of the condo down payment. As of
now she owes me a little over 11K. The vacation will
use up about four of that. Maybe less if I can cut

expenses to the bone as I'll try to do.

Use this free time well. Don't fritter away too much. -- But use it to do precisely what? So much to do I don't know where to start, or know way too many places to start. Talking about my own work here -- talking about jyze. (Plenty to do elsewhere too, shaping up (myself) and settling in (the condo). Can't get really serious about settling in, though, until the big bookcases are anchored to the walls. I've been hoping old Wayne could find a couple of spare hours to do the deed, but that's looking less and less likely. Might be time to hunt up someone else.)

Meanwhile: much to report. As always, yes. With a full lunar orbit between entries scat jyze is set up so it'll never run short of material. Bolts and bolts and bolts of material.

Third-warmest April ever, this town, OMP and FAP say. Also third driest.

And deaths to report. Including pets: Kat's cocker Arnie and Gail's ferret Lahontan. But also Cassie B.'s husband Nash (known to me through Z) and Leola's sister Renny (for whom Gerry and Leola held an Irish-type wake which we attended at their home three days ago, with jazz-pianist/vocalist/"coach" Tetra Y. on hand to provide live music as well as accompaniment for Leola's and Ronni G.'s singing (and Z joined them for a couple of rollicking numbers)).

But closest to me, I learned via Rob that Aunt Shel died several months ago (Barb let him know about it belatedly). While Dad was away in the war and Mother was living with her family in Lahontan, Shel (about three years younger than Mother) was like a second -- yeah, mother to me (as were also her mother, a/k/a Nana, and the youngest of the three sisters, Shar). Shel was also my first official schoolteacher, at the nursery school in MSM #2. (I've never understood what she was doing in that city at that point. Did she follow Mother -- "Big" to her -- out from Lahontan or did Mother perhaps find her the job and ask her to come out because she, Mother, was lonely there with Dad overseas?) I

continued feeling close to Shel and Uncle Vern after we
moved to Gatewood and they set up housekeeping in
Lahontan -- there were many family visits back and forth
over the years, and several times I stayed with Shel and
Vern in Lahontan for a week or two during summer
vacations. But Vietnam split us apart: she and Vern
were hawks on the war and very moralistic about it along
with anything smacking of counterculture values (Vern's
father being a fire-and-brimstone Lutheran preacher).
This also poisoned Mother's relationship with them, and
the difficult situation with Nana in her declining years
during the same period made matters even worse (Shel and
Vern, because they were right there, had to bear the
brunt on Nana's Alzheimer's-caused wanderings and ever-
increasing inability to care for herself).
     And now I feel bad about having nothing to say to
Vern. I don't even know where he is or how he could be
reached. Nor am I planning to try to find out. -- If
the guilt over this rises to a certain pitch it triggers
memories of fierce arguments with him over Vietnam,
writing, hippies, racism and much, much more: and the
guilt vanishes. Not completely, though, really, and not
forever, but enough. I'm open to reconciliation efforts
from those who've dissed me over the years (in major
ways, I'm talking; and Vern was one of those) but I
won't be the initiator. Period. I've done enough of
that to last me a lifetime.
     -- And I suppose I should wander on. Hate to go
though. One whole wall of books in here at the primo
and it's more than twenty feet high. More books spread
on tables. Conviviality. Oil paintings and bricks,
music I can go for and usually do. Rich java whiff.
Fond memories too -- times I've come here with Z-wiff,
with Kat, with many others. Best late-night jyze venue
in town, I'd say now. As in fact I've said more than
once before in jyze itself, which is why I long ago
started calling this place primo.

*   *

     -- Time for the four a.m. follow-up. In the "land"
of the newly "landed" gent. Living-room area -- roughly

125

as it'll be, with lots of details still to be worked
out. Right now the big futon couch stands against the
south wall, Z's wicker armchair faces it at an angle
from room center, the low wooden coffee table squats in
between (Z'd prefer it to take a hike to the dump so
that her pink Nepal dragon rug would show better), and
the two big floor-to-ceiling bookcase sections reach
shakily out at right angles from the south and west
walls, currently anchored only with wire to the couch
and the low dining-area bookcase; but they embrace the
whole area, giving it a warm and intimate feeling -- sez
I. And as far as I can tell Z goes for it too.

About a third of the old plants are gone (to avoid
at least some of the water damage Raphael warned about
from "shedding" windows). No jazz playing at the moment
-- haven't set up the radio yet. Full-length window of
the door to the balcony shows a reflection of the jyzer
jyzing away beneath an extender-arm floor lamp, with a
deep backdrop -- not a reflection -- of scattered
nightlights from the four-story apartment building to
the west. Several of its upper-floor windows look out
across maybe fifty feet of parking lot and straight in
here, so curtains are another priority item, especially
for that door (all our other windows have blinds).

Hot news these days: worldwide furor over
revelation of U.S. torture tactics in Iraqi prisons,
scandalous photos of naked prisoners being humiliated by
U.S. troops. As hoped and expected by many of the
millions who opposed it, the neocon cabal's invasion is
proving to be a disaster. But can the out-party make
election hay of this? And if they do, will their
policies be any better? (I still say they will, or
would, but not by enough to avert long-term catastrophe.
Corporate and military control of the country are too
deeply rooted, middle-class complacency and political
corruption too widespread. Hoping I'm wrong -- but
pretty damn sure I'm right.)

And how's the Z-spouse doing? Buying the condo was
"like getting married again," she confided -- meaning
it was super-stressful. She predicts our relationship's

heading into "a new stage" and fears it won't be a good one: old marrieds in a rut. Wants to stir things up, she says. Also wants the John Thomas of the jyzerman to step up to the plate more often (gee, the jyzerman would like that too). Wants us to do what we can to get back into player shape -- but also asks, "Are you ready for the changes of our bodies?" -- And she told me for the first time one of the main causes of her nine-year hiatus in romance before we met was "heartbreak" over the breakup with Jerry II, which in her telling happened essentially because (and this too she hadn't revealed before) he was "unwilling to commit."

True, we've been a bit distracted by the move, and for quite a long time. But I'm looking for a revival now. Ready to do my part (health permitting) (and if it's not permitting, I'm a goner anyway).

On that happy note, on to other news. -- Or no, first a couple of final move updates. First, the grand old Crest console went out ignominiously. Most of the other superfluous items were claimed by Z's office coworkers or members of Raphael's condo-conversion crew (including the microwave which -- almost a decade ago now -- played such a key role in my shift to reclusive "bachelor living"). But no one wanted the console, except for the CD player which Jim Q. added to it a few years back, and someone stripped that out while the console was stashed in our garage stall (taking up almost as much room as a small sedan). Cuarto, chief of the carpenter crew, suggested we put the thing up for grabs out on the sidewalk, as they'd done with many other items left behind by former 1511 tenants; "It'll be gone in an hour." But it wasn't. It stood there for days, ignored, rained on, a door hanging open and flapping forlornly in the wind. In the end Wayne had to chop it up and take it to the dump, for which service he billed us (the final indignity) fifty bucks.

The big green recliner chair, meanwhile, went to Cuarto himself, for his ailing and housebound father. Just today Leola asked whether that chair was taking up too much room in the new condo. Z's comment to her: "No

comment." It seems telling Gerry and Leola about the
fate of the thousand-dollar chair, which they gave us
gratis (when it became surplus for them because they'd
found an even more expensive one they liked better),
will be my job.

Other news then. Biggest, the visit of the three
Egan sisters. It finally happened after six months of
postponements and it came off quite well, I thought,
except for a panicky couple of hours during which Erin
thought she'd lost her ID and credit cards (but they
eventually turned up in a "secret compartment" whose
existence in her own wallet she hadn't known about; all
on their own they'd somehow found their way down into
it). I discovered I scarcely knew any of the sisters
anymore -- Erin, the oldest, is six years my junior --
but I did know a lot about them that they didn't know
themselves, and especially about their parents. All
three sisters now work in computer services of one kind
or another in the megastate to the south and none share
any of my major interests and yet our similar
experiences in the sixties and seventies enabled us to
relate fairly well (as did the fact that all three were
close to Mother, not only in the period after their own
mother died young -- just forty-five -- in 1969 but also
during Mother's megastate years). The Roar and Sadie
incident, the Beckham scandal, the "lost branch," the
troubles between me and Aunt Greta over Lady S were all
news to them (just as their disabled brother Damon's
death in '97 and several other matters were news to me).

The sisters were here only a little over two days,
coincidentally staying at an HQ hotel right across the
alley from Vic and Jean's loft. Friday afternoon I
showed them around the usual downtown sites, took them
up to the hideaway and then to a nearby pub, gave them
copies of family historical materials and explained
those in some detail. Saturday night Rob and Z joined
the four of us for dinner at the edgeville fish diner on
the cruise-ship dock. I think the sisters were quite
taken with J. City; they're talking about coming back up
again in the fall (and have already e-mailed to Z

several dozen digital photos from their visit).

Also a couple of touching moments with Vic. One,
he gave me a copy of a book that's just come out,
"Leading the Way: Asian American Artists of the Older
Generation," in which he's one of the featured artists;
and he asked me to accompany him "for moral support" to
an exhibition at the pan-Asian museum, "Talking About
Race," in which his work was again featured (and to my
eye it was best of show by far) and for most of the
evening he and I sat just outside the entrance chatting
away, a glorious day, big crowd, good talk -- and an
unending stream of attendees meanwhile coming up to
congratulate him. And we just had a grand old time.

And mention this: the only communication of any
kind Z and I have had in many months from Elgie (who by
failing to send us a photocopy of his birth certificate
blew off a scholarship worth several hundred bucks which
Z's union wanted to award him) was an e-mail mentioning
that while surfing the internet he'd met a woman in MSM
#1 who knew a couple living nearby with the same unusual
last name as his and my own. This turned out to be Josh
(brother Jeff's son) and his wife, Mirelle, and the
internet woman said she would check up on him with them,
so, he asked, if Josh and Mirelle in turn inquired with
us ("Who the hell is this guy Glen Sandefjord?"), would
we please say something nice about him? -- No such
inquiry came in, but we did receive a thank-you note
(slightly delayed) from Josh regarding the wedding gift
we sent them last summer, and also he enclosed a wedding
invitation from his sister, Rosalie, who'll be tying the
knot at Our Lady in Gatewood in June.

-- And for sheer coincidence this is hard to top:
Chris, the purchaser of unit 202, the one we were living
in temporarily, is a June graduate of the medical school
at the university where Elgie's a student and used to
live in the very next room on the same floor in the same
dorm, room 309 to Elgie's 310. (And totally unrelated
except that another condo is involved, today we met the
buyers of the unit below ours and they're two twenty-
something Japusan sisters -- "the sisters N." -- whose

mother, currently living in the north end, was
with them: and how odd, Z and I agreed, for a Japusan
family to arrange things this way, their unmarried
daughters living apart from them in a condo.)
     Could also mention I'm still waiting to hear from
Sverre W. (this is the month he was supposed to send me
the manuscript of "Grenjad and Vaehild" for
copyediting). Haven't heard at all from June; looks as
though she's decided to make a clean break from us.
Learned that cousin Kar quit his most recent job and has
lately been hanging out in MSM #3 -- 120 miles south of
Elgie's MSM #1 -- with his most recent new woman (a
Brazilian he actually "dated" in college and then lost
contact with for almost four decades).
     And: Sylva S. is retiring from politics and moving
to Cambodia. Z's friend Terri in Lahontan, due to visit
us next month, has just had reconstructive breast
surgery. Aida's brother Ray, the firefighter who was
injured in a badly designed training exercise last
summer, keeps turning up in news stories as
investigators dig into the incident. Mama E's doing
better thanks to her new medication. Olwen's son Trent
is trying his hand at writing historical fiction (he was
laid off last year from the same firm for which Tanya L.
does most of her work -- and he's still living with
Olwen, whose brother Carey is doggedly hanging on in his
battle with cancer; the six months to live which the
doctors gave him last fall have run out but he's still
hard at work on completing a novel he started writing
shortly after the terminal prognosis came down).
     And it's been a great month for tuna-salad "snack
packs." The first sale on them in years, half price; I
bought eighty or so in trips to various outlets of our
local drugstore chain, many with Z (because of coupon
purchase limits); and these handy little items will
furnish my 9:30 p.m. lunches (augmented with a banana
and a slice of whole-wheat bread) for the next four
months, helping me to survive the financial crunch.
     Won't even try to describe the exceptional bad-
karma day I had several weeks back except to say the

final straw came when, dragging from blow after blow, I
stuck my key in the lobby door downstairs and it broke
off -- the key, I'm saying, or call it the straw, but in
any case not the door. Though by that point the door
breaking off would've been even more apt. So then I had
to wake up Z -- it took about ten minutes -- to buzz me
in. (And at the hideaway, new light. After four years
of dimness -- just one of the eight overhead fluorescent
bulbs still working -- the dead bulbs were all replaced.
In this time of massive change it's in a way the biggest
change of all. Illumination! Enlightenment! -- And
we're parking in a new stall now here at The Ettore,
across the garage from the old one -- after seven years
I could maneuver into the tight confines of the old one
blindfolded (betcha!) -- and we've shifted to a new
storage closet and a new slot in the bank of mailboxes
as well. (And yes, I'm now writing "The Ettore" without
quotes around it. Must mean it is what it is. Then
again the name might be changed at a condo association
meeting once Raphael is totally out of the picture.)
    Pedestrian jyze, this. -- But no apologies.

17

    Try for some real scat here. No sentence over ten
words long. No sentence even a proper sentence.
-- Such perfection however being beyond reach for any
survivor of Ms. Des V.'s by-the-book high-school-
sophomore English class. And I am one of those, though
just barely.
    But here it is, balcony of the new ZAG & GAZ condo.
Sunny day. A few notes to work from -- LOOK OUT!
    A gust of wind blew my notes away! Scat notes

scattered!
     -- Just checked. Leaned out to see half a dozen
scraps of blue paper blown halfway across the yard of
the sisters N. down below. No way to retrieve them
short of deploying the rope ladder and possibly scaring
the hell out of the sisters.
     Nothing in those notes they'd find too shocking, I
hope. In any case, not half as shocking as I found
their sudden flight.
     Well. Can I keep going here? Of course I can.
who needs notes anyway? Winging it's much more fun.
(And for good or for bad, I'd just reviewed them.)
     Coffee cup, made a long time ago by Kat, calmly
rides the fence rail through all the hullabaloo. It's
too heavy to fly off anywhere. (Knocka knocka.)
     So. Sun. Will the pale night-working jyzerman
burn out here? Does he deserve to? For sheer idiocy?
     -- About a dozen feet to the west, a wall of
laurel trees more than two stories tall and as wide as
the yard itself, and all aflicker now with frisky
leaves. Down below at the far right and left ends of
the yard camellia bushes whose presence much pleases Z-
wiff: they serve as a colorful twin memorial for her
half sister whose name they share (almost) and whose
death Z's still mourning a year and a half later.
     (She sat alone out here last night, Z did -- and in
her mind maybe Camilla joined her -- with a glass of
wine. First balcony sitting of the 201 era. She moved
one of the dining-room chairs out, wicker on aluminum.
Now it's my turn. -- And in two weeks our wooden deck
chairs ordered from the environmental home center will
be arriving. My job: to screw them together.)
     All right. Where was I?
     -- Settling in. It's happening. Suddenly we're
acting like the de facto boojies we've just become:
we're fascinated with furnishings. A new bamboo lamp.
A new (used) armchair for me. New (used) wooden
bookcase for beneath the living-area window. New feng-
shui hallway curtains. New wooden TV trays. New green
metal stand for flowers and plants, almost head height

with four tiers, already doing the job at the far end of
the balcony with red miniature roses riding the top
tier. Also a big wooden hanging basket (not yet hanging
though) of yellow daisies.

Other Ettoreans settling in too. Just yesterday
the couple who attended Elgie's university arrived to
stay, filling the garage with their furnishings before
moving them all up to 202, our former transitional abode
(and the peephole hardware's not even installed yet in
the little wormhole in their door) (but ours is in and
like true fuddy-duddies we can check out all the new
arrivals through it and have done so a time or two just
for kicks).

Earlier, others. One set per week, more or less.
A possibly gay couple (T.J. is one) above us in 301. A
definitely gay couple (Jonas is one) in 103. All in
their twenties or early thirties, I'd guess, and
seemingly quite conventional, clipped, Cawk (except
Jonas's Latino partner, who may live elsewhere), all
working for banks or internet-related companies, all
driving shiny new SUVs. We've been told a single woman
in that same age group is taking over our old 203 abode
but we still haven't met or even seen her via peephole.

Meanwhile the turn into summer. Memorial Day
yesterday. (May's monthly average night-time
temperature was nine degrees above "normal." -- A good
time for the hokey yet not necessarily unrealistic
ecodisaster blockbuster "The Day After Tomorrow" to hit
the theaters, as it's doing. It shows a massive tidal
wave wiping out FCM #1. Otherwise a dud, we hear.)

-- And enough sun already. Broiling forearms and
forehead and scalp. Inside I go. (But this afternoon
brightness, our access to it, how fine it is after seven
years of living in east-facing apartments.)

*

-- Oops, no wonder it's so dark in here. Forgot I
was still wearing my shades!

The notes remain scattered in the sisters' yard,
I'm sorry to report. No sign anyone's home down there.
Maybe we'll luck out and it'll rain hard tonight so they

won't be able to read them (though from the looks of the sky, rain's not too likely).

Next project will be mounting the screen for the balcony door. Just shooed off a big flying ant that buzzed in through the wide-open doorway. No doubt we'll want to be able to keep that door open during the warm season.

Today's scat fullness comes at seven p.m. Today also the oldest dimestore in the AQ holds its going-out-of-business sale. Seventy-five years. One of the Japusan sisters (a different set to be sure from the one living beneath us) whose parents opened the place is now closing it down as she reaches age ninety. Z-wiff was there at noon scoping out possible condo adornments and found a few which she'll be surprising me with later (her phone message says).

And speaking of ninety: today is Mama E's birthday and she begins her ninetieth year. We celebrated the occasion out at Benita's on Sunday with a very fine "Chantilly" berry cake. And later that same evening we indulged in fresh-caught salmon and homemade raspberry pie at Betty and Kat's. (Mama E was complaining about the shakes but was more sociable than usual in recent months. Tomorrow we take her to see Doc F -- still known as "Winnie" to Betty, his former nurse, who first recommended him to us, and on Sunday she regaled us with some previously unheard dishy stories about him.)

And last week was Lwazi's first birthday. (We're celebrating the gamut -- ages one and eighty-nine.) Now that David and Stacy have taken him out of day care his health is much improved -- but their financial state isn't. To no one's surprise, nannies cost much more than group day care; but just how much more is coming as something of a shock to everyone. (A collapsed Lwazi lung was the final straw, as it were, for David and Stacy with the day-care outfit.) -- The kid's birthday present from us is a monogrammed blanket made from organic wool but we haven't been able to get together with them to bestow it. Right here on the arm of the couch it rests in a brown paper bag colorfully decorated and tied up in shiny blue ribbon by the Z-spouse.

And tomorrow is my parents' wedding anniversary. Their sixty-third. Always one more than what my upcoming birthday will be -- waddaya know. (From the earliest years I can remember, Mother worked hard to inculcate the family-togetherness thing in her offspring. She'd have mixed feelings, though, to know that most of our current family togetherness is on the Sandefjord side. Oh the cruel irony of this for her!)

And the J-slinger? Exuberating along except for the health glitches. This left-flank bulge, it's persisting. A hernia of some sort, most likely, I'm thinking now, since all internal organs still seem to be functioning normally. Can it heal itself? Not too likely. But give it time. Try to slim down to the max (or rather to the min) and see whether that helps.

"Going down slow." Also arthritis may be coming after the middle finger of my left hand, knuckle closest to the palm. My hands have taken quite a beating over the years -- piano, bass, baseball, football, basketball (this last-named especially: cause of numerous sprains with major swelling) and all these mixed in with decades of heavy typewriter and computer keyboarding. I'm trying to head off the likely arthritic consequences before they become serious. An over-the-counter gluco/ chond cream with a trademarked secret ingredient, massage it in twice a day and hope for the best.

-- And real or not, this scat's gotta shut down just about now. Today Z-wiff and I return to the WOC together for only the third or fourth time in the past six weeks. (Possibly some overambitious weight-lifting caused this hernia, if that's what it is. Trying to do too much without maintaining the basics: same cause as that for my ruptured left Achilles tendon of three decades ago. Hubris I guess is the word. -- Not even a guess really. Hard truth.)

*   *

Spotted an armchair newly stationed up here on the fourth-floor balcony -- this was the other day when I was paying the rent for No. 225. Trying it out now for

fit. Two hours and forty minutes past scat fullness
(which came at 9:20, not 7:20 -- will there ever be a J-
day when I get it right?)

So -- my life. (Forget the "no 'I' in jyze"
business, except for special occasions.) For me
personally these are terrific times. No "day job" work
until September. Tanya L. has inexplicably dropped out
of sight (hooray!). Excitement of the new condo --
feathering the love nest. Loving the Z-woman. And
summer's here. And I'm whaling away at my own work.
I've even bought a new printer for home use and it's all
ready to hook up. Maybe by next scat-jyze moon I'll
finally have a home desktop computer up and running.

Z-spouse availed herself of one of the loan offers
constantly arriving in our mailbox, every last one in
her name. Three thousand bucks which she's signing over
to me so I can get by until scoping starts up again.
This means her debt to me is already down to about eight
K. If I'm truly lucky some of the three K will still
linger in my bank account when I retire from scoping,
probably about three and a half years from now. Or
maybe if the scoping's still available and the workload
isn't too great I'll try to hang on for another two
years beyond that, thus qualifying for a couple hundred
more dollars in my monthly Social Security benefit.

But for the three-month nonce little "day" work and
maybe none at all. And already I'm learning once again
it's not at all hard to fritter away the free time. So
much to do! Fixing up "the property." Shaping up at
the WOC. Being extra-good to the Z-wiff. Being
sociable. Seeing movies and getting out and doing
things and renewing acquaintances with various friends,
most of whom were Z's friends first. Reorganizing here,
there, and everywhere. And of course buckling down to
lots and lots of reading.

To be a dedicated jyzer you must skimp on all such
stuff, especially if you're also working a part-time
job. So when some extra free time finally opens up, a
big backlog's sure to be crying for attention, and
that's the case now.

[Scat Jyze : Green Monkey]

       But I think I'm doing okay on all this. Okay --
but not really well. Must do better. Roughly 1.4
million words of hardcore jyze to whip into shape.
Maybe six volumes now instead of seven, depending on
whether I decide to fold "Jyzeburst" (Jyze Age Annal 1)
into "Jyzemelt" (Annal 2).
       (Keeping an eye on my pocket watch here. For
several months I thought I'd lost it. Found it buried
in the notes and letters piled high on my chairside tray
at home. -- It's half past the hour. The hour is
midnight. -- Must work on conciseness also.)
       World situation, politically speaking, still every
bit as perilous. Not even to mention eco/climate
matters. The ruling U.S. neocons are quietly reversing
some of their disastrous policies but eating little crow
and admitting nothing. The incumbent high honcho's poll
numbers are way down but has he discredited himself with
enough of his true believers to lose in November? The
formerly antiwar out-party challenger's now tacking to
dead center. Sad to see. If it doesn't work, the price
to be paid will be horrifically high.
       (Such a quiet building tonight. Hum of the fans
and that's about it. Not many vacancies these days, I
see from the lobby bulletin board. Seven floors with
maybe two hundred offices in all, but only five are
posted under "Available." Elsewhere in J-town the
vacancy rate for office properties remains high,
somewhere around fifteen percent, so the hideaway
building's low rents must be what's keeping it close to
full. -- Eight and a half years I've been here now.
All of a sudden!)
       New today, the bag I carry to the WOC with my
workout clothes inside. For more than seven years I've
been using the same bedraggled black vinyl briefcase I
salvaged from the dumpster outside B-2. The other day I
noticed a white canvas carpetbag with a leather bottom
standing by the door in 201, mixed in with other items
Z-wiff was planning to give away at the office (she was
"purging" again as part of settling into her new room).
I put in an early bid -- a "Get out of horniness free!"

card -- and it was successful. This bag's much bigger
than its predecessor and also much better to look at --
I'm proud of it! -- though it does lack pockets inside.
Or rather it has only one large pocket. Have to do lots
of fishing to find my lock and swipe cards in there.

Thinking it's time to pause. Tend to a few chores
in 225, then bus home for the jyze wrap-up. (Wish my
new armchair at home could be this comfy. But then it
would have to be larger and wouldn't fit the allotted
space by the door to the balcony. Everything's tight in
the living/dining zone. (The area enclosed by the
bookcases I privately think of as "the cockpit." Don't
want to say this aloud, though, because the way the
area's set up is mostly my doing and I'm pretty sure
I've convinced Z it's roomy enough.))

*   *

-- Meaning this area right here and this armchair.
Four a.m. and the birds are just starting up. Radio
shuts off at four and then I notice the birds. (Still
having trouble adjusting the volume on this radio, whose
"loudness" knob goes by increments rather than on a
smooth continuum, and the size of the increments seems
to change every time I turn the radio off and on. It's
very difficult to ratchet the damn thing low enough for
tolerable late-night listening -- tolerable for everyone
else, that is -- without making it go entirely silent.)

As I left the hideaway a guy on the third floor
warned me to be very careful out there; said a man was
murdered in the alley beneath his window at two a.m. a
few nights ago -- he heard the screams. -- And the
police shot a man to death by the AQ freeway overpass
near the high bridge a couple of weeks ago (after he
opened fire on them). So, yeah, I'm careful. For one
thing, I can't exactly count on my footspeed the way I
used to. And a punch in the hernia bulge -- assuming
that's what it is -- could probably do me in on the
spot. But still, I've seen the streets much worse.

Z-wiff's surprise items from the dimestore sale
were awaiting me right here on the chair. One's a red
silk pillow with lots of fancy needlework showing

traditional Asian kids (Chinese-looking, I'd say) chasing butterflies; the other's a tray bearing the famous Japanese "The Wave" print (which in truth has become such a cliche it's almost unviewable as anything but parody). Both, though, are very finely made. Our reach for high-flown condo cachet continues. (I kicked in a thousand bucks to it myself by reducing Z's debt to me by that much; so no self-exoneration here.)

Key moment of the month came just a week ago yesterday with the arrival at our unit 201 door of one Richie Y., Cawk carpenter dude. Aida recommended him. In a matter of a little over two hours, at $45 per, he anchored all three of the large bookcases, including the one in our bedroom. Since then I've been going gangbusters unloading boxes. The major task still left for me is to set up the art worktable against the diagonal northeast wall of this large five-sided "great room." The table's there already (nowhere else in this unit it could go); the task is to locate, sort, and arrange all the art goods on it, below it, around it.

(Will say again: I couldn't be more delighted with our new home. And a big part of the reason I feel this way is that I now believe Z likes it as much as I do.)

Big issues of the moment: should we return the new bamboo floor lamp and exchange it for a table lamp? And which of several candidates will serve best as the feng-shui curtain in the hallway? (This curtain is entirely Z's thing; my many run-ins with the negative side of feng shui in Korea were enough to bum me out on it for a lifetime.)

Neglected to mention earlier: I went through another big scare with the FBI earlier this month. After a week of playing phone tag I learned they had more questions about Elgie -- even odder ones this time. Why hadn't I mentioned in the reclearance papers that I had gone to Korea to pick him up? But that preceded the start of the prescribed reporting period on those papers by almost twenty years! It turned out they had him in their records as currently being eleven years old (and attending law school!). Apparently they had carried

forward his age unchanged from the time I first applied
for clearance as a scoper back in 1984 when he really
was eleven. (It's true he looks quite young for his
age, but this is ridiculous.)

     Upshot of it all (learned just last week): I'm now
"officially cleared as a court reporter" for grand jury
and the U.S. Attorney's Office. (Do they really think
I'm a court reporter? The incompetence of this outfit
is stunning. -- But we knew that. And regardless
they're still highly dangerous to any USAn who so much
as dares to think an "unpatriotic" thought. Not much
change here, if any, from the sixties and seventies with
their infamous COINTELPRO and so much else just as bad.)

     From Elgie himself not a word. Is he still
planning to come stay with us for the fall semester? We
don't know. He sent Kat a birthday e-mail two weeks
ago, for some reason thinking her birthday was May 25th
(it's February 24th, five days after his). After that
they exchanged a couple of short e-mails, mostly about
nutrition and healthy living. One of his said, Kat told
Z, "Law school is very hard." (From our new neighbors
we know the semester at Elgie's university ended a
couple of weeks ago, including the law school's.)

     Kat, by the way, has enrolled at the high school on
southwest island for her freshman year starting in the
fall. It's ritzier over there, more burban, and of
course therefore much Cawkier. More like my own burban
adolescent incubator Gatefield High -- which
incidentally was featured in a Sunday "night paper" mag
article this week on contemporary sexual practices of
high schoolers. It's still way ahead of the curve on
such matters, the article states, just as it was in my
day (not that I was myself; I was woefully behind the
curve). "Hooking up" and relationships "with benefits"
are the latest rage. Oral sex with no emotional
attachments. Is this where Kat's headed or is she maybe
already there with her new boyfriend Clive? I'd guess
yes, she's there -- or if not yet, soon. (On Mother's
Day a lovely Sunday-afternoon brunch with Betty and Kat
at our favorite west-side fifties retro cafe. And this

summer I'm supposed to be teaching Kat about writing --
if she'll stand for it. And I'm sorry to say she's
given little indication so far that she will.)

   Aida won a big honor: she was one of four
recipients of the annual Voice of the Community award
from the more liberal of the two AQ English-language
weeklies (same one Z and Vic write occasional reviews
for). We attended a spiffy award dinner at a downtown
hotel, four hundred attendees, mostly Asiusans -- June
sitting next to me. She looked somewhat better, June
did, but didn't have much to say. To me this confirmed
my longtime suspicion that our days as "buddy-buddies,"
as she used to call us, have passed. (And Aida's son,
Charles, sixteen now, failed to show; the seat reserved
for him remained conspicuously empty all night. He's
turning into a problem kid. In their desperation Aida
and Tom, his father, are thinking of sending him off to
a backwoods "boot camp" for hardcore troublemakers.
He's dropped out of school, has no job -- runs, Z tells
me, with a group of "feral" younger kids.)

   What else? (1) Got a flat tire on a loaner car
while the Z-mobile was in for five hundred bucks' worth
of brake work. (2) Attended a wake for the husband
(Nash) of Z's workmate Cassie -- Nash being a good guy
who several times plied me with savvy questions about
writing when we were both present at spouse-related work
gatherings. (3) Visited the classic bohemian Yuke
saloon with Vic on a night that, by sheer coincidence,
turned out to be the seventieth anniversary of the place
-- TV interviews of patrons and the original owner (now
age ninety-two) were in process nearby as we rapped away
in the southeast-corner booth, a favorite protojyzing
spot of mine back in my early J-town period.

   And: These days I'm wearing a rediscovered pair of
deluxe-model red-and-black low-cut chucks and also the
hemp shirt-jac, white, which sat in the closet for years
(too heavy for a tuck-in, too expensive for a spring/
fall everyday carry-along -- until now).

   And: The new central library has opened to an
international chorus of raves. It seems I may be its

only detractor anywhere on the planet (especially of the
structure's exterior -- I never tire of pointing out the
many ways it resembles Darth Vader's helmet). Even so I
had intended to work in a session there for this month's
jyze -- until Z decided she wanted to hit the WOC last
night; and I'd been flacking for these workouts so much
in recent weeks, I couldn't say no.

*

    -- And by the way, last time I looked the jyze
notes were still scattered on the ground down there in
the sisters' yard, seemingly glowing in the moonlight.
Radioactive maybe -- beaming info up this way, helping
propel me through the past few pages.

18

    Sixth moon of the scat year. Also the sixtieth
moon, which I hereby christen the Heavenly Moon,
counting the months we've been married, Ms. Z and me.
    Celebrating first here, Z-geist, outdoors. Was
headed for the HQ plaza less than a block to the west
because tonight is First Thursday artwalk. But here I'd
have a guaranteed seat: it was right in front of me to
grab. Or at least for forty-five minutes I'd have it,
until closing hour at seven. And down in the plaza
crowds would be swarming until eight or later; seats
would be at a premium everywhere.
    The familiar row of aluminum chairs and tables
(small and round) on the sidewalk just outside the
windows. At the far end of the row an "author signing"
is underway, Cawk dude with a stack of self-published
books (could almost be me one of these days if I'm
lucky). Sun's slanting in under the awning. Ballpark

crowd going by too but easily outnumbered by artwalkers
(the baseball club's a bust this year). Ancient three-
story brick hotel across the street is still being
renovated, iron girders bracing the walls damaged by the
earthquake three and a half years ago now.

An open-topped double-decker tour bus stops
parallel just yards away; one of the student women
sitting at the table in front of mine waves and yells,
"Hi, tourists! Welcome to Jyze City!" And a couple of
young women wave back from the upper deck, smiling
weirdly (recalling the delectable "Twisted," its
creator/performer wigged out on a similar bus in London
because there's "no driver on the top").

Jyze zingers, one after another.

Last night in that same HQ plaza (visible from
here, one end of it, half a block west, if you squint
against the late sun), a mob scene: well over a thousand
people lined up while waiting for the most recent of the
ex-presidents of the USA (an authentic politician not a
rock star) to autograph a copy of his new book for them
at the ORB. And that was two hours before the man was
due to appear. When I arrived at the ORB itself minutes
later it was already crawling with cops and Secret
Service agents and numerous photographers and TV cameras
were setting up. The cafe was closed. I'm proud to say
my quasi-grungy presence drew suspicious glares from
several of the security types. And that I fled the
place moments later. (As I left, a guy in a gaudy
silver suit was complaining at the main counter,
"Someone's gonna get killed out there if you don't do
something about crowd control!")

Right now this particular ex-president's starting
to look better to lots of folks -- even some in the
other party. The current cowboy kahuna's popularity is
still falling as the Iraq debacle deepens and more of
the cabal's blunders and deceptions come to light. Just
a few days ago they returned "limited sovereignty"
(wotta crock!) to the Iraqis (the new "interim
government" hand-picked by the U.S. and headed by a
former CIA stooge who supervised our own terrorist

operations over there a decade ago). -- A new antiwar
documentary, "Fahrenheit 9/11," opened a week ago and
has become a national sensation.

   -- Does any of this mean the incumbent will lose in
November? No. But the odds that he will are improving.
And if they keep improving, look out for a nasty October
surprise or two to knock them back down again. (Hey,
brilliant political analysis here!)

   On the way in I stopped to color-copy a photo of
Kat. It's from her graduation ceremony and I'm planning
to splice it into a postcard advertising a real-life
play called "The Book of Kat." The card will accompany
the graduation gifts we'll be giving her Saturday night
(the four of us will also be seeing Kat's choice of a
movie, "Napoleon Dynamite"); my gift is the "Dictionary
of Allusions" (same one I've been browsing through
myself) and four of these fuzzy blank J-books -- in red,
purple, green, and blue -- which she's supposed to fill
in during high school, one for each year. (This is
jyze's second direct attempt to reproduce itself. The
first, the "spree" with Z-wiff seven years ago this
summer, though it seemed to work well at the time, has
turned out to be something she doesn't want to repeat,
or at least not yet.)

   Kat's eighth-grade "promotion ceremony" was the
high point for me of the month just past. The low point
was the death of Naomi's husband, Larry. More on both
of these later. Because any moment now I'm expecting
someone'll be out here to stack the chairs and tables.

   Red-and-black chucks, jeans, dark blue short-sleeve
henley, jyze pendant -- same old jyzer. This is the
life: sittin' and jyzin'. Sippin' at my stubby brown
bottle of root beer. Folks wandering by. Gulls
flapping about. Traffic up close and sometimes personal
(as when a few minutes ago a snazzily dressed ebony-
skinned woman in a sporty blue convertible called over
to me from maybe eight feet away while stopped for the
light, "This how I get to the freeway?")

   My four-month sabbatical now half over. So soon!
But I'm loving it. And using it to firm up the jyze

vision. What good fortune for me to have this time
free! It's inspired me to embark on a full revision of
"Jyze Age," all seven annals (I've dropped the six-annal
idea) and roughly four thousand pages in typed form
(single-spaced with forty lines and 360 words to the
page). More a touch-up really, except for "Heavenly
Year," the last annal, where I expect to either redo or
cut major parts or possibly all of the backstory
sections ("This Is Your Life, Jyzer G").

At home the long settling-in process continues. A
chore or two or three related to this each day. Z's
friend Terri from Lahontan stayed with us for a week and
that cut down significantly on what I could get done.
But things are progressing. And we're both still
delighted, Z and I, with what we've got. (-- And what
is it we've got? Not a condo; we don't like to say
that. "Flop." "Crib." "Love nest.")
    -- And this is it: Z-geist closing time. And just
as a siren starts up somewhere nearby with a big whoop!
*   *
"More later," he says -- but not all that much
more. Jyze is running a few pages ahead of itself.
Must cut back this round.
    And jyze be lazy. Here's that same flowery-
patterned armchair, fourth floor of the hideaway
building. It's official rent-paying day this time. And
it's a whole lot cooler up here tonight than it is in
room 225, where I'm more or less forced to keep the door
closed as protection against the talkative guy -- name
is Baker, and that's his first name -- who's moved into
231 (and unfortunately keeps hours much like mine).

With all my bills paid I now have about two hundred
bucks to live on for the rest of the month, which is to
say the entire month: four weeks and three days. That's
if I want to go into the last two months of my
sabbatical (assuming the scoping work will restart at
the beginning of September but I won't be paid until the
end) with eight hundred on hand for each month. And
that is the plan.
    But I haven't heard from Naomi since several weeks

145

before Larry's death. I'm just assuming she'll return
to work when she said she would. Knowing her, knowing
her situation (three kids at home, no independent
income), I think it's a pretty good bet.

   (Z-wiff and I attended the memorial service held
for Larry at the U.S. courthouse. A special session of
the district court was convened with a number of current
and former judges present. The eulogies were
surprisingly eloquent and moving. The courtroom was
packed to overflowing -- Z and I were lucky to find a
standing spot in an anteroom just to the side of the
first row of seats, within a dozen feet of Naomi and the
kids -- actually we wound up leaning against the edge of
a table. This also gave us a close-up view of the
frantic backstage tinkerings when the sound system acted
up, emitting a high-pitched wheeeee. For the first time
I was seeing the faces and in some cases hearing the
voices of not just the judges but many of the assistant
U.S. attorneys whose words I've been scoping and at
times "cleaning up" -- but that's a trade secret now,
you hear? -- for almost a quarter of a century.)

   Bad month for deaths. The great Ray C. is gone
too. Oh -- and so is a former U.S. president, prior to
the ascension of the current incumbent the public figure
I've most loved to revile in my lifetime (though two
others have come close). The media's beatification of
the man during his funeral week was truly a shame to
behold. Only a lonely voice here and there dared to
observe that "the Gipper" more than any other single
person is responsible for the horrible fix the country's
in now. (What, you don't believe that, jyze reader?
Then you too may be in dire need of some revisionism.)

   -- But I digress.

   Will mention instead my own physical state. It's
not all that terrible, but bad enough. Bulge persists,
as do symptoms. But I still can function well enough
that no one even suspects. And that's how I hope it
stays. Mainly I just have to be careful not to twist
myself too much in the wrong direction, especially if
I'm around people who know me. "Glen, why are you

screaming like a stuck porker?"

Body giving out. Well of course. Nor is it a surprise it's happening in what to me is a surprising way. Now I face a philosophical conundrum of sorts. Should I try to have the bulge repaired? Doing so would go against some of my principles -- self-reliance, living naturally, accepting unbegrudgingly my inevitable physical deterioration -- but then not doing so would go against other, equally important principles: keeping myself functioning at as high a level as pragmatically possible (self-reliance II), living long enough to complete my life's work, doing my best to be a good husband. And there's also the matter of the serious risk involved if I don't seek a repair as well as the lesser but still not negligible risk if I do.

Maybe next month I'll take another crack at grappling with the dilemma.

-- Very peaceful up here. Haven't seen a soul. And I still have an hour to burn until bus time. But will stop anyway so I can sling a bit at home and still keep the page count within the extended limit.

*   *

Now 4:05 a.m. In four minutes the moon goes scat. But it's nowhere in sight out there (as I sit at home by the balcony door). And the explanation for its absence is a persuasive one: it set exactly an hour ago. (But I didn't see it before then either. I was focusing hard on "Annals" matters.)

-- Nor is the new deck furniture holding forth out there on the balcony. And a persuasive explanation is handy for this as well: it still hasn't arrived at the home center. They called to say it left Brazil by freighter last week and should be arriving in J-town by the 5th. So presumably it's now somewhere off the coast of Nicaragua (just a guess).

To my left stands the new tabletop bamboo lamp with the cubical red fabric shade, now warmly aglow. I love this lamp! It rocks the whole cockpit! -- Or just pit. Or nook. Homey little space, enclosed mostly by books and plants. A radio speaker nests behind each ear, just

147

inches away -- I can listen to jazz in true stereo on
the public station at any hour (if the news isn't on).
     So yes, all's pretty doggone good.
     Except things with Elgie. He did answer an e-mail
inquiry from Z-wiff to say he'd just arrived in MSM #1
and was looking for work. So eager was he to get back
home that he collided with a truck somewhere out in the
desert after driving twenty-four hours straight.
Managed to avoid injury and to creep the few hundred
remaining miles in the crumpled (again!) car. Later
another e-mail arrived telling us his grades: three B's
and a C. In this era of extreme grade inflation I
imagine he's not too happy with a scorecard like that.
     And Z-wiff's not too happy with him, nor am I. To
me he's sent not a word, including even on Father's Day
(horrors!). Worse, he's said nothing about whether he's
still intending to come up here and stay with us this
fall. Z's starting to feel uneasy about giving up her
room to him under such circumstances (in part, it's
true, because having Terri staying there for a week
wound up putting a severe strain on both of us, and
especially Z; but then Terri seems to be turning into
something of a tyrant under the influence of her post-
mammectomy meds).
     I'm just waiting for Elgie to make the next move.
That's because he's the one whose move it is -- and then
some. I feel sorry for him but I can't let him keep
jacking us around like this. The lad's a prince, that's
the trouble. No surprise really he's developed this
way. Much that's fine about him. The thoughtful care
and concern of a prince, though, he's sadly lacking in.
(Yeah, and who am I to say. But I'll say it anyway.)
     Other stuff? Heard from Barb and also from Ken D.
The usual bland and cautious and faintly pious few short
paragraphs from Barb. From Ken the news that Diane W.
called him and Jo around the time she and Ray divorced
-- in '99, was it? -- and said, "I've been taking this
man's abuse for thirty-five years!" (And that's very
sad to hear. But what does the length of the period say
about Diane?) I try to keep up with Ray's published

work but the truth is it just doesn't interest me very much (though his cover screed on 9/11 for a national monthly mag was quite good). Ken enclosed a packet of his own poems (I haven't checked them out yet) and asked for suggestions on contemporary fiction to read. I imagine he's having as hard a time figuring out how to handle me -- and especially how to deal with me as a touchy graybeard jyzer -- as I am with him.

Also should mention I still haven't hooked up my new printer (I sneak in every Friday night to use the one at the scope office and that's enough to meet my current needs).

And this: it leaks out that the tallest building in town (standing just across the street from Z's office and four blocks up the hill from mine) was on Al Qaeda's original hit list for 9/11. Supposedly. Do I believe this? Well, maybe. Do I see the leak as part of the cabal's pre-election fan-the-fear tactics? Definitely.

And: I came across an essay that does a nice job of describing the stages of life and preparations for death. Also it provides some potential add-on material for "Heavenly Year": talks about the Hindu celebration of shastiputri, which means "completing sixty" (years). It marks the point at which the celebrant's family responsibilities end and the move into the "forest dweller" stage begins, with the "wandering beggar" stage to follow.

Right now I'm a couple of months short of two years into forest dwelling. Since I was still age sixty and Z-wiff was just past it herself when we first heard our building would be condoizing, it could be the gods are designating this unit right here as our mutual "forest dwelling." Further, it's time for us to scale back, the article says, and focus on self-realization. So I'm wondering if this, when all's said and done, is what scat jyze is really about. This and, as the article also says, preparation for our leave-taking.

So in months to come I'm likely to be looking more deeply into things shastiputrian, yeah. (For starters, exactly when does the "wandering beggar" stage begin?

[Scat Jyze : Green Monkey]

It occurs to me one would probably be well advised to
have most of one's major projects completed before
embarking on that.)

19

     And it's a "blue" one too. Brownishly visible
through the trees. As I sit out on the condo balcony at
half past three in the morning. In one of our new
wooden deck chairs, assembled (by me) just yesterday.
     Hot diggity dog! And not an insect in sight.
Newly screened doorway to the living room at my back;
and at the far end of the balcony, behind the four-tier
flower stand, an exterior door to our bedroom where Z
lies right now, presumably asleep.
     Glass of my usual ceremonial bourbon here. Drained
the last drop out of the bottle. Now a hard choice to
make: blow some of my dwindling sabbatical funds on
another bottle? So I can celebrate my birthday
properly? Suppose I'll probably have to do that.
     Just moments before I came out here our buzzer
sounded. Twice. I went down to the lobby door and
found a drunken young woman standing outside in a cowboy
hat, jeans, and a low-cut, midriff-baring sheer black
teddy top. Quite attractive too. And quite clearly
under the influence of -- something. Said she, looking
at me imploringly: "I just need a place to sleep
tonight." Hm, thought I, a tricky ethical conundrum has
arisen. But no, it turned out she was a friend of
Antonia in 203 -- just hit the wrong buzzer. (At first
she thought I must be Antonia's new boyfriend -- and
he's an older fellow as it happens, although perhaps not
quite to the extent I am.) Antonia did let her in

eventually. And from the sound of it not too happily.

We still know very little about any of our neighbors and have yet to meet several. No homeowners' meeting has been called. Nor has a bill for condo dues arrived. But we're hanging loose on all of these. And The Ettore's "Condos for Sale" sign in front of the building has finally come down.

It's a little chilly out here -- I'm bundled up in sweatshirt and sweatpants and winter moose slippers just in case a blizzard should blow in. But no, it's fine. No breeze, or very little -- just enough to flutter the leaves slightly and make the brown moon half hidden by them seem to twinkle. Second fullness of the month -- which is why it's "blue," of course. Haze from a high-pressure inversion, that's why it's brown.

Earlier tonight, while the summerfest's torchlight parade clogged the downtown with three hundred thousand spectators (according to radio news), Z and I joined six of my "lost" second cousins and nieces and nephews for dinner at brother Rob's. These were Ron H. and his wife Karin and two of Ron's kids, Lynn and Matt, and their spouses, Michael and Libby (all of whom Rob had met last year in Tomsville). Barbecue on the garage-roof deck, Rob doing himself proud as always, even baking a homemade blackberry pie, the berries picked from his own extensive patch bordering the backyard. Classical music piped down from his garret study to the cluster of benches and chairs set up amid the gnarly branches of the corkscrew -- willow, innit? A kerosene lantern hung from one of the branches. Always touchingly idyllic for me, this scene. (And enjoyable talk. How all the couples met. Why the lamentably snooty and pompous "Lincolnesque" -- JRX! -- presidential challenger has just got to win in November.)

It's been the week of the challenger's party convention. About twenty-five hundred miles pretty much due east. It went well enough the incumbent now appears to be running scared. A nasty battle ahead -- and that's at best. At worst, a terrorist incident or some other emergency (quite possibly staged), even a canceled

election (leaks already emerging about detailed
government plans for just such a "contingency"). (The
challenger's a year my junior. In reading stories about
his college days, in a number of places I might almost
have been reading about my own such days just up the
road from his school, which also happens to be the
incumbent's school, and also the school of the previous
two incumbents before him. (Elite enough?) -- And by
the way, back in June I let my fortieth college reunion
slip by unremarked. I'd forgotten all about it. Mezzu
and even Gatefield High have managed to catch up with me
for their alumni mailing lists but Adams never has.
-- So then would I have attended if I'd been notified or
had remembered on my own? Ha! How? But even if I
could've afforded to? Of course not. Unless.... Well,
who knows. It's just that attending such an affair is
scarcely imaginable given my present circumstances and
that's been true for a long, long time.)
     -- Under my maroon sweatpants, new black hemp boxer
shorts. "Unners." Z-wiff smuggled them safely across
the border for me. She and Aida rode the fast ferry up
there to see an Egyptian art show, returning last night.
     Next week it'll be my turn to decamp. Out of the
blue came a call from Naomi asking if I could house-sit
for ten days while she takes the kids down to the
megastate for a family gathering. Since I'd previously
offered to help out in any way she might need, I could
scarcely say no, and in fact didn't want to. The truly
good news from this call is that she'll definitely be
returning to work in September and I'll have my old job
back, probably at about the same number of hours per
week as before the first symptoms of Larry's final
illness appeared. And this means, barring some new
emergency or disaster, I'm probably set for bill-paying
work all the way from here to Social Security. That's a
distance of about four years as things look now, though
I continue to think I might want to stretch it out a few
years further if my health still seems okay.
     Did I say "still"? Not meaning to imply it looks
all that great right now. A spreading rash on my legs,

especially behind the right knee, to worry about. And
of course the "bulge" on my left flank. And I'm not
shaving off much weight even though I'm trying. But in
most respects I seem to be as functional as ever. I
walk almost everywhere, work out with weights two or
three times a week. So yeah, okay, go with "still."

   Last week Z-wiff had a mole removed from her labia.
Yesterday a card arrived from the doc: "Good news:
Benign!" (This would've been a bigger cause for relief
if either of us had realized the doc -- Karen -- thought
it might be anything other than benign. Somehow she had
neglected to spell out the risks to Z.) -- Karen did
advise Z, however, to "tell that stubborn husband of
yours there's a reason women live longer in this
country: they go to see their doctors." She's right, of
course. Well, that's one reason anyway. (Like I say,
I'm not in denial here. -- But enough on that.)

   I'm happy about: writing Ken D. a seven-page
letter. Doing a good altered-art card for Z-wiff last
night. Finding at least some of the writing in
"Jyzeburst" very good indeed. (And I could've put that
last one first and stopped right there.)

   I'm unhappy about: Elgie's continuing failure to
contact us in any substantial way (though he did
recently send Z a couple of photos by e-mail, both
showing himself with his exceptionally attractive
Asiusan (Chiusan I think) girlfriend Faith. "Sex and
the City," Z says of them; "Hormones jumping right
off the page"). And equally unhappy: Kat's still
showing no interest in taking up my offer, repeated
several times, to tutor her in writing this summer.

   (Foghorns sounding now. Must be the kind of fog
that clings to the water. Up here on the hilltop the
sky's hazy but otherwise clear. And brightening too.
News on, I can just barely hear from outside, but it
still cues me it's after five. -- And so maybe I ought
to pack it in. -- Bird flits by a foot from my head,
startling me, loud whirring wings. -- But luckily this
time I have no notes to drop.)

*   *

153

Fourteen hours later and here's the rest of the scat, seventh moon of the Green Monkey (but no it's not my lunar birthday month, even though that too falls in the seventh moon; but strictly speaking this is only the sixth moon according to the Chinese calendar because the second month -- Z-wiff's birthday month -- was doubled this year on the zodiac, for reasons much too complex to try to explain here, even though, amazingly enough, I do know what those reasons are) (and yet as of the midnight when this solar day began some twenty hours ago it actually is the solar month of my solar birthday).

Here where? No. 225. After completing our usual Sunday-evening north-hill provisioning run and driving back downtown by myself. On a two-rolls-in-the-hay weekend, Saturday and Sunday, both in the afternoon. But we canceled the usual Sunday visit with Mama E because Tuesday afternoon she goes in to see Doc F ("Winnie the Doc") and we go with her. The shakes and other side effects of her medication have disappeared now that she's off that nasty stuff, but, after a blessed no-complaints interval of a couple weeks, the hallucinations which the nastiest of the drugs helped block are back. Yesterday she was sure FBI agents were after her and telephoned several times begging us to call them off. (But maybe the FBI really is after her -- say, to answer questions about me as part of the reclearance process. Not likely, true, since I didn't put her name down as a reference, but given the FBI's track record with me in recent years, far from impossible. "I've got it, Chief. The way to suss out the true skinny on this court-reporter guy with the eleven-year-old foreign national kid who's in law school is to shake down his delusional mother-in-law.")

Speaking of incompetence, two weeks ago the incumbent high muckety-muck delivered a campaign speech in my old hometown, Gatewood, that was received rapturously according to the media (bringing to mind the adulation a certain shadowy USAn veep, later a president who resigned in disgrace, received there one evening back in the fifties -- and the jyzer himself was in the

auditorium). -- And the day before that Gatewood
speech, the challenger was wowing them in both Dad's
birthplace and my own: Wachute and Lahontan. (Z and I
did finally see "Fahrenheit 9/11," catching it in a
southern burb with Fred and Eleanor W. (the latter a
grad-school chum of Z's in Lahontan). Not bad, but for
me a yawner anyway because I'd already read so much
about it.) -- And the 9/11 Commission's report has been
released to much acclaim and what a crock it is, casting
no political blame despite all the cabal's blunders.

And Friday evening, I'm chagrined to say, my one
pair of wearable jeans split in the crotch as I slid
into the car after picking up Z and Aida at the fast-
ferry dock. This means I'll have to buy a new pair this
week -- tomorrow -- and will be out thirty more bucks I
can't afford. September is looking likely to bring on
for me a major, major financial crunch. And poor Z-
wiff's just about broke too from the strain of picking
up the full condo mortgage payment for the period of my
"sabbatical" (though technically she's repaying part of
what I loaned her for her share of the down payment).
And she has a lot of anxiety about all this because of
past bad experiences with debts, including loaned money
lost to former boyfriends (the most traumatic of these
losses being the three grand Arvin made off with).

And a few other items. Think I'll just wheel out
the closely paired double stars here:

** For Father's Day (but delayed almost a week)
Kat gave me two boxes of "the leading brand" of
cornflakes, each box individually wrapped and cleverly
and colorfully decorated by hand.

** Godson Lwazi's health has improved dramatically
since he stopped going to day care (but his parents'
financial health is rapidly declining owing to the size
of the nanny bills). And Thursday he took his longest
upright stroll so far, halfway across the living room.

** Amanda made her first cleaning visit to 201.
It turned into an adventure when she pulled the blinds
in Z's bedroom right out of the wall -- the fixtures,
that is -- and I lost most of an afternoon helping her

remount them.

  ** Z tacked the "Get out of horniness free!" card
on the headboard above our bed, perfectly positioned for
me to gaze upon while in the act missionary style. She
took it down, but only temporarily, for Amanda's visit.

  ** And an amusing story I'd somehow never heard
before this past week: A few years back when cousin Ron
H. left the out-of-the-blue message with Gail announcing
the existence of what turned out to be the "lost branch"
of the family, he identified himself as the "son of
Barbara Sandefjord." When Gail passed that message
along to Rob, he assumed the reference was to our sister
Barbara and agonized for days about calling Barb with
the news, since as far as he (and the rest of us) knew,
Barb was childless. But Ron's Barbara Sandefjord, as it
turned out, was a different one, the daughter of Karl
Sandefjord, younger brother of our great-grandfather
Bendyk (and different also, of course, from our
grandmother Barbara Fritsch Sandefjord) (and Ron H.'s
older brother is also named Karl).

  ** Marlon Brando died. Another big influence on
me concerning how to be a cool guy -- right up there
with Paul Newman, John Lennon, Jim Morrison, Otis Spann,
Otis Redding, et al. -- and best not to forget James
Arness in the formative years. Or James Dean. Or Jack
Kerouac (but that was a bit later). Or Peter O'Toole.
Or Jim Brown. Or Elgin Baylor. (A once-in-a-jyze-life
group JRX for the naming of all these heroic role models
of my collegiate or earlier years. Why I'm identifying
them like this I have no idea. Self-subversion,
wrecking the whole jyze concept and the jyzer's public
image as well. But what the heck, all things pass.)

  ** Vic H. and I enjoyed seeing "Zhou Yu's Train"
-- Vic proposed it -- out in the Yuke. Afterwards we
had sandwiches at the cine cafe and drinks at a bar
across the street and I spilled some nostalgia: about
Gatewood, Mentoka, Japan and Korea, even J. City (I've
lived here so long!). Also Vic confirmed I'd "maybe
gone a little too far" in objecting to some extremely
disparaging remarks of Jean's concerning male sexuality

in general which also touched on her own relations with
Ro. So I'm being very careful now not to transgress
Jean's boundaries (but only to the limited extent I can
figure out where they are and in regard to what).
     ** Z-wiff says she's switching her prime reading
focus from mysteries to biographies. Unfortunately the
subjects of the first two she's taken up have been woman
writers -- Colette and Edna St. Vincent Millay -- whose
notions regarding sex, love, and romance and their
influence on their own writings have inspired all sorts
of tough questions from Z about my ideas concerning such
matters. (Okay, two more JRXs. I'm on a roll tonight!)
     ** An excellent article by Charles M. in the alt-
weekly discussed the emergence of J. City's south end
(where we live -- near its northern border) as one of
the country's few more or less fully integrated
"multiculture islands" -- and we're proud to be part of
that emergence, yes we are (and it was one of the main
reasons we chose to move up here to the hilltop).
     ** Having finished a complete read-through of the
"Dictionary of Allusions" I'm now moving on to the
"Hippie Dictionary." To my considerable surprise I'm
finding myself familiar with just about everything in it
and in many cases could offer some quasi-scholarly
emendations. Evidently it all just soaked into me
during the MSM #2 years even though at the time I
thought large swatches of it were sheer nonsense -- and
for that matter still do. Prime demonstration of an old
saw: you're shaped by your times whether you like them
or not. (But then I'd add an important clarification:
actually I did like them, mostly, including many of
those aspects which I thought were sheer nonsense.)
     ** And heard from brother Rob that author Gavin M.
was savaged by a "panel of distinguished historians" in
a TV special about "1421." But I'm still a fan and
still expect his theories regarding wide-ranging Chinese
explorations in the early fifteenth century to someday
be borne out at least in part.
     -- And must go. Bail from this dubious unending
list. As if I've got no serious work to do tonight!

[Scat Jyze : Green Monkey]

20

------

(1)

     So this time it really is my birth moon. And it's
really my birthday, the solar version, Gregorian
subspecies. And three after four in the morning.
     And I'm winging it. Glass of the usual good stuff
in hand (ice cubes crackling portentously). Astride my
new green armchair by the balcony door which is open and
it's cool out there, overcast, no moon in view and
that's how it's been all night. (This will always be
the "new green armchair," is my guess, even though it's
used. The "old green armchair" still sits in the
bedroom just as it did in 202 and 203 and at least five
previous rooms of mine and probably always will here in
201 -- until death do us part -- and this latter phrase
applies to old and new armchair alike.)
     Came up with a six-entry birthday scheme for this
year. Tonight, now, Sunday night, it starts; and it
goes through Friday night, since Friday's my lunar
birthday. Will celebrate all week. Use up all "free"
pages in this volume for the rest of the year. Core of
the Green Monkey scat jyze, right here. (New kind of
extended "lunisolar" birthday sure does beat the lame
old single-day kind. One of these years I, or anyone,
could have a birth "day" lasting three weeks between
lunar and solar celebration, maybe even longer,
depending on how the dates happen to fall on the two
calendars -- need to research that.)
     And come to think of it, it started yesterday.
Birthday party up at Benita's. Chantilly cake (again)
with Mama E. She'd lost track of what day it was and I

had to make myself scarce while she, with Z's help, put
the finishing touches on her card for me. She was in a
so-so state healthwise but came up with a couple of nice
smiles and a big smack on the cheek for the birthday
boy. When conversation lagged seriously we all watched
the TV news together. But she did demolish her piece of
cake, which she quite often does, even after vigorously
protesting she can't eat a single bite. -- And then Z-
wiff and I rushed off to catch "The Corporation." (Good
film. Wish my father could've lived to see it. Then
again it might've brought on his demise all by itself.)

And earlier tonight, Sunday night, another birthday
party for me, this one with Betty and Kat at our usual
retro fifties cafe. My favorite restaurant of them all
these days. I was asked to wait outside while they
prepared the scene. Climbed the steep hillside steps in
back, I did, first time ever. Funky improv garden up
there, giant sunflowers going wild. -- Summoned back
down and inside, I found all three womenfolk wearing
special green "We Dig You!" T-shirts, words emblazoned
over a visual of a shovel. Wuz deeply touched!

Retro-fifties meatloaf, I can't get enough. Golden
oldies playing on the jukebox: "At the Hop," "Mother-In-
Law," "Birthday." I was tempted to ride the mechanical
rocket despite my vulnerable flank but managed to
resist. Betty's homemade raspberry pie was the "cake"
and Kat stuck in eight candles, an arc of six on the
left facing two on the right, lit them -- and then
laughed so hard at something I said (wish I could
remember what it was) she accidentally blew out all but
two and had to start over on lighting the others.

Then a bag of presents for "the big guy," as Betty
often calls me (and no one else ever has except the
occasional small-guy panhandler: "Hey, big guy!" -- but
come to think of it they usually say "big man" -- or
once in a while in recent times "Pops," just like Elgie,
a/k/a "Pups"). Goofy gifts: special incandescent yellow
"hazardous material" tape to indicate my kitchen gear
and various other items and areas are off-limits next
time Amanda comes to clean; a toy tin Jeep made in China

[Scat Jyze : Green Monkey]

(Kat remembered Jeep was my childhood nickname); and the
main present was exactly what Mama E had also given me:
a gift certificate for the only real bookstore. Just
what I was hoping for, and in both cases! (No kidding.
A couple of books I've been burning to read and I'm
broke to the marrow with still more than a month to go
before I can expect a paycheck.)

     My little sweetheart Kat. Day after tomorrow she
starts high school. Most of her focus, of course, is
there, or elsewhere -- certainly not on boring fossils
such as ourselves -- and yet we still had a few shining
moments. My surrogate family, Betty and Kat. Z-wiff's
doing, this. I'm a lucky guy in many ways. (And deeply
happy with my gorgeous and sexy and supremely clever
wife. Have I mentioned? Max-out mush time yet again!)

     Turning sixty-two. Here's where I feel I'm
crossing into true elderhood. Not at sixty or for the
Heavenly Year. That was a landmark but too much of a
high point to be the real crossing. Now I'm more in
shape (that is, out of shape) for it. (That is, body
breaking down. Which is just how it is and I'm even
delighted it's not more broke-down, yes I am, though of
course that will be the case all too soon, and ongoing.)

     -- And I wasn't even present for the symbolic
moment. While I dashed (in a manner of speaking) down
to the Yuke magazine shop to pick up a certain hard-to-
find quarterly (which I couldn't afford, correct, except
for projecting what I might be able to extract from my
jar of nickels), Z-wiff bought our tickets for "The
Corporation." She explained to the cashier that her
husband would be turning sixty-two on Monday and the
cashier gave me the senior discount. Six bucks instead
of nine. This is our local arthouse theater chain
where, in all its theaters combined, I've seen hundreds
of movies over the last quarter of a century -- maybe
close to a thousand. Often noticing the sign for the
senior discount and thinking one day that would be me.

     So decomposition has its compensations. (But the
senior bus fare doesn't kick in until age sixty-five.
So decomposition also has its stages.)

[Scat Jyze : Green Monkey]

On the couch facing me a bedsheet covers a small
mound of gifts. A sign atop the sheet says "For G's
62nd yr. wake-up!"
First, second, and third helpings of both Chantilly
cake and raspberry pie ala mode, all in a single thirty-
hour period: could have something to do with why I've
already gone through ten antacid tabs tonight. (Six of
those were at the hideaway earlier as I finished up my
four months' work on Jyze Age Annals 1 and 2. Both will
be needing another draft or two or ten but I'm still
feeling very good about them.) (Big story in today's
far-coast paper: director of Mezzu writers' workshop
retires. Famous grads are listed. I'm thinking my
stuff's as good as anything I've seen of theirs -- has
maybe even a better chance of living on for a while (as
serious journals often seem to outlast traditional
fiction). And so I can say it with no hesitation: I'm
doing my alma mater proud, yes I am. -- But are they
aware of this? Well of course not. Not yet. Let those
others have their laurels first, sez I. As I think I've
pretty well established now, I'm in no hurry.)
-- And speaking of quarter centuries, maybe I ought
to mention: twenty-five years ago on this very date Lady
U and I first rolled into Jyze City, as it was of course
not yet known at that point, and took up residence in
the Yuke, a few blocks from the theater where Saturday
night I crossed another symbolic line into geezerhood.

(2)

-- Last hours of the standard Gregorian day.
Monday. Solar birthday. Still.
Scattered mind tonight. Here's the same green
armchair (new albeit used) and same jazz station. Z-
spouse asleep in our bedroom. Today she took off from
work but tomorrow she'll be right back in there.
My day. "It's your day -- whatever you want to
do." Well, I didn't think we should be spending too
much money. Maybe take a walk somewhere. Maybe catch

another movie, since they're so cheap for us now that we've both crossed the bar. Or maybe -- maybe just what we'd ordinarily do on a Monday she takes off, but with some special birthday glitter sprinkled on it.

(It's also the day the war party's convention gets underway in FCM #1. Yesterday half a million protested against it outside the hall -- against the policies of the cowboy incumbent and his neocon cronies. Meanwhile slime ads are attacking the challenger, ostensibly for allegedly fabricating large parts of his swift-boat so-called heroism in Vietnam, but actually for daring to express antiwar views that arose from those same criminal boating episodes, among others. More than thirty years later we're still fighting the same battles. Corporate power. "Market uber alles." The bankruptcy of this worldview is so evident now -- as is the corruption that keeps it in power -- it's hard to believe it's not due at the very least for a nominal electoral setback or two. But what happens when a majority of the electorate profits from corruption and the neoimperial policies it leads to and the economic bonanzas they produce? It would seem we've stumbled upon a fatal glitch in the democratic program. We're reduced to hoping millions of people will vote against their own short-term material interests.)

A little nookie at wake-up time -- expressing mutual adoration even while freeing ourselves from mutual horniness. A twofer! Then the ceremonial opening of the gifts. Then the newly reconfirmed elder gets to read his newspapers and drink his coffee in special birthday peace for a couple of hours. Then, after he scratches the normal Monday WOC session from the itinerary, he's off to -- but wait. Hold that as a surprise. Finish up the afternoon at home first.

The main gift is a wonderful bird mola from the SQ folk-arts shop. Very unusual: just two colors, blue bird and jungly blue surroundings on an orange background, except for the bird's eye with its frondlike spokes of seven different colors spinning out from a black pupil. It's like an extreme variation of the bird

mola I gave ol' Mom roughly twenty years ago and which
now hangs on the hideaway wall. I found this new one
ravishing at first sight at the shop last month -- as Z-
wiff noticed, and later she asked if I'd like to have it
as my birthday present for this year.

(I stagger around in green henley and maroon
sweatpants -- the better to keep my rashy right leg from
becoming a topic of conversation or concern.)

Two birthday messages on the phone. One's from
brother Rob, and I'll call him back tomorrow. The
other, a surprise, is from Z's nephew Jacob in
Centropolis. First time ever. What gives? Z's as
baffled as I am. Did his mother's death some twenty
months ago awaken his awareness of the mortality not
only of family members still living but even his Jyze
City in-law whom he scarcely knows?

Also a card from sister Barb. If I were to
decipher the codewords it would be the usual Barb
message -- so I won't try to do that. Owing to neck/
shoulder problems she's still unable to work and
therefore is doing lots of reading. And writing? I
wonder. But if so, she never says anything about it to
me. She and Keith are still together, still living in
the apartment Mother died in. I see no sign that
relations between Barb and me will ever warm up beyond
their present tepid state. Which is sad. As with so
many other things these days, I hope I'm wrong.

-- From Elgie, nothing. But maybe Z will find an
e-mail from him on her work computer tomorrow (the
laptop she keeps at home has been down for months or
maybe it's closer to a year now). Or -- maybe something
will arrive by snail mail. Today's s-mail didn't even
get delivered. Z called up to find out why and was told
there'd been some sort of mix-up with the key to our
building. Who knows -- could be the missing delivery
contains dozens of perfectly timed birthday messages.

(As the jyzer's big solar day moves into its final
three minutes. Any last thoughts? Or possibly even any
first thoughts? Well, how about this: I think I've
developed an easygoing approach to things that -- while

still keeping me at least somewhat politically alert --
will also usher me through unscathed, or only lightly
scathed, to birthday sixty-three and even a few more
beyond that, the health gods willing. Popeye didn't
make it to sixty-three and neither did Barb's favorite
philosopher; both died at sixty-two. Dad didn't even
see fifty-nine. But by taking a step or two back from
the raging cavalcade I hope I can keep ambling along and
also crank out a whole lot more jyze. That's my thought
-- and we're now several minutes into August 31.)
     -- So then to the ORB, Z and I, early in the
evening, where I snapped up a couple of books on local
history (using Kat and Betty's gift certificate). Then
up to east hill, the usual drive-in, for the cheapest
yet tastiest burger-and-fries in town (and a quick look-
in at the nearby magazine shop, but nothing was
irresistible there) and then back home for "berry medley
scones," the makings provided by Z: blueberries,
raspberries, strawberries (all organic to be sure),
French vanilla ice cream, whipped cream. Oh wotta
feast. Oh how I've been pigging out! (But here's a
shocking thought: no more of that. Turn it around as a
wise elder. Now's the time. Even fits right in with
the survival notion.)
     -- "Into the discount era," as one of Z's birthday
cards says (dragonflies on it), referring of course to
those tempting senior givebacks. -- And she made me a
"Jyzer G Bobblehead" by altering one featuring a J. City
soccer player. It's perched on the bookcase right here,
a pen-bearing arm raised in jolly benediction over these
jyze proceedings. (Lucky guy I am to be so hitched.
Will do -- continue to do! -- my best by this Z-wiff for
sure, and will aim for even better than any previous
best.) (Not that I'm unaware tomorrow or any other day
may bring new perturbations. Or for that matter even
later tonight. But I'll still say it: how good it is
right now and has been in general for such a long run.
I'm blessed, we're blessed. -- Looks almost like I'm
turning theosophical here. But no, it's where I've been
for many a moon -- if it means chooshing that all's not

[Scat Jyze : Green Monkey]

just a matter of mere matter out there -- as if you can
even know what it is! -- But of course you can and
that's part of the mystery, how you know and exactly
what it means to know. And so on. -- Otherwise, no, I
haven't been there and will not go there ever, I betcha.
-- And if any confusion's arising here, I'll have to try
to clarify things at some later time.)

(3)

     Last Night in August (by the "Light in August" man
-- not!). Pretty much the usual here except I've moved
to the futon couch facing the green armchair (and behind
it the tall cactus, the swing-arm floor lamp turned on,
the stepped floor-to-ceiling partitional bookcase with
plants riding all the steps and also across the top, and
behind that the darkness of the dining area and kitchen
visible through the gaps). (Why describe all this? I
just love the way it looks. -- Above all, and in more
than one sense, the shadows of plant leaves slightly
quivering on the ceiling whenever I shift my position.)
     The s-mail did finally arrive but there was nothing
for me. It would appear all birthday well-wishings for
this year are already in. Time to move on to other
things. (For one example, the private birthday, the
lunar kind. This year I haven't even told Z-wiff when
it is -- because I don't want her to feel she must come
up with some way to celebrate it. The sweetheart's
already done far more than enough.)
     Believe it or not, I'm jyzing this under the
influence not just of another "berry medley scone," not
just another glass of the same old ceremonial bourbon,
but also a third reading of the best living lit critic's
"Hysterical Realism." Such a fine and wise demolition
of the "Underworld"s and "Infinite Jest"s it is. I
predict those two ballyhooed novels and the many lesser
ones that fall into the same category will always be
known, if at all, mainly by it. Or I certainly hope so.
     It's the end of a Tuesday and so I must've visited

Vic H. in the loft earlier tonight. And did. This time
Jean was present and provided most of the conversation
all by herself. Tonight she seemed to like me again,
who knows why. Tangled tales of the A-mart floral
department, exposes', the new exclusive she wangled on
cloned orchids from Thailand. In two weeks she leaves
for Bali -- traveling with a group of friends. Vic,
meanwhile, will be continuing with his regular part-time
work as a guard at the convention center. He has a big
lump on his right knee from tendonitis -- woke up with
it one day. Breakdown of the body with age -- yike!

     Vic's my best friend these days (Z-wiff excepted)
but he didn't remember my birthday, nor did Jean, though
I've come up with something for both of theirs. Odd,
sez I. I'm this blessing that dropped out of the
heavens for Vic the writer and so I'm to be tolerated in
all other respects -- could that be it? Vic likes me at
least somewhat, I'm sure, and enjoys having me around
for sparking purposes -- and as an excuse once a week to
knock back a few stiff drinks. Oddly, though, I like
both him and Jean enough that their failure to fully
reciprocate as far as attention goes (or just say ditsy
fondness) doesn't really matter.

     -- Did see some moon tonight. Quick looked away
when an image of a certain muscle-bound showbiz governor
speaking at the continuing far-right convention flashed
on a nearby TV. "The Terminator," yeah. Grunt grunt.
The incumbent supreme leader himself is suddenly back to
proclaiming his hardcore conservatism is
"compassionate," the campaign theme of four years ago
we've heard so little about since. Needs to soften his
image a bit, it's said, to attract some of those
independent voters, a majority of whom are women who
view him as being too harsh (and are they ever right).
-- But it seems they really do like him much better when
he says he'll be compassionate. And so we may lose the
world to gain a little show of utterly phony niceness.

     Meanwhile I start packing. Tomorrow I shift bases
-- I become a house-sitter. A dog-sitter too. Whose
house and dog? My one and only client's: Naomi's. She

called on me and I'm responding. It's a bit of a hassle but otherwise enjoyable and she's even paying me to take it on: twenty bucks a day. I'd've done it for free but she insists and I'm broke (because her husband had to go the way of all flesh -- but far too early -- and thus incidentally and, it turns out, temporarily deprive me of a job) and so I accept. I've already put in one ten-day stint up there in early August and now I'll be doing six more days. She and Larry always took the kids up to a lake in the mountains for Labor Day weekend and this year she wants to continue the tradition "despite the changed circumstances," as she wrote in a note to me.

     And the Z-woman is about to do some traveling of her own. In mid-September she'll be flying to Centropolis for the forty-fifth reunion of her high-school class. The Vikings: I still get a kick out of her school choosing a marauding swarm of Norskis as its mascot. She's known about the reunion for close to a year and didn't think she would attend, but one of her old buddies from that era, "Duse" (co-editor with her of the school newspaper, The Log), called a few weeks ago and they decided to do it together. And adding an esoteric dimension to it, the reunion will be held in -- Gatewood! My old home burb! Eight miles (famously) to the north-northwest of Z's birth-to-college raising-up turf. Strangely enough, this will be her first visit ever to my own turf of that era as far as she can recall. During both of our two previous Centropolis trips we wound up putting off the planned Gatewood leg of the visit to a future journey. So I'll have to draw up a few maps for her. X marks the site of G-hub's first kissing party and like that.

     (A pause and I ask myself, will I be doing this every year now? An expanded scat-jyze entry bridging my solar and lunar birthdays? Might be fun. But it sounds too predictable. Too dull. Same birthday nonsense year after year, I'm aging, body breaking down, here's what I got for gifts, here's what I ate, Z-wiff was wonderful, here's who wrote and who called and here's who didn't do either, the schmucks. Of course none of that dullness

would be guaranteed. I could be postmortal instead,
just to name one rather obvious possibility -- but let's
go with it anyway. -- The possibility, I mean, but just
as one of many. The expanded entry on a yearly basis, I
think not. Maybe once in a while on a lark if I'm still
able to. Better, I think, to try to surprise myself.)
     -- After the visit with Vic and Jean I staggered
half-ripped back to the hideaway and worked for over an
hour on a thank-you card for Mama E. ORB card, "Son-in-
law goes crazy," arrows pointing at a guy who could
almost be me as I've augmented him with my set of extra-
fine-point color photo pens. Funny. (Of course it's
just as much for Z-wiff, this card. Of course!) -- But
I'm in the midst of switching gears on book projects and
so it was easy to shunt some energy elsewhere. Now I go
back to the reshaping and revising of "Jyze in Love,"
installment five, due on September 25th, our wedding
anniversary. Got work, work, work to do -- for one
thing cut it down from seventy to maybe fifty pages....

(4)

     -- Some kwikjyze here at Naomi's kitchen table.
Because I got caught up in rereading a section of "Deep
Jyze" (successor to "Jyze in Love") and lost track of
the time. It's 4:25 a.m. already and Z-wiff (asleep in
the guestroom downstairs where I'm also staying) put in
a request for a five a.m. wake-up.
     -- As Missy gives up and wanders back into the
living room. Big white spectral malamute-like dog,
fifteen years old, a bit arthritic in the hindquarters.
She sniffed out the hunk of roast beef I found in the
fridge. For sure it'd go bad by Monday (when Naomi and
kids return); best not to let it waste away. (And damn
good meat too. My first taste of roast beef in years,
seriously. -- And then a spectacular locally grown
peach for dessert, gourmet French vanilla ice cream.
Such a week for eats it's been!) -- But no roast beef
for poor Missy. The vet says special diet only.

[Scat Jyze : Green Monkey]

     -- And I was wrong, though also right. No more
birthday s-mail arrived, but some had already come in
and been misdirected to our old digs, 203. This morning
they were resting on the floor outside our door. One, a
very lovely hand-drawn card from Olwen. The other two
both from -- Elgie! The first of these, a seriously
belated Father's Day card (just as Z had suggested he
send back then); the second, a birthday card. Each
containing two very short sentences. Wishes he could be
here to celebrate with me. Says I'm "the best father
ever" (and oddly enough I don't even think he's being
sarcastic -- just flinging out whatever phrase happens
to come to mind that somehow seems ritually suitable for
the occasion). -- A kind of diss, though, really, when
you think about it, but I say let it go: can't be too
choosy in circumstances like these. Still not a word on
whether he's coming up here this fall, whether he has a
job, whether he's going back to school. The return
address, though, is his mother's place in MSM #1. (My
guess is he's using that as a mail drop while shacking
up with the one whose pictures he sent us -- Faith.)
     Z-wiff made a special call home -- to me, I'm
saying -- to find out what was in those three envelopes
she'd seen on the floor when leaving for work. Neither
of us could stop laughing over the sheer absurdity of
the way Elgie discharges his "family responsibilities."
     -- After work the Z-woman caught a bus for north
hill but it turned out to be the wrong one; she wound up
having to walk all the way to the top of the hill from
the west side. Arrived more than an hour later than
planned. "Greater love hath no wiff." -- Meanwhile
it's a stormy night and she's on flood watch for the
utility, her cellphone armed and ready at bedside just
as when she's on terror alert. The warm and dreamy
summer fled about three weeks ago and it's been cool and
rainy ever since, including one spell that produced
catastrophic flooding in a low-lying east-central J.
City hood (for which Z's been coordinating the utility's
"mitigation") (yes, she's being called on a lot these
days and racking up huzzahs for the job she's doing).

[Scat Jyze : Green Monkey]

     -- But I'm just about ready to drop. So before
that happens, best to transport myself somewhere near
the bed.

(5)

     -- A new site, I do believe. Or new and old both.
In any case it's the conference room at the scope
office, which indeed contains plenty of oldness (the
furniture and artwork, for example, are mostly the same
as always), but also it's in the new scope building,
third floor, my scope office No. 3, "scope east," and
though I've been working here for well over a year, I
can't recall its ever hosting a jyze session before now.
     Today I was called in to make a couple of copies of
old grand-jury diskettes. It's only the second time
this has happened -- or no, third -- since Naomi started
her leave. And I could easily have instructed the day
staff over the phone how to make the copies ("walked
them through it") but I want to do all I can to make
myself indispensable and yet at the same time keep
exactly what I do mysterious, shrouded in government
"secrecy." That this call came the week before Naomi
is due to return to work is just a coincidence.
     But she is returning. The note she left for me on
her dining-room table before leaving for the mountains
says she's been practicing to "lose the rust," and her
steno machine is indeed set up in Larry's study in front
of the desk. (A scary moment this afternoon, by the
way. Somehow the back gate got open and Missy made it
out to the street. How long she was there I don't know
-- could've been just a minute or two or could've been
an hour or more. But some heavy barking from the next-
door neighbor's dog caught my attention and then I heard
a bark coming from the same direction that sounded a lot
like Missy's. Looked around for her in the house just
to be sure and -- holy samoly! Missy was missing! Went
out there, up to the corner, and there she was, and when
she saw me coming she sashayed right over as if she

thought I might have a milkbone (medically sanctioned)
for her, and I was able to grab her collar. Nor did she
put up any resistance to my hauling her back inside.)
     -- But it's been quite a month for bonehead moves
by me. Might even mention a few of the others later,
time permitting. I'm hoping to do a second part for
today's entry because suddenly I'm thinking I'd better
not stick around the scope office too much longer. It's
only midnight or so but the buses to north hill run on a
schedule different from that for south hill and I'm not
sure I remember it correctly and I don't want to screw
up here (again).
     But yeah, the scope office. The janitor's still
the same very likable East African guy, Mohammed --
tall, slim, funny, personable, a dynamic dude with an
irresistible booming laugh. I've been coming here once
a week ever since Naomi's leave began but it's almost
always been on Friday nights when the janitors don't
work. And I picked Friday night for precisely that
reason -- because they come in Sunday night now instead
of Friday night, and this means all signs of my presence
in the office will be scrubbed away by Monday (though I
have to be careful to clean up after myself in certain
areas which the janitors tend to skip over if rushed).
     Advances in technology have made it extremely
unlikely I'll ever run into any of the reporters or the
day crew in here at night. And this, of course, is just
how I like it. I try to leave as few traces of my
presence as possible. (And always did. The less the
day crew thinks about you, the less you get blamed for
their problems. I've been around long enough to be
wrongfully accused plenty of times regardless. And
rightfully accused a few times too, I should fess up.
-- It's all just part of the job, fact is.)
     -- But enough. Onward.
                    *   *
     -- And later. But bleary-eyed. But no, go for it
anyway.
     Because it's now four a.m. on the day of my lunar
birthday. On the solar calendar it's September 3rd. A

few hours ago -- closer to ten, I suppose -- the
incumbent compassionate cowboy who's running for another
term gave his acceptance speech at the convention. If
I'd heard it I'd've no doubt been apoplectic.

Instead I'm thinking about what wake-up message
I'll leave for the Z-spouse when I call her in a few
minutes. Maybe it'll be a reworked version of the very
first song I sang on stage, as part of a quartet,
"Redhead," at age twelve. "They call her Z-wiff,
everybody loves Z-wiff." (Originally done by Somethin'
Smith and the Redheads, I do believe.) "Z-wiff, she's
my best gal -- she is my pal -- and someday, when she's
walkin' down the street, with her two little freaky
feet...." (JRX, yes, on the group name.)

Earlier I managed to keep fooling Missy with the
roast beef almost all the way to the last bite. Then
she caught on and "hounded" me for an hour with her nose
wrinkling frantically. Clearly the arthritis has not
yet reached her nose. -- And all the while I'm reading
a draft of the "Jyzin' with Z" section of "Jyze in
Love." Sorry to say it needs a lot more work than I'd
realized. (Missy now growling in her sleep in the
dining room.) (Z-wiff no doubt sighing and moaning and
thrashing in her own sleep, maybe growling too, but I
can't hear it from here. Not by a long shot, because
she's back at The Ettore tonight, which I intended to
mention when I said I'd be calling her. Or I suppose
technically I could use Naomi's phone to call Z's cell
in Naomi's guestroom. But like I say, she's not there.)

Yawn. Just can't keep going. And judging by the
last couple of paragraphs definitely shouldn't. So I'll
put all my hopes on tomorrow for a rousing finish.

(6)

-- And tomorrow fails to come through. I'm on a
roll with "Jyze in Love." I'm saying to heck with any
more birthday entry. What already exists is way beyond
what I originally decided on as the max for scat.

[Scat Jyze : Green Monkey]

21

      I take my usual favorite seat at the back of the
ORB cafe and before I can even break out the J-book Ned
R. shows up. The kingpin of local and maybe even
national author-reading impresarios. He's setting up
the autograph table right next to mine. On which,
perhaps, he'll someday place a big stack of copies of
"Jyze in Love"? At the very least it might be so
fantasized.
      In the other basement room tonight's reader is one
of the finest writers in Turkey and all Eurasia and thus
the world. And because he's a relatively liberal
Muslim, right now he's in vogue with liberals here in
the USA, and that's good. The wall shutters are open
and the crowd for the reading spills over into this
room, taking up many of the seats in the middle section.
      I still dislike readings, including this one. So
from here on out I'll ignore it. Until I can't, and
most likely that'll be when the action starts to move to
the next table.
      -- Today? Wooden wedding anniversary, Z's and
mine. That's what the almanac says. Fifth. But the
lunar version. Last night at three a.m. I caught a
surprise glimpse of the nearly full scat moon and was
moved. Irony here? Yes, I suppose; always better to
have some around when things get sappy. That's why we
call this jive here jyze (one of the reasons anyway).
But still I was truly moved. Moon through blinds of
living-room window, through leafy branches of backyard
trees, with a rim of softening fog (aura I guess) --
looked like a much brighter and closer Saturn with its

rings greatly bloated. Big romantic moon of the Moon
Festival once again celebrating the fabulous Z&G hitch-
up now sixty-one complete lunar orbits back.

(Just switched caps with the backup J-stick I carry
in my backpack. The one I replaced was losing its
gripping power and wouldn't stay in place on the stick
at the opposite end from the nib to serve as a
counterweight. Without that counterweight, jyzing is
awkward, even for the savviest of veteran J-stickers.)

Fresh from a workout with Z at the WOC.

What news? Mama E's in the hospital for a
"geropsych eval." The incumbent cowboy candidate is
said to be running four percentage points ahead of the
lantern-jawed challenger with the first debate coming up
later this week. Hurricane Jeanne (not Jean, though she
can be pretty tempestuous herself) -- Hurricane Jeanne
has just roared through the far southeast corner of the
nation, the fourth to hit that area this season. (Ivan,
Charlie, and Frances were the others -- all nastier than
they otherwise would've been, sez I, owing to the water-
warming effects of U.S.-led global climate upheaval.
But of course this is only the merest hint -- like four
gentle puffs -- of the tempests that lie ahead.)

And this disquieting personal note. My return to
work is off to a very slow start. Turns out Naomi's not
ready to take on grand-jury reporting -- may never be,
or not for a long time, since it reminds her too much of
Larry (whose words as a GJ prosecutor she transcribed
over a twenty-two-year period) -- and without GJ there
just isn't enough work for her these days, and thus not
enough for me. Probably she's too disheartened to do
the hustling necessary to line up the jobs.

How long will I be able to hang on while waiting to
find out if I can support myself on work done for the
grieving Naomi? Only a few more months -- until the end
of the year at best. Just yesterday Z-wiff arranged to
borrow another two K which she's signing over to me as
loan repayment. After covering my rents I'll have
fifteen hundred in hand and she'll still owe me forty-
five hundred and then that's it for my financial

resources. End of the "deep reserves." End of the nest
egg, the money I inherited from poor old Mom.

Z's understandably uneasy about all this. She'd
hoped she wouldn't have to be repaying this money so
soon. Lots of teasing these days about when I'm going
to get a real job, start bringing home some bacon, hold
up my end of the load. But on the whole she's being
supportive and always has.

On Saturday we celebrated our wedding anniv ---
                    *   *

-- At that point the reading ended abruptly. An
ORB employee came galloping toward our corner and I
heard him mutter, "That was so sudden!" And he glanced
frowningly at me, and I could see Ned R. himself backing
toward my table, arms raised, trying to restrain the mob
of wild-eyed autograph hounds. "I'll ease right on
outta here," said I, aloud.

Circling around the far side of the room I nearly
bumped into the autographer himself -- the author --
where the passageway narrows by the big wooden
periodical case. He was traveling in the opposite
direction, of course, coming as I was going, and he,
just like me, was wearing an untucked and unbuttoned
heavy black cotton shirt as a semi-jacket. About my
height but skinnier and hunched over somewhat in the way
one might expect of a heavy-thinking scholar, which he
also is. Seeming half lost in thought, half resigned to
the autographing ordeal ahead. Our eyes did not meet.

(When I first discovered this man's writing roughly
a decade ago I took a kind of proprietary interest in
him. Recommended his first novel published in English
translation to a number of people, including, later, Z-
wiff. Could see him even then as a world-class talent,
and still do. Literary historians of the Jyze City
scene might someday regard him as the most eminent
scribbler ever to read in the ORB's auditorium. His new
book is stirring up storms of criticism on the right --
a rabid evisceration by a former Brit lefty now gone
near-neocon leads the pack -- because of the book's
failure to disavow radical Islam. If the current "clash

of civilizations" is what really matters about our time,
then this author could be regarded as a central player
in the clash. Certainly one could focus on him as a way
of writing about it. -- But I'm not going to attempt
anything along those lines. I still see the times
differently. I say the looming multifaceted eco/climate
catastrophe is what really matters. The Christian/
Islamic clash is a mere sideshow to this or an early
skirmish within it, though a tragic one to be sure (and
no doubt just the first of many). -- And that of course
is my main reason for saying down with the USAn Empire.
Not to be too crude about it or anything. But the
imperium with its out-of-control power hunger prevents
the entire world from coming to grips with the true
horror, not to mention trying to do something about it.)

    -- So now I'm back up in the hideaway. Brown
armchair. Under my current austerity regime I can't
afford to go anywhere else. And it's too cold to be
doing this outside.

    These days I'm forced to stretch every dollar as
far as it'll go. Simple. No eating out, no buying
books or magazines, no subscriptions, no new clothes.
Necessities only. (I'm cutting aspirins in half with a
knife rather than paying for that rip-off commercial
half-tab version -- that's the way things are going.)

    -- And so back to the anniversary. Did the usual:
revisited the reception site at the garden club, then
hit the wedding site at Jess and Gwen's former house in
Z's old hood and followed that with dinner at the newly
traditional joint near the drawbridge and our meet site
(all these fell into the category of necessities). Then
back home for dessert, which was a deep-dish apple pie
made by Z's work colleague Roy, and champagne and gift
exchange. For me from her, a handsome gray tile (size
of a shoebox top or a little larger) bearing an image of
a galloping black horse in midstride, legs stretched
out. For her from me, the fifth installment of "Jyze in
Love," a big chunk of which she read immediately as we
sat there. Pronounced it "pricklier" than its
predecessors. Since then she's read the remaining pages

and reread the whole thing and seems to appreciate it
more. "I've really never come across anything like it."
That's good, right? And I'm still believing that when
it's completed and can be seen as a whole, "Jyze in
Love" will make a worthy centerpiece annal (literally,
as the fourth annal of seven) for "Jyze Age."
     Best of all was the talk. It's been a damn good
five-year run: we're in full accord on this. She never
dreamed a long-term relationship with a man could turn
out so well. We're more settled now -- and suddenly
she's saying she thinks this too is good! I'm a
"mensch" just as her good friend Manny was! I'm a
"catch"; "you're more rare than I am"! -- But not
true; she's one of a kind and the kind itself is surely
rarer than my kind or just about any other. For
starters, how many Polapinas are there in the world?
Truth is, it's sheer luck that we inspire each other so
much. "Chemistry." She's a delight, a spark, a
provocation, a mystery, a sight to behold and a wonder
to hold, a boggler, a dazzler, a zazzler. (Just the
facts here, Madam Z!)
     -- In mid month she flew back to Centropolis for
her forty-fifth high-school reunion, talked into doing
so by her co-editor of the school paper, Duse, who now
lives in prime hurricane country, the far-coast
southeast. By chance, as noted earlier, the reunion was
held at a motel in Gatewood, on the far western edge of
town. I gave her a map marking some of my main personal
memorial sites, so to speak, but she felt uneasy about
checking them out on her own. "I know you'll never
forgive me but I just couldn't do it." (To suss out the
underlying reasons for her reluctance would be a complex
undertaking. For sure "the class thing" has a lot to do
with it, or rather some ineradicable misconceptions she
has, along with some absolutely correct
nonmisconceptions, about the class thing -- or so sez I
-- but that's all right, Z-Goose, think whatever you
want about all that. We both know we're going to have
the occasional major disagreement on it (not a joke!).)
     Roughly fifty people showed up at the reunion, most

now living in the northern and northwestern Centropolis
burbs. She felt she was one of the better preserved
physically and I have absolutely no doubt she was.
Seven of her classmates have already died, just for
starters (again) (or maybe more apt to say enders), and
several reunion attendees were in wheelchairs -- but of
course that's not why. -- One "famously hoody greaser
type" came up to her and his first words were, "Nice
boobs!" When she told another guy, Paul B., she'd
always had a big crush on him back in the day, he said,
"Boy, I wish I'd known that then." (He was a star
hoopster. She figures her crush on him paved the way
for her to go for an ex-jock like me -- "not that you
didn't have some other good qualities besides
basketball-player legs.") She also decided that the
viking depicted as the school mascot on the yearbook
cover and athletic equipment and all those other
traditional places -- and this Viking logo is unchanged
from forty-five years ago -- looks a lot like me. (No
one else she's showed it to can see this, including me.)
     (Said she, "You're just being modest; you know you
fall into the category of great catch." Said I, "Yeah,
well, if you say that, you also have to say I fall into
the category of 'having major drawbacks.'" Said she:
"Well yeah, you've got a point there. But you could say
the same about me." And I: "Yeah, but I've never come
right out and said it like you do about me." And she:
"Oh yeah? And so which 'major drawbacks' of mine are
you thinking about that you've never come right out and
said something?" -- And on and on. Having fun!)
     -- Also on Saturday some five or six thousand miles
southeast of here -- as we learned from a last-minute
invitation -- cousin Kar tied the knot again. That same
Brazilian woman he's known apparently ever since college
days. Name's Eva, I'm pretty sure. Fourth wife for
him, so he retakes the family lead in number of spouses
-- he was tied with me -- unless I count zen-wife Lady
U, in which case he only draws back into a tie. And now
with Eva he has the same solar wedding anniverary as I
do with Z: September 25th. But the all-important lunar

date differs, of course, since it's not the same this year as it was in '99 for the ZAG & GAZ wedding.

No reply from Elgie so far to the brief letter I sent him (writing him long letters has come to seem a big waste of time) and just a brief card from Ken D. in Mentoka Falls, or rather in Ronikan, a few miles north of MF. But a couple of surprises on the correspondence front:

** Sverre sent me a short section of the English-language version of "Grenjad and Vaehild" and said the full first draft will soon be ready. Will he be mailing it to me for editing? That was our understanding before but he doesn't mention it in this letter. The paragraphs he wrote about me in "G&V" based on our "interview" are still riddled with the same errors. I'm tempted to leave them as they are just to give the biographers something to puzzle over someday (haw -- but it's as good a reason as any to duck the drudgery of correcting them). His main concern at this point is coming up with some info about Barb and Jeff (he's "desperate"; they don't respond to his entreaties). I imagine this'll be a prime topic for Rob and me when we meet at the railcar diner next week for our annual joint birthday dinner.

(And by the way, I learned indirectly -- from "lost" second cousin Ron H. by way of Rob -- that evidence has turned up about the fate of another of great-gramps Bendyk's younger brothers, Anton, whose name appears in some obscure western Mentoka newspaper from the 1930s -- and that's all I know so far.)

** Also, Barb sent a conciliatory and even mildly friendly letter in reply to my birthday message. She suggests we could write each other about literary matters in areas where our tastes "overlap." I'm not so sure any such areas exist -- my hunch is that in those rare cases where we do like the same writer it's for radically different reasons -- but I guess I'll try to eke out letters to her a little more often. I still have the same old fear (or reluctance, call it): that something I say, and I can never guess in advance what

it might be or why, will offend her. And if I criticize
or kid her about anything, look out. And it's not much
fun writing letters if you have to be supercautious
about every last word you come up with.

     -- Here in the hideaway, little change. But some
might be coming. With the "Jyze in Love" installment
out of the way I'm now ready to focus on getting Z's old
computer up and running with my ancient program
installed. If I can't figure out how to do this myself
-- and I'd say the chances are far from good -- I'll
call in the computer expert whose services Z won at an
office auction last year but never used and finally
passed along to me. If he can't do it, well, I'm stuck.
But considering the iffy situation with Naomi I'd better
know sooner rather than later which way it's going to go
with the computer. It might turn out I'll have to put
all my digitized material on ASCII disks and hope up-to-
date equipment can now read them in a way that allows
for changes in the files, i.e., editing (in the old
days, and maybe still, you couldn't do that). Another
option would be buying a scanner and reading all the
hard copies on. But that would be messy and time-
consuming and expensive.

     -- Last month, those bonehead goof-ups of mine I
never did specify, they included (1) a hundred-dollar
error in my own favor in computing the monthly amount I
owed Z; (2) carelessly sitting on the sharp point of Z's
big "Throw Out the Bastards" political button in the car
and nearly going through the roof, afflicting myself
with a sore neck for a week or so; and -- worst of all,
at least potentially -- (3) leaving the Z-mobile in gear
when parking it in Naomi's gently sloped driveway; and
even though I did engage the emergency brake, the car
slowly rolled down the incline and banged into the fence
and the corner of the storage shed near her garage. The
noise was very loud -- it was three a.m., and it took
the car about twenty minutes to roll that far -- but
luckily the damage was minor, not even detectable as far
as I could see. But I was shuddering for days at the
thought of what might've been.

                [Scat Jyze : Green Monkey]

                    *   *

    -- Home style now. Quarter to four in the a.m. I
promise, I'll figure out a way to keep this scat jyze
from falling prey to the dullness so commonly caused by
penury. (Three hours short of the exact moment of scat
fullness. And using a white photo-marker I just wrote
"Five years of wedded bliss," among other mushy stuff,
on the label of the anniversary champagne bottle.)

    Why's it -- I don't want to say "likely." But
why's the risk large that Naomi won't turn out enough
pages for me to make my measly thousand or eleven
hundred bucks a month? Because she has three kids and,
as she says, "no backup." On any given day what are the
odds of at least one of those kids being sick or needing
some kind of parental assistance or attention and thus
forcing Naomi to turn down a reporting job? Even when
she had Larry for backup she couldn't hack it on non-GJ
jobs alone (she did try it once for a spell a couple of
years ago when she was fed up with grand jury but soon
caved and went back to GJ).

    I face a hard choice if scoping doesn't work out:
start Social Security early (and thus receive for the
rest of my days an even more paltry monthly benefit than
I could otherwise expect) or look for another job,
part time or maybe even full time. And I may be too
beat-up to handle the kind of work I'd be likely to
find, which would probably involve being on my feet all
day like Vic in his gig at the convention center.

    -- So I remind myself: I've done pretty damn well
to still be at it -- focusing most of my energies on the
jyze -- especially considering all the risks I've taken
over the years. (Which isn't to say I don't still have
a long way to go or that age won't pile up ever more
risks for me, including the crucial one that my time for
doing all this may be too short.)

    (-- Ooh, serendipity, another accidental view of
the moon, same spot as last night, even brighter now,
and I figured I wouldn't be seeing it at all tonight.
Right then! It seemed to wink at me from up in the
branches as I reached over for my cup of "aronia wine"

                          181

atop the bookcase by the window. -- And for dessert an
hour ago, another piece of that anniversary apple pie.
And jazz playing all along, including the extraordinary
T. Monk, a main man for me ever since the fall of 1960.)
(JRX, and why the heck not for such a phenom.)

     -- And Z-wiff, while in Centropolis (where she saw
a "zooper-zanzy," i.e., great, French Impressionist show
at the Art Institute), solved one of the major puzzles
of her life. Why was it that her half sister Camilla
disliked Z's (and her own) father, Vincenzo? Camilla's
son Jacob had the answer: it was because Vincenzo was a
Christian Scientist for a time when Camilla was growing
up and refused to let her be treated medically for her
diabetes during her teen years. (Odd that Z had never
heard this before. Had she maybe forgotten it? And why
wouldn't Camilla have said something about it to her?)

     Speaking of whom -- Z -- the woman's been working
extra hard this month as the utility's "point person" on
last month's disastrous neighborhood flood. One
Saturday she appeared on the evening news, all four
channels, offering advice to flood victims: "We want you
to bug us [the utility]." The very opposite of what
she's always saying to me! (But a good part of the time
-- maybe most of it -- just goofing, that is, with me.)

     She does admit now that in recent months her
hormones have been less active than usual. At times she
chalks this up to aging, at other times to stress. Over
the past few weeks she's been receiving acupuncture
treatments for stress headaches and the hormone flow
seems to be picking up again. (My own flow is doing
just so-so, I'd say. When it's low I make an extra
effort to keep her sexually happy by whatever means are
available to me, which is to say: mostly good old plan
B. The level of satisfaction this produces may not be
as high as she or I would like but that fact, if it is a
fact, doesn't seem to bother her as much as it might've
in past phases of G-hub low hormonal flow. And this
fact itself pleases us both -- but also somewhat worries
us both, and in part because it pleases us both.)

     I too made the TV news in all but name, but only by

proxy, about the same time as Z did. A bit of a scandal
because the U.S. Attorney's Office "lost" some
transcripts when they moved to their new building this
summer and so had to drop a perjury charge against a
well-known animal-rights activist (which I wasn't sorry
to hear). Actually, though, they didn't "lose" the
transcripts; they threw them out, falsely assuming we --
Naomi and the scope firm -- would have electronic copies
available if they needed them. The fact is we've never
kept electronic copies of the kind of material in
question. (They could easily have blamed us for this.
I had even suggested to Naomi that we keep such copies.
But she checked with the feds -- this was several years
ago -- and they said no: it was too risky because the
material might somehow leak to the media or to a GJ
target.) -- But still, Naomi was the one who recorded
the testimony in question and I was the one who scoped
it and made the backup disk which in accordance with the
feds' own policy did not include the relevant material,
though they somehow had the idea it would.)

    -- Second-best event of the month (after the
anniversary celebration): Jess's forty-sixth birthday
party, held outdoors on the deck at a restaurant she's
crazy about on the inner-city lake with a large group of
almost forty celebrants, most of them lesbians and many
now longtime acquaintances of mine, including Aurelia
who looks a lot like Z at age twenty-something --
Aurelia now a mother -- and she's not a lesbian anymore,
and Z's not sure if she ever was. -- The name of the
restaurant also happening to be the same as that of the
spot near Turtle Rapids where Dad's ashes are scattered,
as I couldn't stop musing about on that evening.

    Vic H. and I, Z-wiff thinks we're "attached at the
hip" just as Jean does (and Jean was the first to use
the phrase) but I wonder if we're drifting apart. He
seems to have lost interest in his writing or hit a wall
on it -- maybe because he can't find a publisher for
"Cicatrix," his book of early reminiscences (up to age
twenty-four) -- and therefore he needs my editing help a
lot less. Under these circumstances our differences

seem to loom larger for him. (Jean's been in Bali with
her friends for most of the month but Vic has shown no
interest in "when the cat's away" messing -- or mousing
-- around; I've seen him up at the loft only once.)

     And Kat, she canceled out yet again on a scheduled
monthly visit with us. Like me, Z is very disappointed
but we're trying to face the facts: the girl's almost
fifteen and she has other priorities now. Attending
high school on southwest island entails extra-long days
for her (she takes a ferry over and back every day) and
she's also got a boyfriend again, another new one, and a
lot of homework. (C'est la vie, Katgrrrl!)

     (THONK, a newspaper arrives. Far-coaster probably.
Between 4:30 and 5:00 is the normal time nowadays and
that's a big change from the previous 1:30 or 2:00; it's
forced me to rearrange my whole late-night routine.)

     -- And finish up with this note. I was thinking.
Twenty years ago this month I visited Lady S in MSM #2
in hopes (soon thwarted) that we could work out a deal
allowing me some access to Elgie. Thirty years ago this
month I was living with Lady S in Korea and, in order
that she and Elgie might be able to leave Korea if they
so chose, she and I had tied the knot some six weeks
earlier. Thirty-five years ago this month she and I
were living together in the fog belt in MSM #2. And
forty years ago as of three days from now -- October 1st
-- we went out on our first date, a spontaneous one,
after bumping into each other at the workshop and
crossing the Mentoka River on the footbridge for what
turned out to be a long chat on the grassy riverbank
below the art museum.

     (Any point in mentioning all this? Only the
obvious. A lot of moons have passed. Now Lady S is
seventy-one years old, living alone in MSM #1 as far as
I know, doting on the son I fathered with her (or at
least decided long ago to assume I did) but also, from
what I can gather, half mad or at least notably
eccentric and a kind of exile. For which, or some of it
anyway, I'm partly responsible, or co-responsible. So
it is. I wish things hadn't ended up this way for her.

And of course I never intended them to and when I
realized what was happening with her tried in many ways
to prevent it. Even so it's just about the biggest
sadness of my life. -- And yet I still believe I acted
honorably and even lovingly all along. With lapses,
sure, but only minor ones, and certainly no greater than
her own. -- So then am I trying to justify it all,
rationalize, explain away my share in it? Nope. I have
to bear it. -- And I mean to bear it with pride and see
no real reason not to. Pride -- and lots of sadness.)

22

     Z-geist again. The right time for this place.
Night of the full lunar eclipse and last week before the
big election. "The toad eats the moon," say the Chinese
of such a celestial phenomenon. -- And it's Halloween
week as well. Time-change week. Baseball World Series
week. And if the line weren't so long I'd go get me
some java right now.
     Big changes happening. Colorful developments.
Comedy and tragedy. "Not just your daddy's kind of
month." (Annoying expression, that, sez this jyze-daddy
right here, and it just won't go away.) And I've got
about an hour before meeting Z at the WOC. (And across
the street the funky old three-story redbrick hotel is
completely swaddled in opaque white plastic.)
     Biggest deal for me personally: the hideaway is now
my one and only office. In effect it's the new scope
office. Atop the desk there, watched over by the newly
arrived Jyzer G birthday bobblehead, two computers stand
side by side, both in working order (though problems
remain). Atop Mother's old TV cart next to the desk,

two high-speed laser printers ride stacked one above the
other, separated by the detached lid from one of my old
cedar boxes to which I added four sixteen-inch legs made
of two-by-fours and then slapped on strip cross-braces
to stop the teetering. Nothing too pretty to look at
but it seems to do the job all right.

As I feared would happen, one day several weeks ago
the word came down: since Naomi was no longer handling
grand jury, the court-reporting firm no longer felt
obliged to provide "secure" scoping space for her and
thus for me. They needed those few square feet for
other things. We had one week to evacuate.

So we did. Naomi describes herself as "a dinosaur
in all things." She drives her cars into the ground.
She's quite happy continuing with our arrangement --
including the ancient equipment -- if I'm willing. And
I am. I'm even desperately willing. Therefore in the
future I'll be picking up her worksheets and steno
diskettes at the same old scope office (meaning No. 3),
taking them down to the hideaway for tranning, scoping,
and printing, and returning the finished rough draft to
office No. 3, all in the same night. And I'll repeat
the process -- minus the tranning -- for the finals.

Therefore a tighter schedule. More walking.
-- It's good for me, sez I. Sez Z-wiff too. She's
happy (also) to see me once again holding down a
moneymaking job, oh is she ever.

Will the money be enough? This month it is. So
I'm more hopeful than before. -- And Naomi was willing
to spring for the new printer (the lead one) and will
pick up the cost of paper since she no longer has to pay
the firm for supplying it. This too is a good sign.
Looks as though she's truly planning to stick with court
reporting, with me as her scoper. (Tomorrow, however,
she's taking off. She'll be discussing Larry's
autopsy with the surgeon.)

*

-- And here's the java. Sunny out there. In just
two hours the eclipse begins. The October scat moon is
known more widely as the Hunter's Moon and also as the

Blood Moon. About an hour or so into the eclipse (which will last a little over three hours) it will be looking bloody all right -- turning a deep red. Apocalypse Moon, some are already calling it. I'm hoping to see at least some of the show.

So...a month of moving things around in my tightly packed hideaway office. The first real "reorg" there since I arrived on the scene almost ten years ago. To move any one thing you must move a dozen others. Also a month of hitting the office-supply stores looking for deals. The new printer is a familiar Japanese brand (same one as my newly demoted backup printer, bought earlier this summer); and both of these printers put me strongly in mind of my Japan days and the typewriter I bought there, made by the same company, a big heavy clunky electric model, such a pain to haul around.

Also a month of visiting Mama E at the geropsych ward. She just returned to Benita's place Monday after undergoing a course of electroshock therapy. It seems to have helped. She's in less pain, and also she's less or even not at all delusional. Some memory's gone, it appears, though maybe only temporarily. If not, enough's left that she still seems herself. She's pleased, we're pleased. So far. But will it hold? Maybe for a year or two at best, Doc F tells us.

And month of presidential debates on TV. The challenger demolishes the incumbent and pulls himself back into the race. I watched snatches at the WOC and elsewhere and heard more on public radio. Great theater. Nastiest campaign of my lifetime. At this point the election looks like a toss-up. Mentoka is considered one of the key states: both campaigns are spending huge amounts of time and money there, and much of it in the old Sandefjord stomping grounds. Today's above-the-fold front-page photo shows the incumbent kissing a baby in Longdale, "lost" second cousins Ron and Karl H.'s hometown near Wachute.

If the incumbent wins, look out. Say goodbye to any lingering notion the United States will ever become the country of our sixties hopes. (What, you didn't know anyone still nursed such hopes all these decades later?) Fascism the USAn way? USA against the world? -- And the campaigns have scarcely mentioned the gravest danger civilization has ever faced. (Yeah, I'm talking about global roasting and metastasizing ecocatastrophes.) (And no, I'm not playing down the grave danger of all-out nuclear war. But the odds of that occurring, horrific though it would certainly be -- possibly even more so than the eco/climate hyper-peril -- in my judgment are much lower.)

    -- But so far no October surprise. For a while yesterday J-town city government was on orange alert because of strange doings up at the watershed and we thought the October surprise might go down right there. (And Z-wiff still heads a terrorism-response team and is on call for it at all hours via cellphone.) In the end, though, false alarm. It seems some locals, unhappy with the new post-9/11 prohibition on hiking in the watershed area, are intentionally setting off tripwires.

    And so much more. Always "so much more." Also always so much else to do. Not that I live a rushed life. The opposite of that! "Not rushing" has a very high priority with me. Therefore, limits. And within the limits for jyze, as an example, compression. And so "always so much more." (What you saying again now here please?)

*   *

    -- Home. First night of the new finals regimen for Naomi. Wanted to be sure it would go smoothly. Double-checked everything. Made a couple of quick stops along the way while walking down to the HQ from midtown after picking up the corrected roughs, then the same while hiking back up to scope east with the printed finals (a trudge of about eight-tenths of a mile, I'm guessing, and uphill all the way). Poof -- evening gone.

    Will do better with practice, I'm sure of it.

    Never did see the toad chomping on the bloody scat moon. East hill blocked it. By the time the moon rose high enough for downtown viewing it was your normal incandescent off-white again, the eclipse eclipsed.

[Scat Jyze : Green Monkey]

     Did see my breath though. And other breaths.
Over and over everyone sticking out, as it seemed to me,
giant bloated diaphanous gray tongues. It's cold,
Smokey! ("Smokey Joe's Cafe" is playing downtown and
when I cut through the alley behind the theater I can
hear the cast on stage belting out live those
surprisingly catchy tunes.) Earlier this week Z and I
fired up our portable radiator for the first time since
last spring. I'm back to wearing my heavy boot socks
again. But I haven't yet switched over to long-sleeve
henleys. (Nor am I trying to macho it. Just haven't
been cold in the chest or armpits. Everywhere else but
not there, my key arousal zones for chills.)
     So where do I start on the compacting of tonight's
jyze? Or yeah, I did already. Will continue, then.
With a spate of bad news.
     First, Olwen's older brother Carey (whom I met
briefly at one of her readings back in "Jyze Millennium"
days) died last month. Cancer of some sort, maybe
colon. (Such a range of vulnerabilities we bring to the
arena!) He in his mid sixties, a teacher and a writer
in much the same way I've been both, but he was both at
the same time and for quite a long period. (Olwen was
highly displeased, as I would be too in her shoes, that
the obit prepared by Carey's wife didn't even mention
his writing. -- Z and I had dinner at Olwen's for the
first time and talked about all this at some length.
Good stew rustled up by Trent -- and lotsa very good
talk dished up by him as well.)
     And Rudy M., like me one of Lwazi's three
godfathers, suffered a stroke while visiting the
megastate and is still hospitalized down there. And
Aida's house was broken into (her son Charles is now
staying with Dak and Serafina, and Mr. D. is hanging on
to life but slowly going blind, and Aida's back with
Mather, the Cawk guy around my age whom Z and I have
been unsuccessfully trying to meet for close to two
years). And Shaw P., the grooveyard jock I used to
listen to quite seriously in B-2 days but gradually
tired of and eventually came to find unbearable -- he

too has died. He was maybe five years my senior.

     And then poor Jean. A few days after returning
from Bali she took a nasty fall on a bus in the AQ and
cracked her coccyx (which, as Vic pointed out, is not
the same as a cicatrix). When I saw her last night for
the first time in six weeks or so she was limping around
in a way that reminded me of Mother when her old
tailbone injury acted up -- a hand dramatically planted
on her heinie and "Oh me!" We all numbed ourselves up
pretty good on some fancy scotch she purchased for a
song in a duty-free shop during the trip. Spirited
Jean. She brought back several huge bags of gifts,
including a print of the goddess Shakashastri (do I have
that name right? -- goddess of knowledge) for Zoelie and
me. For Ro, handmade drums. (Extensive lobbying by Vic
and Ro himself led to restoration of Ro's scholarship at
the U.) Jean gave me a lively tour through her freshly
completed photo album of the trip. On this night anyway
her toleration for me as a hippie white ghost from
Summer of Love days was unusually high. -- And Vic has
started writing again and gave me a piece to look over
and therefore I can again serve a useful purpose in his
life as well as be a reliable drinking buddy (who always
supplies half the booze, I want to note). World Series
on the tube the entire time I was with them, sound off.

     And enough for the bad news side of things. Onward
to some better stuff. But first I need to chow down.

*

     -- And did just that. The usual time, 3:05 a.m.,
right after the public-radio news headlines. (What's
with the world tonight? Palestinian leader's health in
sudden decline -- wife called to bedside. Presidential
candidates trade charges over Iraq. Car bomb goes off
in Baghdad. Red Sox sweep Cards in World Series.)

     And The Ettore, what's happening here? Jyze has
dropped the ball on The Ettore in recent months. But
then not much has been going on. The first official
house meeting was unilaterally canceled by our temporary
president, Drew N., who's already gaining a reputation
as something of a martinet. Factions are forming. But

190

by and large everyone's still hanging fairly loose. Our neighbors in 202, Brent and Laura, hosted a pumpkin-carving party last Saturday and we were all invited, and same's true for next Saturday when the sisters N. in 101 (Tsuyoko and Kagami) will be throwing a costumed Halloween bash with a "celebrities" theme. (Last night when I came in the 201 door I was greeted by a tall besuited man who looked something like Frankenstein's monster but even more like the challenger in the presidential race -- because that's who it was, in life-size cardboard cutout form. Z-wiff bought the cutout thinking that since we didn't want to dress up as celebrities, we could instead attend the party with a celebrity. -- This cutout making a nice partner for the full-size "A Fistful of Dollars" cowboy cutout that's still standing guard on behalf of the Jyze Gang in our bedroom. Maybe we'll ask them both to accompany us.

Four months after their promised installation date the new carpets for The Ettore's halls and stairways are still nowhere to be seen. The word is Drew's about to sic a lawyer on Raphael for this and various other derelictions.

-- And then another startling tidbit. Or maybe not so startling. But one Sunday a few weeks back Betty called up in a lather: she'd just found some weed in Kat's bedroom. Next day an update: Kat had not only smoked it but she'd sold some! (Later Kat denied to Z ever having sold any.) Z-wiff took immediate action: talked "tough love" with Kat on the phone and wrote her a letter containing a laminated flow chart, I'll call it, depicting the ups and downs of the life Kat might face one day if she continues to follow the path she seems to be on now. Very fine of her to do that, I thought. For the time being I'm holding back myself, however, feeling I just don't have much influence on Kat these days and it's not my place to be intervening with her. If she made some kind of move seeking my counsel I might feel differently -- probably would -- but she's just not doing that and hasn't been for a long time. (On my repeated offers to help her with writing she's never even responded.)

So it goes. -- And for that matter, no response
from Elgie either. Still. Or from Ken D. Or from
Vic's son Ro, who six weeks ago said he wanted to have a
serious talk with me and would call soon to set it up.

I did hear from brother Rob. First, our annual
joint birthday dinner at the railcar diner. This year,
as predicted, most of our time there went to putting
together some biographical facts on Barb and Jeff (later
I typed these up and mailed them off to Sverre). Rob's
gift for me this year was a book on Afrusan railroad
porters which Z-wiff snapped up almost the minute I
arrived home with it and I haven't seen since (but I'm
glad she's liking it and I knew it would be a while
before I could get to it anyway). My gift for Rob was a
dozen pairs of the boot socks mentioned earlier (Z
guffawed when I told her about this), a copy of a lit
mag from Lahontan containing a story set during Rob's
days at the U there, and a used paperback edition of yet
another nineteenth-century Englishman's diary.

Also Rob forwarded a letter "lost" second cousin
Ron H. received from our more distant cousin Arna in
Canada. This presented her latest genealogical findings
on the Sandefjords. According to her, three different
Sandefjord farms were located in the same highlands area
above Dale in Norway and intermarriage among them was
frequent over the centuries. She also cited evidence
that a number of relatives -- possibly including some of
great-gramp Bendyk's eight siblings -- emigrated to the
USA under different surnames, meaning quite a few more
"lost" relatives could be out there.

Conclusion, at least for me: it's all getting too
dang tangled, this genealogical stuff. I don't even
want to try to keep it straight, in my mind or on paper.
I'll copyedit Sverre's manuscript if he ever sends it to
me but otherwise I'll be focusing my energies elsewhere.
I feel I've done my bit in helping to start the ball
rolling on family history and now I'll let a new
generation of sleuths take over.

What's my focus? Jyze, of course. Now it's back

to "Jyze in Love," completing Z's draft of the entire
book in time for Christmas presentation. But first I
need to download the steno-translation/word-processing
program from the old grand-jury computer. I can't rest
easy until I've done this, because the GJ computer is at
least ten years old and could expire at any time,
leaving me with no word-processing capability and all my
storage diskettes unreadable. Or worse yet, the FBI
could come after the computer itself, since it wasn't
supposed to leave the "secure" scope east office and now
it's set up in the hideaway down in the HQ. But then
the FBI hasn't offered to replace it either. Why should
they be allowed to make off with it, leaving me
uncompensated? -- But of course they could and probably
would do just that if they got wind of the fact that I
have it. In practical terms it'll likely take months or
years for that little gust to reach them, or it might
not at all. But then again I could get unlucky.)
     -- I'm quickly losing my grip here on my narrative
chops (though I'm certainly hanging on to my metaphor
mixer). So I say it's time to turn to scattered items.
In no particular order, the twin stars again, please.
     ** I'm trying to make some sense out of a thorny
piece on "narrativity" in the current issue of a British
lit review. It could be important to me if I could just
figure out a bit better what the author's trying to say.
In my life I suspect "narrativity" has mattered big-
time, just as has "performativity." In some sense jyze
would appear to be (among a few other things) a melding
of the two.
     ** Z's acupuncturist noticed that Z's headaches
tend to cluster around a monthly cycle. Eureka! The
old female hormones look to be the culprits. Now both
mainstream doc Karen and naturopath Lorraine are saying
something can be done about this. Dueling medicos!
     ** Friday morning Z did breakfast with the Filusan
U.S. Army general who put together the tough neocon-
enraging report on widespread U.S. torture practices at
Iraqi prisons and holding areas. Invited here partly as
a result of Z-wiff's lobbying, he'll be speaking to the

[Scat Jyze : Green Monkey]

Filusan organization of city employees.
     **   Z didn't like it at all when I suggested she
"buck up" one day. In fact I was on her black list on
a number of occasions this month. I chalk this up to
the tension she's been under (for a long time now) and
do the best I can when possible to shape up in the ways
she'd like me to and to shrug the rest of it off in a
cautious, light-touch, loving way. Amen.
     **   A hundred or so miles straight down the
freeway, a certain famous volcano has begun erupting
again -- in a small way -- after a twelve-year dormancy.
     **   Doug T., our former upstairs neighbor when we
were in 203, won a couple of big awards (one of them
with big bucks attached) for his accomplishments as
director and chief fund-raiser at the pan-Asian museum
in the AQ. Next time I see him strolling absentmindedly
along in the area near the museum (as I often do) I
won't let him pass by undisturbed; I'll try to hit him
up for a few simoleons, just as, according to his good
friend Aida, everyone else is doing these days. -- But
all in good fun, of course.
     **   On a Saturday night when we were babysitting
Lwazi (so David and Stacy could have some eagerly
awaited private time together at a hotel), Z-wiff was
channel-surfing as I read next to her on the couch and
she suddenly cried out, "Hey, hey, don't we know that
guy? It's Wei! Look! It is!" And it was -- in a
five-year-old energy-conservation video running as
weekend filler on the city channel (which we don't get
at home, lacking cable). Surprisingly to me, it turns
out he has a very easygoing and pleasant TV personality
(in person he can be that way too -- often is -- but he
can also be -- and Z agrees on this -- seriously touchy
and beyond hypercritical).
     **   Until the weather turned colder it was a
helluva month for fruit flies -- almost as drosophically
proliferatious as some of the peak periods back in B-2
days (not to mention the first apartment of the Lady U
era twenty years earlier).
     **   Our refrigerator thermometer has a case of dial

creep. Every two weeks or so everything liquid in the
nonfreezer section starts freezing up. Only lately did
we realize what was causing this. Also, the freezer
unit itself makes very odd sounds -- a hospital ward
might almost be hidden behind it with people groaning
in different kinds of voices and with different degrees
of pain, including extreme. Could be this fridge is
already on life support. (Hey, what've we got to
complain about? It's lasted a whole six months for us!)
     -- And enough for the twin stars. By the next scat
moon we'll know the election results. Are we doomed or
do we still have a slim chance of turning this thing
around? (What thing? You know, that minor matter, the
rapidly gathering threat to all life on earth. Or much
life, I should say, and all or most human life.)

23

     So the neocons and the paleocons and the
religiocons win. The Truly Dark Age begins. -- But
then hadn't it already begun? If not, and if these
loonies hadn't won, wouldn't the Truly Dark Age be
beginning soon anyway? Truly Dark Age before the
ecoclysm, I'm talking about.
     And the answer? Well sure! Anyone who's been
paying attention has known this for decades!
     I'm cursed with hopefulness regardless. There's no
viable alternative, of course. But even aside from the
rationality of it, there's the dispositionality.
Temperamentally it seems I just can't help myself, even
though I'm well aware how slim the chances are that even
a small part of what I hope for will ever be realized.
     So here it is the day after Thanksgiving. I'm

locked in the hideaway 'long about midnight (almost).
Hideaway a/k/a Jyzer Ink World Headquarters a/k/a (more
to the point right now) Georgianna C. H. Sandefjord
Memorial Office. This on the ninth anniversary of her
death day -- not the date but the day: the day after
Thanksgiving. "Black Friday" indeed. A poster hung on
the wall here showing the hilltop park eight hundred
miles to the south where her ashes were strewn. Her
photos propped in several places (five photos in all --
one with me at age three, one with me at age forty, two
with Dad, one by herself). It's looked like this in 225
ever since I rented the room less than a month after her
death. The small inheritance she left me, even though I
hadn't received it yet, made the rental possible.
     I don't forget! (This hideaway itself is a memory
palace.)
     She was seventy-five when she died. My friend Vic
H. turns seventy-five tomorrow. I've been working all
week on a goofy little memento for him. A wooden tablet
with a painting on it ("Muse Rides the Low Clouds") and,
hanging above, a pair of altered photos of trombone
players sliding and blowing in celebration. It's been
fun but also frustrating at times improvising the
woodwork with my sorry set of tools.
     "Buy Nothing Day." So today's proclaimed to be by
certain factions on the left. But really now, isn't it
a bit late for that? Can such a slogan even serve as a
morale-builder when everyone ignores it and goes on
buying just as before? Much more drastic measures will
be required. (Sorry about that, my shop-until-you-drop
friends. But you were seriously misled. We all were.)
     -- However. At least I'm resting easy on one very
important matter. After two weeks of wrestling with the
two computers on my desk here I finally figured out how
to load the entire old program (and with no further help
from Terence G., the utility's computer troubleshooter
whose private services Z won in an office auction and
gifted me with). As long as the basic operating system
is available, I think I'll be okay now. My own work is
all read on and backed up, with no loss of text during

the ten years or so since the last major backup. I have
everything on diskettes including the steno-translation/
word-processing program itself, one set stored here and
one at home. Even if the FBI comes after the old grand-
jury computer I should be all right (unless they come
after me too for disobeying their crazy security rules).

(This was a great triumph! I mustn't be modest
about this! Who would've thought I could do it!
-- When the troubleshooter expert himself was stumped!)

Then there's a related matter on which I'm not
resting so easy. After the one good month with Naomi
the amount of work coming in from her is again way down.
I'll be able to pay my bills at the end of this month
(three days from now) but as a consequence all but five
hundred bucks of my savings will be gone. December is
almost always a slow month for Naomi. I'll be living as
close to the bone as I can -- again! -- and at such a
bad time for it! -- and then if I do manage to squeeze
into January with a few bucks left over I'll need at
least $1200 worth of work that month or I'll be forced
to find some other way of scraping by (i.e., bridging
the difference between income and outgo).

Yes, Z still owes me $4500. But her credit is such
that it would be very risky for her to seek another loan
in the next few months (if she exceeds a certain
unspecified amount in total debt, the interest she pays
on existing debt could, and probably would, go way up;
it's happening to lots of folks these days). And I've
promised I won't ask for another payment "for a while."
Before next summer, say, or the end of next year.

Well this is, once again, dullsville. You call
this jyze, Jyzer G? (Bobblehead nods vigorously.)

-- At my right knee a mini refrigerator Z-wiff
bought for me, "like new," at another office charity
auction. A total surprise. She be the greatest!

Miracles still crop up. For instance, Jeff called.
That's brother Jeff, yeah. Now Jeff the granddad. His
son Josh and Josh's wife Mirelle have begat Keegan
Lahontan Sandefjord (middle-named after the city, no
doubt, since we've all lived there -- Jeff and I were

born there -- and we all, Z-wiff included, love it a
bunch). And Jeff now has what he describes as a
thriving business custom-designing and building sheds.

    And Barb sent me a second straight unobjectionable
letter, this time without waiting for me to answer the
first one. I still haven't replied to either. I've
been distracted elsewhere, but that's not really why.
She figures we can correspond about things where "our
interests overlap." I'm not sure I can do it. For one
thing, that's not enough for me. For another, I still
feel she owes me one hell of an apology (many, in fact)
for her behavior over the years (let's say the last
twenty-eight for starters) and then some detailed
explanations. And third, as noted before, in the few
places where our interests do overlap, we tend to hold
those interests for widely different reasons which
themselves clash. And she's just way too easily
offended for me to risk writing her about such things.
(Because it's emotionally exhausting to be writing at
all under such circumstances -- that's the main reason.)

    For turkey day we again joined Kirby, Kirby's
mother Mari, and Jessica D. at Wei and Alison's. It's
laid-back and it's a tradition now. It's always
followed by a major acid-reflux night for me but still
well worth the discomfort. (Peculiar about this year,
let's see, I sat too enthusiastically on W&A's newly
repaired antique chair and nearly rebroke it. And: the
stray cat with the raucous purr. And: Mari's several
worrisome mishaps with spilled drinks and such.)

    Earlier in the month a couple of good evenings with
Kat. On one of those she and her tall Cawk soccer buddy
Shasta stayed over in 201, and the four of us hit the SQ
artwalk and the celebrated novelty shop nearby and then
Aida's fiftieth-birthday party at her house at the other
end of town (Z raptly watching Aida unwrap presents as I
raptly watched Z watching Aida) and then back in 201,
after Z went to bed, the fourteen-year-olds and I went
out again, this time to the primo javahaus to play board
games on the ultra-cool upper level until closing hour.

    The other good evening, Z and Betty and I ferried

over to see Kat perform with her high-school chorus. Z
wept at one point and I thought it was because Kat was
one of only two "people of color," other than Z herself,
present in the whole auditorium and Z was reminded of
her own high-school days -- but no, she said she was
saddened by the discrepancy between the plush facilities
at this wealthy burban-island high school and the
spartan ones at the urban high school on south hill
where she's currently working with a student/teacher
group on an environmental-justice campaign.

     Other stuff? (Real quick now -- because I've been
writing too much in here and need to cut back this entry
to leave enough space for the rest of the year.) Z's
taken up a form of Chinese dance/exercise/ritual called
qigong, which somewhat resembles tai chi, and she's
rising half an hour earlier every morning to do a forty-
minute session of it. And: I've read all of "The Broken
Estate" and reread "This Wild Darkness" (the author --
also of "First Love and Other Sorrows," among other
works -- learned he had AIDS and started this latest,
and probably last, book at my age now: sixty-two). And:
Z treated me to a terrific R&B concert in which we heard
one of her idols, and mine too, do her splendid version
of "At Last." This was the second time we've seen her
together and my fourth overall. -- And: that's it. No
place left to stuff the Turkey Day "other stuff."

24

     'Tis Christmas -- not the night before, not the day
after (not quite), but the day itself. Evening rather,
and late in it, a few minutes before midnight (and
nearing the end of a fine Christmasy radio blues show).

[Scat Jyze : Green Monkey]

Rain tapping on the windows -- and it just might turn
into snow before the precise time of scat-moon fullness
about seven hours from now.

Laid out naked a few feet in front of me: Z's right
foot, the five famously provocative toes as well as the
one even more provocative ghost toe. And a shapely calf
as well. And a fine knee. All this poking out from the
quilt originally bought for Z's mother and the purple
sheets originally bought by my mother to liven up her
widow's life in MSM #2 -- and in that they succeeded.

And from all this it must follow that the scat's
going down in the bedroom of Ettore Condo Unit 201 --
and so it is. And what I'm sitting on must be the old
green armchair bought for five bucks at the start of the
Jyze City portion of the Lady U era and covered now by a
patchwork quilt made by Lady U's mother -- and yes, this
is also the case. (So is it Christmas here or is it
Mother's Day or what?)

Straight ahead in the shadows on the other side of
the room, two bookcases, the larger rising almost to the
ceiling. To the left, the open double folding doors of
my closet with my venerable green terrycloth bathrobe
hanging from the top of the door closest to me. To the
right, the shaky end table with the boom-box radio atop
it and, beyond that, a three-wide set of linen-stuffed
plastic storage cubes turned sideways that also rises to
within an inch or two of the ceiling. And hanging just
over my head the lamp on its swing arm. Casting a warm
glow. On the jyzer in his seasonally colored -- though
to assert such a link is a stretch -- sweat gear of
green shirt and maroon pants.

Every now and then Z emits a brief burst of snore
or a sigh and thrashes about for a moment. My stomach
gurgles. I just swallowed the annual post-Christmas-
meal antacid pills. Four of 'em. First time for a hit
of those since Thanksgiving.

On the floor by the bed, my one Christmas present
for Z this year (not counting the small stocking gift
"from Santa," a booklet titled "How to Kiss" --
supplementing one Santa gave me in my own stocking, "How

to Make Love"): the complete bound draft of "Jyze in
Love." She was reading the only part she hadn't seen
before (and reading somewhat unhappily, I thought, or
better to say reading with mixed feelings, because of
doubts about the portrayal of her friend Aida, to Z's
way of reading the designated villain of the piece).
And then she faded out. And so did I, for a two-hour
nap. Then I was awakened by my own loudly gurgling
stomach crying out for over-the-counter medical relief.

Last night she dug out her own "Tandem Spree Diary"
written in conjunction with the August section of "Jyze
in Love." For the first time she read some parts of it
aloud to me (skipping the chunks she thought would
displease me, as she acknowledged). I was touched and
impressed by the writing. Her jyze is much less
detailed than mine but much more direct, and yet also
much more poetic, which is not at all the contradiction
it might at first seem to be. I'm trying to get her to
agree to type it up as an anniversary or birthday gift
for next year. So far she's resisting.

(The word I should've been using more in describing
her, I suddenly realized a week or so ago -- at the
height of the pre-Christmas stress period with its
frequent flights of bristling mygs -- is "bighearted."
And at no time does she show this quality (and quantity)
more impressively than at Christmas. How she cares for
people -- and the trouble she goes through to show it!
-- Another puff piece for the Z-wiff here, yeah. And I
don't even care if I'm repeating myself ad nauseam and
making eyes roll heavenward -- "There he goes again, the
poor guy's loony over his own wife. Pathetic. Classic
extreme uxorcist.")

No doubt like a whole lot of people, the other main
emotion I'm feeling here as Christmas Day peters out
(and for me with just the kind of timing I like, in the
small hours, jazz playing quietly, the really good stuff
that for the most part gets aired only during this long
stretch when few are listening and the DJ can ignore the
station's play list) -- is relief. Finished that damn
draft on which I've been working plenty hard for the

entire past year and then some. Only at six p.m. on
Christmas Eve did I punch in the final revisions and
begin printing up a copy for Z. One page at a time,
what's more, so I could use both sides of the paper and
make the bound copy seem more booklike. (Then dashed
off to the scope office and threw the thing together
deposition style and made it home by ten, which was
still too late for Christmas Eve -- as Z didn't hesitate
to let me know -- but she was equally quick to forgive.)
     -- Earlier this afternoon we joined Mama E, Tony
(the caregiver), and Muriel (another resident) for
dinner at Benita's, with the lady herself -- Benita --
also present. Z-wiff provided most of the fixings by
way of the co-op: turkey dinner with all the trimmings.
We heated up the turkey here and I nearly dropped it
while carrying it down to the car using oven mitts.
Damn thing was hot and it was sliding around in the pan
inside the box, charging from side to side as if trying
to escape (reminding me of transporting my freaked-out
cat Flunkton in a box by car some fifteen years ago).
     This year's dinner was an unqualified success.
Mama E's been doing much better since her electroshock
therapy. A new antidiarrheal medicine has helped too
(especially from Tony's point of view -- he's the one
who does most of the cleaning up after her). Today she
said she wasn't hungry and didn't want to eat (which she
often says), but then she gobbled down everything set
before her -- a full plate -- and even demanded a second
slice of pumpkin pie ala mode. Afterwards we opened
presents in her room and watched TV and she scratched
maniacally away at a stack of lottery cards sent to her
by nephew Jacob. As we drove home in the rain afterward
Z was almost euphoric -- and rightly so. It's been a
long hard haul for her ratcheting up her mother's health
to the point where she, Mama E, could thoroughly enjoy
(or so it seemed to us) an event such as today's.
     Before today, the usual full holiday season but
this year fuller than ever and also differently toned
(as many people we've talked with have observed) because
of the disastrous election results hanging over us, with

the role of fundamentalist Christians in that disaster
being set in sharp relief by the season. My own
Christmas card took on an anti-Crusade theme this year.
Even Barb and Keith, serious Christians both, sent a
card bearing a political message. (By the way, as of
today our state governor's race still remains undecided
more than six weeks after the election, although the
third recount, by hand this time -- and sure to be
challenged in court -- has put the incumbent, a moderate
liberal, ahead for the first time, by about a hundred
votes out of almost three million cast -- the closest
governor's race in U.S. history, the media say.)

As usual, once I got going on my cards I found
myself putting a lot more time in on them than I
should've -- each card took about twenty minutes to make
and they numbered thirty-six in all, including three
extras. And that's before I wrote a word. It's as if I
thought we were still living back in the age when people
had a lot of free time on their hands between the fall
harvest and the spring planting. -- Or more to the
point, it's as if I'm trying to live in a way which
values creativity and human relationships over material
consumption. Because if all cultures and societies
don't soon adopt this kind of valuing we'll truly be
seeing an apocalypse to make the Christian one in
Revelations look mild, quite possibly in this century
(and things are so far gone it will likely happen anyway
-- of course) (this is not even news -- and the
ascendant Christian "fundies" don't even care -- if
anything, they approve of Earth's destruction as "God's
justified punishment for our sins" -- and how astounded
my younger self, say of the fifties and early sixties,
would be to know I'd someday find myself writing this
way because of the rise to power of the fundamentalists,
who back then seemed irrelevant and well on the way to
extinction as a political force -- and that younger self
still exists in me and is still astounded right now).

*

Just poured myself a stiff drink. Wanted to break
myself out of that rant. -- And moved from one green

203

armchair to the other, bedroom to living room. Give
poor Z a break and let her sleep the sleep of the just
(for it's true, if you want to sleep that kind of sleep
in this age -- okay, probably any age -- you can only do
it in the dark (at least metaphorically speaking) -- and
to have any hope of surviving for another day we must go
to that same dark every day).

But didn't I say I was done with the rant?

Same jazz playing here as in the bedroom. So
onward to the full holiday month. But of course in a
condensed account -- because this is jyze!

First I'll note the opening couple of weeks were
tough because of my financial situation. Grim for
me anyway, although only by local standards. I wasn't
starving, I wasn't lacking a roof over my head, I wasn't
a single dollar in debt, I wasn't terminally ill (as far
as I know -- always that caveat) or unbearably painfully
injured (just annoyingly painfully injured with the
likely minor hernia and various other even more minor
complaints) -- but I was in ample doubt about being able
to pay my bills at the end of the month. Each day for
those two weeks it was nail-biting hit or miss: would I
have work that day? And if I did, would it be enough to
make a dent in my overall monthly dues?

But I lucked out. No big jobs arose but the work
was steady. It added up to just over a thousand bucks,
and Naomi tossed in $150 as a Christmas bonus (and
thanked me in writing for "being such a good friend in
this difficult, difficult year" -- referring mostly to
Larry's travails, of course, and his death). And so,
after figuring in the extra expenses stemming from the
season itself (and the yearly Jyzer Ink business-license
fee and city business-tax assessment) I'll be going into
January in about the same shape I was in at the
beginning of December, which is to say: bad shape. And
quarterly U.S. self-employment taxes are due on the 15th
of January. Again I'll be hanging each day on Naomi's
phone calls. But because she was able to do that
thousand bucks' worth of work (by my measure) in just
three weeks in December (with the kids home from school

she's taking off the week between Christmas and New Year's) I'll be a little more confident she can line up enough deps to carry me through to the end of the month.

Meanwhile I'll start working on Z's and my joint income taxes and try to submit them early, figuring we'll qualify for a sizable refund this year (owing to various deductions having to do with buying the condo -- and for the first time in my life I'll probably be itemizing on this return rather than claiming the standard deduction -- and I'm expecting the itemization to be a major headache for sure).

So it goes. You gotta play the games. You hope to scrape by. Aside from a few exceptional years I've been doing this my entire adult life. And am plenty proud I've been able to muddle through while hanging on to a few scraps (or scrapes or muds) of integrity and saving a significant portion of my energy for the real work.

So then the Christmas doings: the second half of the month. Starting with the annual CEU ball, my favorite (and where this year I proved no mere hernia, if that's what it is, can stop me from stepping out on the dancefloor, though I did have to step a bit more cautiously than usual -- and I hope not too obviously so). After that, just to summarize quickly, get-togethers with David and Stacy and family (tree-trimming party, with Lwazi happily dashing about -- Z-wiff saying she was proud of the way I handled myself as "the only white person in the room") (she still doesn't quite get it that for most of the past forty years I've much more often than not been "the only white person in the room" -- and I'm not talking about the rather numerous occasions when I was the only person, period, of whatever skin color, in the room). With Betty and Kat, a couple of mash-ups, one for a movie at the cine-cafe theater, one for gift-exchanging here on "Festivus" night on the 23rd (Kat, at my request, inscribing lots of good stuff on the small toy Jeep she gave me four months ago for my birthday -- things seem to be looking up again for her and me -- she even left me a mushy private note and wants to get together again soon to play gin rummy) (and Z and I gave her a very fancy handmade decorative cat from Mexico, each individual claw all by itself a fabulous multicolored work of art).

And a subdued dinner with Jess P. at the new AQ fusion eatery. And a livelier dinner with Olwen and Trent (scallops this time) at their place. And with Vic and Jean several excellent evenings at the loft (Jean's run of bad luck continuing with the discovery of a lump in her breast -- but after two anxious weeks the biopsy came back benign -- and last Tuesday she lifted her jersey in back to show me the horrific purple welts left by the moxibustion acupuncture she's been undergoing -- and Vic was visibly moved by my presentation of the dodad I made for him to commemorate his seventy-fifth birthday and he's left a Christmas gift for me at my office which I haven't opened yet but I think is one of his paintings -- and I'll be thrilled if it is -- and a megastate university press has shown belated interest in his "Cicatrix" manuscript just when he was about to give up all hope on it. And Ro has finally graduated.

June left a "Merry Christmas" voicemail message for me. "I think about you really a lot." First time I've heard from her directly in many months. (At the CEU ball -- CEU is the city employees' union -- we learned from a former work colleague of June's that this isn't the first extended period of depression she's gone through. There have been at least two others.)

And then the disappointments. All those folks I send cards to every year who never send one back. Gerry and Leola, for instance. Also Wes P., the artist and book-grouper (but this year he has a pretty good excuse: he collapsed while trying to help chase down a friend's escaped dog and wound up in the hospital for several weeks with what was diagnosed as a mild heart attack). Also Betty and Kat -- but lateness is their usual thing.

And then some bigger hurts. Nothing from Ken D. after I sent him that long letter, a post-election postcard, and a Christmas card. Nothing from brother Jeff (though a card written by Angie and maybe signed by Jeff might still straggle in late -- it's happened several times before -- and I'm thinking I might try to call him tomorrow anyway).

And saddest and most hurtful of all -- most puzzling too -- nothing from Elgie. Z's as baffled and disappointed as I am. We've both put a lot into trying to make things work with Elgie. Z suspects Lady S is pressuring him unbearably not to "tilt" toward the man Lady S insists, and I'm certainly not about to disagree, is his father (me) or maintain relations with him at all. Z wonders also if maybe Elgie's just callous and self-centered: he satisfied his curiosity and found out just how much he could squeeze out of us, financially or otherwise -- helping him with school, for instance -- and now thinks the potential returns simply aren't worth the effort. And she wonders if maybe he's shifted his career plans after making such a big deal with us about "medical patent law" and is afraid we'll see him as a failure or a sellout or an unserious person. And I share all these suspicions, with a slight tilt toward the last-named (they're hardly mutually exclusive).

Of course we could call him. But it's gone beyond that now. We refuse to do it. If he can't manage a decent minimum of courtesy and reciprocation we'll keep our distance. (I'm not denying it: it's very helpful to me that Z sees this situation as she does. If she didn't I'd probably be more manipulable and more vulnerable to severe sorrow over our almost nonexistent relationship with Elgie, as it's turned out to be -- and in my case not, by a long shot, for the first time.)

About time to wrap this up. So I can stagger into the kitchen and dig into that turkey carcass. But mention a few last things first. After supper here, for instance, I'll turn to wrapping gifts for Rob and Gail which we'll present to them at tomorrow's annual holiday get-together, this time at the retro fifties cafe (we're going there because the historic log-cabin restaurant, which we had hoped to revisit this year, has abruptly closed down after the death of its owner). Three books for Rob (a used two-volume set of yet another Englishman's diaries -- but a living Englishman this

time -- and a copy of "Memoir of No One in Particular")
along with a liter of the mid-range scotch he likes so
much. Gail's annual ferret calendar I'll wrap in a copy
of the OMP "Living" section which features winners of
its homegrown-Christmas-card contest -- including Gail's
own "Deck the SQ Bridge with Lefse."

And it's quiet around here tonight. Folks are out
visiting elsewhere. First condo-council meeting was
held last month: Z attended and I didn't (couldn't).
But all appears okay with The Ettore. New common-area
carpets are in. Z's wreath bought from an office friend
is filling our enclosed second-floor hallway (shared by
the three units) with a potent seasonal sniff.

And? Call it a night. Save some room for a New
Year's (solar) kwikjyze. Green Monkey scat is now
pretty much back on target pagewise. Turkey carcass
here I come.

25

-- Just crept out of the bedroom. At quarter to
twelve I awoke poor Z-wiff so we could watch the new
solar Gregorian year burst in with fireworks (same old
hyper stuff) at the fairgrounds -- this on Z's ancient
black-and-white TV with the thirteen-inch screen. And
as of now we're still slightly short of an hour into the
year christened by Christendom as Twenty Aught-Five.
But Z needs her healing sleep a good deal more than
usual so I opted against staying on with her in the
bedroom to read tonight.

Hard to concentrate. Public radio has switched
this year to a replay of an earlier broadcast from
various European cities for "Toast of the Nation," the

new year having rolled in over there some seven or eight
hours ago -- maybe in some cases nine or ten -- and lots
of the talking, of which there's been way too much, is
in French or German or Spanish. It's the one night of
the year our locally produced post-midnight shows on
this station take off.

"Poor Z-wiff." Thursday afternoon she had gum
surgery to replace (with grafts) tissue eroded by the
condo-buying and Mama E-tending tensions of the past
couple of years. She's still in pain, applying ice
packs for fifteen minutes every half hour (when she's
awake), eating little (mostly baby food) and talking
less, instantly regretting the slightest smile or laugh
(not to mention her signature hearty guffaw). Deep-
mouth tongue wrestling is obviously out for a while.
And the pain's supposed to worsen from the third to the
seventh day. But so far she's proudly refrained from
taking either of the powerful painkillers prescribed for
her.

Howzit for me? Not bad at all so far. After
warning me half tongue-in-cheek (which itself must've
been painful for her) -- warning me for days about how
nasty she'd be and the "service" she'd be expecting,
she's been a pussycat. The "Get Well Quick!" bouquet of
balloons I presented when picking her up at the medical-
dental center definitely helped the cause.

Meanwhile a horrific week out in the world. The
most powerful earthquake in forty years triggered a
tsunami in the Indian Ocean which has killed well over a
hundred thousand people and made millions homeless and
possessionless. All week the confirmed death toll has
been climbing by many thousand per day and likely will
continue to do so for several more days. It's being
called -- and it must be -- one of the worst natural
disasters in recorded history. (Most of it had already
happened as I was blithely jyzing away on Christmas
night a week ago. On Saturday nights, and it was one
then, the jazz station drops its "News Headlines" and
the post-midnight programming is pretaped. But the
tsunami was probably still in motion during those later

hours, sweeping toward the east coast of Africa.)
     -- And even when Z and I met Rob and Gail at the
retro cafe the next evening for our annual Christmas
get-together we still had no idea of the scope of the
disaster. (And it was a lovely evening for us. The
cafe was almost empty, for some strange reason;
therefore we were able to grab the best table in the
house, by the front windows -- with the fine view of the
cityscape to the east crowned by the only slightly post-
scat moon. Meatloaf with gravy, mashed potatoes, cherry
pie ala mode. Rob and Gail presented us with a
housewarming gift -- at one point we'd all thought we'd
be doing this dinner at 201 -- and I was touched by it:
a set of wind chimes hung from a stained-glass artwork
called "Prairie" which Rob picked out for us because it
reminded him of some murals I'd painted thirty-five
years ago for the sundeck at 1616 in MSM #2.)
     As the tsunami death toll mounted day by day, Z and
I ate turkey leftovers. Every day until Friday. Full
meals: stuffing, sweet potatoes, cranberries, gravy, and
that supremely tasty organic free-range turkey. (One
day will it seem barbaric that people could've been
feasting like this, and on fattened birds and cattle? I
hope so. It'll mean the human race has wised up. More,
it'll mean the human race has survived. -- But at what
cost? -- And so much of that cost utterly unnecessary.)
     From Elgie, still not a word. I suppose we might
as well give up on hearing from him again. -- But a
card did straggle in, as hoped, from brother Jeff and
Angie in which Jeff goes so far as to add a handwritten
quip (yes, in his own hand!) to the effect that, given
the election results, he envies our proximity to Canada.
And a lengthy note in a card from Jim Q., who's off on a
cruise to Australia with his new wife Rae, about whom no
one we know knows anything -- except Jim Q. himself,
presumably, and so far he's not talking.
     Also this: our first condo repair crisis. One
afternoon when I turned on the water in the kitchen sink
to make my coffee, a geyser erupted from the attached
spray hose. Water shot all over the place, including

the kitchen ceiling and the dining table some ten to
fifteen feet away. Somehow the plastic spray head
(which I'd never even used, and Z hadn't recently) had
cracked. I was forced to remove the head, and since
then running water's been available in the kitchen only
through the headless hose; the faucet's useless. And
that's how things are going to be until I can figure out
a way to plug or clamp off the hose. Our financial
condition at present is such that we'll call in a
plumber only as an absolute last resort -- such as, say,
water threatening to leak into the sisters' unit below.

     And a little bit of balancing serendipity. When I
opened my business-license notice from the city I
learned (for the first time!) that the city has recently
adopted a two-tier system, and if your business grosses
less than $20,000 a year your fee is half what larger
businesses pay. Thus I save forty-five bucks. And
believe it or not, that will make the difference for me
(along with Mama E's thirty-dollar Christmas gift):
unless some unexpected major (for me) expense pops up,
I'll now be able to survive financially until my next
paycheck comes in on the 15th of January (Naomi and I
have switched to twice-monthly pay periods).

     This Sumatra quake and tsunami, by the way, is
eerily similar to what happened off our coast here in
the Gregorian year 1700. The experts say monster quake/
tsunami "events" happen on our section of the fault
every three hundred to five hundred years. So as of the
millennium five years ago, one could say we're due. And
this gives us another reason to be grateful the hill we
live atop is, according to my city map, 364 feet tall.

     -- And I'll mention that Z-wiff had a similar gum
operation twenty-two years ago just after her breakup
with the diabolical Arvin. And six years after that she
sent "Jerry II" packing in part because he refused to
offer the degree of "service" she expected after her
hospital stay for fibroid treatment. Those are her two
most recent big loves prior to me. This is another
reason I'm being very, very careful these days (and
lovingly so to be sure).

[Scat Jyze : Green Monkey]

(My dire financial straits didn't prevent me from
buying a bottle of the good stuff, meaning my favorite
brand of bourbon. Because it's become a tradition. And
I'm working on keeping that tradition alive -- sipping
away at it -- right now.)
(Here's a radio tribute to the extraordinary Ray
C., who, as noted before, died this year. They're
playing "Wha'd I Say." I first heard the man himself
perform this at the Jyze City World's Fair in 1962. A
few months later it entered the playlist of the Nomads/
Worried Men at Adams, with each band member -- myself
included -- doing a verse in turn on the vocal. A few
months after that I again heard the man perform the tune
live, at Adams, and just before going onstage he shook
all our band members' hands because we'd helped with
setup. Old Brother Ray, "the Genius," whose career got
underway right here in J. City, at the clubs on the main
east-west drag down in the AQ, just ten or twelve blocks
from this jyze site where I'm now scatting under the
influence -- first such session of the year 2005.)
(And Vic's gift is indeed one of his own paintings.
"The Green Boy," I think it's called. Inspired by a
certain Norwegian land mass, or possibly an Italian one,
if not both, as he told me, being uncertain himself, and
it's abstracted in his unique way. Very, very touching
-- and inspiring. I've hung it up in the spot of honor
above my brown armchair at the hideaway.)

26

Try something a little fractured here. Prow of the
triangular upper level at the primo javahaus. Looking
down past my right shoulder I see: the counter. High

counter or ordering counter, I guess one could call it.
Straight ahead the iconic golf-tee-cum-saucer. The
real thing but through glass, maybe about a mile to the
northwest. All lit up too. But not ejaco-orgasming as
a few weeks ago. Now it can maintain its dignity, such
as it is, until the Fourth of July.

Too many distractions here? Too much? Who's
ordering what down there? Speak up! (Folksy music
playing but some mawkish strings in it. I don't wonder
who it is except as a reflex, meaning I don't like it
enough to wonder who it is. And I suspect that not only
sounds repetitive but is. Must focus harder.)

Turns out this is not Popeye's birthday. I was
thinking it might be. Checked. His birthday's January
11th. That is, thirteen days ago he would've turned
113. Oldest person in the world right now, documented,
I'm pretty sure is 114. And the 24th is the date Kat
turns fifteen -- her "Quinceanera," if I'm spelling it
right. Equivalent in Hispanic cultures to a bar mitzvah
combined with a high-society debut, sort of, but for
girls only. -- Or no, that's February 24th, a month
from now. What am I thinking?

Get a grip. Get an anchor!

Good scat-moon view tonight. To the east. Clear
skies. Floating up there as I, instead of cutting
through the AQ, kept walking north for a mile and a half
or so after crossing the high bridge. "Ah, that's
right, it should be looking just like that. Tonight's
the night." Fully scat at 2:32 a.m. I do believe.
(Even at two years post-Heavenly I still trust my memory
about as much as I ever did.)

Now "My Best Friend's Girl." Tongue-in-cheek rock.
Oldie. Glam and glitter. And now glitch, I happen to
know, because the rocker who's belting it out just had,
some twenty-seven years on, a heart bypass operation.
(At first he thought the problem was a mere pinched
nerve in his shoulder, maybe more like me with my "hip
pointer" than I'd like to think.)

I'm still on my way -- the back way -- in. The new
dispensation. Pick up corrected proofs at scope east,

return there later with printed finals. A new layer of
bother (it still feels new anyway) but it still feels
worth it too. Still still still. Feels feels feels.
New new new. (Fan spinning horizontally about eight
feet straight out from the railing here. For some
unknowable reason its rhythmic little whisk-like
triplets just tripped my conscious auditory awareness
for the first time: tickety tickety tickety.)

Am I still thinking I'll make enough to cover my
bills this month? Yes I am. Will it also be enough to
pay my expenses for the first fifteen days of next month
(that is, until my next paycheck after the 1st of the
month)? That's still in doubt. Probably it will
though. I need at least 150 pages of scoping this week
and I've been averaging twice that number for the weeks
Naomi has actually worked. And she's planning to work
this week. But plans can go awry.

(As they did earlier this month. Her aged mother
died. "Glen, I think I've hit rock-bottom here." But
once again she sucked it up. I was called in for three
days of house-sitting over the MLK weekend while she and
the kids flew down south for the funeral. Tuesday she
was back at work.) (It snowed that weekend. Just
enough to cripple this hilly city for an entire day --
which is to say, it snowed about an inch. Z-wiff and I
crept out from Naomi's place on foot -- slippy-sliding
up and down the summit streets of north hill to a nearly
empty Italian restaurant for dinner. Otherwise cozily
lolling on the sofa with good old Missy the spectral
hound in front of the blazing gas fireplace with its
impressive imitation logs made of heavy iron.)

How's Z? Recovered from the first round of gum
surgery and therefore ready to chomp into round two.
That takes place Thursday -- the surgery itself does.
The pain and suffering go on for the following two weeks
or so. Which means she ought to be ready to roll by
Chinese New Year's. And that falls two days before
Valentine's this year. I'll be one busy dude the next
couple of weeks. (But this is life as I want it to be!)
-- Just to the right of the iconic saucer out

there, one of those three sets of vertical flashing red
lights marks the radio tower a block from Naomi's house
and maybe eight blocks behind, and rising to maybe a
couple of hundred feet above, the saucer.

Lots of screens glowing on the primo's upper level
here. Just what I like to get away from when I go out
(just as I like to avoid them when I go home). But
options in this laptop-crazy city are limited.

Today I'm wearing my old forest-green work jacket
for the first time in years. Left my regular black work
jacket in the hideaway last night (I thought it was in
the backseat of the Z-mobile when I left the building;
when it turned out not to be, I didn't want to retrace
my steps for three steep blocks to fetch it). The green
jacket, I bought it shortly before moving back into J.
City. About nine years ago, say. And it was a full
decade ago this month that we received word about
Mother's lung-cancer death sentence.

Ken D. did write finally, though briefly and in
oddly impersonal fashion. From Elgie, still nothing. I
sent Barb a Year of the Rooster "skinny calendar" (four
inches wide by thirty high) in honor of her Heavenly
Year, with the accompanying letter saying, as tactfully
as possible, that I doubt there exist any areas of
"overlapping interest" which we can write to each other
about without ideological strife, so maybe it's best to
keep any communications utterly banal and -- what? Some
other such word. Maybe it was "impersonal"? -- And
that message was written on a vintage J. City World's
Fair card showing the monorail and, yes, the iconic
golf-tee-cum-saucer. In whose shadow I worked for a
summer the very year it, the icon, went up. (Which it
had to do before the shadow could go down, yeah.)

Two days ago, "Ray" the movie. Brought back lots
of Nomad/Worried Men memories. Ray C. learning to play
boogie piano in the film could almost have been me in
the basement at 636 Cedar despite a whole lot of
sociocultural and talent differences. Saw it at the
refurbed cinema in the south-end entertainment zone, a
theater familiar to me from dozens of visits to it in

its earlier incarnation as a venue for Japanese-language films -- the Lady U era. Faye, mom of Kat's friend Celine, was in town for the weekend and we saw the movie with her and Betty. Looks like Faye's new relationship -- with an old high-school flame -- is already hitting the rocks or, to stay with the flame metaphor, the extinguisher. "Flaming out." (And Z-wiff and Aida are squabbling again. What a piece of work our Aida is. She's a capable leader but also can be extremely pushy. She's pledged to good leftish causes but is also a drama diva and a smarmy religious sentimentalist and moralizer. She has an impish side which often goes over the top into irksome and beyond. -- But I can let it all slide by, yes I can. She's delightful when she wants to be, and she often does, or better just to say is. And -- she's Z's "bestie"! They've been devoted to each other for almost thirty years!)

"Beyond Solidarity" is disappointing. So's "Blink." So's "Bad Education," the new flick by a sexually ambiguous Spanish writer/director whose earlier work I greatly admired. We saw all three this month.

-- Okay, I'm bailing. Too much liquid. Too much pressure for tables. Hit the road, Jyzer.

*   *

-- Just a coincidence here. But too good to pass up. The clock strikes 2:32 a.m. Exact full-scat time!
What's happening, J-man?
Me in my home sweats. Wine here, doctored as usual with aroniaberry juice. Low-sodium veggie juice a bit earlier, the nightly medical dose, self-prescribed, poured from a large plastic bottle into a twelve-ounce mug. My warmly lit little corner by the balcony door. (I've now forbidden myself to touch the wine or anything else before I down the veggie juice. It's the kind of trick I find myself resorting to more and more in my post-Heavenly years.)

Z's feeling "restless" these days. Says it's because the office move's finished. She quarterbacked it for the whole division. Logistics were tough, she tells me, but people problems were tougher. Now the

216

division's located on the forty-sixth floor of the Jyze
City Municipal Tower, a/k/a "The Big Dick" (for its
infamous phallic profile as seen from east hill).

   For twelve or thirteen years her department
occupied the same fifth-floor space of an ancient
building down on the middle road. That period includes
all the years I've known her. It was a rare day when I
didn't pass by that building on foot at least a couple
of times (with my own hideaway building, even more
ancient, located in the far corner of the next block
catty-corner to the southwest). Sheer coincidence there
too, our propinquity, even before we met (and we met for
reasons having nothing to do with the propinquity).

   Now she's four blocks up the hill. And it's a very
steep hill (which I assume is why it was originally
called Profanity Hill). I know how steep it is because
under the new dispensation I walk part of it a couple of
times a night, first downhill and then uphill, on my way
between hideaway and scope east. But her new office is
way up there, higher up the hill than I ever get, and
then it's way up in the building, too high to connect
with or even identify from the street. (She tells me
her view of the bay is terrific but the city's tallest
building right across the street blocks off the HQ
triangle and my hideaway building. I haven't seen this
view of hers yet -- does she think it means I don't care
enough? -- but will as soon as I can. Again the new
dispensation makes it tough: getting to her office
before her quitting time is all but impossible.)

   So now she's needing a new challenge. Thus the
restlessless. It's not our relationship that's
triggering it, or so she says. But she's also said she
thinks the relationship needs some shaking up. Once
again she's uncomfortable feeling so happy all the time.
No lie, that's what she says, and she's definitely not
kidding. (This "too happy" business seems to go in
cycles. She worries because we don't fight more --
except when we do fight, and then she hates it. But we
don't fight much. It's just too damn disruptive. And
besides, we're usually very happy together and that's

just how it is and one could almost say it can't be helped. Not that we haven't worked hard to make it this way. Not that we won't have to go on working hard, and probably quite often, to keep it this way.)
     -- Here on the coffee table, a sheet of the new Chinese-zodiac U.S. postage stamps. Spectacular! It's all twelve animals at once, the stamps from the past Great Year cycle exactly as they were first issued one by one annually except in several early cases the number indicating stamp value has now been adjusted upwards to the current one (37 cents). Turns out the first stamp in the series appeared way back in 1993. Same artist on them all. Wish I could remember his name. But of course if I did the jyze rules would just force me to suppress it -- or swallow my pride and proclaim a JRX.
     Guess I'll attach a Monkey stamp to the inside front cover of this fuzzy right now. And as soon as practiceable, a Sheep to last year's fuzzy. And the other ten animals to the fuzzies already set aside for the next decade. (Rooster coming right up!)
     Yeah, these stamps are a big deal for me. This zodiac is at the heart of scat jyze. Of "Heavenly Year" too -- which scat jyze grew out of. Serendipity here. (And it was Z-wiff who came across the new sheet first, while she was mailing the calendar to Barb -- but I had asked her to check it out because I'd read about it.)
     -- Okay, the Monkey's in place (and the stamp itself is green and the Monkey on it is partly green though mostly gold and white like all the other animals in the set).
     And so it's a good time for a dinner break. Back in twenty or so.

*

"With dawn comes a song." That's what the "skinny calendar" -- one's hanging in our kitchen too -- says for this month of the awakening Blue Rooster.
     Just tried my first sip ever of acai juice (mixed with mango). It's supposed to be "awesomely nutritious" (quoting the co-op checkout clerk). A South American berry. Odd taste for a berry, sort of cucumbery. The

kind of taste one might enjoy acquiring. But I don't
think I'll be trying to do that anytime soon. Which is
fine, because the stuff's too expensive anyway. I'll
stick with my beloved aronia, which also happens to be
the cheapest berry drink going.

Health? The prearthritic condition, if that's what
it was, in the middle finger of my left hand has cleared
up -- presumably thanks to applications of the gluco/
chond cream with the special secret ingredient. I'm
down to once a week on those, just for maintenance.
Otherwise all's the same for me, at least as far as I
can tell, across the broad health front.

Mama E's doing all right too. Just yesterday she
was chatting up a storm during our visit.

-- Speaking of night workers, the best-known
graveyard-shift radio DJ of my lifetime thus far died
yesterday. A Centropolitan. I was a teen-years fan of
his until we parted company over Vietnam and the
counterculture. Maybe he turned antiwar eventually -- I
don't even know -- but a few things I heard him say in
the late sixties turned me off on him forever. Exactly
what they were I've long forgotten. Same thing happened
for me back in the day with many other entertainers,
writers, artists, celebs. For me and for many others.
(Bob Hope: the shame. Sinatra. Mailer. So many.
Abandoned by the zeitgeist. As now many who think as I
do have been. It seems. But I feel no regrets at all
about my political course. As far as I'm concerned,
events have come about as close as they ever do to
validating a few decades after the fact a particular set
of political and ethical beliefs and interpretations.)

Reminding me, last Friday was Inauguration Day.
The shame. The horror.

(Did I hear right on the three o'clock news
headlines just now? I thought I heard the number
300,000 for the revised death toll on the tsunami.
That's up 120,000 from the last estimate -- and that was
just yesterday.) (And of course I should've registered
a JRX for all those celebrity names up there. And my
bad is doubled for waiting so long to do it. Falling

                    [Scat Jyze : Green Monkey]

back, I am, into old protojyze habits. Sometimes I do
it intentionally but others, like the ones above, I
simply space out my own guidelines.)
     A new Ray W. (not Ray C.) short story in a first-
rate lit quarterly. I went ahead and bought it. Read
the story. Was puzzled by it. Why doesn't this story
move me? Is it just me? I don't think so.
     My neoprag hero, two new reviews of his in top-
notch journals, one also serving as a devastating
takedown of the neoconnish evolutionary-psych fad. Good
to see the main man back!   -- But his own piece on
Anglo-USAn analytic philosophy in yet another journal
contained more hedges than I would've expected to see.
I'm afraid the man's been forced to cede a few too many
points in the past six or eight years. His morale does
not seem good.   -- And on solidarity I believe he does
need to make some adjustments. My understanding is he's
in China this year; maybe some Taoist or Buddhist
thinkers there will nudge him a few degrees in the
necessary direction. (I feel if I could bone up on
philosophy for a few years I could give him a nudge or
two myself. But luckily I don't have to prove I could
do that and I'm certainly not about to try. Someone
else will do it eventually, if not to the man himself
then to his thought. Nowadays I'm feeling more strongly
than ever that neoprags will have to admit, somehow, of
a first principle: a form of sustainability in the
ecological sense. Without that, no thought, no
civilization -- a superheated planet. -- Or to put it
differently, we can't simply be pragmatic, whether neo
or not, about our absolute need for air and water and
nutritious sustenance. We've gotta have 'em!)
     Could mention (will!) that Jess and Gwen have
broken up again. That in turn could go a long way
toward explaining ex post facto Jess's subdued demeanor
at our Christmas dinner in the AQ. But this time, Z-
wiff tells me, Jess was the instigator. Why, we don't
know. "I felt sorry for Gwennie," Jess told Z -- then
went off snowboarding with an all-new group of lesbian
friends. But Z's on Jess's side -- they're buds from

                            220

way back. And Gwen was the instigator the first two
times around, causing Jess endless grief, as I saw with
my own eyes during the second of those rounds. To some
degree what's happening now may be a form of payback.

     The Ettore's okay. Council officers are elected.
Drew the realtor is prez. We'll see what happens. Here
in our unit 201 we're finally getting around to "phase
II" of the move-in. The detail work. Put some pictures
up, shelves, a feng-shui curtain, things like that. And
it's my good fortune to say I'm the man for the job.

27

     Might as well crank it up at the ORB Cafe.
Basement just as always, a table in the far left
(southwest) back corner also just as always, if it's
available. The author for tonight's reading is not one
of my fave-raves but she's still a force and she's due
to go on in fifteen minutes or less.
     I did walk through the AQ. Some bustle was evident
but, since most Chinese do family things at home on
lunar New Year's Eve, not much. Flowers, decorations --
brand-spanking-new Roosters everywhere, of course, along
with worn and torn and crumpled Monkeys. Mr. X's
gallery always has the best depictions of the new year's
zodiac animal -- the big new one in the doorway is even
the appropriate color, blue (as the Wood Rooster of the
yin year 4703 surely oughta be).
     What do I know anyway. But I could call myself a
kind of self-educated expert in certain popular and
easily accessible aspects of the Chinese zodiac, I
guess. No, I know. So will.
     And a quick whassup. State of the Union, radically

reactionary not to mention fundamentalist and bent on
ever greater world domination. Frightening. Now the
neocons are going after Social Security and ramping up
to smash Iran. Budget busting. And any program with
even the faintest liberal whiff is out. Object to any
of this and you're not just unpatriotic, you're aiding
the terrorists. To prison or the gallows with you!
(This is not an exaggeration. Many neocons and other
forms of ultra-right life talk openly this way and are
so quoted in the media and among "we the riffraff.")

But a festival is underway -- just -- at the film
forum. A dozen works by the greatest of the great
Japanese directors ("auteurs") from the middle five
decades of the previous century. So for the time being
I'm pretty much oblivious (as much as possible) to all
that political stuff mentioned above. Saturday night I
saw, with Z, "Tokyo Story" and I think it was my fifth
viewing, possibly sixth, of this supreme masterpiece but
the first for which I myself have been an old fellow and
Z-wiff and I somewhat like the grandparents in the movie
(though of course vastly different as well). Also it
was my first viewing of it since Mother died. And so I
won't even try to explain why my eyes were misting up
almost nonstop from start to finish, and especially the
part near the end when the grandmother dies. Afterwards
if a salt block had been present in the lobby I'd've
started licking in hopes, no doubt futile, of
replenishing my tear-duct reservoir. (Might as well
stipulate a standing JRX for the "auteur"'s name even
though I haven't even stated it yet. Because I'm sure
I'll slip up eventually, since I'm intending to see all
twelve films if I possibly can.)

(Folks filing in for the reading. Older, mostly,
many coupled up, and the occasional earnest-looking
singleton female student. I'm drinking root beer.)

And for the previous hour I was poring over "2005
Income Tax for Dummies" upstairs in the bookstore.
Learned enough, I think, to be able to avoid buying the
book. As noted before, I'm gearing up to itemize
deductions for the first time. I've already figured out

[Scat Jyze : Green Monkey]

our nonitemized refund would be about five K. We've
been hoping to double that with the itemized, but now a
gain of one-third to one-half looks more realistic.
Lord knows I'll be needing my share of it. I wish I
could come up with a way to have the check in hand
before the end of the month. But it's not likely, no.

Such crass materialistic concerns. Really. Let's
move on to the spiritual stuff without delay.

Well, but first I'll note Z gets her stitches out
Wednesday. The Mouthful of Hurt era comes to an end, at
least for a while. I wouldn't want to deny it's been a
bit of a strain on me too. But of course nothing like
what it's been for her.

And Barb sent a thank-you note for the Heavenly
Year skinny calendar. A couple of sentences at the end
agree it's best for us to keep things noncontroversial
(i.e., "keep it banal"), as I had suggested. So, fine.
Too bad this is how it is but it's the only way I can go
forward with her at all.

I look back at the Green Monkey Year. Don't want
to say I didn't get a lot done. My "lit legacy" is
finally starting to take shape. I'm pretty well set up
now for the stagger to the finish line. I'm hoping
it'll be at least a ten-year lurch. Of course I'd be
even happier with a few bonus years beyond that. But I
think I can do in ten what most needs to be done.
(Actually most of it's there already. I just need to
undertake some serious culling of the other stuff that's
there too. And beyond that, as much shaping and
polishing as will add more than it will detract.)

Am I healthy? I'm trying to be. Fine-tuning the
vite & supp mix. Under the newly adjusted dispensation
I'm walking a minimum of three and a half miles a day,
and some of those miles are highly hilly. Even by the
standards of the recently revised government guidelines
I make the grade for nourishment, including on average
eight or nine daily servings of fruits & veggies (ol'
Mom would never believe it). But even so, despite all
this, I remain highly vulnerable. When it comes to
medical I'm still flying blind. But then -- aren't we

all? When, again, it comes right down to it? (And it
always does come right down to it, of course.)
     (There goes Ned R. with tonight's author, or I'm
assuming that's who it is. But I'm not hearing anything
yet. I'm not even sure which of the two women he was
escorting is the exalted one. Both sort of resembled
photos I've seen of her. For me her writings long ago
took on too much religious coloration, Roman Catholic to
be specific, even though it's always been a maverick
variety of that. At some point I started thinking she'd
betrayed the cause -- didn't want to waste any more time
reading her when so many others of equal or even greater
talent and with just as much to say and political views
more compatible with my own were clamoring to be heard.)
     Funny how the lifetime flow of one's reading
happens to take the course it does. One reader. A
dribble here, a dribble there, creeks, rivers. Some
dribbles -- most, I suppose -- just drain into the
earth. And are those dribbles of any less intrinsic
worth? (And what's "intrinsic" in this context? Well,
but more to the point, what isn't?)
     No booming microphone tonight. I can't hear a word
out here -- not even a whisper. Only two other sitters
in the cafe at the moment and they're both holding down
a single small table way up in front.
     I did two loads of laundry today. Mama E had a bad
day yesterday -- kept claiming she couldn't see anything
although she clearly could. (The Super Bowl was
blasting away on her TV and I'd swear her eyes were
following the ball every time a pass was thrown.) I'm
carrying a small book on the Tao in my shirt pocket. My
bag contains a big batch of free art postcards picked up
at various venues along the way over the past several
days. No work tonight: I'll use the time for tinkering
with the protojyze files (the electronic typescripts
have been messed up by a recent format change called for
by the courts and passed on to me by the scope office,
but everything can fairly easily, even if also time-
consumingly, be fixed).
     -- Applause. Only now is the reading starting, it

turns out, about forty minutes late. This explains the
long puzzling near-silence. Even better, it gives me a
chance to vamoose before the actual reading begins.

*   *

     Seeing out the year now. Three a.m., so by some
measures, or one anyway, it's already gone. By another
it hangs around until the new moon comes into view
at roughly half past two tomorrow afternoon -- and by
"tomorrow" I mean later today, technically, in
Gregorian solar terms, about eleven and a half hours
from now.

     Odd how I find it so hard to resist the urge to get
technical on these celestial events. But I don't try to
push the oddness even further and delve into the
question of where the urge comes from (as if I know
anyway -- but of course I do have some ideas -- and at
another time in my life I might've thought this
particular kind of question of origins mattered a lot
more than I do now).

     -- These scratchings coming from, as it happens, my
new favorite corner in the 201 "cockpit." It's the end
of the big futon couch farthest from the picture window
and the glass balcony door. Cozy over here, with one of
the big bookcases standing to my right, the heater
brushing against my right leg (portable electric
radiator on wheels), a Christmas poinsettia riding the
end table within reach of my jyzing elbow, and three
slightly puckered balloons floating overhead -- these
left over from picking up Z at the oral surgeon's office
the second time two days short of two weeks ago. Also
photos, kiri ribbons, memorabilia and tchotchkes galore.
Intricate plant shadows quivering a bit as always on the
ceiling. Jazz playing quietly.

     It's my favorite corner but before tonight only to
look at. This is the first time I've actually sat here
for more than a few minutes. If Z's out here it's her
spot.

     (Just a week until Valentine's Day. Several times
already tonight I've heard a grooveyard promo pushing
"roses for your special one." The usual anxiety

225

creeping up. My high-maintenance Z-spouse always
requires a major V-Day gesture and here I am broke
again. And the 14th is an -- JRX here, as previously
stipulated but repeated anyway -- an Ozu Fest day as
well. -- Luckily we both get the senior discount now.
-- And well-earned it is; it's not all just luck.)
     Evan W.'s Rooster card came in today. Great
timing. And again addressed to "Z & G" so we can both
feel we belong. Is there anything in the whole city
that speaks more authentically of Chinese New Year? I
say no.
     (What tchotchkes? Like the Love Train, the wedding
shoes, the Love Ducks, the Mentoka cow, the Kat-
graffiti'd Jeep. Like the display copy of "Pluche: The
Love of Art." The south-hill pendant. The antique
bottle of Original Bluesberry schnapps (JRX, a new one).
The fused back-to-back Horse and Snake Heavenly Year
guidebooks. The Kenneth P. "Caring is the only daring
(oh you know it is)" picture-poem. And many many more.
Not to mention a batch of my own altered-art cards in
cheapo plastic standup frames scattered about.)
     -- So this was a big year. Scene-setter year. We
bought a condo and here it is. We're set (except, true,
for a few legal details, such as the absence of my name
as a one-third co-owner on any of the ownership papers;
instead I'm just there as a literally no-account
husband). And we like it a lot, this condo, yes we do.
(Do I maybe like it a little more than Z does? Could
be. I'm really not sure yet -- about her feelings
toward it, I'm saying. She may have a few more
reservations than I do. I think she probably does. But
I don't want to accept that as fact just yet if I can
help it. -- And besides, having more reservations is
just in her nature. Doesn't necessarily mean she
dislikes it more. -- And I could also apply that
observation to the way she thinks about me.)
     -- Maybe the jazz wasn't playing quite quietly
enough. So I shut it off. Just five minutes until
extended news time anyway so might as well.
     And keep on pushing. (What does someone like me

have for dinner on a night so notable? Chicken stew
from a can, nuked, with a dozen whole-wheat low-salt
saltines for dipping, a few tablespoons of cranberry
sauce, a mug of low-sodium veggie juice (but consumed
earlier). The uneaten half of the stew goes into the
fridge for tomorrow night's dinner. -- And for dessert
a real-fruit cherry popsicle. -- Hey, didn't I say I
eat like a king? -- And this standing up in the kitchen
at three a.m., all of it except the popsicle, which I
sucked and chomped down right here. -- The discarded
cellophane wrapper with the wooden stick swaddled inside
resting in the dried-out water pan atop the radiator so
that it, the wrapper, won't dribble drops of cherry melt
on anything important, like for instance the newly
cleaned futon cover where I initially set it down,
unthinkingly, and it stayed there a bit too long even
though in total it was no more than a few seconds. Just
in case anyone wonders about that tiny, all-but-
invisible red stain there. Right where the left-handed
Z-woman habitually rests her left hand.)

     -- A big year too for my day job. Its nature
changed significantly; I'd say it's the second-largest
change since my nightscoping era began. No more grand
jury. No more working in someone else's "secure"
office. Two computers set up side-by-side on my
hideaway desk and two laser printers one-above-the-other
on the cart right next to it. A new pickup-and-delivery
regimen. (Going down on my knees four times a night
before the firm's door at scope east, two unlockings,
two lockings: the door is all glass except for a two-
inch stainless-steel strip just above the carpet and
that's where the lock is.) -- And I worked less than
half the year. My gross income for the year was under
five thousand bucks. (This means it was just slightly
more than one-tenth the current Jyze City median.)

     which means it should've been a very good year for
my own work. And I'd say it was, yes indeed. For
starters. Now to keep it rolling.

     And healthwise (this again!) I'm still able to do
everything I was doing five, ten, fifteen years ago and

[Scat Jyze : Green Monkey]

I'd say at just about the same pace. That mysterious
bulge is no longer slowing me down on most things. (Not
that I don't worry about it or a number of other health
matters, but probably no more than the typical guy of my
vintage. Maybe even less since I don't have a doctor
stirring up my anxieties. But likely not less since I'm
good at stirring them up on my own. But then I'm also
good at suppressing or denying them on my own, and this
despite the fact that I'm not really denying. -- What,
me with prostate problems? Colon? Skin? Heart? Knees
and fingers? A stroke here, a stroke there? Different
strokes for -- well at least I'm hoping not a single one
of the medical type for me.)

     And I get to read a lot. I'm doing passably well
at knowing what's going on in a lot of different fields.
"Discourses." Superficial knowing, maybe, but not
totally mindless. It's just something I enjoy more than
almost anything else -- jyze excepted.

     Romance? Eight years now, almost, and still going
strong. Not that I couldn't be a more ardently sexual
lover. And I'd like to be! (There I'll acknowledge a
kind of slowdown. And if a pill's what's required for a
speedup, I prefer to stay slow. -- And even here I'm
expecting improvement, if I can just do better at
persuading the Z-wiff that slow loving is usually just
as preferable as slow food. -- Could be I'm a little
jaded too from my wild younger days. And definitely I
have my hands full with this still-pretty-damn-wild Z-
wiff. But then again, that's how I like things to be --
knocka knocka knocka.)

     So that's it, the last mysteries of the Green
Monkey revealed as it goes swinging out -- bare-assed
and springy-tailed as they come or, yes, go. Very good
year, Monkey. You rocked. And I thank you. And I'll
see you again in twelve. Twelve years, that is, or one
"Great Year." And granted you won't be Green then;
you'll be Blue just as the cycling of yin and yang
decree. And granted I'll have to do whatever it takes,
if I can -- and I'll sure as hell try -- to get there
myself.

BOOK C

[Scat Jyze : Blue Rooster]

28

     -- But it's the second day. Sorry 'bout that.
Can't be helped anyway. Jyze can adapt. Let's hope!
(Or why jyze?)
     This is Z-geist. Dusk and less than an hour until
closing time. Quiet streets out there and quiet
sidewalks too. In the shadow of the old rooftop fire
platform, the darkened Venetian clock tower, the
plastic-swaddled Gold Rush-era redbrick hotel. Seven or
eight blocks up the hill stands Z-wiff's massive
municipal tower, all sixty floors still ablaze with
lights long after everyone's gone home. And that's
headquarters for the city's energy-conservation efforts!
     (Oops, surprise, pause for a sneeze. AaaaaCHOOOO!
That got their attention! -- But where does it come
from? -- Lungs, nose tickle, well sure: the usual. Or
it seems. But could a herd of angry rhino-germs be
horning into my nasal passages? If so, they might upend
the rest of my winter.)
     Music turned up loud for the staff's enjoyment
because only a few die-hard customers are still hanging
on here so late in the day. Bass, drums, a jungly sound
with cautious semi-soul on top. Guitar too. Tolerable
I guess. Sounds so familiar, almost the way, say,
animal cries from the forest must've sounded back when
forests still existed around here. -- Or come to think
of it this area was underwater in those days. So not
too woodsy, no. A few barking seals maybe.
     Yesterday pretty much had to be canceled. "On
account of scope expedite." Z-geist is now an opening-
day tradition for jyze and I would've been here in

midafternoon if not for the emergency call-up. Then,
since it was Tuesday, I would've hit Vic and Jean's
loft, and what better place for Chinese New Year's? But
I had to telephone and disengage on that also.

Instead early scoping, a drive up to Naomi's house,
goofing with her kids for ninety minutes while she read
the draft. Freshly baked brownies. Kissy-Missy the
laid-back chalky-white hound, the cozy living room with
a fire going. The "Chinese Love Signs" book I happened
to have with me. Larry Jr.'s a Monkey, it turns out,
the girls are a Rat and a Pig, and Naomi's a Snake like
Zoelie (but a Water Snake, not Metal, because twelve
years younger -- Water like me, but color Gray for yin,
not Black for yang -- and that's it for this latest demo
of my loony esoteric knowledge).

Then back down to the hideaway to punch in the
corrections and print up the final. It was Mardi Gras
day too, as it happened, and even four years after the
infamous riots the HQ was still (again) crawling with
scores of black-uniformed cops in full battle gear.
Without doubt their numbers were sufficient to control
the few dozen costumed Fat Tuesday revelers brave enough
or foolish enough to show up. Hank, the building
handyman -- working late -- informed me that all trash
barrels had been removed from the triangle and nearby
environs to deprive potential troublemakers of the main
traditional source of projectiles to hurl. (But it
continued to be a quiet night, by and large, from my
perspective, except for the distant stomping of police
boots and the clip-clopping of police horses.)

My work was done long before midnight. But because
I wanted to preserve the Z-geist opening-day tradition I
didn't take up the scat book.

For an entry like this I should be looking ahead.
Rooster Year, Blue. "I am Curious (Blue)." "Columbus
Sailed the Ocean (Blue)" (that bleeping Columbus was
even nastier than previously thought, new revelations
confirm). "It'll Be a (Blue, Blue) Rooster Year Without
You."

This year once again, as is now almost a tradition

itself, I want to work a little harder at all the same
things I was already working hard at last year. Staying
in age-appropriate good shape, say. Loving the Z-wiff
right. Readying jyze for the ages (in hopes they'll
make at least a skosh of room for it). In addition I'd
like to start closing down the old home-port storage
unit. And it's time to come up with the last will I'm
always talking about (to go with the aforementioned jyze
testament). And I want to whip that condo into fully
livable shape. And I hope to resume churning out
altered-art cards for Z-wiff. I'm still short about a
hundred cards -- maybe ninety-five at best -- to meet
the wedding pledge of a thousand.

(The floor's already been mopped here at Z-geist.
A young Asian-looking guy in a ragged cloak and pushing
a grocery cart full of bundled sleeping gear and bags of
salvaged trash just stopped right outside the window at
my elbow to pick through the contents of an ashtray --
stopped to do that twice, in fact, within maybe ten
minutes. The first time I thought for a second the
scavenger was Ro, Vic and Jean's son, about to tap on
the glass to say hello. But no.)

A front-page story reveals the mega dot-com may be
about to move out of the orange-brick DC castle. Our
hill would lose its biggest claim to contempo eclat.
But the move-out, if it happens, will take a long time
and couldn't begin for four more years under the current
lease. By that time, who knows, the entire hill might
be below sea level and the dot-com economy not even a
memory.

Meanwhile the U.S. secretary of state is in "Old
Europe" trying to mend relations. Be wise, Europa, I
say, and go your own way. Please let's work for a
multipolar world. Resist the hegemon. Force Uncle to
compromise, to play by rules which we all set together.
This is not the plea of a sentimentalist; I'm saying
play hardball, world, or we'll be dragging you down with
us. Now may be your last chance to do something about
it. (Economic weaknesses are evident in the huge U.S.
trade deficit, the sinking dollar, the massive national

debt, the busted budget, the billions of people
worldwide ready to boycott U.S. goods. Exploit these
weaknesses! Leverage them! We deserve it!)
     Coming up in just two weeks Kat's big fifteenth-
birthday celebration ("Quinceanera" -- the dictionary
spelling). But before that, Valentine's Day. And a
month and a day after V-Day, Z's sixty-fourth birthday.
Just today she came home with the Sergeant Pepper CD
containing "when I'm 64." And we've got the continuing
monthlong Ozu (JRX for the new fuzzy) Festival, with
tickets already in hand for two films this week, "An
Autumn Afternoon" and "Late Spring" (and so life for an
Ozu-loving soul can scarcely get any better than this).
     -- And the minute hand on the clock is pointing
straight up and some raucous "time for everyone to
scram" country music is blasting and the aluminum chairs
and tables outside are being stacked on one side of the
entrance vestibule. What's the meaning of this?
(Opening day will have to continue elsewhere, that's
what it is, among others.) (But not before an important
note: no more sneezes so far.)
                    *   *
     -- "Elsewhere" turns out to be nowhere else but the
old green armchair in condo central. Or no, not old;
this is the new green armchair, relatively speaking.
Just looks and feels and is old, but not as old as the
one in the bedroom. At quarter past three in the a.m.
     (Pause for a sip of wine/juice mix. Three-Buck
Chuck -- JRX! -- and aroniaberry, the usual. In the
fruit-stained cup that never needs to be washed because
it's always in service. Next use after I drain the
wine/juice mix: thawing frozen fruit for tomorrow's, by
NUT count, wake-up cereal.)
     Awaiting me on this chair when I arrived home
tonight was a fine obscene "red bone" card handmade by
the Z-woman. This was a reply to my own obscene "red
bone" card left on her pillow this afternoon. And that
in turn was a reply to her fine obscene Year of the Cock
card left on this chair last night ("Love your doodle-do
too"). And so on, and on and on, on back to the

beginning many hundreds of cards and notes ago (but only
a healthy fraction of those profane and/or obscene).

      -- And I ought to mention this: unforeseen
anomalies caused by changing the format when I copied my
files onto new diskettes are forcing me to reread all
the jyze, proto and ur as well as current. It's speed
reading, more like skimming, but still the gist comes
through. My thought now is that this is no bad thing.
It's my first real overview -- looking at all of it in a
short period -- of something that's taken decades to
write and more decades to type up. Each day I'm
scanning through several hundred pages. The big picture
is emerging. Life of the protojyzer. Patterns coming
into view that were invisible closer up. (Invisible to
me, that is. Others saw them -- some of them -- and
occasionally tried to point them out to me, but it seems
I was focusing elsewhere. Or maybe just stubborn or
willfully blind, as some did assert at the time.)

      I'm still thinking it makes a worthy part of the
legacy, the urjyze/protojyze testament. But I should
give prospective readers a break and prune a whole
petrified forest of deadwood. I must acknowledge that
as a J-slinger I frequently fall prey to a variety of
syndromes, and the one of greatest concern to me is the
dreaded repetition kind. (And I might even be falling
prey to it again right this instant. Haven't I made
this repetition point a few times before? A few dozen
times maybe in the "Scat of the Green Monkey" all by
itself? And this point about making the repetition
point before, doesn't it sound familiar too?)

      So maybe I need more like twenty years, not just
ten, to whip it all into shape for final distribution.
So perhaps I'd better start right in on a beefed-up (but
not with beef!) good-living campaign.

      -- And so much for opening day. A big stack of
newspapers awaits bagging before dawn. (And also a new
tax manual to look over. Coupla mags to glance at.)
-- As the news comes on. Lead story, North Korea says
yes, it really does have nukes. And the reason it gives
for having them? Well of course: self-defense against

the U.S. threat. Makes perfectly good sense too, since
we've been threatening them for decades with our own
nukes and before that bombed them "back to the Stone
Age," in the infamous U.S. Air Force general's boast,
with conventional ordnance. Nobody's surprised really.

     Where's the loose cannon in the world? Right here.
We're riding it. Like that other U.S. Air Force maniac
riding the nuke in "Dr. Strangelove."

29

     -- Can I pull this off? I think so. And want to,
I guess I don't need to say -- not once I've mentioned
it's chilly out here and a little dark too -- because
the time is just about right. Or so my notes suggest.
And this dim light could almost be lantern light.
     Where? Hillside-steps park across from the art
museum, one level down from the edge road. Fountains
murmuring above and below. And just overhead a cherry
tree -- I think it's cherry -- maybe a day or two away
from bursting into bloom. And if I stood up, my face
would be disembodied and floating amid the buds, a great
big bewhiskered and bewithered jyzer flower (sort of
like a demon mask hanging in a tree at Halloween) -- as
seen from the edge-road sidewalk perspective above the
steps here, I'm saying.
     When is it? About the time more or less formally
attired folks start streaming into the symphony hall two
blocks straight up the hill. Just moments ago I was up
there myself, listening to an orchestra, presumably
recorded, booming schmaltzy classical stuff to the crowd
of waiting bus-riders and other hangers-on huddled
beneath the loudspeakers at the stop outside. And then

on the lower level of the symphony hall -- war-memorial
level along the middle road -- a security guard was
going after a trio of skateboarders, just as some six
years back a different security guard (same security
outfit though) went after the jyzer himself at that very
spot. For what crime? In the jyzer's case, for doing
the jyze thing on public turf! (I was even thinking of
trying my luck there again tonight -- until I saw the
guard in action and deja vu said no and I kept walking
down the hill to my present perch.)

No moon in sight from here. Two young Taiwanese
couples posing goofily for photos with big black
Hammering Man pounding away in the background in front
of the art museum. Huge towers all around with lights
still wastefully ablaze just like the ones at the
municipal tower two weeks ago (or why not, these could
be special holiday lanterns lit just for the festival).

One block farther east and up the hill beyond the
symphony hall I stopped at the outdoor bank machine near
the former scope south and scope north buildings (and
within sight of the inappropriately head-dressed -- like
a Great Plains Indian -- Native visage carved into
stone). Two twenties and a ten (both twenties brightly
marked with red bank-robber dye) to eke me through the
week. Again the coffers are low and my ability to pay
all bills at month's end is in doubt.

But (to continue in reverse order): two blocks
still farther up the hill and half a block north I
arrived at scope east to find Naomi unexpectedly present
and all in a tizzy -- today's deps had run very late,
until 6:45, and she had to rush off to pick up the kids
and didn't have time to type up a worksheet. And she'd
be taking several more witnesses in the same case
tomorrow -- another full day. And if those order too,
my finances for the month should be okay after all.

(Otherwise I'd been planning to ask for an advance.
That's something I've never done before, or at least not
that I can recall -- with Naomi I mean. But I knew I'd
be able to repay it quickly even if work were slow,
because I've already done the taxes, Z's and mine, our

joint return, and within the next few weeks a refund of just over five thousand bucks should be coming in and almost twenty-four hundred of that will be mine. Mine, mine, mine! And the hope is that this windfall -- "the marriage bonus" -- will provide sufficient cushion to ease me through any monthly shortfalls in income over the next year. -- So hurrah!)

But by the same token -- Naomi's long day -- a heavy load of scoping work awaits me right now and so I'll have to be continuing this entry later tonight or possibly tomorrow (which by the way is Kat's fifteenth birthday, her Quinceanera -- to repeat -- which we'll be celebrating with her and Betty Saturday night at a happenin' east-hill "Hispanic fusion" restaurant).

-- And why is this tree (the one I'm sitting under) almost in bloom on Lantern Festival day? Same reason the daffodils are already out and the cherry blossoms at the U as well: lots of warm and sunny weather. Climate upheaval, exactly! (Study after study confirms it's happening. In this country only the hard rightists and the U.S. government -- same difference there in many respects -- insist otherwise and direct national policy accordingly, to the world's horror and our everlasting shame.) Meanwhile all or most of our rain has literally gone south: the megastate's awash in it (wettest winter in recorded history down there). And it's likely we'll be facing drought conditions up here this summer and those'll be keeping Z-wiff plenty busy at the utility, which supplies most of the water for the metro area.

Well, it's a trip being right where I am, outdoors and at night in February, jyzing away, and I certainly don't want to stop but -- onward.

*   *

Flick off the radio. Earlier I saw the scat moon high in the clear night sky. Before that I heard someone out in the hall at the hideaway talking about snow. "Out there." Or so I thought. I even left ten minutes early for the copy-delivery hike up to scope east -- just in case. Found the streets dry. As always, a few disreputable characters were out and about (on Wednesday nights they're pretty much all the HQ offers for nightlife). But snow? No, no snow. Could it be the hallway informant was fooled by the silvery moonlight bathing the cobblestones?

At the bus stop outside the symphony hall, San from the kitchen crew at a highly popular nearby restaurant is in a goofing mood. We're weird together. For riders of the last bus of the night to the hilltop no symphonies are played on the outdoor loudspeakers as they are in earlier hours; instead you've got to do some sort of playing yourself -- like running in place -- if you want to stay awake and warm. (Usually I arrive at scope east at 12:51 a.m. Tonight it was 12:49. Considering my early departure from the hideaway, the walk took eight minutes longer than usual. That's because, knowing I was ahead of schedule, I walked slowly, as if the streets really were snowy. Took it real easy. -- And then for fifteen minutes or so at scope east glanced through new issues of the two alt-weeklies. At present both come out with near-perfect synchrony late Wednesday afternoon.)

Z-wiff was awake when I arrived home, sitting up in bed, reading "Memoir of No One in Particular" (which I recommended to her and she likes tolerably well). Darkened bedroom, just the bed lamp on and it's mounted on the sideboard lower than her face -- and the underlighting makes for a warm and pretty picture. Then out in the "cockpit" I found she'd earlier left me a couple of handmade cards, one apologizing for failure to put a "love token" on my chair before leaving in the morning, the other crowing because her weight's down to two pounds below what it was on our wedding day. And then a note: shouldn't I add Betty's initials to ours and Kat's on the silver backing of the Scrabble "Q" tile and bracelet (one of the gifts for Kat on Saturday -- I broke out my old electric engraving tool to "personalize" the metal backing of the tile this afternoon -- and it was tricky work too because the tile's small size made for fumbly handling). -- "Q" for Quinceanera, of course. (And JRX for "Scrabble," I

guess. It's sort of a gray area in the rules.)
    Over the long Presidents Day weekend just past, Z-
spouse was away house-sitting for Jess P. on southwest
island. I joined her there Saturday night. And a
lovely night it was. Dinner at a fine and what's more
blessedly informal restaurant in town -- I had rack of
lamb for the first time in ages (Z's treat) -- and then
a cozy night at Jess's with the two pets curled up
nearby in the high-ceilinged main room after Z hit the
sack. Cy-dog who's now stone deaf and Chootchie the
poignantly clumsy cat. Jess left some strange luxury
bourbon out on the table -- "Strong stuff, Glen," her
attached note warned; "Try it!" -- and it fueled me up
pretty good. Glass walls looking out in all directions
on woods that might almost have been the ones I came to
know way too well in my peninsula era. A book on so-
called radical hermeneutics soon had my head spinning
even faster, like a booster libation for the bourbon.
    Still no curtains in the bedrooms. Not good for a
daytime sleeper on a sunny day, and Sunday was as sunny
as they come. And then Z rejoined me in bed and we had
to be careful not to stain Jess's sheets (Sunday is
almost always a "hump day" for us regardless of whether
any other day is also; and in a normal week in recent
times there'll usually be at least one more, and that's
not counting the fairly frequent plan B action).
    Riding the ferries again. Ah the memories.
Couldn't resist the popcorn, either going or coming
back. Missed the early boat on the return, though, and
so couldn't catch "Equinox Flower" at the film fest
until the next night, and then "Floating Weeds" last
night. And earlier, last week, my other favorite (along
with "Tokyo Story"), "Late Spring." Awesome flicks.
The pinnacle for me. Moving far beyond my power to
describe. It's as if I've spent a lifetime preparing
myself emotionally and intellectually just to be able to
watch these films. (And I'm hoping to catch four or
five more, some with Z and some without, before fest's
end. -- The audiences so far numbering from ten to
twenty-five tops per showing.)

[Scat Jyze : Blue Rooster]

    And this: already one of our Ettore Condo dwellers
is moving out. Breena, the nurse, unit 302. Received
an offer from a distant city which -- despite the frigid
winters there -- she couldn't refuse. Everyone's eager
to see if the value of her unit has increased as much as
the news reports are saying it should've.
    And this: the tax laws are screwy enough that
despite the availability of large itemized deductions
for mortgage interest and home-buying taxes we find
outselves better off going with the standard deduction
on our income taxes (the main reason being the extreme
disparity between Z's salary and mine -- after deducting
office rent and business expenses, my net income for the
year was under three K, or about a twentieth of hers --
whereas in a typical year it would be about a sixth).
    -- So okay then. Gotta hit the sack early tonight
because tomorrow I take the Z-mobile in for a tune-up.
                    *   *
    -- Sun streaming in through big windows at an SQ
chain coffee shop. We're right across the main drag
from the newly refurbed Scandi park with its ever
hopelessly corny "Friendship Mural" featuring a sister
city likely well known to my Norski ancestors -- just
some fifty miles down the coast from the family farms.
We're also looking straight down another main drag --
here in the SQ, I'm saying -- toward the auto repair
shop four blocks to the southeast, where earlier I read
in the waiting room for an hour and a half or so while
the Z-mobile got its vrroom back. And also rapped a bit
with the desk guy, Russ, who not long ago ruptured his
Achilles tendon playing tennis, so we had plenty to
commiserate about. What's more, he recently bought a
condo himself, and it happens to be just a few blocks
from the film forum (site of the Sacred Ozu Fest -- and
yes, "Sacred" is part of the actual title -- and
rightfully so, sez I) -- and he'd seen the marquee and
wondered what it was all about, this "Sacred Ozu," and I
did the best I could to fill him in. (From now on again
assuming a stipulation on the Ozu JRX.)
    So, situated.

241

[Scat Jyze : Blue Rooster]

Am I a happy fellow today? Well sure, I'd say so,
once I discount all my many grievances with the powers
that be (talkin' 'bout the neocons and the corporados,
and they ain't no friends of mine). And such
discounting, I should probably be ashamed to admit, is
not so hard to do, usually, unless I'm grimly focused on
specific content, which I try to avoid being for more
than an hour or two a day if I can help myself (reading
the papers or politically oriented mags and journals,
listening to the hourly news headlines overnight).
    Why happy in particular? Because my jyze stuff's
coming along well, that's why, first and foremost (and
because I'm part of a stable and loving "dyadic pair,"
which makes so much else possible, and I scratch out
just enough of a living to be able to get by, and the Z-
spouse is able to tolerate this and even encourage it).
    No complacency though. So much still to do (always
and forever) and so little time. (But enough time? I
still say enough time, yeah. Of course with fingers
crossed, and especially J-stick-holding fingers.)
    -- So it's Kat's big day. While in the shower at
one p.m. (after rising an hour early!) I cooked up a
song for her based on "Stranded in the Jungle":

> I crashed on the futon
> and had myself a dream
> about that krazy Katgrrrl
> who's almost sweet fifteen....

-- and continuing like that for several more verses and
choruses, and later delivered by phone as a "hip-hop
singing telegram." Not only did she pick up the
receiver live (she's on spring break) but she's already
back from the next state to the south, where she and
Betty were visiting Betty's friend and former nursing
colleague Maggie (whose father recently died at age
101). Opined Kat about my hip-hop style: "Hey, that was
pretty good!" (In Z's view I'm still the closest Kat's
got to a father. That's why we're going out to the
Hispanic restaurant Saturday, and I'm dressing up: so

Kat and I can do the traditional Quinceanera "father and daughter" dance. And I'm pleased and proud to be the one she wants to do it with.)

That other kid, Elgie? No word from him. Still. Z and I sent him a birthday card but neither of us holds out much hope for hearing from him anytime soon. "My guess," Z says, "is he'll keep himself on the far periphery until his mother's gone." (And I remind Z that Lady S's mother lived into her late nineties.)

Elgie turns thirty-two. I have vivid memories of my own thirty-second birthday. That took place, as it happened, in Seoul, just a few weeks after Lady S and I tied the knot so Elgie would stop being an official nonperson under Korean law and thus would be able to leave the country with his mother (if and when they wanted to). Otherwise he would've faced a very tough life there as a biracial kid. (It was not one of my happier birthdays. I hope his own thirty-second is working out much better. But his long silence makes me fear it's not.)

Other news? I should think so! Even after only a two-week gap a bunch should be spooled up and demanding playback. ...But what exactly? Memory, I test thee. (Slowing reflexes, body falling apart, clouds blowing across the eyescape -- why not dimming memory?)

But no. No noticeable dimming memory yet, or if some, minor. You can't be much of a senior without at least an occasional "senior moment" to prove your vintage mettle. Doesn't matter if these moments are no different (at least as far as you can tell) from any other such lapse you might've had earlier in life.

Valentine's Day, for instance. Day before, a stop at the public market for flowers (special price on two dozen tulips) and then up to Z's new office -- it was a Sunday -- for my first visit. Wow, some view, including our own modestly forested and impressively castellated hilltop just 1.5 miles to the southeast. I pressed a fingerprint high on the window to distinguish the floor from others for viewing someday from our hilltop lookout park with super-high-power binoculars, just in case.

She's on forty-six, I think it is -- or forty-four?
(Senor Senior, another moment is here!) (I'd just read
a magazine piece on a famously pluralistic political
philosopher in which it was mentioned that the great
man's dislike of the United States crystallized as he
looked out a forty-fourth-story window (or forty-second
story?) in FCM #1 at people moving antlike far below.)
     -- Next day, V-Day itself, tradition decreed that
we meet at the AQ teahouse at the end of Z's workday.
As I parked the car outside I was so distracted by the
touching sight of the Z-woman struggling up the steep
hill with her wheeled backpack in tow that I hurried
down to give her a hand and forgot to feed the meter.
While we were inside -- presentation of the single rose
-- of course a meter-gendarme slapped the car with a
ticket. (Z graciously insisted on paying it.) Then off
to the Ozu Fest, both of us. (And her gift to me,
presented earlier, was a mash note inscribed on a piece
of floorboard, auctioned off for charity, from the old
downtown library: "I love you, MBAO / from the ceiling
to the floor of X," where "X" is an infinity sign.)
     And I'll mention that a hero of mine died. Flawed
hero, freaky hero. Shot himself dead at age sixty-
seven, he did. The premier political commentator of my
MSM #2 era. Counterculture guy, at least to a degree.
For several years I'd often hear he'd attended someone's
party the previous week or been sighted in a certain bar
night before last. His typewriter repairman was my
typewriter repairman. But I never did meet him or see
him in person, even though for much of that period we
were working in the same city and the same line of
counterculture ("alternative") journalism. -- And: I
didn't think much of his extreme drugginess and still
less of his violent streak, his obsession with guns, the
nasty side of his self-dramatization. But as a writer
he made good use of them all. An original. And most of
the time pretty much right-on politically. (His day is
gone, some current commentators say. Well yeah, I
guess. -- Or is it that his day is still to come? The
only kind of culture able to survive the catastrophe now

looming, I continue to insist, would be one as counter
to the present version as could be, and in many ways
more like the counterculture of the sixties.)
    And on the same day, goodbye to the woman who
played Gidget in the eponymous movie. A few months my
senior. The role model deluxe for all those cute goody-
goodies of my high-school era. Some of her in Cindy L.,
for example. And a lot in brother Jeff's Jamie and
Jess's Gwen. And scarcely any at all in the fabulous
Zoelie B., thank the deities, the subdeities, the muses
-- and most of all, of course, thank Mama E and Papa V.
    -- And the sun going down on the Scandi quarter.
It's gonna be another long night of scoping. I need
some red meat to power me through. Also need to stop at
the magazine shop (where Z and I met, first date, first
caught sight of each other) to pick up a certain journal
only they carry, although the new issue may not be in
yet. (Yah, a day in the life once again.)

30

    It's Big Date Broke Day so of course I had to hit
the ORB cafe. Nabbed my favorite table too. The most
crucial table of them all.
    Eight years ago today I "met Z's spirit" at this
table after the lady herself had decided not to show up,
having broken our very first date (by leaving a curt
message on my answering machine). And about five weeks
before that -- but also right here, this very chair
location (maybe it's the same chair, maybe not) -- I had
first come across her spirited ad in the alt-weekly.
And although five days after Big Date Broke Day (BDBD)
the delayed first meeting in the flesh took place

elsewhere (as noted last entry), our second meeting in
the flesh, four days after that, came here. So to me
this is the real life-changing spot.

     And Gregorian spring just rolled in a few days ago.
And we're midway through Easter week (it's very early
this year), so tomorrow's not only Domesday but also
Good Friday, and today's -- what's it called again? --
something Thursday. Whelpy Thursday, I want to say,
although that couldn't possibly be it.

     Domesday, that's March 25th. As of tomorrow it'll
be exactly a thousand and five years (give or take a few
crucial calendrical adjustments) since Christendom
celebrated its first millennium, because New Year's Day
fell on March 25th in that era; and tomorrow it'll also
be exactly five years since jyzedom celebrated
Christendom's second millennium. That happened to be
the same day J. City's sports dome was imploded before a
crowd of sixty thousand or more, most of them perched in
the prime viewing spots along the south hill high bridge
and in the outlook strip park just above it. The
biggest crowd in hilltop history. Domesday. The True
Jyze Millennium. As memorialized in Jyze Age Annal 6
that goes by the same name minus "True." Or to me, TJM.

     Sunny day today -- and sunny week, sunny month.
The global broil continueth ever more broiling. Down
here in the ORB basement it's quiet and unusually warm,
aptly enough, and the door's wide open (to the staircase
leading up to the sidewalk). Just three chess players,
all extremely serious, and me hangin' about. (As now
the waterfront streetcar rumbles by up there and gives a
couple of toots on its steam whistle.)

     The quietness down here may have something to do
with the recent opening of a new coffee shop just a few
blocks to the east. If not for today being BDBD I'd be
laying down this Blue Rooster scat over there. I have
high hopes for the place. It's on the ground floor of a
newly opened city-subsidized lofts building and it's
independently owned and operated and it's open until
eleven on weeknights. Hallelujah! A nightscoper's
dream! (Well, no. The real dream spot would be open

all night. But this one's a start on that. And for the
HQ it's beyond compare.)

     Busy scoping week too. Busiest scoping month ever,
in fact, during my time with Naomi. (And the security
muckety-mucks at scope east pick this week to reprogram
their elevator swipe-card reader, causing me all sorts
of after-hours grief -- I'd guess about four lost hours
so far. Twice each night I've had to call for a guard
to escort me up to the office and then back down again.
The guard usually takes about twenty minutes to arrive.
It's the kind of thing which reminds me that being a
night worker has its downside even after you've safely
made it inside the building.)

     And then the wild ups and downs of my pecuniary
status. At one point this month (and by no coincidence
it came on the day Z-wiff turned sixty-four) my bank
account was down to under five bucks. In the end I did
after all have to ask Naomi for an advance. The very
next day after I did that our tax refund arrived -- I
was up $2400. Two days more and Naomi left me a note
saying she'd be taking off the whole month of August and
a couple of isolated weeks in June and July -- and so I
was back to worrying, this time about bridging the
cumulative gap of more than six weeks without income.
But then another day or two and Z-wiff suddenly offered
to start paying off her five-K debt to me at a hundred
bucks per month, which would certainly provide a few
sturdy planks for that bridge over the gap. And now it
appears I'll be reaping over two K on scoping for the
month of March all by itself. So I can't very well deny
it: all of a sudden I'm sitting pretty.

     Of course it could all flip back to crisis mode at
any moment.

     "And so it goes."

*

(It was time for a coffee refill. The guy charged
me a quarter! Just! I'm living right today! -- And
Maundy Thursday is what it is, not Whelpy Thursday.
Where'd I get that from? "Maundy" came to me as I
maundered back from the refill counter. Confirmed it in

the handy coffee-stained unabridged dictionary lying
open like a very fat orchestral score on its own stand
by the condiments.)
      Earlier, on the way down from south hill, a stop at
A-mart in search of items for Z-wiff's birthday present.
I'm still doing this, nine days after the big day
itself. And will be for 356 days more. This is the
downside of the idea I came up with for this year's gift
-- except I'm enjoying it and I think I'll continue to.
And, what really matters, I think she is and will also.
      It's a new tradition: when you're sixty-four you
celebrate your birthday sixty-four times over the course
of the whole year you're that age. "64 Birthdays When
You're 64." Happily enough, 64 breaks into 52 plus 12,
so every week on Sunday Z will have an envelope to open
containing a tag for her "When I'm 64 Wish Tree" and
every month on the 15th -- her birthday date in March --
she'll have a little gift box to open. (They're wrapped
already and sitting in two big paper gift bags on our
living-room coffee table. Unknown to her, though, the
contents are all dummies. Each week I work on the
upcoming tag or gift -- then undo the wrapping on the
appropriate box (they're all labeled) and substitute the
finished item for the dummy. It's a trip!)
      I'm so pleased with this little scheme. On her
actual solar birthday I gave her these two gift-laden
(seemingly) paper bags and also two plants, one for home
and one for the office, and both pots labeled "When
You're 64 Wish Tree." Each of the 64 gift boxes and
envelopes contains two more or less identical tags with
a short length of string attached, one tag per tree. On
these tags -- each relating to a year in her life, going
in chronological order from 1 to 64 -- she's obliged to
write a wish on one side and a "gratitude" on the other;
that's the rule, decreed by the new tradition. The tags
also are decorated with decals and rubber stamps and
other good stuff from the art worktable. And each of
the monthly gift boxes includes a larger tag
commemorating one of the months of the Chinese calendar.
She was born in the month of the Rabbit so we're on the

[Scat Jyze : Blue Rooster]

Rabbit now.

Ooh, so elaborate! So participatory! So kinkily spiritual! So utterly bonkers and over the top!

The idea was sparked by reading a news story about a Southeast Asian city-state's ancient wish tree (which collapsed this year, or rather one of its big limbs did, from the weight of thousands of tags placed on it). And Jean H. assisted by finding me a couple of plants in her floral department that would suit the purpose: a Narihara bamboo for the condo and a weeping ficus (or "fica," also known as "weeping Italian cunt tree," as she bawdily called it) for Z's office.

Z-wiff went for all this in a big way. And well she should've! Wotta production! It's right up there with the Heavenly Year spectacular!

-- And so now, the big item out of the way (take that, Spirit of Zoelie B.!) it's time to crank out some scoping work. Over three hundred pages to go, four witnesses, each with a large, unwieldy exhibit binder frequently quoted from, requiring me to hunt up the quoted material each time to be sure we've got it right.

(But I'll just say: I'm spending money again. Buying books. Renewing a few subscriptions. Laying in a big bottle of the good -- but not the special fancy version of it -- bourbon. Filling up the vite & supp coffers. -- Fun while it lasts. The hard part being to dial the celebration all the way back to normality while the bank account still has something left in it.)

*   *

All right, feelin' pretty good now. Poured myself an unusual weekday glass of the aforementioned good stuff. Grabbed some chips, which I don't indulge in too much anymore, even if they're baked, as these are. (Got to stretch it out as much as I can now -- "it" being, of course, my life. Can't afford the really sophisticated approach, the 150 vites & supps and whatnot, not to mention the even fancier longevity nostrums I assume the super-wealthy are pumping themselves up with but most of the populace never even hears about.)

Three gorgeous views of scat moon tonight.

Already. And it's only 3:21 a.m.

So I gave Kat a congratulatory kiss smack on those splendid lips of hers. "I always wanted to do that!" crowed the bad, bad surrogate pop. But all too quickly she spun away rather than dance one more step of "the Quinceanera of the streets" -- this right outside the Hispanic fusion joint, where the food was tasty but the aisles too crowded for dancing (and sadly the only brown faces in view other than Kat's and Zoelie's belonged to the bus crew). And earlier Kat gave me a two-foot-by-three-foot oil-crayon depiction of a lighthouse she did herself, a slightly delayed Christmas gift. -- All this back almost a full month now. (And back almost as far, what would've been ol' Mom's eighty-fifth birthday.)

Well, the times are just about as nasty as they can get for the world (yet also rapidly worsening) but for me personally, embarrassing though this be in a sense (not to say criminal), they're terrific. I ought to mention this more. Express my gratitude and also my uneasiness. Admit I don't deserve this -- no Cawk USAn does -- and especially not now.

For instance, March 19th, a few days ago, was the second anniversary of this country's unprovoked invasion and occupation of Iraq. The resulting war there rages on, though of course our lying government says all's well in Iraq and for that matter just about everywhere. Except, that is, for our own Social Security system and a few other leftover liberal programs from New Deal days. Those must be dismantled immediately. Our recently re-elected and supposedly compassionate supreme leader is at this moment barnstorming the country in pursuit of that very end.

In the news today I notice both a USAn chess ace (newly made a citizen of Iceland) and a USAn soul diva are exactly my age. Therefore it must be correct that, like them, though I often can't believe it, I'm now sixty-two. Never to be any younger. And yet still possessed of some wicked energy, all that "vintage" stuff referred to above notwithstanding.

Narihara bamboo poking up above my feet. A heart-

shaped doily at my back, sewn directly into the fabric
of the chair by Z-spouse a few weeks ago. And she left
a row of pup-tent notes on the floor for me tonight
saying I'm "neither unsung nor unloved" (as if I ever
thought anything like that) "nor unjyzed." And in the
mail today a postcard from sister Barb, perplexing and
distressing in the classic Barb mode, urging me to read
a certain maverick sixties theologian's "Jesus Comes to
Harvard." (Does she still not know I don't run with
Jesus? Or is this yet another intentional irritant?
-- And I still recall how my eyes rolled heavenward over
that same theologian's "Are You Running with Me, Jesus?"
when I sampled a few paragraphs of it a mere thirty-
seven years ago, approximately.)

The Z-woman likes to torment me too, though more
just to keep things lively. Lately she's back to doing
it with dreams, accounts of a certain anonymous
"dreamboat" she's hanky-panking with, or maybe even
more deeply engaged, until with a sudden guilty frisson
she remembers (in the dream) she's married and announces
to the hard-breathing dreamboat that she's really sorry
but she must immediately go find her husband.

(A strange clicking sound we've been hearing
outside in the afternoons the past few weeks -- a
woodpecker, we both thought. But people in the know at
the utility say it must be a squirrel. Now each time we
hear the sound Z is reminded of her girlhood pet
squirrel Squeaky. And the other day Z ran into a guy
with a squirrel on a leash, perched on his shoulder.
She mused aloud to me that maybe we should get us a
"companion squirrel" too. -- But no, she wasn't
serious, thank god.)

New for supper, a hunk of smoked salmon from a
fancy box of same on sale at the discount mart. For
eleven bucks Z and I score three meals apiece, plus our
fingers smell of salmon for roughly ten days in a row
because that smell is all but impossible to scrub off.
Nothing you can do but wait for new skin to grow in.

Meanwhile Elgie's moth orchid of a couple of years
ago has been supplanted, so to speak. Kay E. gave Z a

new one for her birthday. Elgie's orchid had long since
stopped blooming anyway. (Six or seven birthday parties
the Z-spouse had this year, thrown by different circles
of friends, colleagues, quasi-relatives (i.e., D-clan).
For our generation exposed at such an impressionable age
to the mega-hit "When You're 64" it turns out sixty-four
is big.)

Ozu, the month. "Sacred" (as in the name of the
festival) -- yes indeed. Eight or nine of his flicks in
all I saw, maybe ten, including a couple with Vic. For
long periods watching the master's work I'm in a kind of
karezza-like near-orgasmic state (but of the aesthetic
nervous system, I'm saying).

Jean, I'm worried about her. So wonderfully
animated she was the other evening after waking up and
wandering out in her PJs at nine p.m. as Vic and I
rambled on in a scotch haze. She put an arm around each
of our necks and hugged us simultaneously, almost as if
she loved us equally. But walking her home from the AQ
one day I learned that the docs have detected "abnormal
cells" in her cervix. (And I bought a twelve-foot
dragon banner from her, red on black, for brother Rob
the Water Dragon. Proceeds go to Aceh tsunami relief,
for which Jean's serving as a local coordinator.) Once
when I gave her a big hug from behind, it was almost as
frissony (and jouissancey) as kissing Kat flush on the
lips. I like 'em both a lot (but of course with all due
propriety and proportion because there's only one Zoelie
B. and only she can make the beyond-mere-frissony/
jouissancey happen for me and that's a fact).

Here's the start of the five-hour-long public-radio
news, four a.m. Got to snap it off -- more Christian-
oriented nonsense, the brain-damaged woman in Florida,
that sadly disturbed baby-dangling Afrusan pop star with
the great dance footwork and big collection of platinum
albums made by himself. And freshen up my glass of the
good stuff for this rare occasion, sure, why not, with
several pages still to go in tonight's hazy jyze ramble.

*

-- Back minutes later, and what else is new these

days?

Do know my male member is still working okay, at least for the time being. And by the way, that's still without any pharmaceutical boost. (But it turns out the vitamin E supplements I've been taking for years do nothing but make matters worse. It seems. But is that just for some concerns and not for others, for example, protection against prostate cancer? They don't really say. Who knows what to believe? Don't research scientists ever speak to each other before rushing out their studies? Nothing new here really; we live in primitive times as far as knowledge about nutrition goes -- not to mention numerous other crucial realms. But I still ply myself with as many vites & supps as I can afford on which the science looks good, and lately, and for a while now, that's about twenty-two a day.)

Do know I'll soon have to own up to letting the green lazyboy chair go, the one Gerry and Leola gave us. It'll probably be this coming Saturday night, when we're going out dancing with G&L at a club on their side of the lake. No way to avoid it really. Subject of much humor with Z-wiff at pillow-talk time. (She's been reading deeply in the tao-of-sex books, have I mentioned it? But now an evening with several of her feminist friends -- all Cawks -- has convinced her the Asian sex-advice stuff's too patriarchal. And of course those friends are right, though that doesn't mean Z can't get something zingy out of it regardless, just as she does from "Lady Chatterley's Lover," say, and of course her favorite of them all, "The Story of O.")

Ray W., another book published. Glowing reviews but -- but -- I'm sorry again, yes, but I'm just not moved, except for feeling sorry for the guy himself. And I suppose I owe Ken D. a letter exploring why I see Ray's stuff this way. What, am I just biased because of his over-the-line messing with Lady C almost forty years ago? Or something? But then -- Ken's last letter didn't even begin to reply to my passages about same in my previous long one. So should I carve out some time for working up a reply to him anyway? (When I could be

working on my own stuff?   -- And a big thrill this month
when I printed up the last of almost two reams' worth of
single-spaced and double-sided pages of 1980s protojyze,
many of which I'm pretty damn proud of.)
     Reading, I finally gave the tome on so-called
radical hermeneutics the toss. Wotta buncha hooey.
Religious transcendence even, absolutes up the kazoo.
(So now I'm trying a highly literate nineteenth-century
Englishman's "Essays of Elia," just getting started.
And a very good East Indian novelist and critic's Buddha
book when I can take it, just because I love his
understated style: every last tentative conclusion
hedged in with far more qualifications than I can ever
muster for any of my own conclusions, tentative or not,
or at least most of them (and this one right here is a
good example).)
     Health again, why not. Rash worsens gradually in
several spots, but now with the tax refund in I can go
for a different option, a visit to one of the new chain
health clinics -- and hopefully next week. Because I'm
tiring of this rash nonsense, yes I am. How many months
now? (And just hope nothing has to be amputated.)
     Dinner with Olwen and Trent, lamb stew quite good,
and Z-wiff and I both said some dumb things but it seems
neither of them much noticed. And a visit to the Museum
of Glass with Wei and Alison -- it's not really my kind
of thing, glass art, I'll confess, except for neon --
and then afterwards dinner with them at a new Vietnamese
restaurant in the upper AQ, where one of the "servers"
was almost a double for Lady U and (in the spirit of Z's
frequent mentions of oneiric dreamboats and boyfriend
look-alikes) I told Z as much and she wasn't all that
impressed -- "Cute, but I'm cute too."
     And old Marcus G. from the WOC, one of our mutual
acquaintances there saw him on a local cable channel, a
cooking show, Marcus the main man -- with a beard -- "He
wasn't bad, really!"
     -- And now I've earned the right to pack it in for
another 28 or 29 less-than-scat-mooned days with a fully
full conscience and the pride of a scat well shat.

31

Two a.m. straight up. So just over an hour until
all-out scatness. And I've got news. (And the usual
Saturday-night glass of bourbon -- just one glass total
per week -- but this time it's the dregs. As Z-wiff
sleeps. Jazz plays, I know not what or who or by whom,
though I can guess the when: postwar forties. And I
ride the green armchair by the balcony door. I wear
gray sweatpants and olive long-sleeve henley, my usual
off-hours outfit in these cold early months of the "Blue
Roo'." Which sounds marsupial but -- jyze knows better.
    And here, almost at the top, is the big news.
About three weeks ago, and for only the second time in
thirty-two years, I visited a doctor (the first time was
eight years ago next month to submit to an AIDS test to
clear the way to relations with a certain Zoelie B.).
And now I know what it is I'm afflicted with (causing
the rash) and that it can probably be made to go away.
    In the end I didn't call on a commercial chain
clinic. I went directly to a dermatologist. I recalled
noticing a dermatology clinic on the first floor of the
building where we take Mama E to see Doc F. Turned out
that clinic had recently moved to a new office on the
far side of downtown (and it's a good thing I scouted
out the address there in advance via Z-mobile or I
would've missed my appointment by an hour or more,
because I had a ludicrously wrong idea of where the
office was and I was planning to hike over).
    Clyde L., a peppy young Chiusan, is the doc. First
male person to lift my scrotum for a peek underneath (or
for any other purpose) since good old Doc F (another Doc

F, this one of Gatewood provenance) did it half a
century ago. Other than myself, of course, usually
while deploying a mirror to check on crotch rot.

    It's not a hot-tub bug I have. From the start Doc
L suspected it wasn't, but just in case, while a biopsy
was being done, he prescribed a ten-day course of an
antibiotic -- intended more as a kind of placebo, I'd
guess, or pacifier. Ten bad days: I had to give up
caffeine for the duration (and maybe even worse: all
vites & supps, and also all tomatoes). This antibiotic,
alas, had no effect at all on the rash.

    Understandably, it turns out, because what I have,
the lab says, is a nasty and poorly understood and hard-
to-treat autoimmune malady called lichen planus. (Ooh,
that's ugly; just to say the name is to feel ill.)

    So now I'm on a three-week course of prescription
topical ointments, one a powerful steroid and the other
some bizarre concoction so new and experimental it's not
even covered by Z-wiff's city medical insurance. (But
thank the gods and Z-wiff and the city, I myself am
covered by that insurance. I'm out about 265 of my own
real dollars so far -- on the copays and the
experimental drug -- but without the insurance I'd be
owing a whole lot more, maybe ten times as much.)

    So this is why my forearms are glistening as I
grind out this jyze. Both ointments are oily. I apply
them twice a day, legs and arms and a few small isolated
patches elsewhere (but not under the scrotum, no).

    And for now I'm keeping it all a secret. Why?
Because Z's got plenty to worry about as it is. (Monday
she's accompanying Aida to a doctor's office: Aida's pap
smear came back positive.) And: I didn't, and don't,
want to worry Z too much over something trivial. And
I'm still awaiting results on a blood test. Lichen
planus is sometimes associated with hepatitis.

    But I feel fine (except when I say the name). And
the ointments' effects thus far seem mostly positive.
So even though Z's sure to find out eventually (the
health plan sends her regular accountings), I'll try to
keep flying under the radar as long as possible. (How

is it she doesn't worry about my rashes? Well, they're
fairly inconspicuous and she doesn't see them that much,
and when she does the light isn't good, and she knows
I've had sporadic outbreaks in isolated spots in the
past from a chronic skin condition related to toner
allergy. And she knows I prefer to let things heal
naturally if possible, even if it takes longer. So she
chooses not to comment too much on what she does notice,
and I'm very glad that's the case.)

   What's the actual cause of this condition? Doc L
says medical science doesn't know. In his view it's
possible I've had it in a low-grade form for fifteen
years or more, since minor outbreaks have appeared in
pretty much the same spots from time to time for at
least that long. It might be allergy-related. It might
be related to my battles years ago with poison ivy and
poison oak or to diet or to overuse of vites & supps --
or to who knows what. Just about anything, it seems.

   But I did go through some bad times over this, not
knowing. Worrying. Craving caffeine. (On the other
hand, it's good to know I can quit the stuff cold.)

   -- All right, enough on that. (Though of course
this is only an early trial run -- I'm assuming trial --
for age-related medical adventures lying ahead. And I
do hope to keep this scat jyze going until the end, or
close to it, without letting the near-inevitable major
crisis or crises during the intervening years or months
or weeks, whatever may be the case, overwhelm it.)

   What else is new? Well -- well! -- to my left,
twelve feet or so, shimmers Z-spouse's newly installed
feng-shui curtain. Earlier tonight I mounted the wall
brackets for the bar (actually a bamboo stick about six
feet long) holding up the curtain. I don't much like
the curtain itself (gauzy, shiny, goldish) and don't
worry too much about the flow of chi -- not after my
unsettling Korea experiences with feng shui -- but if it
makes Z happy to have the curtain hanging there (and it
does), I can certainly live with it.

   Also I finally managed to clear off the art
worktable -- it took me only a full year to do this.

[Scat Jyze : Blue Rooster]

(Next Tuesday is the one-year anniversary of our signing
the condo papers.) And I steadied the bathroom towel
rack by using the mollies Wei recommended. (And Z and I
are both sad, but she especially is, because it appears
Wei and Alison will soon be moving about twenty-five
hundred miles southwest across the Pacific, to the
tropical U.S. state where Lady U grew up and is probably
living right now. Z tells me she's been "really close"
to only two other men in her life besides me. One was
Betty's husband Manny (Z's nonlover crony for ten years,
and housemate for several of those, before he met
Betty). When he died in 1995, Z called Wei -- they'd
met five years earlier when both were home-insulation
advisors for the city -- and asked if he would fill the
gap left by Manny's loss. He said yes. And he's been
that kind of friend to her ever since.) (By the way,
the J-town school district this week announced a school-
closure plan -- the district's under severe financial
pressure, essentially owing to Cawk flight over a period
of years -- and it's possible, maybe fifty/fifty, Betty
will lose her school-nurse job as a result -- and this
in her Heavenly Year!)
     -- And to my right, a new "Mother fern" we bought
this afternoon, along with a hundred bucks' worth of
pots and soil for the balcony. (A few weeks ago Z-wiff
and Leola attended the annual spring sale at the fuchsia
society and -- knowing how fond I am of the hardy
variety -- Z came home with no fewer than seven of them.
At this moment they're all still stashed in their black
plastic temporary pots out on the balcony awaiting my
ministrations. -- And, yeah, no question, I love 'em
all, these glorious flowering vegetables that you don't
have to eat (unlike nasturtiums), and they'll almost
certainly feature in many a future scat-jyze passage.)
     And the "64 birthdays" scheme is going well. The
Ides of April (Dragon Month) was a knockout. (Actually
the Ides falls on the 13th in April, it turns out -- I
finally researched this -- but we're sticking with Z's
birth date of the 15th for all months.) Last night I
made up the tags she'll be unwrapping tomorrow. We're

up to 1948 now, Z at age seven. -- And I don't really
see all this as a "scheme," no. One of my best birthday
ideas ever. (Several weeks ago it inspired her to bring
out her babybook and she read aloud from it for an hour
or more, howling with laughter at times, bawling at
others -- and a marvelous afternoon it was. And this
led to another afternoon every bit as good when we
hauled the babybook up to Benita's and took turns
reciting passages from it aloud for Mama E, its proud
author, and she seemed to enjoy the reading almost as
much as scratching lottery tickets or watching soap
operas or horse races or football games on TV.)
                            *
     -- Back from a quick dinner break. We're now
twenty-five minutes past scat moon. It's not visible
from this chair tonight, but last night the near-scat
version was, misted and leaf-laced by the flowering
laurel trees: breathtakingly lovely, and I'll even come
right out and say so in just those well-worn words.
     (My first-string J-stick, No. 5, busted its barrel,
by the way. Nasty cracks. This one I'm using now is
backup No. 4 and it's both leaky and rusty, its flow
frustratingly obstructed at times. Behind it I have one
more backup, No. 6, and the two together must last me
however long I last. This particular model isn't made
anymore. J. City's one and only J-stick shop, where I
bought No. 6, itself is gone. If push comes to shove --
or just to push, really -- I'm sure I could find some
other acceptable instrument to keep the jyze flowing.
But because of my long history with this brand and model
I doubt I could ever be as pleased with anything else.
Give or take a few months it's been thirty-six years
since I bought the first one.
     -- My mood right now might be much worse if not for
a single happy fact. After a very good month in March,
the past two-week pay period for scoping was the best
ever. $1150! What's more, Naomi agreed to start paying
me a dime per page for materials expenses -- because
that's what the scope firm charged her for the same
materials -- and since those materials (toner,

diskettes, paper, etc.) cost me altogether only about six cents a page -- and I did tell her this -- it's as if I've racked up a three percent wage increase. So moneywise things are looking better now than they have for quite some time. (And I'm knocking on all the wooden bookcase shelves in sight when I say this, knowing how easily and quickly things could change.)

   -- Out in the world what's happening? The big stuff is mostly religious. A pope dies. The hard Christian right in the U.S. flexes its muscles, trying to oust "activist judges" and do all sorts of ugly reactionary things. And a fine book co-authored by my No. 1 neoprag hero appears (though it's skinny and way too expensive) and it's called "The Future of Religion." Once again I'm stunned by how my thought chimes with so much of his and by how beautifully he writes.

   And gas is now up to $2.59 a gallon in J-town. And the insurgency in Iraq cranks up to an even fiercer level. The U.S. embarrasses itself again and again in international affairs. Our state of denial on global eco/climate crisis is so appalling everyone on the knowledgeable side of the issue is paralyzed by it, it seems. (This is not new, no. It's just one blow after another. Pick yourself one inch off the mat and BAM, you're flattened again.)

   Meanwhile what? The author of "Augie March" dies. That novel seemed pretty good to me when I first read it in college and so did "Henderson the Rain King," but after those two I couldn't abide anything else the man wrote as he moved ever deeper into cranky neocon territory in reaction to the rebellions of the sixties. The unconditional Israel supporter. The Committee on Social Thought -- nasty stuff! -- at Z's and my father's and grandfather's old school, the U of Centropolis. Hanging in there with the ultraconservative right on "The Closing of the American Mind." Yikes! For my favorite Centropolis writer I'll take poor old Nelson A. of "The Man with the Golden Arm" fame anytime.

   (The "Stop-Time" guy dies too -- he a successor to Karl Muller at Mezzu. He's now to be succeeded there by a Chiusan woman for whom I hold out high hopes. The preppyish "Stop-Time" I could never get into but I acknowledge the author's role in making my jyzey and refictionalized kind of "creative nonfiction" potentially more palatable to the wider reading public.)

Another postcard came in from Ken D., a black-and-white photo of the railroad station in the tiny Mentoka town of Hotchkin where Jo grew up (and I the best man at their wedding almost forty years ago). News that brother Rob's son Zach has suddenly married a Cawk woman first-named McKenzie back in the next state to our east here, panhandle portion. A visit (inaugural for Z and me both) to Rob's lair at the big new company store near the fairgrounds. Naomi presents me with a bound copy of the transcript of Larry's entire memorial service (reporter Fran did the transcribing). A newspaper article says the Al Qaeda-related terrorist now known worldwide as the Millennium Bomber, nabbed at the border ninety miles north of here in December 1999, is no longer yielding information these days about the terrorist network, perhaps in part because Larry's not around anymore to direct the feds' dealings with him.

And: Z-wiff and I did a godparents dinner at David and Stacy's. Fellow godfather Rudy M., recovering from his stroke, was present, mellow but also just barely alive, it seemed, and even heftier than before, as was his wife, Serena, who's fighting breast cancer and whose elementary school, where she's a counselor, has just been slated for closure by that same J. City Public Schools shake-up mentioned earlier. But godson Lwazi, nearing age two now, was a delight, zooming about in his PJs and "reading" -- out loud! -- from a newsmagazine.

Jess's breakup with Gwen seems to be holding. She, Jess, already has a serious new love interest, a professor down in MSM #2. And for unknown reasons Jess is about to sell her hand-built (and the hands were her own!) digs on southwest island, intending to ask 600K for them. Gasp. (But real-estate prices in J-town keep soaring. Over the past year they've shot up another fourteen percent. This means our own modest condo is

now worth somewhere around 210K. That's about thirty
percent above what we paid for it. On paper we're
$47,500 richer than we were a year ago -- which actually
means we're that much less deeply in debt -- and the
debt too, of course, is on paper.)

And we had a one-day fight, Z and I. She thought
I'd been too irritable. Maybe I was: this was during
the no-caffeine period. But I wasn't telling her about
anything related to the medical treatment for the rash
and so she couldn't factor in caffeine deprivation as an
excuse. Instead she thought maybe I was losing interest
in her -- no longer finding her as attractive. But no,
that definitely was not it. (And I'm sorry if I'm a
weird fellow. But that's how I am. Not at all
secretive on most things but there are a few exceptions,
and I'll grant this might make me weird, yes. But then
she can be plenty weird herself. Fortunately a good
many of our weirdnesses are bizarrely complementary.
All in all I still think we're a helluva good match and
I believe she does too.)

And in addition to all this, what? Saw "The Wild
Parrots of Telegraph Hill." Most of it appeared to be
set along the same lengthy and very steep staircase
about a hundred feet down from where we scattered
Mother's ashes. My eyes misted up again and again. The
protagonist, a St. Francis-like figure with parrots
eating from his hands and perched atop his scalp, was a
likable younger and far more mystical version of my very
own MSM #2-incubated and antiquatedly longhair
protojyzer self of a decade or two back.

(And it's been a good month for jyzing. Or pruning
the jyze really. I'm now working on the early protojyze
period, the first five and a half years, for which I've
got several thousand pages of text -- single-spaced, 460
words per page -- which I'd like to cut back by at least
a third. And I'm jolted again and again by the memories
evoked. Also I'm finding a good deal more fairly decent
writing than I thought would be there, especially for
the very earliest "chron/urjyze" stages.)

(And this has been a good month for reading as

well. And yet: nowhere as good as I'd like. So much I
want to get to, so little time! "Fencing with Words" --
about the English 1-2 program at Adams in which I
participated my freshman and sophomore years. "The End
of Suffering." "Beyond the Gray Flannel Suit." "The
Asian Mystique." And much, much more. -- My neoprag
hero's co-authored religion book, for another one.)

Oh life is good while it lasts. Oh I'm lucky and
I'm privileged. Make the most of what I've got and just
hope I can increase thereby the sum of readerly pleasure
and social hopefulness available to the world in the
face of the horrifying reality that's looming (and it's
even doing that where it's already arrived -- more and
worse still to come -- I mean the truth is we've seen
nothing yet -- with what Iraqis and Afghanis are going
through at our hands an obvious exception).

32

"So let's jyze on down to tinsel town."
Well, no, tinsel town is not where I've wound up --
it's about a thousand miles south of here and known to
these pages as a subdivision of MSM #1 -- but for some
reason the phrase has been echoing in my head like an
old-time radio jingle I can't get rid of.
Instead it's the new HQ coffee shop. At last!
"Kind of quiet in this joint today," sez I to the
young woman behind the counter (she's in a short denim
skirt and cowboy boots). "Oh, yeah," she monotones.
But it is. I'm the only customer in here. Which
means I've been able to snag the best seat: a two-chair
table up in the prow of this quasi-triangular corner
storefront, with floor-to-ceiling picture windows up

close to the left and right.

And what a view. South and east, five-way intersection right outside. I'm facing straight toward the orange-brick DC castle atop our hill (the castle's all craggily lit up by the late sun and backdropped by a big billowy cloud, snow-white and even craggier than the castle, which looks provincial indeed by comparison).

In between me and those two castles, the AQ: mostly nondescript century-old brick buildings six or fewer stories tall, many in less than top shape, but still one of my favorite places in all of J-town -- all the world, really -- and so it's been for a quarter century.

Stretching due south from here, a double set of railroad tracks maybe thirty feet below street level in an open cut a third of a block wide -- and right now a northbound blue-green-and-white commuter train is entering the hundred-year-old tunnel pretty much directly beneath our feet. You'd almost think you could dash down to the basement and hop right on. Metallic screeches -- a klaxon blast coming up through the floor!

To the immediate right of the railroad cut, still looking south, massive stadia and more old brick buildings (one nearby with an art gallery's balcony sculpture garden hanging out over the tracks). To the left of the cut, a bustling main north-south avenue choked with a vanishingly long line of buses, in places two, three, even four abreast.

Across that avenue and just a block down, a low-income residential hotel, half-a-block square, a grimy ten-story wedding cake of a building I used to dream of putting up in during my years of long-distance commuting (as several other night workers I knew actually did do, sharing a single rented room for daytime sleeping during the workweek). And straight to the east, across a block of hillside parking lots, an east-west side street ascending steeply to the Japanese theater (now mostly a drama and community-meeting venue) and the hilltop peace park, with the intricately terraced AQ gardens (which a few decades back Z-wiff helped build) off to one side.

A wonderful spot here, visually fascinating, even

though directly outside this shop the diagonal (fifth)
street's all torn up. Half a dozen buses are parked at
a slant on the lower slope of that same east-west side
street. Scores of hard hats at work. Foot traffic
threading by through taped-off sidewalk sections. No
one I really know but an occasional semifamiliar face.

     I linger over this description because I'm hoping I
can come back here fairly regularly for jyze sessions.
If, that is, the joint survives. With such late hours,
much as I love them, it's not too likely it will. The
core of the entertainment and shopping strip with its
big crowds is probably a bit too far away.

     Finishing the setting, then, hills to the far
south. And just to the east of the busy one-way north-
south avenue, local plutocrat #2's east-depot complex,
including the fancy all-glass green diesel-engine-shaped
twelve-story tilt-a-building just behind the depot
itself. And above the shop here (as another train, a
long freight, rumbles and screeches by endlessly down
below) are four floors of artist spaces in this brand-
new city-subsidized lofts building. At one point Vic
and Jean were thinking about moving over here but then
decided they couldn't give up their current space:
despite its many drawbacks they loved it too much (and
it's much larger than anything here).

     -- I said I "jyzed on down" but I didn't really do
that. I limped. My right Achilles tendon is acting up
again. It's not too bad yet, maybe something iatrogenic
(the most likely culprit being the steroid ointments I'm
still applying here and there twice daily) or temporary
for some other reason, but emblematic regardless: it's
been a month dominated by things medical.

     Z-spouse first. Her flu's relapsed twice. She's
been out from work the past two weeks straight and
returned for the first time today, easing in for just
half a day. In all, including the gum-surgery recovery
period, she's missed more than five weeks of work since
Christmas.

     And it's wearing on her. Yesterday she told me she
thinks her body's trying to tell her something --

namely, that she should retire at age sixty-seven,
meaning a little less than three years from now. It may
turn out to be just temporary but at this point anyway
she seems quite serious. If she really does it, a bumpy
time would likely follow. Her income would fall
abruptly by close to two-thirds. And she's not used to
living frugally and definitely prefers not to. (And
it's probable I'll be retiring at about the same time.
That could well add to the transitional troubles. But
retirement won't have much effect on my income. I might
even wind up better off than I am now, especially if I
can stay with scoping part-time after starting up Social
Security, and I probably will try to do that if the
option's still open.)

But no point in delving further into all that now.
Or later either, I suppose, if I can help it. But one
can't always avoid obsessing on the basics, and this
income stuff is about as basic as it gets. Along with
the health stuff, of course. But I'm still aiming for
major suppression if not outright denial in both of
those realms for as long as I can get away with it.

-- But...did I mention health? My own? I'll go
ahead and say the ointments are working, albeit slowly.
And: other than, to an extent, the new limp, along with
the need to keep my arms and legs covered to conceal the
rash, my current problems don't inconvenience me in any
way, except temporally. I lose about forty minutes a
day applying the damn ointments and my walking speed is
cut by a third or more, meaning I lose maybe another
thirty to forty minutes. -- Oh yeah, and moneywise: I'm
out about eight hundred bucks now on the rash alone,
with plenty more yet to come. I didn't figure on little
things like copays and deductibles, off-list doctors,
experimental drugs which insurance doesn't cover at all.
(Without the insurance, of course, I'd be far worse off.
The steroid, for example, costs $166 a tube, and I pay
only $30 of that, and by the time of my next appointment
in late July I'll have gone through nine tubes. And
that's the cheaper of the two ointments I use! The
other one, the experimental one, I have to pay full

price ($199), but I use much less of it; I'm still
working on my first tube.)

The point here being that after all my crowing with
respect to money matters in the last entry, I'm already
back to living on the edge. Medical expenses have eaten
up the gains of the unusually good scoping months and
then some. Z-wiff has offered to double her monthly
debt repayment to $200 and that just might enable me to
squeeze through the summer (when Naomi is still planning
to take six weeks off). But at the new rate the entire
debt would be wiped out in less than two years, and then
I'd have no cushion at all to carry me across the last
year or so before Social Security kicks in.

So that's where it stands. It's gonna be chancy
whatever way I decide to go. But then it always has
been and it was always gonna be. I just temporarily
forget those facts once in a while during the good
times.

And so: onward.

Because otherwise I'm a happy fella (and this
despite the state of the world, of course, along with my
personal degree of complicity as a Cawk U.S. male in the
making of this world state). Work's going well (my own,
that is). I'm now deep into the early protojyze years,
and enjoying the rereading of certain key books from
that era which I've picked up again just for the hell of
it (but also because I might write about some of those
books when the time comes for revising the backstory
parts of "Heavenly Year," if it ever does).

And reading for the first time various books about
the Mentoka State Writers' Workshop and some of the
people associated with it. Fascinating stuff. Who was
I then and who am I now -- that's another topic I'll be
mulling for the possible "Heavenly Year" revision. (But
when I actually get around to tackling all that I might
well find I've already written enough about it.)

Pocket watch on tabletop sez 6:03. I made one
lousy mistake in punching in thousands of corrections on
Naomi's latest job (which was a nine-hour videotaped
deposition and those are always rife with corrections

[Scat Jyze : Blue Rooster]

because she double-checks the scoped rough against the
tape itself) and so I have to go all the way in to pick
up the job just to redo the one recorrected page along
with the storage disk. I routinely double-check my own
corrections to try to avoid this kind of situation.
This is only the second such screwup since the scoping
operation shifted to the hideaway.

   So I should mosey on. Because I have no other
scoping work and I want to put in a full night on the
protojyze. But I know it could be tough getting back to
this jyze right here, scat type, later at home. Why?
Because the Z-woman's sleep patterns are all messed up.
Lately she's been sleeping most of the day and staying
up most of the night. This has its good side for me but
also its bad side: I get a lot less done. We tend to
yak a lot. She likes to bug me if my attentiveness
("service") levels start falling short. I even like it
myself! -- But then a time may come when I don't like
it anymore. And it's hard to be firm with her about
something like this, and especially so when she's ill.
(Aida's comment to Z this week, at least according to Z:
"Why can't I find a man who'll treat me like a princess
the way Glen treats you?")
                    *   *
   -- All right, I'm geared up with the decks cleared.
Sequestered in our bedroom which these days is mainly
mine because the Z-wiff has once again banished herself
to the foldout couch/bed in her room -- "the sick room."
Four a.m. is what it is (and that's fourteen hours past
scat fullness and about twenty-six hours past my last
lunar viewing: Moon over Stadiums (from the bus windows
looking west as we rolled across the high bridge last
night, meaning the night before the one we're in the
early a.m. hours of now)).
   First this (I'm already all oiled up too, by the
way, meaning salved and ointmented). My attempt to keep
Z from knowing about my doctor visits didn't last long.
Busted! Of course I knew it would happen sooner or
later, but I hoped it wouldn't be quite so soon as this.
Alas, notice of a bill came in, and it arrived in her

name, unsurprisingly, since she's the primary person on
the insurance. She thought the insurance company
must've made a mistake or, worse yet, I'd been a victim
of identity theft. When I fessed up she laughed and
laughed. Then she grumped out: I must never do anything
like this again, never ever, and especially I must not
do it thinking I'm doing it for her own good. Okay,
fine: so sworn. And quickly she cut me some slack. (It
wasn't only her own health and her mother's and Aida's
she was worrying about a month ago, I should've noted
back then; it was also her friend Kendra's. And now the
doctors have told Kendra they can do nothing more for
her and have given her two to four months to live --
ovarian cancer, I think it is, that's metastasized to
her brain.)

Second, this: someone broke into our mailbox (thus
Z's fear of identity theft). A thief shadowing the
letter carrier smashed the outside key box with a hammer
and used the keys to gain entrance to the garage and
then to open both tiers in the double bank of mailboxes,
casting all catalogs and other bulk mail on the floor
and making off with the first-class mail (probably
including a medical bill or two for me, which means my
tally for the month will eventually mount even higher).

Z-wiff was the one who discovered the break-in
since she was home sick at the time and was the first to
go down to check for mail at two p.m. Drew N., our
Ettore prez, was also home and he acted quickly when Z
informed him. By that evening the cops and the postal
authorities had already been out to the scene, all locks
had been changed, and a new lock was installed in a
place where we lacked one before: on the internal-access
door between the garage and upstairs. Very impressive.
It seems we've lucked out on condo management. If I
haven't gotten around yet to taking back in writing my
early doubts about Drew, I hereby do so. (Everybody
else in the building is shocked that a break-in could
happen here. Not Z and me. We've seen far worse in our
time in this building -- including the robbery back in
"Deep Jyze" days some seven years ago involving a

smashed-in door on our own floor, in unit 202.)

Third, this: a good month with Kat. We saw "Wild Parrots" with her and Betty (second time for Z and me) and then twice during the following week I helped with her school paper on "Depression and Teens." Z and I were both taken aback when she suddenly announced (and apparently quite seriously) she wants to be an editor when she grows up -- just like her subunk, that is. Right now she's in a period between boyfriends and seems to have more tolerance for the old folks. She's even consented to accompany her mother on a tour of Guatemala this summer. (The one piece of bad news is that "Uncle Nick," husband of the late Manny's late daughter Ruth and thus Kat's adoptive brother-in-law -- though he's about twenty-five years her senior -- has decided he needs to break off all contact with the people of his former life "in order to be able to move on," and he and Kat have always been quite close.)

Fourth, this: a big miscellany. (But I'll try to limit it in here.) It's been a month of freaky weather in J. City and environs, squally, thunderstormy, with a lightning strike on the hilltop one afternoon last week that nearly knocked me out of my chair (and did knock out power for parts of the hill for several hours). A month of flowers, with the three-story-high, yard-wide wall of laurel truly dazzling just ten feet or so from our balcony (and the flowering hardy fuchsias on the balcony itself, all seven of them, quite delightful in their own right). And month of anniversaries: Jolt Day, It's Love! Day, and FF Day for Z and me, one-hundredth anniversary of Norway's independence from Sweden on Syttende Mai (still quite the big deal out in the SQ, and for us as well, in part because it's the eighth anniversary of the day Kat and I met out there). And -- not quite an anniversary -- the annual celebration of Mother's Day with Mama E, who was in rare good form and tore right into the wrapped gift Z and I brought her (a nifty running suit) and then with equal relish into the specially decorated (by Z) Mother's Day cake. And also the 25th anniversary of the spectacular eruption of the

volcano ninety miles to the south, and the memorial for
this was an even bigger deal locally than the Norwegian
anniversary (especially because these days the
mountain's rumbling again).
     -- And could I go on? Sure could. But (as the
papers arrive downstairs one after another -- thwap!
thwap! thwap! -- and the noise awakens the birds, who're
now going at it so loudly it's more like a pack of small
dogs barking and yapping) -- but, I say, this month is
different. Jyze is slated to make another appearance
just a week from now. No need to shoot its wad tonight.
Instead I'll try to push a little bit ahead of the game
in newspaper reading because tomorrow looks to be a very
busy day (and I'm thanking my lucky stars -- and Z's
lucky stars too -- that she was able to sleep through
the night for the first time in a while).

33

     Here's the bonus. It's a week later and the place
for the opening jyzeburst is the same as last time, not
for any particular reason but just because I like it so
much. The new HQ coffee shop. Kwik J-burst only.
Fifty minutes and the bell rings for work. Scope kind.
     This time it's Memorial Day. No workers out there
in the torn-up diagonal street but a few folks are
threading by between the pylons on the sidewalk just
outside, most of them clearly on their way -- the folks,
I'm saying, not the pylons -- to tonight's game. Five
after seven it starts, Jyze City versus I don't know who
(the team's prospects look bleak this year and so it's
easier than usual for me not to follow them, the team,
at all, though Z and I do need to know when games are

scheduled so we can take measures to avoid the all-but-certain traffic tie-ups they cause). From here I can see that the portable roof of the baseball stadium has rolled in over the field, meaning weather gurus are predicting rain. But the sun's shining at the moment.

And across the east-west side street just outside, the back of the big billboard (standing on stilts, so most of it is raised above my level and thus I can see southward beneath it) -- the back side, I say, is undergoing a texture shift every five seconds or so, from one colorful random abstract pattern to another. The other side, the front, may convey more meaning in conventional terms -- whatever scam the animated billboard might be hyping today -- but our side is much more visually appealing. One of the artists sitting upstairs in here might well be dashing off a watercolor version of it even as I do a jyze one down below (or rather resist the temptation to try my hand at same).

What's new? -- Memorial Day's not new, that's for sure. Same old nationalistic hokum. (During our early years in Gatewood when Dad was still in the army reserves, he marched in the parade there. He did that a couple of times at least -- was required to perhaps -- although I can't bring back any images of him in action. I do recall inspecting his old dress uniforms in the attic at 2015, but I don't remember seeing him wearing those at any time, ever, other than in photos, and mainly the wedding pictures, an eight-by-ten framed exemplar of which now stands atop ol' Mom's antique glass-doored bookcase in the hideaway. -- Except this year the nationalistic fervor is about as bad as I've ever seen it, with our world-hegemonic aims now openly acknowledged -- trumpeted! -- by the neocon warhawks currently in power and our outrageous war of aggression in Iraq still raging on, as is the somewhat smaller one in Afghanistan. The news coming out of the capital continues to be nothing but all disgusting all the time.

(So what can we do about this? Not much. We can hope it eventually proves self-destructive. We can try to identify positive risk-taking counterforces and

support them without putting ourselves too much in the
line of fire, because in the long run that would just
prove self-destructive for the good guys. -- All pretty
elementary, yeah.)

Three days from now Mama E turns ninety. Z-wiff
came up with a fine celebratory angle, asking Mama E's
friends and family to send photos and enclosing a self-
addressed envelope for them in her letter. And almost
all did send photos. Thursday we'll be taking Mama E
out to the big north-end bookstore arcade -- it worked
for us once before -- and presenting her with, among
other things, an album containing all the cards and
photos.

-- For Z and me it's been a fine laid-back holiday
weekend. I did little else but read and repot plants.
Z's health finally seems to be approaching normal again.

Coupla two-star items:

** One night I miscalculated and finished up my
scoping work at the hideaway twenty minutes late,
meaning I'd left myself just fifteen minutes to make it
up to scope east on foot and then to the bus stop,
slightly less than a mile in all and several blocks of
it steeply uphill. I did make it but every hobbly,
pain-stabbing step of the way I was wondering if I was
signing my own death warrant (thinking of Karl M. of
Mezzu days keeling over as he hurried through the
Centropolis airport to catch a plane -- but then it's
true he was twenty years older than I am now).

** Saw a movie that jumped right onto my list of
all-time favorites, the six-hour Italian-made -- and for
TV originally -- "The Best of Youth." It played at the
Yuke multiplex in two parts. Its politics turned out to
be a little dubious in the end but the acting and
writing were superb and the storyline could scarcely
have been more personally relevant, following a set of
four siblings from the mid sixties up to 2003 or so, the
ages of the four about the same right down the line as
those of my own sibling foursome, myself included.
(Similarly I read, and was much moved by, the two self-
published books that Olwen's brother Carey finished

writing and polishing just before his death last year.)
   -- And so much for the bonus. Not much substance
to it, I'll grant, and even less poetry. No flash! But
I do what I can do and I still enjoy doing it just this
way. (Realizing this month I'm exactly the same age
Popeye was when he died. He who said the Dantean (JRX)
halfway point of thirty-five was also his own high point
in life and thus implied all that remained was downhill;
and his first grandchild -- that's me! -- didn't even
appear on the scene for another fifteen years. For me
the reverse is the case: thirty-five was more like a low
point and things have been improving ever since. I
insist! -- Today anyway. Maybe not at every single
moment during the intervening twenty-eight years.)

34

   Just a little chilly out here. The 201 balcony --
flower-bedecked. And it's the shortest night of the
year. It's coming to an end right now (as foghorns
bellow in the distance and birds awaken nearby).
   I'm still in jeans and khaki workshirt. Had to
take an early bus home at midnight so I could drive back
in at one a.m. A two-hour standard dep to scope plus
five hundred pages of video-dep to final -- the
combination proved to be way too much for my usual
worknight of five hours max ending at one a.m. When I
finally finished everything and drove home at half past
three (zipping down the totally empty "very, very high
road" in the heart of the city and then hitting the even
higher high bridge), gray was already seeping up into
the night sky to the east, dimly silhouetting the
mountains.

Madly proliferating hardy (but also hearty!) fuchsias out here, blooms like I've never seen before, many hundreds of them dangling all around me, floating, quivering, colors gorgeous -- reds, pinks, purples, and of course fuchsias. It's a little bit of paradise (and just the right amount of paradise too -- so proclaimeth the jyzer).

-- And a lovely J-moon it's been. Well, mostly. From start to finish I've been among the halt and the lame and I'm still slathering on the ointment for my weird rash -- or set of rashes really -- and the rashes are no longer going away anywhere near as quickly as before and in some places maybe not at all. But otherwise a most excellent twenty-two days (not counting the pre-"bonus" period, which I seem to recall was pretty good too).

But "lovely," you say, J-man? How so?

Well how's this for starters: a bank error of $1100 in our favor!

It seems the bank that holds our mortgage overestimated the amount of property tax we'd be paying (probably because they based their estimate on the average amount all the units in the building sold for). My share of the $1100 is one-third, $367, just about exactly one month's "rent" on 201 for me. And our monthly tax payments will also be going down by $45!

Not bad, eh wot? And it's also been another good month for scoping, and this means I've suddenly made up most of my losses regarding unexpected medical expenses and should now, and once again (what a roller coaster this year has been!), be able to scrape by for the rest of the summer without any serious problems. And the same's true for the rest of the year as well, just so long as scoping income holds steady at two-thirds or better of the ongoing average.

But money -- who cares! Once you know you have enough to get by on, you don't even want to think about it. (Because you're not the kind of guy who does that. Of course you're not!)

Z-wiff, I'm happy to say, appears to be back in

truly good health. Her cough started up again briefly but subsided just in time for her to fly off to the long-planned five-day weekend at a mountain gambling resort in the megastate two hours to the south with "the girls": in this case (she has several different sets of "the girls") her old grad-school pals Flor and Terri. And we have a thriving sex life again (even by pre-geezer standards) and we're getting out and around as a couple again in most of the usual onbeat as well as offbeat ways, whether making routine grocery-shopping rounds or boogalooing down the east-hill corridor or up The Ave in the Yuke.

While she was away I went over to the old home port two days in a row, by ferry the first time and by Z-mobile the second. Something a bit momentous about those journeys too. Not only did I begin cleaning out the storage unit in preparation for a shutdown (though I'm now thinking that's probably a year or more away) but I started tossing out the voluminous research material for those pre-Jyze Age novels I now accept I'll never (A) publish, (B) rewrite, or (C) write at all, depending on the case. What preposterously ambitious plans I once had!

-- And I'm still hoping to do at least some of my writing at Elgie's old desk, which I brought back in the Z-mobile. This is the narrow "student desk" Mother bought so he'd have a place to tend to his homework during overnight visits in their mutual MSM #2 years. It's only sixteen inches deep (by forty-four long) and so makes a perfect fit for the niche in the southeast corner of our "great room," beyond the big protruding bookcase on the east side of the "cockpit," in the hall-like space leading to our bedroom and large bathroom (the one with the tub). The next step will be to bring home one of my two computers at the hideaway and set it up there. And since the steno-translation/word-processing program will then be installed in two different places, and I'll have digital copies of all my writing on both machines, I'll no longer need to worry about losing any of that writing to fire. I'll have gone just about as far I can go to safeguard my writing setup as well as the writings themselves.

    Yeah, so I'm a happy camper overall, except I sure do wish I could feel at least a little more confident I'll have enough time to complete the major works. (I'd still like fifteen to twenty years. The actuaries are now saying -- in a recent article I came across -- a USAn male who's made it as far as I have will keep on going, on average, to eighty-two. How healthy he might be in the later years of that period is another matter, however, and likely even more so in my own idiosyncratic case. -- And by the way, those same actuaries predict Z-wiff and I will die within a few months of each other (this time assuming we hit the averages on the nose), just as we'd both prefer, though we'd rather it happen in, say, 2063. Not that there are any guarantees even on 2024 (when I'll turn eighty-two and she eighty-three), needless to say. But I say it anyway, and the same thing makes me say it that makes me churn out everything else in this paragraph: dread of death, pure and simple. But never mind that now, and for as long as possible. Let's get on with what's doing right here. And, okay, as far ahead as the eye can see, which to be sure is not all that far. And yet may be far enough.)

    -- Mildly powder-blue sky. Other than the birds awakening I see no signs of life this early in the a.m., in or around the building or for that matter the entire hood -- no lights shining anywhere so far as I can see (which, again, is not so far) -- but the morning papers have arrived with their usual thwacks (and then a slide on concrete and sometimes a second, echoic set of thwacks if the papers bang up against the back wall) (and sure, this newsprint fixation dates us; everybody else in the building and probably a majority in the city, the state, the country now prefers scoring their news from the internet, relying on network TV and news radio for any desired quick augmentation -- and fine for them, sez I, though I do think they miss out on a lot) -- and so I'll call it a night (now that it's day, sure!) and figure on popping back up again later. And

why not, since authentic scat fullness is still about
eleven hours off.

*   *

    -- Twenty-one minutes past said fullness and where
do I find myself? Not at any of the places I thought I
might be, all of which are outdoors. But not to
complain either, because it's my most favorite non-201/
225 indoor spot of them all in the present era (as of a
few months ago now): the new HQ coffee shop!

    Just as I left the house a long, deep, very loud
peal of thunder rattled the hilltop, lasting at least
twenty seconds. It seemed to be announcing this would
be no ordinary walk in. Or hobble in, I should correct
myself, since that's what "ordinary" still means these
days in the realm of movement by me on foot. But then
the hobble in proved ordinary after all. My unfurled
foldable black umbrella (which now goes everywhere I go
year-round, usually folded up in my bag) encountered
only scattered light sprinkles, not the downpour which
had seemed imminent. But even so, just a few such
sprinkles suffice to prevent alfresco jyzing.

    From this window table facing south I again have an
excellent view, between two large buildings, of the DC
castle atop its -- our -- hill. Today, though, just
above and behind it, fuzzy round dark-gray clouds are
scudding briskly by, charging northeast as if on an
urgent mission. And I have an even better view across
the street here of the kaleidoscopic mutable billboard
backside I mentioned last month. And what else? Many
soaring gulls. And another ancient iron fire tower I
hadn't noticed before, complementing the one over by Z-
geist. And lots and lots of orange and red brick, most
of it dirty, but all of it handsomely aged, composing
the walls of nearby buildings, the vast majority four to
six stories tall and about as boxy as buildings can ever
get. -- And the familiar reassuring trains passing down
below, freight and passenger, long-distance and short.
And buses rolling by just outside, including many headed
in from the hilltop and loaded with the usual mangy cast
of swing-shift workers (on rainy days I'm sometimes one

278

of them, and of course almost always one of them on the last bus going back up there). And trekking by, ballpark habitues with their telltale J-town caps and pennants, because this is another one of those days for "the boys of summer" to do their thing (but the first this year that's actually in summer).

The sidewalk just outside the window to my left is still rendered all but impassable by fat orange pylons and yellow construction tape. When the work's finished I imagine it'll be much harder to find an empty table in this joint -- of the dozen or so tables currently present -- at half past four in the afternoon.

As it happens today I'm just passing through the area myself. I have work to pick up downtown (it's another videotape dep, "probably an all-day affair," Naomi warned in her phone message, and "it's that same boring case I just hate," bringing several possible candidates to mind, but she didn't specify further) and I have checks to deposit and an ointment prescription to fill and I'm still moving just as slowly and pathetically as ever because of the Achilles flare-up.

On Sunday Naomi and kids leave for family visits in the megastate (two different smaller cities in the northern half) and I move into their house for a week to watch over the premises and keep Missy company. In August I'll be doing the same thing again, twice, a week at the beginning and another at the end of the month. But neither, as I recall, will be at scat-moon time. Too bad, because it's very comfortable there, especially on the back patio -- which is literally "in the shade of the old apple tree" -- and thus ideal for some laid-back elder-by-his-lonesome jyze musing (as would be only appropriate as I make ready to cross over into my own sixty-fourth year at the end of that month).

Boisterous low-flying dark round clouds still rolling by much like huge tumbleweeds just above the DC castle, I see, but now they appear to be dragging patches of blue behind them. The rain, at least in nearby areas, seems to be at an end. (A longtime favorite soul/funk singer pops up on the sound system

here, some cuts from the "Coffee and Cigarettes" album I
listened to almost obsessively way back in Mezzu days.)
     -- And it's been a month of celebrations. The
three best: Mama E turned ninety, Lwazi turned two, and
I turned into a pumpkin, I guess I can say, on Father's
Day. No word from Elgie, my only surviving fatherly
creation in DNA terms so far as I know; but Betty and
Kat came through, along with Z-wiff, treating me to a
Father's Day dinner at the retro fifties café (which is
now under new management, and both meatloaf and roast
turkey, my two longtime favorite entrees, have vanished
from the menu; but at least the funky retro decor,
including the crucial golden-oldies jukebox, is still in
place). Kat showed off the A-plus "Depression and
Teens" paper Z-wiff and I helped her with. She
mischievously observed (forewarning: "I know you won't
like this, but here goes anyway"), "Even your nose hairs
are turning gray, Glen." But she's still in a
heightened palsy-walsy phase with me, and with Z too,
making for a time we're both relishing.
     (Reminding me: a week earlier, while Z was
cavorting in the gambling mecca, I joined Betty and Kat
for dinner at their place. Kat was showing me her new
computer setup and how she can "find out anything I
want" by googling. Suddenly she posed this question:
"Hey, that old girlfriend of yours who looked sort of
like me, what was her name again? You know, the one
who's in the movies." I told her, she googled the name,
and out scrolled twelve pages of Lady V cites. One of
these was called "Autobiography" and we checked it out,
finding an updated version, as it turned out, of the bio
the lady herself sent me back in the mid eighties. One
change I noticed that's not merely an update, however:
the kindly former boyfriend in MSM #2 whom she used to
credit with helping to launch her career in moviemaking
-- I'm pretty sure she was referring to me -- had been
edited out. -- And now at the retro cafe a week later
Kat slipped me a downloaded copy of the current bio.
-- And I hesitate to show it to Z. Should I? It would
probably just stir up trouble. So then instead risk

another charge of being secretive? -- It seems I've
once again worked myself into a bit of a moral quandary
here. -- But my first impulse is to let it all slide
quietly back into the mists. Recognizing, of course,
Kat might not permit that to happen.)

      Mama E has been in unusually chipper form. On her
birthday she let us take her to the bookstore arcade
again and then on a ride along the nearby lakeshore --
and for the first time ever during her J-town stay she
said she wanted us to keep driving; she didn't want to
go home! (In the end we elaborately hand-decorated the
"90!" scrapbook for her containing all the
congratulatory cards and letters and photos which,
thanks to Z's group letter, arrived in the mail. In
fact I'm still working on it -- to make the cards more
accessible to Mama E -- when I have a chance.)

      Lwazi's party was held outdoors at a park in a
rapidly gentrifying part of eastern east hill on a
gorgeous spring Saturday afternoon. (His father, David,
attended a nearby elementary school when it was
virtually all-Afrusan.) Lwazi was a bundle of energy,
cute and fun and affectionate even when the scary old
Cawk godpoppa puffed up his cheeks with orange slices.
The sad news is that it looks more and more likely
Lwazi and family will soon be moving to the megastate
so Stacy can be near her soon-to-be-octogenarian mother.

      (That same soul/funk CD is still playing. "Tramp"
now. -- And even in my Mezzu years I would've said this
man was a good candidate for the short list of vocalists
who would more or less permanently be fusing synapses in
the culture's evolving musical memory. And here I'm
being reminded just what that means. -- He whose "Dock
of the Bay" (playing now!) rose to iconic stature in MSM
#2 during my years there, even lending its name to the
first underground newspaper I worked for (extremely
briefly). He whose plane crashed, killing him, into the
lake along the shores of which I played as an infant, a
couple of miles from the hospital where I was born.)

      -- And now a longhair guy strolls by outside, I
have to double-check to be sure it's not brother Rob and

[Scat Jyze : Blue Rooster]

I'm already up and headed for the door when I do it.
But it's not. (And lookie there! Late sunlight all but
igniting the hillside to the east and I turn to see a
big nasty near-black storm front suddenly looming like a
massive granite wall above the old redbrick buildings to
the west! And the sun making an end run around it!)

     If I had the money to do so I'd come here every
day. How fine it would be to have a regular haunt
again! But nope, no hope on that one. Whatever extra
coins I can scrape up must go to feed my main habit:
books and magazines and quarterlies. And that's how I
want it to be! -- And this way my once-in-a-scat-moon
jyzeday outings take on a little extra meaning (since
only on these outings do I sit in cafes for lengthy
spells anymore), and if I'm lucky that extra meaning
will jazz up the -- jyze! Yes! Right on!

                    *   *

     -- Now about ten hours later and the new peg is:
it's Z's conception day. (I won't try to explain again
how we know this; it's laid out at length in, as I
recall, TJM.) I left a C-day card on her pillow; she
left a drawing of a bouquet of heart-blossomed cut
flowers here on my green living-room armchair (the one
with the shade of a floor lamp right now suspended, at
the end of an elbowed swing-arm, a few inches above my
head, shedding a warm light downward -- more than
anyhing else it's this lamp and the jazz station that
get me through the deeper parts of the night -- this
night and most every night).

     A few feet to my right, through the balcony
doorway, squats the wooden deck chair where this entry
launched just about exactly twenty-four hours ago. That
door's open at the moment, but just a crack; it's a lot
chillier out there tonight.

     And atop the low bookcase to the left of the door,
the "When I'm 64" Narihara bamboo now boasts seventeen
dangling tags, no two alike in size or content or
imagery: an increasingly delicious sight for me. (And
of course I hope it's the same for Z-wiff. A lot of
love and devotion -- not to mention time -- is going

into making this tree, and also the one in her office,
sprout a new tag each week, and in weeks when the 15th
of the month falls, two new tags.)
     News of the world this month? "Deep Throat" from
the Watergate era is finally outed (and he did the
outing himself). To many people's surprise he's an FBI
insider whose basic motive back then was a grudge
against the villainous president in office at that time
for passing him over in choosing a successor to the
odious previous FBI director. This insider guy was
himself deeply implicated in some of the worst outrages
of the era, including the infamous COINTELPRO with its
smear tactics against civil-rights and antiwar groups.
Not a good guy at all, but his act of petty revenge in
'73 and '74 inadvertently had some very good effects.
Not until roughly a decade later did the bad guys
succeed in undoing most of them.
     Also: a new constitution for the European Union is
rejected by voters in two countries (France, Holland)
and suddenly the Union itself, which many people
(including me) have been hoping would eventually serve
as a strong counterweight to the U.S. in a multipolar
world, is in trouble. At the same time another
potential candidate for a counterweight role, China,
neglected for a spell by neocon warhawks focusing on the
Middle East, is again increasingly being portrayed by
them as a dangerous rival (with a slick far-coast
monthly mag in its latest issue running a particularly
disgusting "Yellow Peril" cover for a breathtakingly
foolish China-bashing story inside).
     And I read the excellent "The Long Emergency." If
the author's anywhere close to right, things will start
getting nasty owing to depletion of oil reserves even
sooner than I'd been thinking. (Some, including this
author, are saying we're at the "Peak Oil" turning point
right now. Oil prices are at an all-time high -- just
short of sixty dollars a barrel -- and rising rapidly.)
     -- And a paragraph like that poses a familiar
dilemma as this jyze entry nears its end: what can
follow it that won't make for a pathetic anticlimax?

[Scat Jyze : Blue Rooster]

35

    At 1:35 a.m. when I stepped off the bus at the
usual stop I saw the full moon surprisingly low on the
horizon, seeming to be hanging in the nearby trees.
From my angle a glowing clamshell button appeared to be
affixing the crowns of two of the trees to the sky at
their widest point where they overlapped, sort of like a
patterned black velvet vest on an extremely busty woman.
Pop that button, it seemed, and the whole sky would come
tumbling down. -- This as I looked straight south, with
city lights twinkling peripherally in the valleys far
below on both sides down the corridor formed by the
east-west street.
    Now it's four a.m. and that happens to be the exact
time of this month's scat moon. Right on the clamshell
button. So sez Chicken Little.
    And speaking of buttons, I've arrayed some real
ones here, pin-on type, that I bought today at the ORB.
One's an enamel called "Full Moon/Mauve." Now I need to
figure out how best to add the words "Scat Jyze" to its
surface. -- Another's the famous side-profile portrait
of the greatest of all jazz pianist/composers and I'm
planning to send it to Ken D., who loves the man's music
(as do I!); and two are enamel typewriters with the
words "Write Hard, Die Free" emblazoned across the top
(and between the "Hard" and the "Die" a skull and
crossbones, with a pencil and a fountain pen serving as
the bones). After somehow changing "Write" to "Jyze"
and "Die" to "Live" and the fountain pen to a J-stick,
I'll give one of these pins to brother Rob and keep the
other for talismanic personal use.

[Scat Jyze : Blue Rooster]

     What extravagance! Does this mean I'm suddenly
rolling in dough? Hardly. But August's already
covered. If I can make a few bucks in the next ten days
before Naomi starts her month's vacation, September
should be good as well.
     -- And so the months tumble by. Or scrape by. Or
fly by. Whatever kind of motion the jyze gods happen to
decree.
     And here I sit in my old green short-sleeve henley
and the way-too-big black hemp boxer shorts (complete
with gaping buttonless fly) which Z-wiff gave me last
year. It's summer! But it's a shade too chilly to be
going at it out on the balcony, much as I'd like to be
doing just that. So it's back to the old green
armchair, which, I hasten to add, is still a very fine
place to be anytime.
     And from now on it appears I'll have to make do
with an hour less of radio jazz after I arrive home at
night. For some unfathomable reason -- never explained
on the air so far as I know -- the jazz station's
suddenly decided to start its weekday-morning national-
public-radio news coverage at three a.m. instead of the
longstanding four a.m. This means I shut the radio off
an hour earlier than I'm accustomed to (for the past
eleven years!) and sit here in silence for that time.
Reading, usually. (Fortunately on weekend nights,
Friday and Saturday, the jazz will still be playing
until five a.m.)
     Other personal news of import: yesterday, under
buffoonish circumstances, I reinjured my right Achilles
tendon yet one more time. Yes, I'm back on the hobble
again. Back where a blockhead is a blockhead. And it
hurts! And it's farcical and pathetic! And more than
anything else it's just plain lame!
     Not yesterday for the reinjury, actually, except by
NUT reckoning; rather Tuesday. That's when I took an
awkward step into the gutter after hopping off the bus
at the usual hilltop stop, winding up on my hands and
knees in the muddy strip between curb and sidewalk. And
also winding up, of course, right back on the I.L., the

injured list, and this just as I was about to declare my strained (frayed?) Achilles one hundred percent healed.

And why was I in such a hurry that I would hop so awkwardly? Because I was late to see Doc L. And I was late because I'd hoofed it all the way across the high bridge when I realized I'd forgotten something important back home. And so I grabbed a bus which conveniently happened by going in the opposite direction, back up the hill. And that was the bus I soon hopped awkwardly off of.

What I'd forgotten was to don underwear. (Not the black shorts I'm wearing now, heaven forbid; rather one of the two other pairs of underwear I own, the flyless olive (A) and beige (B) hemp ones.) See, Doc L always asks me to pull down my pants so he can inspect the rashy areas on my thighs and calves and behind my knees, and at least one other observer always accompanies him on his rounds and the observers are always (so far) female. Under such conditions it would not be kosher to obey the doc's request and reveal a shocking absence of "unners" (my normal absence of same, I should note). (And if the doc wants to explore further, as he's actually done only the first time, he asks the observers to step out, or at least he did that once.)

I'd neglected to don "unners" (a term I picked up years ago from Z) because I was having an inspired afternoon -- eureka after eureka after eureka. Very distracting. But for me the best excuse imaginable.

(The rash, meanwhile, continues to improve but very, very slowly. This is par for the course, says Doc L, although he's also told me lichen planus has no established course. So I guess when he says "par" he must mean something more like "not an extreme outlier." But in any case he seems satisfied and so I am too. Next appointment, two months from day after tomorrow. During the interim I'll still be applying the same two ointments twice a day on my legs and cutting back to once a day on my forearms, which have been healing faster.)

(And by the way, I still made it to the appointment

on time. Broke down and drove. And did so not knowing
whether Z would be needing the car that evening -- it's
her car, after all. I called her from the doc's office
and it turned out she didn't need it, luckily for me,
because I also had a heavy worknight ahead and was due
to visit Vic at seven for our usual Tuesday night cheap-
scotchathon, though we wound up cutting that short. And
my right foot was throbbing painfully the whole time.
Wound up doing the alternating ice/heat thing with it
when I arrived home. Some night it was!)

Meanwhile Betty and Kat are off touring Guatemala.
Day after tomorrow we pick them up at the airport. No
word yet on how the trip's going. But Z and I enjoyed
helping them prepare for it and then dropping them off
at the airport. And a few days before that Kat stayed
overnight with us and she and I wound up talking for
three and a half hours straight -- until five a.m.! --
while Z slept.

And the next day Z called to let me know her
friend Cassie B. (who's in the recycling section of the
division or unit of the department or however that's
configured) had just won the state lotto. And not just
some small win either. Two-point-six million
smackeroos! Cassie from MSM #2 whose husband Nash died
last year. (She claims -- quite seriously, it seems --
his guidance from Beyond (with a cap on "beyond" for
sure where the seriously Christian Cassie's concerned)
enabled her to choose the winning number.)

So you never know. (But once in a while you almost
know. For instance, I almost know Cassie will soon quit
her job, even though she insists she won't.)

Oh it's been a fine month. Fascinating too. All
the usual, the gamut, the horror, the wonder, the
sublime indifference out beyond the rest of it. "The
Magical Hummingbirds of The Ettore Condo." But I'll
have to wait until later to go into any of that, and
even then only as superficial scratching. Now the clock
flashes double zeroes and I need to move into the day's-
end regimen. (Even though this is quarterly budget week
at work for Z, she's taking the day off to shop at the

south-end discount supermart and then to visit Mama E by
herself so we'll have Sunday afternoon free to picnic
with Olwen and Trent. And since she doesn't need to get
up for work she might be a little friskier than usual in
there on a weeknight -- or then again she might sleep in
-- but in either case the G-hub had best not dally.)
*   *

     -- About thirteen hours later. Nabbed me a bench
beneath the pergola in the HQ triangle. Just finished
my first run-through on tonight's job, 137 pages of
highly technical expert depositions -- two of them -- in
an environmental suit involving a tire fire at a city
dump. It's not too likely, but the Z-woman herself
could be called as a witness in a case like this. It
happens to involve a contract which she oversees.

     And another example of a scoping job with real-
world ties: today's headlines reveal a link between this
month's subway bombings in England that killed dozens
(and an attempted second round fizzled just last night
when the bombs inexplicably failed to detonate) and
one of the Al Qaeda cases that came before the grand
jury here in J-town a few years ago. It appears the
mastermind of the England bombings may have been one of
the Al Qaeda "scouts" who back then checked out a ranch
in the wilds of the next state to our south as a
possible training base for terrorists, and then resided
for several months at a mosque over on the east side of
the next hill to our north (Z-wiff and I sometimes drive
by the site -- the mosque itself has long since been
shut down -- after making a pickup at her naturopath's
home, usually on Sunday evenings).

     And while noting the news, I might as well mention
this: a conservative-heartland Eurusan dude has just
been selected as the nominee for the open Supreme Court
seat. The battle over his confirmation will no doubt
take lots of heat off a developing scandal at the White
House involving the neocon cabal's nastiest and most
successful political strategist and the administration's
attacks on inside dissenters during the run-up to our
invasion and occupation of Iraq (which occupation

continues, to be sure, and is proving to be even more disastrous for both the U.S. and Iraq itself than just about everyone, except for the U.S. right wing and its Iraqi stooges, had already predicted back during that same run-up).

And it appears the plan to build a new Jyze City monorail is about to collapse. Have I ever mentioned this plan before? Even if not, I won't try to describe what's involved; it's way too complicated. The collapse is a shame, though, I think. And it means the hideously ugly "sinking ship" parking garage I'm looking at right now just across the street from the hideaway building's side entrance may not be coming down after all. A monorail station was supposed to go on that site.

(But plenty of changes are still in store for the HQ, including several highrise condos soon to be built and a new car barn for the waterfront streetcar. All this is part of the developers' push, abetted by the mayor, to raise height limits and boost population density throughout the city. Another shame, I'd say, and a big mistake which will quickly reveal itself as such when energy costs start skyrocketing as we pass Peak Oil (if we haven't already -- because they're skyrocketing now). -- But at that point, or not long after, our whole way of life will be seen as a colossal mistake, and so who'll give a damn about a few more highrises standing empty?).

-- And the tour groups keep shuttling around the triangle before heading down to the underground. For them it's peak season. The century-old six-story redbrick building just the other side of the "sinking ship," I recently learned, was headquarters for our local aerospace/defense colossus during World War II. Overheard one of the tour guides talking about it.

Lovely evening, yes it is. And the foot's better today, the "bad pin," as someone referred to it as I pathetically limped by in the upper AQ (my gait closely resembling, at least as I saw it in window reflections, that of the clubfooted medical student in "Of Human Bondage"). "Got you a bad pin, eh?" (Also got me a new

little suspicious mole growing on my nose, right next to
my right eye; I can actually see it in blurry form now
as I write. Just one more of many suspicious body
developments, though; and any one of them could, of
course, at any time take me down for good.)

     -- A rabidly conservative congressman from the
mountain state where Lady U and I met (in my city No. 11
lifetime) has said recently, just in the past few days,
that if the "Muslim terrorists" keep coming after us we
should "take out Mecca" with a nuke. These are insane
times, all right. Yet again! -- Nor did this
congressman, nor do any of the other warhawks, say
anything about the effects that our "going after" Islam
for the past hundred years (or in truth more like the
past thousand years) are having on their "coming after
us" in recent times. And not that we're failing to "go
after them" ourselves right now, no, and what's more
with, of course, massively "asymmetrical" power, as it's
called, "shock and awe" and the full nine circles of
hell. But we have a God-given right to do this, as all
good Christians know, not to mention a holy duty.)

     -- But as I was saying, lovely evening. And I mean
it! Odd truth is I'm still a hopeful kind of guy.
Optimist of the will. Hey, we can beat this global-
broiling thing! If everybody pulled together I bet we
could hold world casualties under five billion!

     -- The barbecue joint over there on the far side of
the intersection, I've recently added it to my worknight
cheap-eats circuit. In the current era I eat out only
once a week on a weeknight; this joint is now one of the
certified options. Large pulled-pork sandwich, no
sauce, six bucks. It's a lot to pay, relatively, for
me, but worth it. And that's the option I'll be
exercising tonight in about twenty minutes.

     The usual weeknight mix out here: drunks, druggies,
drifters, crazies. Dubious Cawk dude trying to peddle a
hand-carved walking stick he probably just snatched from
a tottering elder with a bad pin -- mugged him or her in
an alley maybe. (Or maybe not, right. Maybe he really
did carve it himself as he said. But I didn't want to

inquire too closely, for instance by asking to see his whittling knife.) (We are talking "skid row" here, the original, the source of the term itself, as seven or eight different tour groups have learned, if they didn't already know, within my earshot in the past hour. At this point I could almost do the spiel myself. -- And add a few colorful new historical factoids of my own.)

And otherwise what kind of month has it been? Why, most excellent! It included a one-week stay at Naomi's house on north hill during which Missy's sixteenth birthday happened to fall (Z-wiff and I bought her a bag of fancy vet-approved dog treats) (Missy was born just a few months after Naomi and Larry's wedding). -- And we hit several summer festivals this year, including Bon Odori, the AQ fest, the street fair out in Z's old hood (where we bought a handsome African fish banner to serve as a cover for our drawerless gray rolling cabinet, which we've now moved into our bedroom to make way for Elgie's desk in the passageway to the big bathroom). On the Fourth we drove down to the electronics megastore to buy a narrow-based flat-screen monitor so that I'd be able to fit my keyboard along with the monitor on that same desktop; otherwise we stayed home that day. Saw a couple of movies during the month and one wasn't half bad: "Saving Face," a romantic comedy about Asiusan lesbians which had me thinking a lot about Vic and Jean's respective family homes and hoods back in MSM #2.

For me, good reading. I was much moved by a number of tributes in various publications to the recently deceased poet Thom G. (whom I met during alt-newspaper days in that same MSM #2). A book called "Counterculture Through the Ages" kept me interested (though I couldn't buy its major innovative move: postulating the Enlightenment and the development of modern science as instances of countercultural change -- but then the authors are a couple of, yes, MSM #2 techies and libertarians, it appears, so you can't be too surprised by it).

-- And end-page time has arrived: onward to the pulled pork!

        [Scat Jyze : Blue Rooster]

                       36

     Got a leaky J-stick here. Leaky resolution too.
But it's scat-moon night and here I am back in jyze
action.
     Maybe I won't keep this scat thing going, though.
For the past hour or so I sat in the Z-mobile mulling
the matter. Nor is this the first time for such
mulling. Maybe just finish out this year and that'll be
it.
     And what about the big stack of blank fuzzies in
the hideaway, enough to last me a good part of the long
haul to Jyzer G Heavenly Year II? Not even that major
investment, it seems, can keep me committed.
     The preference now, as I'm feeling it anyway -- and
feeling it strongly -- is to give my all to upgrading
the big stacks of work I've already completed in draft
form of one kind or another -- but mostly jyze or urjyze
or protojyze -- or at least the portions of those that
show the most promise.
     -- This going down outdoors at the downtown plaza.
Friday evening about eleven p.m., warm August night,
lots of folks still out and about. Wall of Water
fountain thundering away. A guy sleeping it off on the
bench next to mine, his head resting on a spiffy new
backpack (and he's wearing a tan knit cap pulled down to
cover his eyes and seems unusually trusting for a park-
bench sleeper).
     Arrayed in a circle around us like a miniature
Stonehenge (JRX), an exhibition of decorated wooden
doors, maybe thirty in all, each on a separate stand.
"Art Doors." I've tried my hand at a few of 'em myself

                      292

over the years, including the extremely well received
"Calvin & Lenore U. 1983 Visit Memorial Door." A photo
of it stands on a half-hidden bookshelf at the hideaway.

I stopped to drain some cash from the bank machine
that stands midway between the two former scope
buildings on the very high road. Lucked out on a street
parking place only a block away on a Friday night in the
heart of downtown J. City. Then sat there -- couldn't
move. Tried to think of an inspiring place to do the
scat thing. This is the best I could come up with. Two
blocks due north of the bank machine.

I'm wearing my black jeans so I must've been out
somewhere dressy earlier tonight. And was, yes. Holly
R. threw a farewell dinner for Wei and Alison, whose
mid-ocean move is scheduled for next week. Just the
five of us, and then Wes P. showed up late after getting
lost. Poor Wes, much thinner now and sadly halting in
his speech, presumably because of the drugs he takes to
counter a heart problem. As Z observed afterward, "The
two of you always seem to hit it off so well." True,
and I don't really know why. (But think of all the
friends you might have had in this life and the few with
whom things have actually worked out.)

Last Sunday was the big farewell party for W&A,
held at their place. Z and I served as the cleanup crew
(this in return for a plumbing repair Wei did a week
earlier on our kitchen sink with its malfunctioning --
again! -- hose). For close to three hours straight I
washed dishes in W&A's kitchen (and had an amusing
conversation for much of that time with a Japusan woman
from MSM #1, as it happens, named, of all things, Dani
-- though in her case the last name does not start with
a U and the Dani itself is a simplified form, and at the
same time one could say a corruption, of her real given
name, Dawnae -- and she's a big fan of Japanese lit and
that's why we had plenty to talk about).

The view from Holly's deck of the scat moon rising
above the eastern mountains an hour after sunset, framed
by large nearby evergreens and the house-and-tree-
studded, steeply canted hillscape a few blocks away --

if jyze included photos, one a neighbor of Holly's took
of all six of us with that view in the background would
be among them for sure.

Only yesterday did I return from my second weeklong
stint of Missy-sitting at Naomi's. Again it was peach
week at the hilltop market a few blocks from her house,
just as during my stay last year. Every single night
a peach shortcake and every single morning peach-slice-
studded cornflakes. The best-tasting peaches I've ever
come across anywhere. -- And at the end of next week I
go back to north hill for my third and last stay there,
at least for this year (barring another emergency).

So I'm basically on vacation this month. More than
five weeks of it in total with only a couple of very
small back-order jobs to tend to so far, no more than
three hours' work for the two combined, corrections
included. Of course more back orders could pop up, but
that's unlikely. This is prime time for cranking out a
big chunk of my own work. And I'm going at it as hard
as I can. Like the button says but with the sentences
reversed as I prefer: "Live free. Jyze hard."

Also I'm reading a fair amount. The Lawrence J.
bio and then another go-round with his "Destiny Drive."
It's still impressive, or maybe I should say it's back
to being impressive (but not all the way back to where
it once was for me, which was at or near the top of the
USAn fiction stack). The man himself, though, is
haunting me. "Revise, revise, revise!" Also his
excruciating life. Poor Adele W. (And I wonder: did
she ever tell him exactly why it was she transferred to
Mezzu? Which is to inquire: did Lawrence J. know one of
his own students preceded him with Adele? The bio does
not answer that question. -- But the jyzer knows who
the predecessor was, yes he does, because he was it.)
(Dish, dish!)

-- And I've finally established a fully functioning
computer setup at home. It replicates the hideaway
setup down to the last file -- redundancy to the max! --
and so I'm highly pleased. At last I can breathe easy.
If one of those computers fails, there's still another

one left in the world running the same program. (And
most likely not many more than one. The program was
already antiquated ten years ago.)

(And we've mounted large molas on all bedroom and
bathroom doors, so four in all -- not including the one
which remains on the hideaway wall. And Z-wiff's
bathroom shelves are up. Now I move on to hanging the
paintings and framed art cards of the altered kind, and
when that's done we've agreed we'll finally consider
ourselves fully "settled in" at Ettore Condo Unit 201.)

(But the wonderful balcony hardy fuchsias are
proving to be less hardy than expected. Four of the
seven are struggling to survive. Possible causes are
numerous but Z suspects too much direct sun exposure is
the main one and so the other day she brought home three
large Chinese paper parasols -- quite handsome in their
own right -- and set them up over the worst-hit plants.
It's too early to know if the parasols will perform as
hoped but I do like having them out there -- each panel
on each parasol bearing a large stylish black ideogram
on papyrus-like paper, the parasol handles and spokes
made of bamboo, blossom-laden fuchsia limbs protruding
around the edges and the occasional hummingbird zipping
in or out or hovering nearby, issuing little clicks --
squirrel-like almost -- as it decides which dazzlingly
furbished nectar pot to quaff next.)

Buses rolling up here at the plaza. Tourists
strolling by and admiring the "Art Doors" and casting
wary eyes at the jyzer and the next-bench sleeper.
Other shadowy characters slipping this way and that
beneath the trees. Leaves rustling just overhead and a
few early fallen ones skittering restlessly underfoot.

-- And financially I'm right back to just scraping
by these days. That extra week Naomi decided to work
yielded not a single new job order. Excluding what I'm
committed to pay for rent and mortgage and other monthly
bills, I'll be living on about seventy bucks a week
between now and September 15 (and paying mostly for
groceries with that). And I'll have only three full
workweeks in September to make enough to pay bills

[Scat Jyze : Blue Rooster]

falling due at the end of the month. Chances are I'll
be forced to ask Z to resume the accelerated loan-
repayment schedule, $200 a month instead of $100.
     And health? The foot's no better and neither are
any of the other ailments. Everything seems to be
plateauing, which is to say possibly turning chronic.
And so I'm telling myself: well, this is what aging's
all about. You surprised or something? One part gives
out and you're forced to use other parts in new ways, or
overuse them in old ways, or not use them at all for
fear of aggravating other injuries, and before too long
those other parts start giving out too. It's a slow-
moving, and in more respects than one, cascade.
Presumably I'm only in the very early stages but the
general picture of how it's going to go is all too clear
(and this is at best -- that is, if there are no short
circuits leading to massive or total malfunctioning of
larger systems or the whole organism).
     But as of today I'm feeling -- fine. I'm charged
with new energy. At this stage of the cascade I'm still
able to follow my old regimen, the same kind of daily
schedule I've been on since moving back to J-town (ten
years ago in January, approximately; that's when the
anniversary of renting the hideaway comes up). I can
even walk limp-free if I don't try to go too fast
(though it's not exactly the same gait as before, and
this new way of carrying myself seems to be stressing
different parts of my feet and slowly rearranging some
of the bones and tendons down there and possibly in my
knees and hips as well and thus promising other new
developments of possible orthopedic concern).
     During this vacation month I've been making a big
effort to work out three times weekly at the WOC and to
treat my dysfunctional Achilles to, and with (in another
sense of "treat"), an hour of jacuzzi whirlpooling after
each workout. The hope is I'll be able to walk normally
by the time I start back into a regular work schedule
around September 7th. And even if that hope fails to
realize itself, maybe I'll have established a strong
enough workout rhythm to be able to keep up the thrice-

weekly sessions and eventually they'll do the trick or
at least some part of it.

    -- And here's what I'm thinking now. I'm four days
away from my lunar birthday and then another seven until
the solar. Why not finish up this entry on one of those
birthdays, or maybe on both, and then I'll have several
weeks before the next full moon to decide whether I want
to continue with scat jyze. My hunch is I'll go with
doing what our neo-crusader high-USAn-muckety-muck ought
to do in Iraq right now: declare victory and withdraw.
I think maybe I'm all jyzed out. (Well no, not really.
But I want to conserve such writing energies as remain
for the more important task of completing that part of
the existing work which merits it.)

    -- Could be this scat jyze has just been my way of
winding down from the big blowouts of "Jyze Millennium"
and "Heavenly Year." And now I want to go back and
start whipping those two unwieldy word masses into some
kind of readable shape -- the best I can come up with.
Better those as a legacy than more scat.

    That's the hunch. But we'll see.

37

    Raise the glass of good stuff high.
    Why? Two reasons.
    First, it's my birthday, the lunar version.
    Second, and a whole lot more important, it's the
last entry of this volume and the end of "Scat Jyze."
And it's also the end of the entirety of "The Jyze Age,"
meaning the series of eight annals, this one included.

    Holy carumba, what's happened here? I mean, dude,
isn't this a bit abrupt? Don't you at least want to

throw in a caveat or two and think things through later when you're a little calmer?

But no, I'm calm right now. The jyzer is here to take a last bow, a victory lap, and then that's it. Lights out.

But I still feel I owe the trusting reader an explanation, to the extent I'm capable of giving one. And I should attempt to tie up some of the looser of the many loose jyze strings. And maybe I can even come up with a few final comments on the "Jyze Age" project as a whole as well as this "Scat Jyze" annal of most recent vintage, or tri-annal really.

The last-named first. The astute reader (of course I'm hoping there will be readers and at least a few will have gotten this far) will observe I'm suddenly capitalizing and enclosing in quotes the term "Scat Jyze." And I'm doing that because in the past few days it's become clear to me that the three volumes of (lowercase) scat jyze, two of which, including this one right here, are only about half full, will make an at least minimally shapely and minimally appropriate (not to say inspired!) single final volume for the series. Annal 8. A kind of extended afterword or epilogue or coda but with a few new twists. Title: "Scat Jyze."

It's especially appropriate because "Annals of The Jyze Age" as a whole is beholden to the Chinese lunar calendar not only as a principle of organization but as a prime source of inspiration. And as I've come to realize in these same four days, jyze is now in the twelfth and final year of what can be seen as a full "Great Year" cycle. Next year we're back to the Year of the Dog -- the year in which jyze first "burst into being." And I like the symmetry -- the symbolism -- the shapeliness of stopping with the twelve-animal zodiac cycle complete. It just might be that this "Great Year" period is what a Jyze Age is.

(And where is this last entry going down? In the green armchair in the living-area "cockpit" of Ettore Condo Unit 201. As is only right. With the jazz station on. At about half past two in the morning.

[Scat Jyze : Blue Rooster]

With the Z-wiff asleep in the next room and the four-
days-past-scat lunar-birthday moon partially visible
through the picture window to my right and the branches
of the laurels to the southwest at the corner of the
Ettore lot -- and also through tag-hung branches of the
Narihara bamboo jauntily riding the top of the case for
oversize books located just beneath the picture window.)
     But Jyzemaster, sir, why not keep going with the
scat jyze? Why not do that for another whole Great Year
cycle? Wasn't it the plan to keep churning out this
scat jyze all the way to the bitter end? Maybe even,
under the greatest imaginable "realistic" dream of
longevity, for three more Great Years after that second
one, or almost three, until the advent of Heavenly Year
II, which is to say 2062, the year the Jyzemaster hits
age 120?
     Well, yes, that was the plan and that was the
dream. But let's get really, and not just "really" with
scare quotes, real here. -- And that's exactly what I
think happened: I got real here. Real fast. Real
suddenly.
     It's not enough to say I noticed the jyze was
starting to sound a little dutiful at times, though I
did notice that. The question is, why was it becoming
that way?
     And the answer. These injuries and illnesses. I
guess I've realized at some level I don't want to be
chronicling my own slow demise. "Going down slow." It
sounds way too much like whining and self-pity, such
chronicling, that's what. (As in "This Wild Darkness"
even, let's squarely face it.) I'd much rather go out
at the top of my game. Or near it. And no boasting
here, but that's where I am now. Or so I'd like to
think. And any objectors can just go hang. Because I'm
not saying my game's the greatest game on earth. I'm
just saying it's about as good as it's going to get for
me and from here on in I can't promise anything. And
somehow I failed to realize the ramifications of all
this before now.
     But whatever remains of what game I've got I'd like

to apply to the retrospective, the existing
accumulation, shaping it up, yes.
     -- And in addition to this extended array of
abstract justification, our "Fookin' Fogeys" action
clock that's been faithfully ticking away atop the big
white cabinet by the kitchen ever since we moved into
this building (or almost that long, and in all three
units we've lived in), it suddenly started losing time.
The second hand started limping and hobbling in a kind
of parody of what I'm doing myself these days. It gave
me a helluva start. I still can't look at it without
feeling a pain that goes all the way down, to the very
bottom zodiac animal on which all the others piggyback
(and it's not a turtle and it's not a pig either; it's
the big black steed of J-slinger mammalian essence).
-- And changing the battery for "Fookin' Fogeys" doesn't
help, no. The whole dang apparatus is a goner.
                            *
     -- Back. Celebratory drink refreshed. Time for
the attempt at tying up whatever loose jyze strings I
can.
     But first mention this. For me the writing began
(in urjyze form, what I back then was soon calling
"chrons") along about age twenty. If the actuarial
tables hold true, about twenty years remain to me now.
And again I like the shapeliness. A twenty-year blank
at the beginning and another at the end, my first
childhood and my second childhood (or just as apt, I
hope, my first wisdom and my late wisdom, and both
wisdoms such as they are or were and no more, period).
     That said. Now. Jyze strings.
     The theory first. And it's simple. We like to
know how it all comes out. But we don't need to know
all of it, strictly speaking, and if we do know all of
it, or almost all, we feel it's too pat. It's
disrespectful of the mystery and also of the nature of
mortality and therefore of nature itself.
     Jyze string theory, that's what this is.
     So I still say I'm a lucky guy. I still say I've
stumbled upon a heckuva woman with whom to journey to

the end of my years. (She left me a fine lunar-birthday
card; it basically says she feels the same way about me
as I feel about her -- yay! -- and she wants us to go
even deeper, because she realizes she's maybe been
confounding "long" with "deep," and she wonders if I
have too. And I like it very much that she's always
questing in this loving way and never willing to settle
for mere security or certainty or the illusion thereof.)

   And we have a good place where we can end our years
in as fine a fashion as can be imagined, at least by me,
all realities considered (to the extent such
consideration is even possible). "Our condo." We're
almost settled in. We're almost ready for a long (to
the extent it is long) ride into the sunset. And a
feisty ride it'll be, yeah, much of it; I don't doubt
that at all.

   Financially we should be secure enough, thanks
mostly to Z-wiff's city pension and to Social Security
-- may the program carry on with full vigor despite all
current and future egregious right-wing attempts to do
it in.

   -- And then there's the world. Look out. Peak
Oil, the crisis: it's even becoming a popular topic
(cover of this week's far-coast paper's Sunday
magazine). And Peak Oil or not, climate upending. All
the other looming ecocatastrophes. Look out again!
-- But as they're rising, we'll be fading, Z and I,
along with the rest of our cohort. And in our
increasingly vulnerable senescence one or more of these
catastrophes might just be what does us in, the two of
us, individually or together, the coups de grace, and
possibly a little earlier than would otherwise have been
the case if, say, industrialization and modernization
had been a bit better managed. (Yeah, and if Water
Horses could fly.) (But of course we could also have a
major earthquake and disappear into a chasm, and this is
especially true for Z and me, since that major fault
line still runs more or less directly beneath this
chair, this unit, this Ettore, this block; and the fault
definitely isn't going anywhere except with a series of

very large jolts. However, like everyone else around here we're in full and mutually agreeable denial about this fault and its inevitable rupture, beyond the various emergency supplies we've stocked up on, so not to worry. -- And besides, the experts are still saying our fault here isn't the type that would open a chasm.)

(And this good old backup J-stick No. 4 is leaking again. Black-ink thumbprints on the J-book page! It's not the first time, but still: another startlement a lot like that fostered by the decline of the Fookin' Fogeys clock. Shock, that is. Nudge, nudge. It's time to pack it in, pal. -- Though I do still have that one last backup warming the bench, the stiff-writing vintage rookie No. 6.)

As for the folks who matter most in our lives, Z's and mine, and I mean really matter a lot in a personal way, they're all still hanging in there (the ones who were hanging in there, I mean, when this "Scat Jyze" began) and most seem to be prospering. Kat and Betty, just back from Guatemala with exciting tales to tell. Wei and Alison, equally excited about soon sailing off to their mid-Pacific paradise. Mama E, in her tenth decade and adult-family-homed but seemingly healthier than she's been in years. David and Stacy and Lwazi, though most likely moving to MSM #2 (Stacy grew up there). Jess P., now about 750K richer after selling her southwest-island place (not quite the 800K she wound up hoping for) and soon to start living in friends' driveways in her vintage streamlined aluminum trailer -- and though Cy-dog died just last week. Vic and Jean and Ro, though -- oh, the heck with the story on this particular "though," which is complicated; on balance all's well with them and Vic and I still meet weekly to "get sane and/or get crazy if the daemon so ordains."

And Paz and Tobey, Gerry and Leola, Jay and Melanie, Aida and Sera and the rest of the D-clan, Madge I., Holly R., Cassie of "I won the lotto!" fame, Bitha and her adopted Chinese daughter Josie (both living on the far coast now, northern sector) -- all still pretty much as before, or so it seems anyway.

[Scat Jyze : Blue Rooster]

     June Q., my onetime close friend, it's sad, she's
still tailspinning and is no longer in touch or even
reachable in any sustainable and non-nominal way.
     And the same for Elgie, the biggest disappointment
of the past several years (and after hopes soared so
high!).
     And Rob and Gail, Jeff and Angie, Barb and Keith
(the siblings and their spouses almost right out of "The
Best of Youth" -- our version of the generational film
now rolling into its final reel), no notable changes
with them over this entire Jyze Age epoch, really.
     (Wait -- going back, I didn't mean to imply Elgie's
been in a tailspin. He may've been but I don't know
that for a fact. He's simply vanished. Or maybe I
should say: he's gone back to the silence he cloaked
himself in for so long before our reunion, at least with
respect to me. And now with respect to Z-wiff as well,
because I believe she's almost as saddened as I am to
lose touch with him.)
     And our life, Z's and mine, hasn't changed much
since the day almost eight years ago when we moved into
the nondescript gray three-story apartment building now
so pretentiously called The Ettore (but we like it
anyway and have gotten used to the name). And my work
life hasn't changed a great deal since I moved into
"Suite 225" at the hideaway building back at the start
of the year Jyze 3. The main difference is I now do
there the scoping work which provides my sustenance
rather than do it in the court-reporting firm's "secure"
office, wherever that happens to be. (For a while in
the years Jyze 1 through 3 it seemed almost certain the
nightscoping life would soon come to an end. But "the
nightscoper" is still who I am, along with "the jyzer.")
     -- Holy holy holy, how many more jyze strings to
tie up?
     Okay, enough with the strings. (But I ought to say
Kat's still right up there when it comes to zinging a
different kind of story of a special type: heart kind.
But these days she's more than a bit constrained by her
busy teen life. And further: I want her to truly want

303

[Scat Jyze : Blue Rooster]

the closeness. I still think it's possible she will
someday. Other than Z-wiff she's been the person I've
cared for most during most of the Jyze Age, though Vic's
come on strong in the past few years. And of course
brother Rob: with him the attachment goes just as deep
and much further back.)
     -- So anything more before I jump into my own big
silence?
     (Well, reading. My cravings in this realm remain
much the same. Same mags, same reviews and quarterlies
by and large. Same newspapers, three a day because I
feel I'm missing too much with fewer. For books, the
novels of my teens and twenties aren't holding up well
on rereading -- "Letting Go," for instance, I abandoned
just last night at about page eighty. Plenty of talent
there, no question, as with so many of the best USAn
novels of the second half of the twentieth century, but
to my mind much of it has gone aglimmering. More than
any others the Chinese poets and Japanese diarists and
novelists still do it for me, along with a Pessoa here,
a Tsvetaeva there (two JRXs!). Most fiction of the
traditional variety being produced currently seems a
waste of time: it's just not grappling with the really
hard stuff. It has little purchase. Sez I. I now a
vet of the prose wars. As we move into the post-print
age, so they say. And I figure I'm as well situated as
anyone to make such grandiose pronouncements -- or to
reject them for myself. Which I'm doing.)
     -- And so there's still work to attend to, yeah.
And I'm hungry. And I'm determined. And I'm pleased
with how it's all turned out so far (speaking of the
personal stuff now). And will keep pushing. And if
jyze wants to come back in some form or other, I'll keep
an eye out for the signs and listen to whatever case it,
the spirit of jyze renaissance, wants to make.
     Otherwise, it's goodbye to the Jyze Age. Finally,
the last goodbye. Right here.

END